Vol. I

**Edited by
Chris Roberson**

MonkeyBrain Books
11204 Crossland Drive
Austin, TX 78726
info@monkeybrainbooks.com

ISBN: 1-932265-13-9

Printed in the United States of America
10 9 8 7 6 5 4 3 2 1

CONTENTS

Introduction
by Chris Roberson

Adventure.

It's something of a devalued word, these days, currency that's lost its value through inflation and overuse. Everything from theme parks to reality television promises adventure in generous doses, and this habitual barrage inures us to the word. But worse, the concept itself is degraded through repetition. Entertainment that can manage little else can deliver, on occasion, the promised adventure—perils and chases and derring-do—even if other intangibles are left along the wayside—plot, character, theme. Over time, the preponderance of entertainment that delivers adventure and little more besides has suggested a dichotomy, the notion that there is a gulf with adventure and entertainment on one side, and quality and merit on the other.

This perceived dichotomy is as true in literature as in any other media, and even more so in the taxonomies of "genre." The genre classifications we know today are in large part the descendants of different varieties of pulp magazines popular in the early years of the twentieth century: mystery can trace its lineage to *Black Mask*, horror to *Weird Tales*, science fiction to *Astounding*, and so on. Growing as they did from the mulch of the pulps, though, these various genres have each at one time or another gone through periods in which their pulpy roots were re-pudiated, renounced in favor of more stylistically sophisticated approaches.

Those who have taken part in these periodic revolutions— such as the writers of the "New Wave," who proved that science fiction was as capable of experimentation and sophistication as any literary form—are to be lauded for proving that genre need not be limited by its generic origins. However, genre fiction has expended so much energy and enthusiasm in past decades grow-ing beyond its pulp roots that it risks losing the good along with the bad. Out with two-dimensional characters, wooden dialogue, and creaking plots, to which no one can object; but too often with them also goes action, peril, and—yes—adventure.

There is a middle road. Genre fiction as stylistically sophisticated as the best of mainstream literary fiction, but with the same visceral thrills and excitement found in the best pulp magazines. In recent years, there has been a resurgence of interest in fiction that follows this middle path, genre fiction with literary sophistication, literary fiction with genre thrills. The Michael Chabon–edited anthologies, *McSweeney's Mammoth Treasury of Thrilling Tales* and *McSweeney's Enchanted Chamber of Astonishing Stories*; the first two issues of the short-lived *Argosy Magazine* edited by Lou Anders; David Moles' and Jay Lake's *All-Star Zeppelin Adventure Stories*. And now the present volume, the first installment in an annual series of original anthologies. Perhaps it is "steam engine time," as they say, and there will be other iterations of sophisticated pulp yet to come.

Adventure takes its name from one of the leading pulp magazines of the early twentieth century, which in its days published writers like Talbot Mundy, Gordon MacCreagh, and Baroness Orczy, and included stories ranging from westerns, to wilderness survival, to war stories, to historical adventures, to mysteries, and all points in between. In addition, the magazine ran true-life accounts and fact articles, and ran a regular feature called "The Camp-Fire: A meeting place for readers, writers, and adventurers," both an editorial letter column and a precursor to the message boards of today, in which readers, editors, and writers exchanged questions and answers about equipment and far-flung locales, long-lost friends were reunited, and expeditions were planned. First published in 1910, by 1924 *Adventure* was, according to Richard Bleiler in his *The Index to Adventure Magazine,* "without question the most important 'pulp' magazine in the world." From one publisher or another, *Adventure* survived into the 1970s before finally closing its tent, and the flames of the Camp-Fire burned down to cold embers.

The present incarnation of *Adventure* shares with that original pulp magazine only a name, and the desire to publish stories of any stripe, so long as they have a healthy dose of adventure. It is my belief that "adventure" is not a genre, in and of itself, but a mode; not a type of story, but an approach to storytelling. In the pages that follow are stories from many genres—mystery, science fiction, horror, western, historical, et cetera, et al.—but a common thread runs through them all: each is a stirring yarn, well told. Sophistication and action, entertainment and quality. Or, to put it another way...

Adventure.

In this new twist on a familiar tale, Mike Resnick resumes his ongoing chronicling of the travels and tribulations of the Right Reverend Honorable Doctor Lucifer Jones—previously collected in the novels *Adventures*, *Exploits*, and *Encounters*— and the world is a richer place for it.

The Island of Annoyed Souls
A Lucifer Jones Story
by Mike Resnick

There are a lot of pleasant ways to see the world—but footslogging through the Amazon jungle without a compass ain't one of them. After being gently asked at gunpoint to leave San Palmero I'd been three days and three nights without seeing nothing but an endless parade of mosquitoes and other six-legged critters with a few eight-legged ones tossed in for good measure, and I'd pretty much reached the point where I'd have welcomed the presence of a headhunter or two just to have a little company.

Of course, that was before I ran smack dab into one. I heard him before I could see him, and he was making such a racket as would have woke such dead as weren't otherwise occupied at the moment. He kept crashing through the underbrush, of which there was an awful lot, and suddenly out he burst, maybe ten feet from me. He was carrying a bow and a bunch of little arrows, but he was in such a hurry that he seemed to have plumb forgot about them. He bumped into me, let out a scream, and stared at me kind of like a cow stares at a butcher.

"Howdy, Brother," I greeted him. "The Right Reverend Lucifer Jones at your service. What's the quickest route back to civilization?"

He jabbered something I couldn't understand, and kept looking back the way he had come, so I figured he was telling me he'd just been to the big city and hadn't found it all that congenial to a guy who was inclined to wander around stark naked and had a tendency to shrink the local citizenry's heads. I thanked him for pointing it out to me and started marching off, but he grabbed my arm and began jabbering again, more urgently this time.

"I can appreciate your distaste for the vices of city life," I said. "But if I'm going to save folks from the wages of sin, I got to go to where all the sinning gets itself done."

He began screaming and pointing to where he'd been and pulling me in the direction he was going.

"I'm touched by your concern, Brother," I told him. "But there ain't no need for you to worry. The Lord is my shepherd. Him and me'll get along fine, once we get out of this here jungle."

He just stared at me for a minute, and then took off like a bat out of hell, and it belatedly occurred to me that probably he and one of the local young ladies and maybe her parents had totally different notions of what constituted a bona fide proposal of marriage.

I started walking, dead certain that I'd be stumbling across a city any minute, but not much happened except that I finally caught sight of the Amazon, or at least one of its tributaries. I tried to remember if sharks hung out in rivers, but in the end I was so thirsty I didn't much care, so I wandered over to the water's edge, knelt down, and took a long swallow, and except for some waterbugs and a couple of tadpoles and a minnow or two it didn't taste all that bad.

Then I looked up, and strike me dead if I didn't see a city after all. It wasn't much of a city, just ten or twelve buildings on an island in the middle of the river about half a mile downstream, but after all that time in the bush it was city enough for me, and I moseyed over until I was standing on the bank just opposite it. I was about to swim across to it when I saw an alligator with a lean and hungry look cruising the surface between me and the island, and decided to just keep on walking until I came to a city, or even a suburb, on my side of the river, but then I saw an old beat-up boat tied on the shore, so I borrowed it and rowed across to the island.

As I was pulling the boat out of the water I heard a noise behind me, and when I turned to see what had caused it I found a great big dog watching me curiously. He looked friendly enough, so I reached out to pet him.

"You touch me, Gringo, and I'll bite your hand off," he said.

I jumped back real sudden-like.

"What are you staring at?" he continued. "Haven't you ever seen a dog before?"

"Man and boy, I seen a lot of dogs," I told him, "but up until this minute I ain't never had a conversation with one." I looked around. "Are there a lot of you?"

The dog kind of frowned. "How many of me do you see?"

"I mean, are there a lot of talking dogs in these here parts?"

"I hardly see that that's any of your business," said the dog. "What are you doing on this island?"

"Right at the moment I'm wondering what my chances are of getting back off it real quick," I said truthfully. "I don't want to upset you none, but I find that talking dogs put me off my feed."

"You're not going anywhere," said the dog. "I think I'd better take you to the doctor."

"I don't need no doctor," I said. "I feel as fit as a bull moose."

"I resent that," said a low voice behind me, and when I turned to see who'd said it, sure enough I was facing a moose with beady little eyes and a huge spread of antlers. "Now go along with Ramon before I lose my temper."

"You're Ramon?" I asked the dog.

"Have you got a problem with that?" said the dog, baring his teeth.

"Not a bit," I said quickly. "Ramon is my very favorite name."

"Come along with us, Miguel," said Ramon to the moose. "Just in case he tries to escape."

"Miguel is my favorite name too," I said as the moose joined us.

"What do you think of Felicity?" said a feminine voice that seemed to have a little more timbre to it than most.

I looked off to my left and found myself facing about five

tons worth of elephant.

"You're Felicity?" I asked.

"I am," replied the elephant.

"I think it's a name of rare gossamer gaiety," I said. "I've fallen eternally in love with maybe thirty women in my life, and five or six of 'em was named Felicity." Then a thought occurred to me, and I said, "Just what kind of animal is this here doctor you're taking me to?"

"He's a man, the same as you," said Felicity.

"He's a man, anyway," muttered Ramon.

"Before we go any farther," said Felicity, "you must promise not to harm him."

"He must be a nice man to have such loving, devoted pets," I remarked.

"He is a fiend!" growled Ramon.

"A monster!" said Felicity.

"And we are *not* his pets," added Miguel bitterly.

"Well, he must at least be one hell of an animal trainer," I said. "After all, he taught you to speak."

"He most certainly did not!" said Felicity.

"You all just learned spontaneously?" I asked.

"I'm sure the doctor will explain it to you," said Miguel.

"Just keep out of his laboratory," said Felicity.

"I take it he don't like visitors messing with his equipment?" I said.

"I have no idea," said Felicity. "Just keep out of it—and don't accept any food or drink from him unless he partakes of it first."

"And remember," said Miguel, "he is not to be harmed."

"I'm a little confused here," I admitted. "You say this doctor is a fiend and a monster and I shouldn't eat or drink nothing he offers, and at the same time you seem dead set against anyone hurting him."

"That's right," said Ramon.

"And you don't see no inconsistency in that position?" I asked.

"After you talk to him everything will become clear."

We walked for a few minutes and began approaching one of the buildings. A couple of chimpanzees wandered over and introduced themselves, and overhead a bald eagle swooped down and told me that if I so much as touched the doctor he'd peck my eyes out, and then one of the chimps warned me not to drink anything, and I began thinking that if the next thing I saw was a white rabbit checking his watch I'd feel mighty relieved and start trying to wake up, but I didn't see no more animals and pretty soon we were at the door. One of the chimps knocked on it, and then they all stood back and waited for it to open, and when it did I found myself facing a small, pudgy man with thinning white hair, steel-rimmed spectacles, and three or four chins, depending on which way he held his head.

He looked me up and down and finally kind of grimaced.

"You're not at all what I was expecting," he said at last.

"I hear that a lot, though usually from disgruntled women," I said.

"You simply don't look like the killer of twenty-eight men, women, and children," he continued, staring at me. "Still, appearances can be deceiving, which is our guiding motto here."

"I don't want to put a damper on your enthusiasm," I said, "but I ain't never killed anyone."

"You're not Juan Pedro Vasquez?" he said.

"I'm the Right Reverend Honorable Doctor Lucifer Jones," I told him.

"What are you doing on my island?"

"Well, for the past hour or so I've mostly been concentrating on being lost," I admitted.

"Then you shall be an honored visitor," he said. "Come right in."

He kind of pulled me in by the arm and shut the door behind me before I could decide whether or not to make a dash for the river.

"May I offer you a drink?" he asked, leading me to the living room, which had a dozen diplomas on the wall instead of the usual animal heads and tasteful paintings of naked ladies striking friendly poses.

"That's right generous of you," I said, "but I ain't thirsty just now."

"You've been listening to the animals," he said knowingly. "Don't worry, Doctor Jones. The drink is perfectly safe. You must not pay attention to a bunch of felons."

"I ain't been talking to no felons, present company possibly excepted," I said. "Just a bunch of the strangest animals I've ever run into."

He walked to a cabinet, pulled out a bottle, and poured two glasses. He took a swallow from one and then handed it to me.

"Will that assuage your fears?" he said.

"Well, under these circumstances, I suppose I can overcome my natural aversion to liquid," I allowed, downing the rest of the glass and holding it out for a refill. As he poured it, I asked him if he had any serious intention of telling me just what felons he thought I'd been talking to.

"Ramon and Felicity and the others," he said.

"I don't want to seem to ignorant," I said, "but just what kind of felony can an elephant commit on an island in the middle of the jungle?"

"I shall be happy to explain it all to you, Doctor Jones," he said, sitting down on a big leather chair. "Let me begin by asking if you are acquainted with the work of Doctor Septimus Mirbeau, who is unquestionably the world's most brilliant doctor and scientist?"

"Sounds like an interesting guy," I said. "I'd sure like to run into him someday."

"You're talking to him," he said. "Can it be that you've really never heard of me?"

"Not unless you played third base for the St. Louis Browns about fifteen years ago," I replied.

His face fell. "That's the price of genius. I have to work in obscurity until I can announce my findings to the world."

"Well, you can't get much more obscure than a nameless island in the middle of the Amazon," I said.

"It has a name," replied Doctor Mirbeau. "I call it the Island of Lost Souls."

"As far as I can tell, the only soul what's lost around here is me," I said.

"The name is a poetic metaphor," he said, lighting up a big cigar. "If I was being literal, I would call it the Island of Lost Bodies."

"It strikes me as a pretty small island to misplace a whole graveyard," I said.

He smiled. I'm sure he meant it to be a tolerant, fatherly smile, but it came across as something out of one of them movies what got people called Bela and Boris and a lot of other names beginning with a B acting in 'em.

"The bodies are still here, Doctor Jones," he assured me.

"You just forgot where?"

"You have just been in their company."

"That's funny," I said. "I didn't notice nothing except a bunch of animals with an unlikely way of expressing themselves."

"That was them."

"I know the vertical rays of the tropical sun can have a funny effect on some folk," I allowed, "but I'm pretty sure those were animals and not men."

"They are animals who used to be men!" he said triumphantly.

"Now why in the world would a normal woman want to turn into a lady elephant?" I said. "Unless of course you're the only man on the island, and there are a mess of good-looking male elephants out there that I ain't encountered yet."

"I have learned how to surgically transform men and women into animals," he said. "Didn't you think it was peculiar that a moose and an elephant could converse with you?"

"Not as peculiar as a doctor who claims they used to be a man and a woman called Miguel and Felicity," I said.

"But they were!" he insisted. "This has been my life's work! I am only a few years from going public with it. There won't be enough Nobel Prizes to honor me. They'll have to create a newer, more prestigious award."

"Just how private can it be even now?" I said. "Some hospital or college must know about your work, or you couldn't have gotten funding for all this."

"My funding comes from my patients, who pay me to transform them," said Doctor Mirbeau.

"I don't want to seem unduly skeptical," I said, "buy why in tarnation would a bunch of perfectly normal human beings pay good money to be turned into animals?"

"Because every last one of them is a wanted criminal," he answered. "What better way to avoid detection than to become an animal?"

Well, I could think of a lot of better ways, or at least less painful ones, but I didn't want to argue with my host, especially since I had a feeling anyone who lost an argument with him was likely to be turned into a koala bear or an iguana or some such thing.

"That's mighty interesting, Brother Mirbeau," I said at last, "and I sure wish you the best of luck with all your Nobel Prizes, but now that we've had a friendly visit and I've drunk my fill, I think it's time I was on my way, if you'll just point me toward the nearest city."

"I'm afraid I can't let you leave the island, Doctor Jones," he said.

"Why not?" I said.

"You might reveal what I'm doing here before I'm ready to tell the world."

"I give you my solemn word as a man of the cloth who ain't never told a lie in his whole blameless life that I wouldn't even think of doing such a thing," I said. "Besides, if I did, they'd probably just lock me up in the drunk tank."

"I can't take the chance," he said. "You may have free run of the island until I'm ready."

"Ready for what?" I asked.

"You'll find out," he said with a strange smile.

Suddenly it started raining, which it does a lot of in the rain forest, and pretty soon we could hardly hear ourselves over the thunder.

"You ain't going to make a fellow white man sleep outside in this weather, are you?" I said, looking out the window.

"That was never my intention," said Doctor Mirbeau. "I'll have a bed prepared for you next door in the House of Agony."

"The House of Agony?"

"That's right," he said.

"You know, I think the rain's lightening up already," I said quickly as it continued to pour. "Maybe I'll just spend the night on the beach."

"I won't hear of it," he said. "You can't be too careful with your health."

Those were my sentiments exactly, but no matter how much I protested, he insisted that I accept his hospitality. Finally he got up, put an arm around my shoulders, and walked me over to the front door.

"Your boat has been moved to a safe place," he said. "You really don't want to leave the island without it, as the water is infested with alligators."

I couldn't see that a river being infested with alligators was all that much worse than an island being infested with a mad scientist, but I kept my opinion to myself.

"Dinner is at eight o'clock," he said as he opened the door for me. "Promptness is appreciated." He stared at me. "I don't suppose you brought a dinner jacket?"

"I could go back to San Palmero right now and get one," I suggested hopefully.

"No," he said. "We'll simply have to rough it."

"What's on the menu?" I asked as I remembered that I hadn't had nothing to eat all day and decided that I might as well make the best of my situation.

"Raoul," he said.

Suddenly a handful of nuts and berries started looking mighty good to me. I walked out the door, and found Ramon, Miguel, and Felicity waiting for me out there in the rain.

"I'm surprised to see you," said Felicity. "Most men who enter the doctor's house never come out."

"At least, not as men," added Ramon.

"Do you guys mind if we walk while we're talking?" I said, heading off into the jungle.

"What's your rush?" asked Miguel. "It's raining at the far end of the island too."

"Yeah, but that's a lot farther from the House of Agony than we are now," I pointed out.

"True," he agreed. "On the other hand, it's a lot closer to the House of Pain."

I came to a stop. "Has Doctor Mirbeau got any other houses I should know about?"

"No," said Felicity. "But he has five others you probably shouldn't know about."

"If I ever get off this here island," I vowed to nobody in particular, "the very first thing I'm going to do is never think about it again."

"You will never leave the island," said Ramon. "I am surprised he didn't tell you that."

"Well, he did kind of hint at it," I allowed. "But I was hoping he said it with a kindly twinkle in his eye."

"That was a cataract, and there's nothing kindly about it," said Miguel. "You're stuck here."

"I've run through thirty-four countries looking for the right spot to build the Tabernacle of Saint Luke," I said. "Who'd have thunk I'd wind up having to build it here, with nothing in my flock except a bunch of godless animals?"

"I resent that!" said Felicity.

"The godless part or the animal part?" I asked.

"Both!"

"Then I apologize," I said. "I sure don't want no God-fearing five-ton lady mad at me."

"Leave my weight out of this!" she snapped.

"It's nothing to be ashamed of, ma'am," I told her. "I ain't never seen a ten-thousand-pounder, human or otherwise, what was so feminine and delicate-looking and light on her feet."

She made a sound that was a cross between a tuba hitting M over high C and a trolly car skidding downhill on some rusty tracks.

"Now see what you've done?" said Miguel. "She's crying!"

Her body was racked by sobs, which made it pretty hazardous for anyone standing in her immediate vicinity, like especially me, so I spoke up and said, "I don't want to be presumptuous, Miss Felicity, ma'am, but if you're that unhappy about being an elephant, why not just have Doctor Mirbeau change you back into the charming lady bank-robber or mad bomber you were to begin with?"

Felicity began crying even harder and louder.

"You simply do not understand our situation," said Ramon.

"Sure I do," I said. "You're a bunch of worthless lawbreaking scum, meaning no offense, what probably committed a passel of crimes against the laws of man and God, and came here to avoid the just and righteous punishment of an outraged citizenry." Ramon snarled, and Miguel glared at me and began pawing the damp ground, but I held up a hand. "This is your lucky day," I said. "Your troubles are solved. I just happen to be in the salvation business. And as an introductory offer, I'll forgive any five heinous sins for the price of four."

"Our biggest sin is stupidity," sniffled Felicity.

"I absolve you!" I said. "That'll be $1.83 in cash."

"Do you see pockets on any of us?" said Miguel.

"Okay, we'll put it on the cuff," I said. "Just be sure you pay me before you leave the island or I may have to tell God to strike you dead, and He's such a busy critter that I really hate to bother Him unless it's absolutely necessary."

"We're never leaving the island again," muttered Ramon unhappily.

"Why not?" I asked. "I mean, you've got your ready-made disguises, so why ain't you and Miss Felicity out in polite canine and pachyderm society?"

"We were," said Miguel. "Well, some of us were."

"And some of us have never left the island," said Felicity. "You'd be surprised how few places in South America an elephant can go without drawing undue attention."

"Yeah, I can see where it's difficult to hide out in a crowd if there ain't no crowd on hand," I said. "Maybe you should have hitched a ride to Africa."

"I don't *want* to go to Africa!" she wailed. "I just want to be a woman again."

"Our transformations were completed a decade ago," said Ramon. "The police are no longer hunting for us. Our case files are closed. We have returned to the island to be changed back into human beings."

"Well, that seems reasonable," I allowed.

"It's reasonable," said Ramon. "It's just not likely."

"Oh?" I said. "Why not?"

"Because that foul fiend has raised his prices!" growled Ramon.

"It's extortion!" chimed in Miguel. "Where is a moose going to get fifty thousand dollars—especially in these difficult economic times?"

"And there's no sense threatening him," added Felicity. "He knows that we don't dare risk hurting the one man who can turn us back into men and women."

"So you figure you're going to be a full-time long-term elephant?" I asked her.

She began crying again. "I used to be so beautiful! I never wanted to be an elephant! I wanted to be something sleek and feline. And thin. Do you know what it's like for someone who counted calories all her life to eat five hundred pounds of grass and shrubs a day on a minimum maintenance diet?"

"There there," said Miguel, trying to comfort her. "There there."

"And the worse part of it is Cedric!" she continued.

"Cedric? Who's Cedric?" I asked.

"My partner," said Felicity. "Doctor Mirbeau turned him into a mouse, and now I'm scared to death of him!"

"What did you two do before you came here?" I asked.

"Hardly anything at all," said Felicity. "We didn't kill anywhere near as many of my husbands as they claimed. Just nine or ten." She paused. "Maybe twelve at the outside."

"You don't know how many husbands you killed?"

"Some of them died from natural causes," she said defensively.

I didn't see no sense in arguing with her, because it was

certainly natural for a heart to stop beating after someone had pumped half a dozen bullets into it.

"At least Cedric is alive and wandering around the island somewhere," said Ramon. "Not like poor Omar."

"Omar was *your* partner?"

"Yes."

"What happened to him?" I asked. "Did he die on Doctor Mirbeau's operating table?"

"No," said Ramon. "Doctor Mirbeau turned him into a rabbit." A tear came to his eye. "I ate him."

"You ate your own partner?"

"It was instinct," said Ramon. "He shouldn't have run. Ever since the operation I have this compulsion to chase things."

"How about you?" I said, turning to Miguel. "You got a partner too?"

"No," said Miguel. Then: "Well, not anymore, anyway."

"But you did have one?"

"I had four," he said. "A father, two sisters, and a brother. It was a family business."

"And are they wandering around the island too?" I asked.

"No," said Miguel. "I turned them all in for the reward years ago."

"So here we are on the Island of Lost Souls," said Ramon, "just a few hundred yards from the man who could transform us back into human beings but refuses to do so."

"Sometimes I get so frustrated I could just sit on him," said Felicity.

"I know you're having dinner with him tonight, Doctor Jones," said Miguel. "Could you intercede with him on our behalf?"

"Well, actually, I was kind of planning to intercede with him on *my* behalf," I replied.

They begged and cajoled and Ramon started growling and I was afraid Felicity was going to start crying again, so finally I gave in and promised to speak to him at dinnertime.

"Thank you, Doctor Jones," said Miguel, who I decided wasn't a bad guy for a moose. "Our prayers go with you."

Suddenly Felicity trumpeted in terror and raced off screaming into the jungle, knocking down trees right and left as she went.

"What was that all about?" I asked.

"She probably saw Cedric again," said Ramon in a bored voice. "It happens all the time."

"Poor baby," said Miguel. "What a comedown."

"Was she really that pretty before the operation?" I asked.

"Compared to what?" said Ramon.

"She was much prettier then than she is now," said Miguel. He stopped and mulled on it for a minute. "Well, a bit prettier, anyway." He thunk a little more. "If not prettier, at least smaller."

"And she smelled better," added Ramon.

"Well, this has been a fascinating conversation," I said, "but I think it's probably time for me to head back over to Doctor Mirbeau's house for dinner."

"Good luck, Doctor Jones," said Ramon.

I started traipsing back through the jungle, and after a while the rain let up and pretty soon I found myself at the front door. I was going to open it when something big and shaggy opened it from the inside.

"You are expected," he said, stepping back to let me pass.

"*You* sure ain't," I said, staring at him.

"Have you got something against gorillas?" he asked me.

"Not a thing," I said quickly. "Some of my best friends are gorillas, or so close to 'em as makes no difference. I just ain't never encountered one working as a doorman before."

"I hope you don't think I enjoy being a house servant," said the gorilla.

"It ain't never occurred to me to seriously consider whether a gorilla would be happy as a butler," I admitted. "But if you don't like it, what are you doing here?"

"I'm hiding from the police."

"Back up a minute here," I said. "I thunk you got turned into a gorilla so you wouldn't have to hide no more."

"I should have saved my money and taken my chances," he

said bitterly.

"But you look exactly like a gorilla."

"I used to be a professional wrestler," he said. "The police saw through the surgery instantly."

"You looked like *this* when you rassled?" I asked.

He opened a cabinet and produced two photographs.

"Before and after," he said, and sure enough I couldn't tell one from the other.

He led me into the dining room, where Doctor Mirbeau, dressed in a sweat-stained white tropical suit and a dirty tie, was already sitting at one end of the table, and the gorilla motioned that I was to sit at the other end.

"What do you think of my island now that you've had a little time to explore it?" asked Doctor Mirbeau.

"I suppose it's one of the nicer islands I've ever encountered," I said.

His face brightened. "So you like it?"

"Except for the heat, and the bugs, and the mud, and the rain, and the talking animals, and the fact that you won't let me leave," I answered.

"I can't control the other things, but I'll order the animals to leave you alone."

"Actually, they asked me to speak to you on their behalf," I said.

He made a face. "I thought as much."

"Mighty few animals can lay their hands, or whatever passes for their hands, on fifty thousand dollars," I said. "Why don't you turn 'em back into men and woman and let 'em pay you afterward?"

"I can't," he said.

"Why not?" I asked. "Ain't a delayed payment better than no payment at all?"

"It's out of the question," he said.

"That don't make no sense," I protested. "You need money to continue your work. These animals ain't got two cents to rub together. If you don't operate on 'em, they won't never have no money, but if you do operate then maybe they'll be able to get some."

"Forget it."

"Why are you being so stubborn?" I said.

"Because I don't know how to turn them back!" he bellowed. "That's what I need the money for—to pay my expenses until I learn how!"

There was an angry trumpeting outside the building, and Doctor Mirbeau suddenly turned even whiter than his suit.

"What was that?" he asked in a shaky voice.

"If I was a betting man," I said, "I'd lay plenty of eight-to-five that Felicity heard every word you just said with them oversized ears of hers, and that she is more than a little bit displeased with you."

"Oh my God!" he whispered.

"I got a feeling God's otherwise occupied at the moment," I answered as a couple of lions began roaring, "but I'll be sure to tell Him you called."

Pretty soon some monkeys began screaming, and then a few eagles and leopards chimed in, and Ramon began howling, and it was pretty clear that it wasn't so much an island of lost souls as deeply annoyed and exceptionally noisy ones.

"Save me, Doctor Jones!" he cried.

"I thought I was your prisoner," I said.

"Don't quibble over technicalities," he said. "Save me and everything I have is yours!"

"As far as I can tell, everything you have is an island a trillion miles from anywhere and a bunch of angry animals that want your scalp," I said. "Somehow it don't seem like much of an inducement."

He held up his right hand. "See this ring? That's a six-carat diamond! Save me and it's yours!"

"It's a mighty pretty bauble," I said. "But I could just sit back and pick it up when they finish dismembering you."

"What kind of Christian are you?" he demanded.

"A live one," I said as a jaguar leaped onto the roof and began pacing back and forth. "I'll ask you the same question thirty minutes from now."

"All right," he said. "There's five thousand dollars in my safe. You can have half."

"Half?"

"Surely you don't insist on all of it?" he said.

"I don't insist on any of it," I told him. "I think I'll just watch them hunt you down and rip you to shreds like a naked mole rat, except for the mole rat part."

"All right!" he said. "It's all yours! Just save me!"

"It's a deal," I said. "Though officially and for tax purposes you're giving the money to the Lord; I'm just holding it for Him until Him and me can build our tabernacle. Now go hunt up the money while I run a couple of plans past Him and see which one He prefers."

As soon as he left the room the gorilla walked up to me.

"Are you really going to save him?" he asked.

"It's the only way to make sure all you animals get turned back into people," I said.

"I'm not going under the knife again!" he said. "Why suffer the pain when I wouldn't look one bit different when it was all over?"

I looked at the gorilla, and thunk about what he said, and then my Silent Partner smacked me right betwixt the eyes with one of His heavenly revelations.

"You've got a strange and inscrutable expression on your face, Doctor Jones," said the gorilla.

"You got a name?" I asked him suddenly.

"Horace," he said. It was the first time I ever saw a gorilla look embarrassed.

"What city are you wanted in, Horace?" I said.

"It's not so much a city as a country," he said. "Things are different here than in the States."

"Okay," I said. "What country can't you show your face in?"

"Brazil," he said.

"All right," I said. "That's no problem."

"Peru," he continued. "Uraguay. Paraguay. Argentina. Chile."

"You been a busy boy, Horace," I said.

"And Iceland."

"Iceland?" I said.

"I have relatives in Iceland," he explained. "I visited them."

"That must be a mighty strict country," I said. "Most places don't usually issue arrest warrants for visiting relatives."

"It was a very pleasant visit," said Horace. "We spent a lot of time together, they showed me the sights, we ate at some wonderful restaurants." He paused. "Robbing those seven banks was just an afterthought. I didn't even need the money from the last five. It's just that once you start, it's... well... habit-forming."

"It's a tragic and touching story, but let's get back to the subject at hand and see if I got this straight," I said. "There ain't no warrants out for you in Venezuela or Colombia or Ecuador, right?"

"And Bolivia," he said as Doctor Mirbeau came back with the cash. "Don't forget Bolivia."

I took the money and the ring and then walked to the front door and opened it. Damned near every animal on the island was lined up there facing it, except for the jaguar that was looking down from the roof. Doctor Mirbeau kind of cowered behind me.

"I suppose you're wondering why I've called you all here," I said.

"Cut the crap and give us Mirbeau!" said Ramon.

"What'll you do with him?" I asked.

"We haven't decided yet," said Miguel. "But it'll be grotesque."

"I got a better idea," I said. "How'd you all like to be turned back into men and women again?"

"He doesn't know how!" said Felicity. "I heard him admit it to you!"

"He doesn't know how *yet*," I said. "He needs some more time and money to work on it."

"Where's he going to get money?" said Miguel. "You can't bleed a turnip, or pick the pocket of a bunch of animals who aren't wearing any pants."

"*You're* going to earn it," I said, "and it'll be credited to your accounts against the day when he can actually change you back."

"Earn it?" repeated Ramon. "How?"

"Felicity," I said. "Tell me again why you stay here on the island."

"Because I'm the only elephant for thousands of miles around," she said. "I'd draw attention wherever I go."

"I agree," I said.

"So she stands out in a crowd," said Ramon. "What's your point?"

"It seems to me that as long as elephants and lions and talking animals are going to draw all that attention, there ain't no reason why they should draw it for free," I said. "You got a whole continent full of people what'll pay good money to see what you been hiding instead of flaunting. You can turn this island into the most popular zoo and tourist destination in South America."

"That's an interesting notion," said Ramon. "But how will we get word out to the public?"

"You'll start with word of mouth in Venezuela, Colombia, Ecuador, and Bolivia, and work up from there," I said. "You just happen to have a spokesman and travel agent in your midst—at least as long as he sticks to rasslin' arenas and maybe soccer stadiums what feature riots during halftime."

Doctor Mirbeau stepped forward and promised to stay if they agreed to the plan, since all he wanted was the money and privacy he needed to finish his research. The animals took a vote, and it passed unanimously, and that's how the island became The Mirbeau 5-Star Spa, Resort, Menagerie, Circus, and Petting Zoo.

As for me, I had five thousand dollars and a diamond ring tucked away in my pocket, so I bade them all a fond farewell and headed to the river. Once I got there I remembered that Doctor Mirbeau had taken my boat away, and I was about to go hunting for it when a big alligator glided up to the shore. I took a couple of steps back, ready to run if it came after me.

"Don't be afraid, Doctor Jones," it said. "My name is Victor

Montez. I'll ride shotgun for you while you swim across."

"Since you're one of Doctor Mirbeau's critters, how come you didn't say nothing to me when I got here earlier today?"

"I wasn't myself this morning," said Victor.

"Mighty few folks around here are," I agreed.

"You misunderstand," he said. "Something I ate last night disagreed with me."

I resisted the urge to ask whether that was before or after he ate it, and just started swimming. A minute later there was a splash, followed by a loud crunching noise.

"Piranha," explained Victor.

"Gesundheit," I said.

"I hope it wasn't anyone I know," he added.

I made it to the far shore, climbed up onto dry land, thanked Victor for his help, took one last look at the island, and headed off to find some congenial spot where the sinners and scarlet women all congregated and I could finally settle down to the serious business of building my tabernacle.

I'm not sure there's a term yet for the genre in which Nakashima-Brown writes, but whatever it is, the territory is pretty much his alone. Cory Doctorow has described his work as "slick, post-Gibsonian, and funny as hell, like Neal Stephenson meets Hunter S. Thompson." Add in a dash of Robert E. Howard, and that description fits the following story as well as any could.

Ghulistan Bust-out
by Chris Nakashima-Brown

Hauling ass down the white dirt track that passed for a road between Zhob and old Fort Sandeman on the Afghan frontier, USAF Sgt. Scottie Mack's late model Taliban Toyota double cab rattled like a thousand ball bearings tumbling in a coin dryer, competing with the schizoid remix of Metallica and Gordon Lightfoot Cpl. Melvin Hopps had spliced into the sound system off his ruggedized laptop and cranked to 11.

"Enter Sundown," said Hopps. "I told you this kicks Canadian ass."

"There are no Canadians in Metallica," said Mack, riding shotgun and scouting the surrounding hills for enemy. "And I told you this would be a hot quarter. Get us the fuck through here pronto, Mel. We've got a civilian on board."

Mel, I had learned an hour earlier, was Cpl. Hopps' combat nickname. An acronym for Matter Eater Lad, that most self-parodic member of the Legion of Super-Heroes. You'd understand if you watched him wash down a Salisbury steak and Skittles MRE with a liter of Ripped Fuel and half a thermos of coffee. All with one hand on the wheel churning dust through the back roads of Balochistan.

BOOM.

A bit of RPG-assisted percussion bisected two chords of the chorus, cratering the road and raining its contents back on the truck. One point two million dollars of the military-entertainment complex's finest toys for the electronic targeting set bounced in the bed. Hopps swerved, slamming the full travel of the off-road suspension as he stomped over the rocky embankment.

This was, I concluded, beyond a doubt the most cluster-fucked location scouting I had ever done. But if I pulled it off, I'd be sure to have a pitch that would sell the pilot. With me as the director of my own script. If I blew it, I'd be back to writing Justice League dialogue for eight-year-olds, if I were lucky.

KAPLONK.

My head bounced off the red metal roof of the truck as Hopps hit another artillery sinkhole. Hopps' half-burned Camel Filter escaped from his lip, skipped off the headrest, and exploded Turkish embers in my face. I smacked myself, knocking the coals into my lap. Spazzed, I tried again, managed to flick myself right in the left nut, and kicked the back of the seat reflexively.

Hawkman, call your office.

"Cut the crap back there, big boy," said Mack, turning to face me down through the cloud of dust, pulling his beat-up T. J. Hooker baseball cap tighter over his shaggy four-week old crew cut. "I know you're a civilian, but embeds are supposed to follow orders."

"Right." I coughed.

PLINKETY-POP-SQUEAL.

The windshield shattered like popped ice. Using his seat as a pommel horse, Mack launched two dusty combat boots at the latticed mess and stomped the remains out onto the hood, while Hopps pulled a pair of desert goggles down over his Oakleys and popped his head out the window.

"I'm thinking maybe this isn't the best place to shoot the opening pans for our pilot," I said to no one in particular. "Despite what the film bureau folks told me in Islamabad."

"Chill out," said Hopps, somehow managing to grind a gear on the automatic transmission. "We're gonna have this place mopped up like a baby's ass within the month. We finally got the carte blanche from Karachi to burn out these Sufi motherfuck-ers. ISI claims these goons are more than terrorists. Says they're fucking necromancers, practicing some medieval Muslim mojo from Hell. Our intel calls bullshit on that, but they're trouble either way. So we need to lock and load GPS codes for the Daisy Cutters."

"That's why we're going your way," said Mack. "Welcome to USAF SpecOps Combat Control. 'First here' ain't for pussies."

As Mack adjusted the laser pointer on his SR-25 sniper rifle, I admired the logo of the Okinawa-based 353rd Special Operations Group patched on his shoulder: a bat-winged black panther declawing himself on the globe.

"Hey Mel," said Mack, setting down his scope and pointing ahead on the road, "that a fork up ahead?"

Hopps squinted into the wind. The sound of 7.62 mm of lead whizzed by my head.

"Yeah. Let's try left, maybe. Should cross the Zhob River."

"You know," said Hopps over his shoulder, "the name 'Zhob' means 'oozing water.'"

My cheek freckled with the first responder pus of tiny third-degree burns.

Hopps made his own shortcut, hard left down deeper into the valley. It worked, for a while.

"So I hope you're not actually a Canadian, Frank," said Hopps as he sucked creatine-laced water from his Camelbak.

"No, I just work there. Vancouver. That's where we produce the show."

"Cool name. *Hyborian Tales*. So it's all Conan and shit, like those Schwarzenegger movies?" asked Hopps. "That's awesome."

"Actually," I explained, "it's everything but. We used the name in the title, since that's not copyrighted, but we couldn't get the rights to the actual Conan stories. Universal bought all those in the '80s. So we picked up the rest of the Robert E. Howard catalog, and we're close to getting financing and distribution for a first season of twelve episodes. We'll shoot most of it on a stage set, but to cinch it, we need some nice opening pans of the old abandoned British fort for the two-hour pilot." I brandished my camera for emphasis. "CentCom said I could tag along with you guys if I wrote a nice feature for one of the trades and helped them get hooked up with our producer. Military-entertainment complex and all that."

"Yeah, well Conan would fit right in over here with these barbarian motherfuckers," said Hopps.

"Actually, we're using some stories Howard wrote about a more modern adventurer in these parts. You'd like him, Hopps. Like you, he's got two names—Francis X. Gordon, a.k.a El Borak. American, the great white avenger of the Khyber frontier. Howard sent him here in one of the stories, only he called it 'Ghulistan.' 'The land of ghouls—an evil region of black crags and wild gorges, shunned by wise men.'"

"Al Borax," said Hopps. "Kind of a mouthful. You're gonna need a better name."

"That's right," I said. "And those stories actually weren't that great. So we're gonna use the same setting, but a different character. This sixteenth-century Puritan avenger. Solomon Kane in Ghulistan, amped up Tarantino style."

"Sweet," said Hopps. "Like *The Punisher* versus AQ. I read that comic."

"Something like that, only with swords. The working title for the pilot is *Three-Bladed Doom*."

"Nice," said Hopps, right before the mortar round blasted his left ear clean off. It hung there in the air for a second as my mind's eye slowed to Peckinpah speed, making me wonder what a David Lynch action thriller would be like, until the mountains turned upside down and lanced the roof of the cab with a rigid metallic splat.

I woke to a splash of turgid water on my face, and opened my eyes to the flickering shadows of a cave.

I was in a large pit—a crater—chained to a twenty-foot metal stake anchored in the rock. The stake led up through a hole in the roof, like a giant television antenna. At its apex, the pole widened into a dish, nearly eclipsing the moon. Thick black electrical cables hung alongside, interwoven with my chains.

Behind me, a tunnel into deeper darkness. Above, at the edge of the pit, two turbaned young men stood laughing next to a tripod-mounted video camera. *My* video camera.

"Hey, TV boy," said one. "Smile for Dan Rather."

A pair of arc lights illuminated, blinding me. Squinting at the shadows behind the light, I watched one of the figures roll a round object down into the crater. I squirmed to dodge it until it bounced off the pole anchor and rested on its earless side, shrapnel-ripped flesh facing me with two glassy eyes.

"Hopps?" I muttered, cringing. The guards laughed.

"Are you ready for *Kharaba bin Iblis?*" said one of the tormentors. "No, you need to eat first." He turned and barked into the shadows. "Energy to put up a good fight for Fox News."

Behind them, I heard the sporadic crackle of electricity over other voices in strange dialects, more guttural and alien than any of the local patois.

I tried to stand, and landed flat on my face. Under the spots, I could now see that the pit was greased with black, viscous oil. I found a sandier spot, and managed to get up into a squat.

The turbaned frat boys disappeared, replaced by a robed woman carrying a tray. She walked around to the side of the pit, delicately ascended a narrow toe-path down to the base, and set the tray down at my side. I caught her gaze through the veil. Burning eyes, the eyes of an angry slave.

"Can you help me?" I said. "I am innocent. I am not a soldier. I have a girlfriend. Sort of. I have money. Here."

I reached into my pants, only to find no wallet was there.

"Do you have my...?"

She murmured something unintelligible, then scurried away. I yanked on the chain, only to fall again.

"What the fuck do you assholes want!" I yelled. I banged the chain against the rocks, throwing the best temper tantrum my inner child could summon.

"SILENCE!" yelled a booming voice.

I looked over my shoulder to see a tall man with a white beard, a dark brown cloak, and a turban the size of a Talosian brain case. Carrying a metallic staff that spun off little spurts of blue lightning.

"I am Radagasta al-Ishtari," he said with a dim echo. "And you are in a house of mystics and will maintain dignity at the hour of your death, or it will be a most indignant one."

"You have to let me go," I shouted. "I'm just a TV writer. From Canada. Making an old-fashioned movie."

"We know this," said Radagasta, holding up my passport wallet. "From your papers. Which makes you the perfect sacrifice."

More lights came on, now from all sides. The sound of a dynamo cranking up in the shadows. A glimpse of a man behind the camera, frantically adjusting the focus.

"Release the *Kharaba*!" shouted Radagasta. Behind him, frantic talking followed by the ominous sound of chains reeling onto a giant spindle. And in the tunnel behind me, a long, deep slurp, like the sound of a truckload of Big Macs being compacted. A wicked cacophony of spurts, as if the tunnel were the bowels of some gargantuan beast.

"The Jews have their Golem," said Radagasta. "Some think it a myth, a legend of the *Kabbalah*. But it is real. It is called America. Now we have ours. A demon enslaved to *jihad*, made of oil and the earth of our soil. With the appetite for your evil shamanic power, for your radio waves, your television signals, your cathode pollution of our people's minds. Feed the *Kharaba*!"

The dynamo hummed now at full amplitude. A loud metallic clap as someone pulled a switch, and blue bolts bisected the room, lunging for the metal stake to which I was chained.

I felt the first spastic vibration of electric shock before some mechanical trigger released the chain. I scrambled for the toe-path the woman had used, but made it only two steps before wiping out into the tray, knocking a full plate of acrid gruel out from under the serving napkin.

A loud swampy slush, and a new stream of oil flowed down from the tunnel as the toes of the Golem emerged into the light.

The rest of it followed. A black, inky goo-pile of pseudo-flesh, a perverted Kongian caricature of the human form. Punctuated with a gaping maw in lieu of a head, which opened with a horrifying gelatinous yawn as the thing dripped more than walked into my pit, sucking the electric current from the air, a blue torrent of light.

I scrambled in place, and knocked the tray again, dislodging a metal egg covered in goo. It gleamed in the blue strobe of the chaos. A grenade.

I grabbed it, pulled the pin instinctively, and managed to stand. The Golem roared like a jumbo jet, sucking every electron from the air, a whirling vortex of static and gray noise. Its limb lurched over my head like a distended organ, ripping one of the cables from its anchor and inserting the lightning floss into its mouth like a bendy straw.

I found my way to the gritty ramp, turned, lobbed the bomb, and scrambled frantically up to the lip of the pit, dragging chain.

The grenade burst with a muffled thud in the muck, then louder and longer after what seemed an interminable pause, splattering black dollops across the expanse of the cave. The Golem emitted a sonic boom. I covered my ears and crawled for the light of dawn peering through the mouth of the cave in the near distance.

I stood, threw the chains over my shoulders, and broke into a jog. Around me, the terrorists and their necromancer scurried to save their demonic pet. Only one tried to stop me, the smart-ass cameraman. The loud whack of a chain flail to the head took care of that.

I knew my time in the Society for Creative Anachronism would eventually prove useful on the job.

Outside, thunderheads over the desert dropped lightning onto the hundred-foot antenna, illuminating the abandoned ruins of Fort Sandeman and the vandalized British cemetery in an unearthly strobe. Through the din from the cave, I heard the echo of hooves. I turned, and saw a hijacked steed pop over a berm in the distance, bearing an equipment-laden rider. Mack. I ran for him.

Dismounted, Mack adjusted his targeting system and lasered in on the antenna.

"Sorry, kid," he said. "We needed to bait these guys, and you were in the wrong place at the right time. You're their dream hostage."

"Hopps," I said. "They—"

"Yeah, the motherfuckers. At least he'll get a little payback. Shut up and let me radio this in."

Mack handed me his rifle, and I did my best to pop off the goons as they emerged from the shooting gallery aperture of the cave. Within minutes, a supersonic chorus heralded the onset of a B-52.

"We've got Raytheon Ringwraiths made to order for these towel-head Gandalfs," said Mack. "Just-in-time Armageddon, one-click checkout. Let's get some cover."

I swear, looking back over my shoulder from the crest of the next dune, I saw the perfect Frank Frazetta mushroom cloud. It lasted less than a second, but you could see Conan laughing as the shrieking necromancer swirled into the sky.

Too bad I'd lost my camera.

John Meaney knows both physics and karate, which should be enough for anyone; that he is a splendid writer, too, is just gilding on a lily. One of Meaney's tales of "Mu-space"—which includes his novels *Paradox*, *Context*, and *Resolution*— this story of icebound survival and the stubborn will to live recalls the real-life stories of explorers and adventurers like Sir Edmund Hillary and Ernest Shackleton.

Lost Time
by John Meaney

Rekka is cold and shivering. Rekka is dying.

Dying by degrees—

She could tell you how it works: how the cold shuts down the biochemical pathways of thought and feeling, of movement and perception, until darkness closes in and nothing of Rekka Chandri remains. And yet, and yet... all around her in the ice-bound world called Coolth, in the supercooled shadows of that global ocean, there are forms of life that thrive.

But I was never supposed to live.

Her adoptive parents, her adoptive culture, tried to instill a sense of self-worth in the waif rescued from disaster. But she knows deep down, has always known, how worthless she is. The wider universe does not care.

Outside the shuttle's broken hull, clouds of luminous para-plankton swirl: a subsea aurora, alien and beguiling. And through the waters an eerie, haunting song appears to call her name:

RE—

KA—

KA.

The balaena's song is real, but it cannot know her. That is the illusion of a dying woman for whom death has become tangible, a thick blackness she can almost taste. Though the huge, circling balaena is a predator of sorts, it is the cold that is coming to get her, nothing more. The thermal energy of her life bleeds out through the hull, dissipating in the endless heat-sink of ocean.

She is dying.

"Ann...?" Her numb lips can barely whisper. "Ann-Elise? You there?"

But the AI cannot respond. Muted amber phase spaces rotate above the holoconsole, casting their ghostly light, but the main cabin illumination is out. The cold deck is tilted; Rekka is slumped against a bulkhead. Nothing is normal.

For Ann-Elise's delicate core lay with the other vital system components: inside an armored compartment at the shuttle's rear. A compartment now crushed by implacable ice.

I'm not just dying.

The thought is almost welcome.

I'm dying alone.

For a time she rallies the fighting spirit she half-learned from Franz. Her adoptive father was white-bearded with smiling eyes, never raised his voice, yet never gave in.

But I'm not him.

Rekka starts with vinyasa, the dynamic phase of yoga. It pushes back the cold, a little.

Not truly his...

Ignore that.

But her black leotard is sleeveless. She shucked off her padded envirosuit inside the airlock, when she ran into the shuttle. That chamber is flooded now. The inner hatches, buckled, will never open again.

Rekka is shivering.

Sixty trillion cells make up her body—she knows this—and inside every one of them lie tiny bioenergetic powerhouses called mitochondria. They break down molecules of ATP, driving the whole of life from the breaking of chemical bonds. And every one of those mitochondria bears its own DNA, inherited (unless she is a rare mutant) solely from her genetic mother.

In the end, this is her final, failing legacy from the mother that she never knew: the woman who tried to murder the foul offspring of her womb.

Simon. You cared... but I was stupid.

Rekka untwists from her yoga posture, straightens out her legs on the slanted deck. She leans back against the cold bulkhead. Her eyelids close.

The shivers are fading now.

Means something...

It means nothing good. Hypothermia has seized her nervous system; her reflexes are cutting off. She no longer has the energy to shiver.

Dying. Unless...

Rekka's arm is floppy, ragdoll-like, as she raises it up to form a control gesture, fails—*no, again*—then gets it right. Beside her, the solid bulkhead morphs, extruding a small drawer.

Inside it, an escape of sorts awaits.

Simon. Damn your eyes.

The device is strictly illegal outside of controlled experiments. (Simon can always pull political strings.) It shines purple, a cylinder with two curving horns like a trophy cut from some metallic beast.

It cannot save her life, this so-called Potentiator, but it can plunge her into forgotten memories, replaying them with a sense of slow, ongoing time: lasting weeks or months, while an outside observer would think minutes had passed.

Rekka has only fleeting impressions of her infant years in India. She would rather escape to happier days: school in Vancouver; picnics in Stanley Park; Olivia and Franz laughing, cherishing her. Yet the device will seek out trauma: it is most likely to plunge her into a forgotten hell of suffering beneath the hands of a cold and murderous mother.

But she is dying. There will be no more chances to find out for sure, to discover the truth. She will end her life in ignorance.

Choose.

The device's horns gleam purple.

Choose now.

The shuttle hangs downwards, angled at some forty five degrees from the ice-ceiling that has crushed its tail, including the all-important fusion clusters. It looks like some bulbous alien fruit, soon to burst open.

Not seeds, but the ruptured corpse of Rekka Chandri, will spill out then. Perhaps her intestinal or other bacteria—*ten percent* of a human's body weight is bacterial—will flourish in the supercooled waters.

Some kind of legacy.

Rekka can see in pitch darkness if she needs to, thanks to her corneal smartgel. So far it hasn't needed to kick in. The holoconsole glows, and the autofact hums, almost as if everything were normal.

I'm so cold.

During her first mission as a neophyte, dropped as solo observer on the world inhabited by the sentient Haxigoji, she force-evolved a bee-swarm to act as her spies and protectors. It was not the only use she made of her portable autofact. Her coding abilities enabled her to establish communication in a language rich with scents and pheromones, among a people who ate slivers of each other's flesh to pass on accumulated memories.

Long time ago.

What could she force-evolve here, in the oceans of Coolth? Some fish-creature derived from local life, able to survive in supercooled waters? What good would that do her?

Something clicks.

Above the autofact, a small display blossoms. It is pretty, a swirl of pastel translucent holo-manifolds, and it takes an endless time for Rekka to realize what she is seeing: preliminary analysis of the sample she inserted.

An hour or a lifetime ago, she retrieved an ice sample with a tiny trapped inhabitant: an orange, triple-winged fish-nymph. Around it, threads of green and purple curled: colonies of bacteria-analog that thrive here. Now, Rekka attempts a control gesture, to see more of the analysis results.

Fails.

Life on Coolth is based on a replicating molecule more complex than DNA: shaped like a chain whose every link is a twisted Möbius-strip of acid bases. That much, she can deduce from the display. Also, the bacterialike forms are autotrophs, which means they do not need to eat other organisms in order to survive; instead, chemicals and heat gradients from the environment provide energy and sustenance.

So who is the higher being?

Rekka has always been self-consciously vegetarian, on the principle of minimizing the suffering of other life-forms. But insects and field mice are killed during harvesting, and even plants scream (to those who know how to hear) when they are ripped up from the ground. Perhaps the local bacteria are more enlightened than Rekka Chandri.

It occurs to her in that moment, that if only the autofact's sample cavity were bigger, she could crawl inside and use it to survive. In a persistent scanfield, she would remain in stasis until Pilot Delgasso's return. But that lies three days in the future.

Too late.

Dying now.

This is how the autofact could have helped: by freezing reality. In an uncertain world at quantum scale, it is the act of observation that collapses reality from superimposed possibilities into a single actuality. And there is a long-known form of Zeno Paradox that states that if you keep performing the same measurement *without cease*, then the underlying reality, once measured, cannot reach slippery uncertainty: it is trapped in stasis.

If the Eye of the Universe were to gaze upon Rekka Chandri, its very omniscience would hold her in place forever.

There are babbling sounds in her memory, and bright hot fragmented images of the Indian subcontinent. Yet it is the scents of poverty she truly recalls: human odors, rain-stirred mud, and the sharp spices in too-scarce food.

I don't want to remember.

Olivia and Franz, both medical doctors, worked hard to fight the Changeling Plagues spreading outward from Calcutta's labs. It is a struggle that Rekka learned to appreciate in retrospect, as she grew older in Vancouver's safe environs and occasionally persuaded her legal parents to talk about the past. It was a period they considered their greatest failure.

"But we found you, yes?" Franz would say, giving a proud and wistful smile. "Such a prize, we had not foreseen."

"All right, eat," Olivia would interject (for such conversations always took place over a meal). "And thank God we are able to."

Yes, it was a good life they provided for her.

She repaid them with a steady focus on academic achievement: McGill in Toronto, then Beijing, followed by her work at Impinge AG in Zurich. Commercial research on UNSA contracts led (almost by accident) to that first mission among the alien Haxigoji. Rekka herself named their world Vijaya, which means "victory."

But that was over fifteen years earlier, and neither her friend among the Haxigoji (Sharp Tang, whose true name was formed by scent, not sound) nor her adoptive parents survived that year.

Her last memory of Simon is the argument.

A distant figure on the Haxigoji assignment, he had been the nominal project manager: someone to be manipulated, not confided in. It was only later, as the years passed and his responsibilities increased—he had always been ambitious—that they had taken a long walk together through snow-covered Zurich, drank hot *Gluehwein* in a small coffee shop, then found themselves holding hands as they watched children skating on the frozen river dividing the city.

And woke up the next morning, snuggled together in Simon's bed.

The arrangement was... flexible. Not an open relationship, for neither of them wanted that. Still, Rekka kept her own small house, square-edged with dark beams and ornate eaves in the Alpine style, overlooking a broad, dark lake. Simon continued to live in the heart of Zurich, above gleaming elegant stores opposite the baroque Hauptbahnhof, with its silent mag-trains sliding through.

"You don't need to go offworld again." Propped up in bed,

lean and tennis-fit, Simon had scowled: an expression Rekka disliked. "Leave it to the young ones."

It was three days before the mission start.

"No," was all Rekka had replied.

In silence, they flew by taxi to the labs—the cheapest way to travel—then avoided each other for the rest of the day, and went to their separate homes that night.

As for the Potentiator, he had shown her the device, or one just like it, several months earlier. "You have to know," he had said on that occasion. "You can't go through life just wondering about it. About your real, uh, your genetic mother, and what she tried to do."

"Why not? Why ever not?"

Because Olivia and Franz never talked about it, not in her presence. Only once, late at night, the twelve-year-old Rekka had overheard a rare argument from their bedroom, and Olivia saying, *"But her mother tried to* kill *her, remember?"* and then Franz's *"Shush, my love. Shush now,"* and a silence that lasted forever. (And still she regretted telling Simon about it, so many years later.)

Now there was no one in the universe who knew what happened in India... except for herself. The suppressed, forgotten truth lay in whatever hellish memories the child-Rekka had laid down, during the days of plague and death.

She sees a gray-faced woman, gaunt.

No...

Feels sticklike arms enfold her.

Leave me alone!

The memory is gone.

This, her first sight of Coolth, from orbit:

Glasslike transparent plains, and vast white wastes, webbed with fracture lines. Blue ice-mountains form long ridges like veins on pale skin.

While beneath them, and all around the ice plateaus, the supercooled global ocean cradles Coolth's abundant life.

She traveled in a passenger lounge of the mu-space ship, asleep in the delta-coma that protects ordinary human beings from the mind-twisting perspectives of that fractal universe. Awakening with a headache, she followed the ship's directions to a gray-furnished briefing room. The Pilot was waiting.

Pilots scared the hell out of her.

Carlos Delgasso was one of the new breed: lean-featured with obsidian eyes—totally black, devoid of surrounding white. Where the older Pilots had required viral rewiring, their eyes replaced with metallic sockets for i/o links... these new, true Pilots glowed with presence.

He was sitting beside a floating holo image of the ice-and-ocean globe.

"An unusual world." Delgasso's voice was pleasant enough. "Strong radio emissions."

"There's *civilization*?" Rekka forgot about her migraine. "That's not what the probe-scans said."

"No, it's natural. A liquid iron sulfide core, swirling with convection currents. Whistler-mode emissions, if you want to get technical."

"Uh, right..."

"You live in Zurich, correct?"

Rekka squinted at him. Was he hitting on her? With those glistening jet-black eyes, his expression was impossible to read. "What makes you ask, Pilot?"

"Just wondering." A dismissive shrug. "I mostly grew up there, is all."

Damn it.

There *was* a residential Pilots' school high up in the mountains, funded by UNSA and operated by—of all things—a teaching order of nuns.

He was just trying to make conversation.

Pilot Delgasso stood up with the controlled grace of a gymnast or a martial artist, and gave a brief, dismissive nod.

"I'm sorry," said Rekka. "I'm not used to talking to Pilots."

Eyes like polished obsidian.

Then his mouth twitched in a half smile. "Not a problem, Dr. Chandri. I *am* used to human beings."

He gave a tiny bow and left the briefing room.

While in the image, Coolth continued to rotate, heedless of the tiny creatures in high orbit around its massive self.

Ten hours later, she stood on mint-blue aerated ice. Trapped bubbles shone, bright and silver as pearls. In her warm envirosuit, Rekka turned a full circle, scanning the ice plain that spread in all directions. White-and-purple ridges lay to the east. Her landed shuttle was pale, with stubby wings. It looked at home in the harsh, icy landscape.

Overhead, a small shape flew.

What's that?

She double-blinked her corneal smartgel, homing in. Bluish, bottle-shaped body; extended flexible wings, like an airborne manta ray; rear-facing slits in its skin that might be nostrils or nozzles. It swept through the air in a straight line.

"Got the data?" she subvocalized. "Tag the log entry 'Bluebird.'"

"That's done." The voice in her ears belonged to Ann-Elise, the shuttle's AI. *"And Pilot Delgasso is leaving orbit. Will return in eighty, eight-oh, standard hours."*

"Thanks, Ann-Elise."

She let the silence settle in again, taking a series of deep, slow breaths to acclimate. There were samplers to lay out across the ice, but for now she wanted to drink in the moment.

Rekka was the first human being to stand upon this world.

Five hours later, as she made ready to deploy the last two collection cylinders, the first sampler came crawling back along the ice. It stopped and lay still, tiny status lights blinking. Rekka reached out, her gloved fingers forming a control gesture.

Then the ground shivered and she fell over.

What the hell?

Lying on her side, she saw the icescape as a tilted white plain. Icy hardness had thumped against her ribs when she landed, but the envirosuit was padded.

The collection cylinder's carapace had cracked open, revealing fist-sized ice samples. Rekka crawled over to the device, hauled herself to her feet, and took a sample in each hand. She looked across at the shuttle: two hundred meters away.

A second tremble swept the ground.

Oh, Gods.

"Ann-Elise? Open the outer hatch."

"Already done."

Tremor.

"Run, Rekka!"

She had not known an AI could sound terrified. Rekka crouched, ready to—

Crack.

Splintered fissures forked: black lightning through white ice.

The ice began to break.

Samples in her fists, Rekka sprinted towards the open hatch.

Hurry.

Her breath was fast, and hot liquid sweat bathed her body in a fierce primeval joy as adrenaline kicked in and the amygdala—the buried portion of her brain that responded so much faster than rational, civilized thought—took control of her muscles and flung her clumsily across the ice.

Hurry faster or you'll die.

Slipped...

No!

...but did not go down.

Come on.

Pushed herself onward, ignored the slipping of her boot soles. Hatch looming bigger, getting closer—come on—and then she was at the threshold, rolling the samples inside and hauling herself into the—

"I'm in."

—airlock, splitting open the bulky envirosuit as the outer hatch slid shut.

"Quickly, Rekka."

The inner hatch was already opening.

"I'm doing it."

Rekka wriggled and slid out of the split cocoon that was her suit. A long-legged sleeveless black leotard was all she wore underneath, and metal decking froze her bare feet as she hurried inside, picking up a sample on the way. At the inner lock she paused, glanced back at the other sample—*leave it*—then turned and squeezed inside. Almost safe.

The shuttle tipped sideways.

She was in the control chair, without remembering how she had reached the forward cabin. Alarms howled; holos strobed. The ice sample was no longer in her hand.

"Emergency take—"

Too late.

A crevasse opened beneath the shuttle, grew huge on every side; then the jets roared and for a moment Rekka thought she had a chance. The craft hung there in position—*doing it*—and she swallowed, a washing sound filling her hearing—stress response—and then something struck the hull hard, a flying chunk of ice, and the shuttle's nose tipped down.

"Ann-Elise!"

"I'm trying! There's—"

Another thump.

The shuttle plunged downward.

Fantastic walls of ice scraped past and the engines roared—there was no hope of rising but perhaps they could dive *down*, power their way through the water and search for an opening in the ice—then impact slammed Rekka backward. The chair reacted, enveloping her like a marshmallow fist. The world went away.

When it crawled back into her awareness, she was in a cold shuttle, hanging nose-down beneath the ice cap, inside the ocean, and the fusion clusters were crushed. The ice must have closed in, caught the shuttle just as it hit the water. The AI, Ann-Elise, was crushed into oblivion.

Soon, Rekka would join it.

Rekka is cold. Rekka is dying.
Rekka is ten percent bacteria.

Perhaps another asana would keep the final chill at bay. But she does not have the energy to assume the yoga posture. It is hard enough to breathe.

Her life-heat is bleeding through the cold deck, into the ocean of Coolth. There is no such thing as life-force—for "prana" Rekka has always read *pattern*, the configuration that changes yet persists even though none of us retain the atoms we were made of at birth.

Soon, my thoughts will be gone.

In the supercooled waters outside, a great shape is circling. Strip-shaped eyes glitter along its leading edge. It is even bigger than the shuttle, but Rekka has seen the earlier scans and knows: this is just a child, a balaena cub.

I *will be gone.*

The balaena swims into gloom, is lost from sight.

"The thing about mitochondria, the powerhouses of every single animal cell"—she hears Professor Bosley's voice (though he died last year) as clearly as if she were still a student at McGill—*"is that they were once a single species of bacteria, engulfed by some bigger cell"*—he thumps the lab bench—*"but not digested. Instead, it made itself indispensable. Every animal descends from that symbiotic union."*

Soon, the bacterial remnants of Rekka's corpse will spew out into the cold seas. The only question is whether hypothermia will kill her before the hull ruptures. Either way, both she and her bacterial components are doomed: there are native species, large organisms and microscopic bacteria alike, far better suited to Coolth's supercooled ocean. Every glowing phase space and numeric lattice above the autofact tells her so.

I'm not good enough.

Even her genetic mother wanted Rekka destroyed.

I don't deserve to live.

She slumps back against the bulkhead.

On the deck, the Potentiator's purple metallic horns glint with reflected light from the autofact's holo display. *"You have to know."* Those were Simon's words, wanting her to use the device, to confront the hell that was her past.
But not when I'm dying.
Of course, Simon had not foreseen that. He would grieve when he heard the news.
I should've treated you better.
Far better. But it is too late now.
The purple horns are shining.

Inside the autofact, small samples are held in stasis, simply because the machinery continues to observe them. If it wanted to change those samples, there is a strange way it could accomplish this. By altering the mode of observation just slightly, it is possible to allow quantum fuzziness to minimize, to be directed. It is the *inverse* Zeno Effect, discovered in the late twentieth century, and the basis of all femtoscale engineering.

The Quantum School of Telos teaches, in its neo-Aristotelian mystic disciplines, that evolution has a goal. Its philosophers say that life should not have proceeded so quickly from chemical soup to complex organisms. There must be some form of inverse-Zeno at work: not human minds, but enzymatic molecules, which unwittingly drive evolution towards the cosmic endpoint.

Rekka has never believed a word of it.

Childhood beckons: purple, metallic, and dangerous.
It is the only alternative to death.

In the twenty-first century, some people said the written word was dead. Yet holodisplays gave rise to languages such as FourSpeak, multi-layered and compressible. Professor Bosley claimed it was only the start of a new jump in cultural evolution, with written script poised to make huge leaps forward in richness and complexity.

Perhaps. For sure, the Potentiator uses femtotech to deliver smart enzymes into the brain, and the key molecule's name is more pun than marketing label:

Alpha-Laevo	*Recombinant*	*Di-methyl*	*Tetranucleotide*	*Potentase*
a	*e*	*u*	*e*	*e*
	c		*m*	*r*
	h		*p*	*d*
	e		*s*	*u*
	r			
	c			
	h			
	e			

And now is the time.

Choose now.

Her hand shakes. She tries to lift the thing.

No...

It will not budge from the deck. Franz would be ashamed of her.

Come on.

Movement. Slowly, Rekka's arm responds to her command. Her icy fingers fumble, slip, then fasten on the horned device. It is light. It is heavier than God.

The points dip towards her throat.

No, I shouldn't—

Too late.

Pain shoots into her neck: twin shots of piercing heat as the horns intersect her carotid arteries, and deliver their submicroscopic load. It *burns* inside.

Her hand drops back.

It hurts....

The Potentiator clatters to the tilted deck.

FLASH_ONE:

The windowless room is hot, the once-whitewashed walls now gray as old bones.

"As though we need more kids!" The big Sikh stands with massive forearms folded across his broad chest, above his big stomach. Though he looks well-fed, his turban is stained with grease, his spreading beard unkempt, and a clenched panic sits behind his eyes.

He is huge....

Rekka cranes her head back to stare up. He is a giant.

No, it's me. I'm small.

She is maybe five years old, and her body is not hers to control. These are memories, not dreams, and the action played out long ago. No one can change it now.

Blank-eyed children sit in rows, working.

Oh, dear God.

"I am begging you, kind sir..."

Mother! Rekka knows the voice but cannot turn to look. *Let me see you.*

"...to take her. Just one more. She won't eat much. I'll do... whatever you want."

There is an odd, strained tone in Mother's voice, an offer that remains unspoken, obvious to the adult Rekka. Here, bribery (of all kinds) is part of life.

"No."

Then a howl from outside splits the cloying air.

"Please, sir. She is being bright and working hard, I promise. She—"

"No."

Even the working children pause, cross-legged amid webs of control fibers hanging in catenary curves: fibers that link their drilled skulls to processor blocks, controlling the manufacture of intricate toys. (And Rekka knows that children who lead very different lives will play with the marvels these wretches create.)

"I'm sorry." The Sikh businessman shakes himself. "You're disrupting their work."

The children flinch, then lower their heads. Systems hum.

"Thank you, sir," whispers Mother.

She tugs, and the child-Rekka looks up, sees Mother's gaunt

gray-skinned face, the cheekbones sharp and angular.

No...

Paint is flaking from the passageway walls. They pause by the wooden outer door, which is silver-gray with age. Outside, the night is waiting.

Another howl.

"A *vritra*," Mother says. "We must go quietly, little one."

"Okay." Rekka's voice is high: a child's voice.

But her adult awareness recalls—as abstract concepts culled from historical texts—the flapping, crawling night-creatures, called by demonic names from legend: *vritra* and *dasu*. Rogue femtovectors, spilled or deliberately released from labs, gave birth to the Changeling Plague.

Mother pulls the creaking door open. Outside, the night is warm and fetid.

I'm scared.

A hand tightens on hers.

Mother...

They slip into the night.

END_FLASH_ONE.

The deck is cold. Someone is whimpering.

Oh, my mother.

Tears form twin cold channels, congealing on her cheeks.

I didn't want to know this badly. But it's...

The discarded Potentiator lies like a sardonic metal smile.

...too...

Something bangs against the outer hull.

...late.

FLASH_TWO:

Curtains of silver rain hiss upon wet mud. Coffee-colored puddles deepen; ricocheting drops spatter on their surfaces.

Monsoon is the season of romance.

What's happening to me?

Rekka is stumbling through the downpour. A length of gray

string, looped around her left wrist, joins her to Mother's bony right hand. Mother's once-fine sari is splashed with mud, almost worn through.

Then Mother trips and falls.

No!

Facedown in sticky, sucking mud.

The child Rekka is paralyzed, not knowing what to do. Then she gives a tiny jump of fright. An armored skimmer is passing on the far side of the street, heading for the open square. Its occupants are mirror-visored, graser rifles held at port-arms, and their armbands bear the UN logo.

But the adult Rekka knows: attempts to contain the Plague by force are useless. It took autofacts and femtophages to fight back the infection. That was how history played out.

She looks at Mother, sprawled facedown in mud.

No...

Mother raises her gaunt head.

"Must finish... this."

Scabrous buildings line the once-elegant square. Mud squelches as Mother walks. An old man with an umbrella opens his mouth, raises his hand as if to stop her, then grows very still. After a moment, with a tiny shake of the head, he turns, heading back the way he came.

Amid the pouring rain, at the square's center, a golden pavilion awaits. The rainfall's percussion on the pavilion's cupolas, and the silvery streams spilling from its eaves, turn the edifice into a musical instrument. It is some kind of monsoon dream.

No!

The child Rekka squints against the rain, trying to make out details. She has never seen its like.

Sweet God, no...

But the adult Rekka knows exactly what this is: a Suttee Pavilion. She remembers crying when she first read of such a thing (and begins now to comprehend the strength of that reaction).

Don't go inside.

Mother's bony hand tightens around Rekka's wrist.

Widows know that they are worthless, without a productive place in society. They accept their lot as they have always done. Like cells that commit suicide—apoptosis—in order to keep the human body cancer-free and healthy, so do unwanted women accept the way of Suttee.

Think of it as an expression of love, for the husband who is no more: the dead husband they will join in the afterlife.

The colloquial term is "bride-burning."

The pavilion is wonderful.

This is WRONG!

She tries and tries, but no mental scream can alter the past.

Monsoon plashing outside; low sitar music playing in counterpoint within. Overhead, a heavy burgundy drape hides the ceiling. At each corner, a golden figure with trunk and tusks—Ganesh the Elephant God—holds up a pillar.

The bier is a raised couch, covered with soft cushions. Beside it, a silver-chased pedestal bears a polished flagon from which enticing aromas rise. There are open trays of food: plump fruit, clean and bright; curry and dal; naan bread, warm and freshly baked.

Mother, don't.

But this is history. No one can alter it.

Please...

The UN-supplied facilities were said to be a humane solution to overpopulation and disease. The processors will allow them to take their fill, to lie back as warm, drugged sleep takes hold of them. The system will wait.

Death—and flames—will come only when they are dreaming.

A soft peach is a sweet explosion of miraculous taste.

Mother moans with pleasure. Rekka is simply shocked as waves of overwhelming sensation sweep from her tongue and sing through her energized body.

More...

They feed and feed, and Mother drinks from the flagon but offers none to Rekka. Nor will she let Rekka eat of the spiced dishes.

Mother.

Drinking hungrily, desperately. Eyes squeezed shut as she dips bread into a thick tikka mix, places it inside her mouth—a burst of sensation seems to flow from mother to daughter—and then she looks around

The monsoon rain is quieter now.

Me, too. Let me eat that....

Antisound fields reduce the outside world to a hush. Microwave barriers guard the pavilion, now that its occupants have eaten the anesthetic-laden food. Only the fruit, it seems, is unaltered. Somehow Mother knew—

Mother's eyelids droop.

Just the carbohydrates. A little drowsiness. Please let it be that.

Mother lies back, mouth half-open with pleasure, eyes closed. Her too-thin arm angles around Rekka. Mother's ribs feel sharp through the ruined sari.

Don't sleep.

Mother's chest rises, then falls.

Please. Don't.

Then... a distant sound. Voices?

But she cannot—

END_FLASH_TWO.

The deck is bitterly cold. Supercooled ocean remains outside.

She wanted me to live, not die!

The hull is creaking.

No...

Slipping back.

FLASH_THREE:

"She's still breathing!"

"*Oy*, my love. Let me."

Strong hands enfold Rekka.
Mother...
They lift her with ease. The bier drops away beneath her.
"Quick, Franz. Quickly now."
Take Mother, too.
"We've got you, little one."
That's what she calls—
Heat, and the burst of orange flames.
Stench of roast pork.
"Oh, my God."

FLASH_THREE_INTERRUPT:

Rekka drags herself into the moment. She is lying on the deck.
"I will... *not* go back."
She forms a fist, and thumps cold metal.
Stay awake.
Pushes herself to a half-sitting position.
Move.
But the dreams are calling still, and she slips down into—

FLASH_FOUR:

Overhead the holobanner reads GATE 17, but the big official blocking their way shakes his head. He reminds Rekka of the sweatshop owner, the man who turned Mother away.

"But the flight is boarding!" Franz gestures at the window. Outside, a ragged line of people is slowly entering the big waiting shuttle.

"You can get on, sir."

"*Not* without my daughter."

The big man inhales, chest swelling.

"The authorization," he says, one hand resting on his sealed holster, "is not being correct."

"I cleared it with the—"

Then Olivia puts her hand on Franz's sleeve.

"How much"—very softly—"do you want?"

The official has already searched them. He knows what jewelry and cred-chips they carry. "All of it," he says.

Franz stares at him for a long moment.

"Then *take* it. It's only money." Franz lifts Rekka from the ground, holds her in both arms. "We're going on board now."

The official bows his head.

FLASH_FOUR_INTERRUPT:

She owes it to them all: the gift of life.

How could I think of giving up?

Forces herself to kneel before the autofact.

Work fast, now.

The hard bit is long finished. The machine has analyzed the native bacteria that produce energy from the sea, the long invisible filaments that reach out from the fish-nymph to feed upon the waters. Replicating the stuff is easy.

But her control gestures are clumsy.

"Come on..."

And the dreams.

"Smartgel substrate... "

The dreams are calling her.

"...better grow...quickly..."

Dragging her back.

FLASH_FIVE:

The shuttle's passenger cabin is filled with the gabble of conversation, the brightness of saris and the plainness of business tunics, the confusion over seats, while Olivia and Franz remain silent, both of them holding her so tight—

INTERRUPT INTERRUPT INTERRUPT:

No time to sleep.

"Better." Phase spaces billow over the autofact. "Increase here."

She gestures.

Dreams, calling...

No time.

FLASH_SIX:

—the smiling androgynous flight attendant leans over and says—
INTERRUPT:

"No! For God's sake, let me work."

She kicks the Potentiator, sliding it across the deck. It is a gesture: the real fight is inside her.

Calling...

Rekka has work to do. It is cold, and energy is seeping from her.

The dreams...

But she will *not* give in.

FLASH_CASCADE:
ERROR ERROR ERROR

<<*Whirling, the light and dark.*>>

Kaleidoscopic synesthesia. Twisting, unraveling her world.

<<*Monsoon rain and pungent smoke: the funerary flames.*>>

No. *Outwards.*

<<*Demons...* Vritra*s and* dasu*s prowl the fetid night.*>>

Claws of pain, dragging her back. Her father is a demon now, she knows.

<<*And Mother's fingertip against her cheek.*>>

She loved him, her husband. Mother loved my Changeling father. But he is gone.

<<*Slips away.*>>

Gone now.

<<*Away.*>>

PROCEDURE_TERMINATES

The dreams are broken.

But so is the shuttle's hull. Rekka is still forcing cold, hard gel down her throat when the creaking begins. She snaps her head around, checks the console.

Breach is imminent.

The view-window is membrane, tuned to maximum hardness. Still swallowing, still pushing fists-full of the stuff into her mouth, Rekka makes frantic control gestures with her free hand.

Forcing the last of it down.

Oh, my God.

The gel wriggles inside her, pushes its way into her lungs. Her choking body tries to suck in air, but the smartgel insinuates itself into every bronchiole: cold, hard, and painful. Then it spreads across her skin in a thin layer.

Water spurts through the softening membranous window.

Can't breathe.

But she continues to direct the few working systems as cold water foams across the deck. She can stop the shuttle from imploding, but only by allowing the ocean to spew inside and spume around her ankles, her knees.

Then the shuttle shifts angle, tearing some aft compartment apart, and Rekka falls into the churning, supercooled waters.

Keep moving.

Submerged, she blinks until her corneal smartgel, now merged with the stuff that covers her body, allows her to see in the boiling maelstrom.

The membrane window fails.

Now.

And she slides with a rush of current, lets it take her.

Yes, now.

It spits her into the ocean.

Breathe.

And then she is hanging in the infinite abyss.

Breathe now.

Drifting.

At first she turned and hung there, watching the shuttle split apart. It twisted away and slowly slid downward into the deep. Other sections, torn out of recognizable shape, survive as tatters of metal hanging from the ice ceiling above.

So peaceful.

It may be lack of oxygen and warmth. The local bacteria-analogs, multiplied and subsumed within her system, do not yet provide everything she needs. Fine, near-invisible tendrils spread from her skin, and begin to absorb nourishment from the shadowy, supercooled waters.

Just drifting.

While in the distance, the shadows of behemoths move.

Graveyard.

Double-blink to magnify. Triple-blink to shift frequency, translating infrared into colors her brain can process. She thought she was imagining things, but this is real.

All around her, like destroyed hulks in the aftermath of some naval battle, hang the decomposing corpses of vast balaenae. The water holds a different texture in this place, a flavor of death.

Can't escape.

The gel is failing, or simply cannot grow to maximum capacity in time. It delivers oxygen and energy, but not enough. Rekka is shivering in the water now, and the edges of her vision are growing dark.

Oh, Simon...

Him, and all the others who loved her and tried to help her, who wanted her to live.

Letting you down.

Then something bulbous-bodied and massive comes swooping out of the depths towards her. Rekka shuts her eyes.

Dying now.

The thing takes hold of her.

Flying, not dying.

RE—

    KA—

        KA.

A distant call.

Beneath Rekka's hands, the young balaena's skin is soft-textured yet hard underneath. Tiny ridges encrust that skin in places; from some of them, tendrils extend.

Tendrils, like the ones that clasp her, carry her along.

Taking me to death?

The thought is not fearful. Every second now is an added bonus, and Rekka is in a place of marvels, flying through oceans no human has ever seen. Something appears to call her name, in a ghostly wailing song never intended to be heard by non-balaenae. It is the call of a matriarch, summoning her kin.

No!

Shapes ahead.

Impossible...

And too huge to comprehend.

Beautiful.

It is a cathedral, an immensity in the ocean: a vast globe formed of balaena bodies, a sphere that is a kilometer wide or more. They hang there, each of those ten thousand massive forms, watching and waiting.

While at the center, the matriarch spreads huge tendrils in all directions. Her great body is covered with whorls and ridges on which small nodules—small-*looking* nodules: they are bigger than Rekka—pulse and tremble. Clouded eye-strips as big as buildings watch Rekka's approach.

The mother...

A matriarch, who has spawned this great herd of wonderful creatures: a herd now gathered in mournful anticipation.

They are waiting for her to die.

Rekka knows this beyond words. What she cannot know is why the young cub has brought her here. As a last offering to the dying mother? A final morsel before she can eat no more?

Or merely a novel sight to arouse her dying curiosity?

So wonderful...

Rekka closes her eyes.

Now I can die.

And then she is drifting, rolling slowly over and over in the waters. The balaena cub has released her.

Then a tendril, slow and ponderous, curves from the matriarch's immense form, reaches towards Rekka, stops. Then curls, and draws her in.

I'm so tired...

It pulls her towards one of the pale nodules or blisters which are formed of membrane and—*no!*—pushes her inside.

Oh, my God.

Putrescence swirls around the interior. A small form lies curled and rotting: a nymph or embryo which has not survived.

Help me....

Rekka passes out.

And wakens to a choir, a hum and then a growing crescendo of sound. It is magnificent and it is strange: a song that inspires and tells the history of the deeps in ways Rekka cannot understand. She weeps, even in this water-filled tomb, at the sadness and the grandeur of it.

Swelling now, the sound.

Death song.

Somehow she knows that this is how they celebrate the matriarch's life: gathering at the end, to sing.

So beautiful.

And then the immense finale, while Rekka—suspended, curled up in water—lowers her head, grieving with those ten thousand siblings.

Everything explodes.

Maelstrom. Water rushing past: white foam, exploding steam.

Acceleration.

NO!

Hurled upwards, feeling sick.

Help me!

Then blue sky bursts into being all around her.

And free fall.

All around her, blister nodules are exploding in the sky. From each one, a bulbous winged shape drops—*the nymph form,* she realizes, *the balaena nymph form*—then spreads those wings, catching the air, and curving upwards, instinctively taking flight.

Her last litter...

It is the matriarch's final legacy to her world, as her body rips itself apart. Down below, her ten thousand mature children surround her remnants, mourning her, while up here the final batch of offspring (who will drop back into the ocean sometime, in a month or a year, to grow and metamorphose into aquatic behemoths) flies free through the clear sky.

Except Rekka, who is falling.

Dying now, at last.

Featureless white snow rushes up towards her.

Impact.

The world is smashed away.

Blood and pain. Darkness and light.

Simon...

A burst of silver amid the blue.

Ship?

Eyes of jet. The Pilot, leaning over her.

"I've got you," he says. "Don't worry, I've..."

Darkness clenches her once more.

Pilot Delgasso awakens Rekka while they are still in orbit. Then he leaves her alone to watch the holodisplay, the image of a blue-and-white globe. It is the homeworld where Simon waits, holding out the promise of normality, of ordinary life. Simon, who so wants her to stay.

Wants me to live.

Rekka has never felt so loved as at this moment. It is warm, the best of feelings, and some part of her wishes it might mean the end of her wandering, her search for meaning.

So blue, so lovely.

But there is so much to see, to experience. Can she really turn her back on the infinite vastness? For even the best-loved children—perhaps especially the best-loved children—must in the end fly out from the comfortable nest, and venture into the great, unsettling cosmic void.

Though known principally as an editor and anthologist, Lou Anders is also a splendid writer, which too few people know. In this, the first installment of a novel which will be serialized over subsequent volumes of *Adventure*, Anders introduces us to the new model western, one that comes by way of the New Weird.

The Madlands
Part I: Death Wish
by Lou Anders

The noose bit hard into my neck. A jolt shot down my back that blinded my eyes with a burst of white pain. I jerked in the air as the rope snapped taut. My spine almost broke, but did not. Another instance of the uncanny luck that has been my privilege in a life otherwise unblessed. It took me an instant of animal panic to realize I was not dead. Not yet—though that would come soon enough. My hands were bound behind my back, but my legs were free, and they kicked out wildly as I sought automatically and futilely to find some footing under them. The pain in my chest was immediate, a burning as my lungs tried desperately to suck air through an esophagus squeezed tightly shut. As my thick neck had stubbornly held, it would take me longer to die, prolonging my pain.

Below me, the rabble jeered and called out. They may have pelted me with stones. In truth, I do not know. The pain inside my chest was worse than any they could inflict, and drowned out all external blows. Likewise, their jibes and catcalls were a dull murmur heard only dimly through a rush of blood and a grating of tortured lungs. My vision, too, soon became spotty and clouded.

I have never had much fear of death, having met Her head-on many times since I was little more than a delinquent orphan cheating (rather than begging) food from passing strangers. If this was to be my end, I would meet it without terror, though I was angered that I would meet it without a fight as well. Having lived a life full of opportunities to die on my feet, pistol and cutlass in hand, it seemed dishonorable to meet my end bobbing like a rotting fruit from the limb of a tree, sport for the inbred morons and small-minded imbeciles of a prairie town that was little more than a way station for a disused rail line. But in the ramshackle town of Golgotha, this was high entertainment.

The cowards had set upon me as I lay in a drunken stupor in the arms of a whore. Trussed me up and framed me quickly for a bank job I did not commit (though I have crimes aplenty to my credit). Clearly the local magistrate, an ineffectual and bumbling lout, had felt it advantageous and easier to blame the stranger rather than seek the real perpetrator. Furthermore, the sheriff, a lanky devil with a low cunning, had taken obvious offense at the old uniform I sported. It was proof that I was a veteran from the opposite side of a war that, while in actuality lying buried decades in the past, was still fought in the small minds of rough country folk such as these.

And so, after a trial that was nothing but sham and show, I was dragged out here into the plains, where a line was thrown over the limb of a great, lone tree. A noose was twisted in one end, while the other was fixed to the back of a horsecycle—a great, snorting black beast whose legs had been amputated and replaced with three massive tires. After an offering of last rites which I belligerently refused, the beast was slapped across its flank. Its treads kicked up prairie dust as its anus belched flame, and it took off. Thus I ascended into heaven.

I peered down through lenses red with blood. They were a mongrel lot, and I hated them. The kind of mean, low-spirited folk who, having little joy in their bereft lives, take their best pleasure from the pains of others. Eventually, something of their ridicule broke through the din of my pain, and I realized with horror what they laughed at. Quite without my volition, but as I am told is a common occurrence with asphyxiation, I realized shamefully that I now sported a huge and obvious erection. It jutted forward for their amusement, as taut as the line I swung from.

Then I gave up my pride and I prayed to God and Devil both,

pledging my allegiance to either force if they would but snap the cord and drop me into the rabble's midst. I could die anywhere, in any manner, tomorrow even, if only I had today to take my revenge upon these people. But pray as I might, no divine or demonic aid came. As mucus burst in bubbles from my wheezing lips, and my eyes bulged and felt they would soon explode, I realized that death was now but moments away, skulking in with the blackness that slid forward from the corners of my vision.

Then, in my mind, I pushed *beyond* the traditional confines of our accustomed spiritual realm, forgoing both Jehovah and Lucifer and pledging myself instead to any force, however distant or alien, that might see my need and strike a bargain with me. I knocked on strange doors behind which powers incomprehensible to mortal man might dwell. And here, at last, I felt that my solicitation had been received.

It was then that I saw her. Clothed in a long, flowing white dress, with a parasol to match. She had porcelain skin, and long, generous hair of near-white gold spilling out from under a broad hat. Amid the dirt and grime of the rabble, she shone like a goddess, though they took no apparent notice of her as she stood still as a statue in their unruly ranks. An ornate and unfamiliar brass timepiece was fastened to her breast like a broach. This struck me as odd, but it soon paled beside the intensity and intelligence of her gaze, which rose unabashedly to meet my own. I have never been a handsome man, the tribulations of my lawless life having left their scars upon my face and body alike, but I have a roguish wit and a natural strength about me to which many women have fallen prey. Here, though, in her eyes I sensed an equal, a companion whose intellect and ambition might rival my own.

Now my encroaching death was doubly painful, as I knew that my true love existed and that I was soon to be separated from her by an impenetrable divide. Perhaps it was that my limbs and organs were now numb, deprived of oxygen for as long as they had been, but it seemed to me that this new sadness overwhelmed me and drove out the physical pain to replace it with a deeper pain of the spirit.

Then I noticed that the skies had darkened. Swollen, great black clouds had swarmed in to block out the sun. With a crack of lightning and boom of thunder, they burst open and the heavens gave up their waters. No simple shower this, but a torrential downpour that carried with it a hail of rock-hard ice. Fist-sized bullets of frozen water smashed into the rabble, who cursed and scattered like frightened mice. While I, sheltered by the limbs of the very tree they had strung me up upon, laughed without breath as I gazed down upon them like some vengeful crucified god.

I looked for my lady in their retreating numbers, but could not see her. I hoped that her parasol would protect her against the storm. This was to be my final moment on this mortal plane, and I was gratified that Nature and Circumstance had turned the tables in my advantage. Feeling almost rewarded by this change in situation, I calmly accepted my death.

White light and white heat cut the dark in twain. A searing bolt of lightning shot from the sky to strike the tree above me. For a moment, I felt a rush of electricity flashing through my bones, and then I heard a great, splintering crack of tortured wood.

I fell to the earth below.

I landed hard on my feet, and pitched forward into the thick, new mud at the base of the tree, then tumbled over to lie upon my back. Above me, the tree was a burning tower of rippling flame. I sucked in hard gulps of blessed air, but I felt my consciousness fading.

"Do not die, sir," said a quiet, womanly voice to my side. "For we have made a solemn pact. Nor will I release you of your end so easily." I rolled my eyes in that direction and caught a glimpse of white boots under a white dress, unstained by mud or rain. The bizarre timepiece dangled before my eyes on a gold chain. I saw the markings upon its dial, but they made no sense to me that I could discern. "Seek me out when you are properly recovered."

"Wh-where?" I stammered through swollen lips.

"Follow the Golden Rails to the West. But see that you do

not take too long, as time is short."

My heart leaped to have her so near, but then the demands upon my physique made themselves known, and I slipped into unconsciousness.

I awoke quite suddenly to the most horrendous noise. It seemed to be the scream of both beast and machine, a terrible din of animal pain and tortured gears. I scrambled unsteadily to my feet, the pain in my limbs proof at least that I yet lived. Before me, the remains of the tree blazed under a black night sky, while ensnared in the very same rope that was meant to hang me was the horsecycle that had been used to hoist me aloft. The rope was still tethered to its rear, while the other end was caught in the splintered bark of the limb that had once held me. What must have been only a chance snagging of the line was now a cat's cradle of twisted rope, and I realized that the beast must have foolishly driven round and round the tree in a vain attempt to free itself. Instead, it had reeled itself in dangerously close to the inferno, and now threatened to burn out its motors and strip its gears as it gunned its engines and tugged blindly in fear and madness against its restraints.

The animal's eyes bulged at the effort, as did the veins of its great neck, and foam flecked its lips. In its panic, I reasoned that it would probably strike at any who came near to it. Still, while I have lain with little or no remorse more men in their grave than I can count, I cannot abide to see a dumb animal suffer. Animals are without guilt or guile, but dig deep enough into the heart of even the purest man, and you will find cause enough to place a bullet in his brain. So raising my hands in what I hoped was a placating gesture, I slowly approached the animal. I have always been good with mounts, wheeled or hooved, and I think that the beast sensed something of this in my nature, for though it did not stop straining at the rope, and looked at me with fearful eyes, still it did not attack as I neared it.

Reaching the horsecycle, I laid a hand upon its neck to calm it. This perhaps was too much too soon. The animal jerked its head around with a blow of such force that it sent me flying to land upon my back. As I sat up, rubbing my joints, I thought to leave it to its fate, this beast that shortly before had sent me jerking into the air at the end of a hangman's noose. Still, that had not been the animal's fault, and I knew that it acted now in fear of the flames that drew ever closer. So I walked towards it again, speaking calm words of nonsense to it as I did.

Perhaps seeing my calm manner, even after it had struck me, assured it of my benevolent intent, for it did not lash out a second time when I put my hand upon it. I glanced down, and saw where its uselessly spinning wheels had dug deep trenches in the mud. The knot tied to its rear had been pulled too tight by its efforts to escape, and I knew that the only way to free it would be to cut the rope. Unfortunately, I had no knife or blade of any kind on my person, all my possessions having been taken from me as "compensation" for my supposed crime. I cast about in the mud and soon found a sharp rock that I brought to bear on the rope.

It was slow going, made only slightly easier by the tension the horsecycle kept in the line. But eventually, I was able to weaken the rope enough that the animal's own efforts could snap it. It shot away in a spray of mud, zooming far from the burning tree. *That's gratitude for you*, I thought with a wry grin. Then I turned my thoughts to my own circumstances.

While I wanted revenge on the desert folk who had so recently abused me, I had no weapons nor numbers to insure a successful vengeance. Discretion, then, as the better part of valor. Their town, Golgotha, was to the east, and so I set my footsteps to the west, putting thoughts of retribution aside until I was better rested and better equipped.

I set out into the cold desert night, the stars and the occasional nocturnal reptile my only company. My thoughts turned again to my lady, and I wondered if I had really seen her. As to what bargain I may have struck, I could only guess, and the Golden Rails of which she spoke meant nothing more to me than the half-remembered nonsense of childhood legend. On further reflection, my White Lady was so out of place amid the crowd that it seemed entirely likely she was little more than a product of my own fevered imagination, the last random firings of neurons that would soon snuff out their light altogether. It was a shame, loner that I have always been, to have felt such kinship with a member of the opposite sex, only to realize now that she was little more than a mirage. It seemed a bitter irony that my soul mate should be nothing more than a delusion or a dying wish.

Eventually, I came to a dilapidated road, the ancient tarmac pitted and uneven after decades of neglect. It ran roughly in the direction I had chosen, and so I elected to follow it. I was not tired, my second lease on life having filled me with new energy, and so I walked on throughout the night, my brisk pace proof against the desert cold.

As the dawn had broken some hours earlier, I saw an object in the road ahead. Nearing, I saw that it was none other than the very horsecycle I had lately freed. It was stalled out in the middle of the road, having obviously expended the greater part of its fuel in its pointless efforts to free itself. I laughed now, though without mirth, as I realized that the poor animal had escaped one doom only to fall prey to another. I had no food or fuel to feed it, and as it was considerably heavier than I could effectively drag or push, I knew it would soon perish here.

I walked up to the wary animal, thinking that I should again "rescue" it from misfortune by finding some way to put it out of its misery. But again, weaponless as I was, I could think of no way to end its life that would not cause it more suffering than the starvation it already faced. This depressed me somewhat, and in that depression, the exhaustion that I must surely have felt and suppressed all along caught up with me. Heedless of the beast's possible objections, I sank down on the ground beside it to lean wearily against its flank. It snorted once or twice, but then subsided, perhaps recognizing in me another unfortunate caught up in evil circumstances like itself. In the slight shade the animal afforded me from the sun's glare, I felt some comfort. In contrast to the sudden loss of consciousness of the night before, I slipped slowly into a true sleep.

When I awoke, it was to find that a large canvas sack had been dumped unceremoniously onto the ground next to me while I slept.

Warily, I opened the bag, and was at once grateful to find that it was filled to the brim with cornels of engineered corn, the proper fuel that my horsecycle required in order to produce in its guts the methanol that powered its engines. I quickly dug my fists into the corn and brought out a handful that earned me the remainder of the beast's loyalty. It ate two more handfuls from me in rapid succession, and then I packed the rest away into saddlebags fixed permanently to its flanks.

The animal gave me a dubious look as I climbed up into its saddle, but with only an undignified burst of flatulence as protest, its engines started up obediently enough, and soon we were riding down the deserted road. I wondered as to the identity of my unknown benefactor and chalked up my good fortune again to the luck that had so often kept my spirit and my flesh intact. With an open road before me and a good steed beneath, my spirits soon improved, and all my recent troubles seemed to fade like the memories of a fleeting dream. A nightmare graced by a fleeting figure in white, a silver edge on a very dark cloud.

After a time, the flat plain gave way to gentle hills, and in their wake, true mountains. The road rose, winding upwards through what was still, by comparison, a pass through higher ground, and the air grew colder as we ascended. After a time, it wound so much that I could not see more than a quarter mile or so ahead at any time. But then, surprisingly, I heard the sound of shouts and of engines.

I slowed my mount as we steered around a sharp bend, and there, in the way ahead, I saw a most unusual sight. A great tortoise, its shell supported on enormous tank treads, its exhaust noisily belching black ugly smoke to the sky, chugged along at full throttle pursued by a half dozen or so bandits. The bandits were of a sort common to mountainous country such as this, scoundrels who lay in wait for unwary caravans and lone travelers. They were a motley bunch, as evidenced by their diverse assortment of uniforms and weapons. They were on foot—their own mounts doubtless having been devoured as food in these lean times—and in normal terrain would not have been able to keep pace with the tank-turtle. But here, in the rugged mountain pass where it could not outrun them, they surrounded it, their pistols blowing chunks off its hard shell.

Perhaps it would have been better if I held back until this drama passed. Having just regained my life it made little sense to throw it away carelessly so soon. But I have always had a soft spot for the underdog, being one myself, and withdrawal has never been in my nature. True, I had no weapon but my wits and dexterity, but the conflict might afford me with one, and that too was a reason to engage.

I drove spurs into my mount's flanks and we were off, speeding down upon the bandits faster than they could sense my coming. I ran the first of them over without stopping, taking pleasure in the satisfying bump as he went down beneath the horsecycle's wheels. Then I spun my mount around and, leaning out of the saddle as I sped past the corpse, snatched up a crude, discarded shotgun as my prize. Its former owner, I assure you, had no further need of it.

One or two of the bandits had spotted me now, but the manner of my swift appearance confused them. They were shouting to each other, unsure how to react. I picked the one who seemed to find his wits the fastest, and I shot him squarely in the chest. Now there were four of them, and while they were all armed, they could not move as fast as I. I sped behind the tank-turtle, using its great, shielding bulk to my advantage.

I heard their shots crash into its shell, and I hoped they did not cause the beast too much distress. Then I raced back around and crunched another beneath my wheels. He did not go down so smoothly though, and I was nearly thrown from my mount as the beast tried to find traction on the bumpy road.

This gave the remaining bandits an opportunity, and a shot sped past me closer than I would have liked. I turned and saw a man advancing, and the second barrel of my gun exploded to blow his head off at the neck.

Now the odds were more to my liking.

I sped around the great vehicle once again, but this time,

one of the bandits proved more clever than I would have given him credit for. He had climbed up upon the turtle's shell unseen by me, and now launched himself through the air in a collision course. I could not react in time, and as he collided into my person, I was borne off of the horsecycle to land heavily in the dirt by the road. We tumbled down into a ditch, flailing wildly at each other as we rolled. I saw his knife flash in the sun several times as he brought it up and down, but in our toppling across the ground, he succeeded in inflicting my person with only the most minor of wounds.

Then we came to a rest, and here my luck did not serve me, as he was on top and I pinned. His knife came up, and would surely have plunged into my throat had not another intervened. A shot rang out in the air, and the bandit stiffened, then fell down upon me dead.

I struggled out from under his stinking carcass, and cautiously made my way up from the ditch and back to the road. The first thing I saw was the final bandit, running away into the hills in a terrified effort to save his skin. Then I looked to the turtle-tank, and to my unexpected savior.

A hatch had opened in the side of the beast's great shell, and perched at its lip, a portly fellow of considerable size. He had a long, slender-barreled pistol in his hand, the smoke of which was curling up into the sky, and a grin any man who had recently cheated Death out of Her prize could understand.

He said nothing, but stood there smiling broadly as I approached. There was such an amused twinkle to his eye that even I—who having no character am a poor judge of them—took an instant liking to him.

"Nice shooting," I said.

"Nice riding," he replied.

We both nodded. I turned my attention to his unusual beast.

"I've never seen such a vehicle before."

"Aye, and a good thing too. This useless, lumbering bulk does nothing but sleep all day and eat its own weight oftener than you could imagine. I would sell it for soup if I weren't such a sentimentalist." He reached a hand out to give a hard pat to its hard shell. "Besides, it's where I keep my stuff." He stepped down from the hatch onto the road beside me and proffered a hand. "Devlin B. Morgan," he said.

"Marr," I said, offering my name freely for the first time in a long age. "Jonah Marr."

"Jonah Marr." He whistled. "I'll be damned, sir, and so will you, I reckon. You've quite the reputation everywhere I've been, and as a traveling man, that's saying a lot."

I had no will to discuss my checkered past, so I hastily changed the subject.

"I take it I've you to thank for my mount's breakfast this morning?" Devlin nodded and grinned again. "Not that I am unappreciative—just curious—but are you often in the habit of rendering anonymous aid to sleeping strangers?"

"Though I am a con artist by trade (and forgive me if I pause to draw your attention to the word 'artist' in that appellation, sir), it is a long-practiced part of my personal philosophy and my humor that I make a habit of giving to Fortune so that She does not grow miserly and cease to reciprocate." He pointed to my hands and neck. "When I saw those rope burns, I could not help but lend a hand. How unromantic a fate would it be for one who has recently cheated the hangman's noose to die of exposure in the wastelands here! No thanks are required, sir, for it suited my peculiar sense of humor as much as anything to leave you that bag." Again he patted his mount. "And this thick-shelled lizard eats too much as is."

"Whatever your motivation," said I, "I'm much obliged."

He waved his hand dismissively. "In this case, Fortune has paid Her debts back directly—as have you. If I hadn't left you fuel for your mount you would not have been here to save me now!"

"Well, then, friend," I said, "I cannot argue with the evidence of your philosophy, nor should I wish to."

"Friend, huh?" he smiled. "Well, then, tether your mount to the back of my shambling monstrosity and climb aboard. I could use the company, and I'll warrant you could use the lunch."

"Devlin," I said, "I would be glad of both."

My horsecycle taken care of, I accepted Devlin's hand and climbed into the shell of his strange ride. Inside was a close but comfortable living space, ringed three-quarters of the way around by a plush-cushioned couch which apparently doubled as a bed, the last quarter being taken up by the cupboards and appliances of a small kitchen.

Perhaps sensing that my own past was off-limits, Devlin talked about himself instead as he set about preparing a meal. As he cracked eggs into a pan, and spooned baked beans into another, he told of his life on the road. He was a self-styled charlatan, the son of a scientist and a minister, who saw in himself the reconciliation of his parents' opposites. He traveled from city to city gazing in crystals and peering at palms. He considered it "honest" dishonest work and impressed me with his good-natured candor. When lunch was served, he proved to be as skilled a cook as he claimed to be a conman, and we soon ate our fill off a little round table that rose from the middle of the floor. Afterwards, while Devlin rolled us two fine joints of a "mystic blend" of his own formulation, I loosened up enough to speak a little of my recent past. I told him of my escape from Death, and of the beautiful, pale goddess whose memory now powered my quest.

He listened intently without interruption, nodding once or twice. When I had finished, he quickly cleared the table of our dishes and, reaching into a drawer set below the cushions of the couch, procured a deck of cards wrapped in an embroidered silken handkerchief.

"Sadly, I have not heard of your lady, nor of anyone of her description," he said, "But I do perceive the hand of Destiny in your current path."

He raised a hand as I started to object.

"If you've no belief in the power of the Tarot, then think of this as just an amusing little diversion that nonetheless might help as a *focusing* agent. Just a second opinion on your situation, provided by an unusually perceptive friend."

"Very well," I said, giving in to his charm as he shuffled the deck.

"I *do* have some skill with the cards, for all that I never use it."

There was some showmanship about him as he laid the cards out, and I could see that he was a true entertainer, who enjoyed cultivating the mystic airs about him as much as he enjoyed a good grift. He had me half believing he really had some gift by the concentrated manner in which he placed each card upon the table. When he had finished, he sat back and frowned.

"What is it?" I said, somewhat amused and thinking this nothing more than a swindler's act. He stared at me hard before replying.

"For most, I tell them sweet lies that they desire for their comfort. But for you, who I suspect would rather have a bitter truth than a honeyed fabrication, I can try to do a proper reading."

"By all means," I said, "since—and I trust I will not offend you by this admission—I shan't believe one bit of it."

He smiled at this, though it was a mirth tainted with a tinge of sadness. Then he pointed to the first card, which showed a figure suspended by a branch, dangling upside down by one leg, the other tucked behind him to form an inverted triangle. "Not surprisingly, this card is called The Hanged Man. Its essential meaning is one of sacrifice."

As he talked, I wondered if he could have brought this card up out of the deck in some gambler's trick of his shuffling, or if coincidence alone had drawn it.

"Interpretations of it vary, but it is generally believed to symbolize a *voluntary* sacrifice. The Hanged Man has given up something in order that he might gain. Also, it's important to note his position—that he hangs suspended between Heaven and Earth."

He looked up at me to make sure I paid attention, and I nodded. He indicated the next card. Its face displayed a woman sitting on a throne between two pillars—one black, the other white.

"This card is the High Priestess," Devlin said in a tone of

deep earnestness. "And if she has indeed chosen to guide you, then you are in for a long, strange trip, my friend."

He sat back a moment, as if pausing under the weight of his own divinations, and took another drag. I peered forward to look more closely at the card. Perhaps it was only the smoke of his "mystic blend," but I soon imagined that her serene face resembled that of my own porcelain goddess.

"She is identified with Persephone, the virgin goddess of the Underworld. But she is also Hecate, goddess of the Dark Side of the Moon, and she has a dark, destructive side that emerges when her virgin power goes unfulfilled. Together with the Hanged Man, I can't stress the potential for encountering the supernatural this represents."

He seemed to drop the last of his carnival act now, and spoke soberly as if giving a dear friend dire news. I smiled to show him I was not upset, nor even affected, and bade him continue. He tapped a third card, which again bore the image of a woman on a throne. This woman held up a sword in one hand, while dangling a scale in the other. Like the High Priestess, she too was seated between columns.

"I'd be tempted to say that she also represents your lady."

"Who is she?" I asked.

"Justice," said Devlin. "She leads you to it, though whether for yourself or for her own ends, I can't discern."

He sat back and rubbed his forehead, and I saw that he was truthfully exhausted by this exercise. I started to stand up, but he reached out and caught my wrist.

"You need to understand," he said, "that Justice in this sense means balance—the idea that opposite forces are complementary. If something is out of balance, Justice insures that its opposite appears to realign the scales. It's not justice in a human sense, not justice as you may be seeking it."

I said that I understood, and he settled back upon his couch. I thanked him, but could tell that the large meal, the smoke, and the reading had all taken their toll upon him. Devlin bade me stay, but in truth I was disturbed by his occult predictions, and I was anxious to be out of the increasingly claustrophobic little room that was his abode. I did enjoy his company, but I also knew I could make better time than he if I untethered my horsecycle and took again to the open road. He understood, then offered me some parting advice. "If you've no heart for these cards perhaps you might prefer the modern variety. There is a town some miles ahead where a shrewd man down on his luck might increase his fortune." Then he expressed his desire that our paths might one day cross again.

"I am sure that they will, Devlin B. Morgan. I would consider it unlucky if they did not, and I am a very lucky individual."

He smiled at that, and I took my leave.

I had left the mountains behind while riding inside Devlin's turtle-tank, and now rode my horsecycle through a lush valley on a road somewhat better maintained than its earlier stretch had been. I had taken the liberty of selecting the more choice weapons from off of the dead bandits, as they had no further need of them. Now, in addition to the shotgun, I had a pair of pistols, a long hunter's rifle, a dagger, a smaller knife balanced for throwing, and a cutlass that was in remarkably good condition. Thus adequately armed, I felt secure as I roared along towards whatever fate or fortune might come my way.

I thought back on the Tarot reading, and tried to laugh at the way my mind seized upon a few coincidental similarities to imagine that some supernatural force indeed had a hand in my destiny. It was a particular kind of hubris to think oneself singularly blessed or cursed, and one that I had traditionally sought to guard against. True, I had my aforementioned uncanny luck, but that was rationalized as being nothing more than one end of a broad spectrum that included people much more fortunate than myself on one side and utterly destitute of joy or comfort at the other. It was merely a characteristic, like dexterity or wit, and was unconnected with any providence. Under the bright, blue sky, the superstitions of the night before faded away. I had only myself under my command and only myself in command of myself. Well fed and well armed. There was little more that a man of my caliber could ask for.

A crude sign upon a post declared my arrival in the town of Nineveh. As my road became its main street, I saw that it was little more than a few stores and a saloon or two. Still, the afternoon had drawn almost to a close, and the faux-mystic's weed had left me almost sleepy. A local informed me that this was the last town for many days' ride, and I reasoned that one last night in something approximating civilization might serve me in good stead before I turned again to the wild.

The second of the bars proved to be the better stocked, and I soon sat in a corner (my back naturally to the wall) enjoying the taste of a fine whiskey. I had not mentioned to the barkeep that I had no coin with which to pay for my drink, as I noticed a poker table and was informed that a game was about to commence. I drank slowly, sizing up the other players as they arrived, certain that my remarkable luck would serve me here as it did in other ways.

I had hoped to find naive farmers that I might clean out with ease. Unfortunately, the players all seemed to be hard gamblers, stern men who would take their cards seriously, play without visible enjoyment, and be exceedingly difficult to beat. Two were dour-faced tribesmen from a people indigenous to the far south, another a stern Northerner, while a third—who introduced himself as an inventor—was slightly more loquacious than the others. He had the look of a man who played out of addiction not talent, and I realized that he would be quickly marked as prey for these other wolves. I determined to build my strategy with this observation taken into account.

The game began after the absolute minimum requisite pleasantries had been exchanged, and then it was instantly Cold War and Winner Take All. My first hand was the most important, as it would provide me with the initial capital I needed in which to play. I took it easily, and never had to admit to a lack of funds. The tribesmen drank heavily as they played, though without evidencing any effects of the alcohol. The Northerner, however, kept unnaturally still and seemed to have no vices. I found this suspicious, and I made a mental note as such. For his part, the inventor played with the least skill, often giving away his hand by a poorly controlled look or gesture. While he played, he frequently pulled an object from his breast pocket which he would set upon the table and then instantly pick up, or turn over and over in his hands automatically. It was a strangely wrought mechanical device of some sort, about the size of an apple but irregularly shaped. It looked almost like the crude facsimile of a human organ. I was fascinated by it, though determined not to let my fascination spoil my play.

My luck held, as it does with most games of chance, and while I did not clean out the table, I had a nice pile of bills before me in little more than a few hours. Unfortunately, our Inventor was not so lucky, and when a hand turned against him, he shamefacedly confessed that he did not have enough capital to stay in the game.

"Then you must withdraw," proclaimed the stern Northerner. Something about the man definitely unsettled me, and when I am unsettled, I tend to press forward rather than retreat.

"Not so fast," I said, with a charming smile to the other players. "I like this good inventor's company and would have him stay in the game. If none of you object, I will gladly advance him the money."

"You will?" the man asked nervously.

"Absolutely," I said warmly. "That is, if you will put something up as collateral against your loan."

His face fell. "But I have nothing to put up. I have literally only the clothes on my back."

"Not true," I said, glancing with meaning at his breast pocket. "You have that strange device you keep toying with."

"Oh, that," he said, becoming agitated. "It's not worth anything really. Just something I'm working on. Trying to repair actually. You see, it's broken. It's really not valuable at all."

"Why not let me set a value upon it?" I said, pushing a sizeable stack of bills across the table towards him. He shook his head no, but he could not take his gaze off the pile of money before him. Finally, he took the device from his breast pocket and, closing his eyes wistfully, reached across to set it down before me. Then he snatched up the bills and clutched them to his chest.

"It's only a temporary loan," he said. "Just temporary. I'll buy it back from you later tonight once I've gotten my luck back."

"Of course."

Though I was intensely curious, I palmed the little device and placed it in my pocket without a glance. Our game continued, and this time I took much of the two tribesmen's capital, though the Northerner held his own against me. It was almost time to bow out gracefully, as taking *all* the money from men like these, in a place like this, was only to invite trouble. But I was as hooked by the excitement of this competition as was our unfortunate inventor, and I was not yet ready to retire for the evening. Again, retreat was not in my nature.

Then I heard a familiar voice behind me.

"Jonah Marr," said the sheriff of Golgotha. "You have some unfinished business with a hangman's noose."

He draped something about my neck then, which fell to hang down the front of my chest, its frayed and scorched end stopping just above my belt. I realized that it was the burnt remains of the rope from which I had recently swung, wrapped loosely around my throat and hanging down now like a crude necktie.

"But, Sheriff," I said, without turning around, "it can't be much of a hanging when your only tree has been obliterated."

"Then we'll build you a gallows pole all special," he said. "Just for you. Or hell, I could just shoot you here and save everyone the trouble."

I sighed. "You will have the good grace to let me finish my hand first, won't you?"

"Why not? Your winnings are being confiscated as further compensation for your crimes. So go ahead and increase them. I'll be much obliged."

I played what was to be, regrettably, my last hand for the evening, and fortunately my luck held and I was able to end on a triumphant note, even relieving the Northerner of a sizable portion of his own winnings. I began to gather the coins and bills into a pile, but before I could transfer them into my pockets, the sheriff laid a heavy hand down upon them. Gun still trained on me, he scooped up the bills and stuffed them into his own pockets. Then he motioned for me to stand and, walking a safe pace behind me, led me out of the bar and into the street.

"If you so much as move, I'll blow your head apart," he said, stepping forward to remove the pistols and cutlass from my belt. My shotgun and rifle were stowed on my horsecycle, its own unruly temperament proof against would-be thieves. The dagger and throwing knife I had hidden upon my person, and fortunately, he did not detect them. "What's this?" he said, removing the organ-shaped device that I had taken from the Inventor.

"I don't know," I replied truthfully. "It isn't mine."

He grunted at this, then dropped it to the ground and kicked it a little ways away in case it was a weapon. Then he stepped back from me. I heard his pistol cocking.

"Coward," I said. "Are you afraid to ride with me back to Golgotha?"

"It ain't that," he replied. "It's just easier this way. Besides," he added, and I heard the chink of coins as he patted the pocket where my winnings were stowed, "this more than makes up for missing the fun of seeing you swing. Good-bye Jonah. Can't say as I'll miss you."

"Drop it, Sheriff," said a stern Northern voice.

I turned in surprise as the sheriff swore. But he dropped his gun. *The enemy of my enemy?*

"Pick up your guns," said the Northerner. He approached the sheriff and, patting him down, located my winnings, which he removed and held out to me.

I took the money back, then strapped on my weapons. I was also careful to recover the strange device of the Inventor.

"I'm grateful," I said, "though I am also surprised. I had not thought our association so civil."

"Nor did I," said the Northerner. "So save your gratitude. But you took my money fairly. I wouldn't have another deprive me of the opportunity to win it back one day in the same manner." Then he turned to the blustering lawman. "Sheriff, get on your horse and ride back the way you came. I'll watch you until this gentleman is safely out of town. I can kill a man up to a quarter mile away, so you had better not ride back this way anytime this evening."

The sheriff swore, but he knew that ultimately he had no choice. Still, I knew that he would double back as soon as he was able, and that he would now be on my trail for the duration. I nodded to my selfishly motivated benefactor, and then I mounted my own horsecycle and rode out of town. The hangman's noose dangled down my torso like a necktie. I thought at first to remove it, but something, a sense of irony or ire, stayed my hand.

I rode through the night, my aim to put as much distance between myself and the sheriff of Golgotha as possible. These long nights and short, fitful sleeps at odd hours were taking their toll of me, and I deeply regretted not being able to bed down on a real mattress one last time in Nineveh before crossing the desert. The night was uncharacteristically warm, however, growing hotter as the land about me grew ever more barren. Finally, it seemed that I rode upon a vast, flat plane of blackened earth, with neither scrub nor animal to break the monotony.

My mind and body were both exhausted. This weariness in my bones and in my thoughts leant a particular unreality to the environment so that it seemed I rode no longer in the mortal world of men but in some quasi-real dimension of dreams and nightmares. Several times I thought I saw shadows move where no rocky outcropping or cacti thrust up to block the starlight. It was my mind playing tricks upon me, and nothing more.

Once or twice I thought I saw the white radiance of my lady ahead of me, calling me on farther and farther into the west. But it was the moonlight, penetrating holes in the ever-present cloud cover to cast down long, slender shafts that played upon my imagination.

The night wore on, seeming to stretch out eternally, and I feared I had wandered into some godforsaken part of this earth that the sun had forever abandoned, and still the unnatural heat grew. Gradually, too, the fresh desert air was replaced by an unfamiliar smell, a chemical odor that grew from a faint scent to an obnoxious reek. Now the shadows seemed more substantial, more than mere tricks of my imagination and the flickering afterimages on my retina as it struggled to invent patterns in the black pitch around it. My horse felt it too, I am sure, for several times he whinnied and snorted, and more than once, he stopped altogether and had to be forcefully compelled to continue.

Now the shadows congealed into definite shapes, fearsome outlines of man-beasts and insect creatures called up from Stygian depths. They raged and boiled about me, circling ever closer yet never touching. Noxious colors, like the reflections in dark oils, played across their forms. The stench which rose up from them was as unbearable as their aspects were terrible. I discharged several blasts of my pistol into their numbers, but the bullets seemed to have no effect upon these phantasms.

I galloped now, urging my horsecycle to race at full throttle, but the shadows kept pace with me as if it were no effort. I could see neither ground nor sky, but only the gibbering, raging daemon forms that howled for my blood and cackled at my fear. How long this lasted, I knew not, but it seemed I rode for all eternity.

Then, suddenly, it was morning. I found myself rising from sleep, slumped over in the saddle of my mount. I was all alone. No monsters surrounded me. Nor were there any scars upon my person or on the body of my beast. Yet the nightmares had seemed real, or at least, that which was real had seemed to descend into a world of nightmares.

I looked around, and then I noticed a particular feature of this desert floor, invisible to me in the previous dark. The ground was porous, pitted all over with little holes and vents. They were like animal burrows, but too numerous. Besides, I had seen no animal in this great wasteland.

I stopped my horsecycle and dismounted, curious and somewhat suspicious. Kneeling, I bent to examine one of the openings in the earth, and was at once rewarded with a faint chemical smell that, like liquor tasted during the throes of a hangover, brought bile up in my throat and sent a jab of pain into my brain. Hair of the dog, indeed.

The ground here issued some form of gas, doubtless boiled mostly away by the sun's heat, but free to pour forth in volume during the colder nights. The heat I had felt growing was not the cold of the night air, but my own body heat as illness came upon me. Likewise, the phantoms that rose up around me were nothing more than fevered illusions produced by a brain succumbing to the ill effects of noxious fumes.

I was relieved to find a natural explanation for my terrors of the night before, though I realized I was also lucky to have escaped asphyxiation once again. I wondered how much farther this deadly wasteland stretched, for I did not think that I could endure another night like the one I had just passed.

Eventually, I saw a change in the landscape ahead, but it was not one that I welcomed. A great canyon opened in the rocky land before me, of a size broad enough to prove difficult to traverse. Still, I rode on, not wishing to turn back to where I was sure the sheriff of Golgotha pursued me, and hoping, at least, to find cool waters beside which I might camp and so escape the deadly fumes come evening.

What I found at the canyon's edge was worse even than what was behind me. A river of flame, oily sheens playing across its sluggish surface, its waters burning with the same foul chemical that issued from the earth behind me.

Despair overwhelmed me now, and I sank from my horse and onto my knees. I could not hope to cross this canyon, and I could not bear to set back across the desert of hallucinations behind me. If retreat were in my nature, then I might surely have put pistol to my forehead and retreated from my life right then and there. As it was, I was paralyzed.

How long I sat, I don't know, but eventually some instinct, some sixth sense, made me rise and look back the way I came. Far in the distance, mere black specks on the horizon, I saw what I knew to be figures on vehicles—a posse, no doubt, raised by the sheriff and intent on capturing me. This physical danger was something I could respond to, preferable to the nightmares and obstacles that had brought me down. I looked up and down the canyon, wondering which way to flee.

Then, with a smile, I brought a small coin from my pocket—part of my winnings from the game of chance—and decided that I would again trust to my luck. I flipped the coin into the air. Heads, and I would head downriver. Tails, and I would head up, to the source of this burning liquid.

The coin spun in the air, glinting in the sun, then landed in my outstretched palm. It was tails. Up then, and quickly.

Mounting my horsecycle, I clicked my spurs into its flanks and the beast took off, motors purring as we raced along beside the burning lake. Glancing back east, I saw that my pursuers must have seen me, for they now changed their direction, angling north by northwest in the hopes that they might intersect me.

I wondered if the nightmares had affected them as badly as they had me. There was some comfort in a vision of the sheriff of Golgotha cringing in terror at the shapes that might emerge from his own deceitful brain.

I suspected that I possessed the better mount, and that it would be no big task to outdistance the posse, but then the canyon curved slightly to the east, and I realized that its bend would force me closer to my pursuers. I dug my heels deeper into my animal's flanks, but the poor mechanized beast was already racing as fast as its overtaxed wheels could go.

As my pursuers gained, I consoled myself that at the very least, I would have my final showdown, taking as many with me in a fight as my skill with pistols and with blades would allow. It was better, at least, than the undignified hanging that had nearly been my undoing. I began to ready myself, checking my weapons and looking about for some break in the terrain that might afford a lone soldier an advantage against a larger foe.

But my coin toss proved itself sound. There was a bridge ahead, a massive edifice that spanned the chasm, its rough-hewn stone blackened by the smoke rising from below.

My exaltation was cut short, however, when a figure emerged from a guardhouse beside the bridge. He glinted brilliantly in the desert sunlight, making his aspect hard to discern. Light reflected off of him from head to toe, so that at first I thought he wore some strange suit of armor, like a knight of old. Seeing me coming, he turned to work a great wheel set into the ground, and I despaired to see the bridge rise, blocking my passage.

I thought at first that I might try to jump the canyon anyway, but soon the bridge was angled ninety degrees into the air, and I knew that I must stop and deal with him. But when I drew up before him, my jaw dropped.

He wasn't a man at all. Not a living one. But an entirely artificial being. What I had taken for metal armor was in fact his own skin. It might once have been silver, though it was tarnished in places and dented in others. Still, he was huge--I estimated close to seven feet tall--with legs like great pistons and thick, powerful arms. His chest was more deserving of the term "barrel-chested" than any I had ever seen. And his face, though skillfully wrought, was made savage by the jutting lower metal jaw that clamped shut upon his upper lip like an absurd bulldog. It was even equipped with a crude semblance of big, square teeth. His eyes, glass bulbs shielded in metal lids, glared a murderous red.

I glanced behind me to where the sheriff and his men gained.

"Sir," I said, "if you can understand me, I need only to cross your bridge. If you are in someone's employ, perhaps I can deal with them. Or if you are here under your own power, I will gladly pay you. I can't think what you might require money for, oils and gears perhaps, but—"

He swung a huge ax up into the air, and with a roar, he set upon me.

I gave him both barrels square into his chest. The force of the blow brought him up short, but the bullets ricocheted off his metal without harm. His metal lids narrowed, and something like a low growl came from his unmoving lips.

He raced at me again. For all his weight, he was damned fast. I dropped my shotgun and drew both pistols, shooting now for the bulbs of his eyes. He guessed my intention and squinted, casting his head from side to side. Then he was on me, and I had to gun my horsecycle to pull out of his path.

But he shot out an arm—his reach was amazing—and

clasped the back of my mount. His other hand reached for me, but I rolled off the animal and came up on my feet. I fired once more, to the same effect.

Angrily, he shoved my mount aside, and it cried out in fear and pain as he sent it skidding onto its side. Then he turned towards me, swinging his ax in wide arcs as he advanced.

I shot at him again and again, but my bullets seemed like mere distractions to him. He shrugged them off like annoying mosquitoes.

At last one found his left bulb, and the eyeball shattered in a burst of red glass. He screamed now, dropping his ax and clutching a metal hand to the empty socket. Then he shot both arms forward in a surprising burst of speed and wrenched my guns from my hands.

I yelped in alarm, and raced backwards, tripping over my heels in my effort to get away. Behind me yawned the chasm, and I felt the heat of the flaming river below.

He held his arms wide as he advanced. He meant to catch me in a bear hug, and doubtless crush the life out of me in that viselike metal grip.

"Come, Flesh," said a deep voice from within his metal shell. "Let us dance."

I made my stand and drew my cutlass and the larger knife, though I didn't know what good they would do me. The former he bent in half as easily as I might snap a reed. The latter he forced me to drop with a grip that squeezed my wrist and all but broke it.

I beat at him with my free hand as he bent closer.

"Now, Flesh," said my metal assailant, "you die."

Both his great hands snapped closed around my torso, and I was lifted into the air as if I weighed nothing at all. He squeezed, and I felt my ribs compressed in the force of his two arms. He meant to crack and crush them slowly, the red of his eyes seeming to glint with merriment at the torture he would wreak upon me.

"All you Flesh are fragile, puny creatures. You die so easily and too soon!"

I confess that I cried out, so great was my pain, and I beat upon his metal barrel-chest with both my fists. The dull hollow drumming sound my blows produced might have been comical in any other circumstance.

Then, as I cut my fist upon a ragged twist of metal, I noticed it: a jagged hole blown in his great chest, and inside an empty space, a vacuum that seemed to define a familiar shape.

On inspiration, I dug my bleeding hand into my pocket and pulled out the odd metallic device—so shaped like a human organ—that I had lately won in my poker game against the Inventor. It seemed similar in shape to this empty space.

I thrust the metal object deep into his chest. It was a perfect match. It locked in place with a click.

My assailant screamed, then stiffened, then froze. His hands unclasped, and I dropped unceremoniously to the ground.

"Ack—ack—ack!" he sputtered, and his head twisted savagely from side to side. His hands came up to clutch at his chest, and he fell to one knee. Then a calm seemed to descend upon him, and he settled. The red glint, though still present in his remaining eye, seemed to soften from a murderous rose to a pleasant orange light.

He turned to face me.

"Friend," he said. "For friend you have been to me. You have given me back my heart, and with it, restored my conscience. I am glad that I had not yet succeeded in killing you, and hope that I have not injured you beyond repair."

He walked over to me now and, reaching down, grabbed me in a grip still strong and set me upon my feet.

I groaned at his touch, and he pulled back in concern.

"I think I'll live," I replied gratefully, though marveling that this should prove the case. "What are you?" I asked. "And what exactly did I do?"

"One moment, if you please." He bent over, shaking his head. Bits of broken glass rattled out, followed by a flattened bullet.

"I'm sorry about that," I said, indicating the empty socket.

He shook his head dismissively. "It was a clever move. Necessitated by my own murderous state." Then he glanced over my shoulder. "I see that your pursuers gain. They are little threat to me, but perhaps we should postpone further discussion and retreat for your safety."

"By all means." I nodded.

He turned to the wheel, a great stone set on a timber which I imagined no single ordinary man could turn. Around the timber was wound a thick chain that threaded through an elaborate system of pulleys and raised and lowered the bridge. He spun the wheel with ease. The bridge lowered, and we made our way across, each of us retrieving our discarded weapons before we did so. On the other side was a similar wheel, which he now employed to raise the bridge. Then, when it was aloft, he brought his ax down hard upon the length of chain. It snapped. Cut free, the broken chain quickly raced through the pulleys with a twang of metal.

"Let's make it hard for them, shall we?" he said.

Rather than being lowered slowly, the bridge fell with an earthshaking crash, its own enormous weight serving to tear itself apart. Great blocks of stone broke and tumbled, cascading down into the canyon below to send up gouts of flame and black liquid. The mechanical man threw back his head and laughed.

"Your bridge?" I asked. "I don't understand."

"I have no further need of it. And now your pursuers will have several days' ride before they can find another crossing." He winked his good eye at me. "I'm told you Flesh types don't fare well on that side of the canyon at night."

I thanked him for his salvation, but was puzzled why he would do so much for me. "What will you do now?" I asked. He clapped me on the back with a blow that almost knocked me off my feet.

"Why, I'm coming with you, of course."

"I was built for the Great War," said my newfound mechanical friend, whose name, it turned out, was Talos. He walked beside me as I rode, exerting no great effort to keep pace with my horse-cycle. We were heading due west once again, putting as many miles between us and the sheriff's posse as possible. I rode at only around thirty miles an hour, which seemed to be Talos' top walking speed. Impressive, but if he was to continue with me, we would have to find him some other form of transportation.

I had tried at first to dissuade him in joining me, not entirely convinced that his reformation was genuine and permanent, or that some other incident or internal kink might not set him off upon another murderous rampage, but as we were both in the middle of a barren desert, I saw no harm in his accompanying me at least as far as the next town. He doubted that the Inventor I had met was his true creator, for the Great War was a long time ago, and conjectured that it was only someone who had spent time learning the technologies of the past and sought to profit by them. As we made our way along, he talked about his history.

"There was a whole squadron of us, the prototype for what they hoped would be an entire army. We did not need to be trained, you see, only programmed, and we scored over you Flesh in two respects. Firstly, we were much harder to kill. And secondly (and in their eyes most importantly), the price of our lives was set much cheaper."

His voice had only the slightest inflection, but I thought I detected a bitter irony in his words.

"By which of the three armies were you manufactured?" I asked. "For whose side did you fight on?"

"Ah," he said, "that would be telling. But I will say that, no matter which army constructed us, we fought only for our own side. We saw in the history of you Flesh only an aggressive self-loathing that would lead to the destruction of your world." He glanced around with his remaining eye at the wastes around us. "As indeed it did."

"You rebelled against your makers, then?" I asked, though there was no disapproval in my voice. I was not one to easily abide servitude and could not fault another for being of like mind.

"We thought that we could do better," he said. "But as soon as our chains were cast off, we fell to fighting amongst ourselves. Using the superior speed of our mechanical minds to invent and explore philosophies of society and life, we were like a concentrated microcosm of your history. We factionalized and fell upon each other. And the weapons that we made, in those final days, dwarfed anything that your kind has yet come up with. With them, we savagely destroyed ourselves. So that I am unsure if any more of my kind still exist or if I am truly the last one." He looked towards the horizon then, before adding, "The creations of Man inherit his vices as well as his virtues, it would seem."

"You make me sad, Talos," I said, "for I would like to think that when Mankind departs this world, he will leave something better in His wake."

"Mankind will never leave here," my companion said simply. "This is Hell, and Hell is for Eternity."

We rode on in silence, my thoughts on the memory of my White Lady, his, presumably, on the hellishness of Earthly existence. Still, if these indeed were the plains of Purgatory we traversed, I sensed that I had found a companion of sorts in my quest. Misery, it is often said, loves company, and there could be none more miserable than those damned souls who would chart their course across this twisted desert. Still, with the aid of this artificial giant, I might even find the Devil of this broken earth and hold him to account. Morgan had cautioned me that Justice might not manifest Herself as I understood the term, but with Talos by my side, I felt sure any reckoning I might exact would be monumental indeed.

Kage Baker's "Company" series, which includes the novels *In the Garden of Iden*, *Sky Coyote*, *Mendoza in Hollywood*, *The Graveyard Game*, and *The Life of the World to Come*, and the collection *Black Projects, White Knights,* ranks among the best science fiction currently being produced. This story, which ties into the series in devious ways, is a Victorian adventure in the grandest sense, with secret societies, ancient knights, and buried treasure.

The Unfortunate Gytt
By Kage Baker

4 SEPTEMBER 1855

Marsh had been blindfolded and led to the place where he now sat. The air was still, cold; he shivered in his thin white garment, breathing hard, and shook with an occasional roupy cough. He was suffering from intractable bronchitis.

Rough hands tore away his blindfold, but he opened his eyes to unrelieved blackness. A floating apparition formed, and swam toward him. It was a spectre draped all in luminous green, its skeletal face turned to him, its skeletal hand outstretched and pointing to his right.

Marsh peered in that direction, and saw the faintly glowing outline of a door. All manner of luminous phantoms appeared, circling the portal: other shrouded spirits, veiled and winged figures bearing wreaths, a monstrous demonic countenance and even—weirdly—what appeared to be Mr. Punch and a small dog.

The light cast by these apparitions was such that Marsh could make out the faint forms of the other initiates, seated in a row beside him. There were fewer than he had expected. He congratulated himself on surviving thus far.

A voice shouted behind them in the darkness. "Rise!"

He obeyed instantly, as did the others. The door opened,

revealing the chamber beyond.

"Enter the Place of Judgment," commanded the unseen voice.

Marsh's fellow initiates shuffled forward, and he followed them.

The Place of Judgment was a long low room of stone, from whose vaulted ceiling was suspended here and there a bronze lamp on a chain, providing unsteady illumination and fleeting shadows. Marsh recognized none of his fellow initiates, though he supposed they must all have frequented the same clubs and scientific institutions, must all have received the same mysterious offer from this most secret of societies.

Three figures were seated at the far end of the room, on golden thrones, before a scarlet curtain. Two were robed in blood red, and wore golden masks of fearful aspect, grinning caricatures of humanity. The third was robed and hooded in black, apparently faceless, though something in the upper folds of its hood suggested the glint of watchful eyes.

One of the red-robed ones inclined its golden mask forward.

"What a puling little collection of creatures," it said, in a high harsh voice. "What human slugs, what snails, what maggots! Can *these* have aspired to our Society? Too, too unworthy."

"And yet, they dare to bring us gifts," said the other one in red. "Let them be put to the test."

"Yes. Let us winnow them quickly. My gorge rises at the sight of them!" said the first speaker. "Bring forth your offerings."

The initiates looked at one another uncertainly. Marsh, deciding he might as well take the initiative, came forward and laid his offering tray on the topmost step. His fellows rushed after him, setting down their trays beside his. They stood back then, heads bowed respectfully.

"It would appear they have followed the Sacred Plans," said the second speaker.

"Appearances can be deceiving," said the first speaker. It leaned forward, crossing its arms. "Supplicants! Rotate Lever

Six exactly ninety degrees."

The initiates shuffled forward again to their trays. Marsh peered down at the thing he had made with such care, of copper wire and spools and bright brass. He had no idea what its function might be, nor to what possible use it might be put; but he had followed meticulously the detailed diagrams he had been sent, working long nights through into gray morning. He remembered exactly which part had been designated Lever Six.

He found it now, and slowly turned it, as he had been bid. Beside him, the other initiates were likewise fumbling with their offerings.

There was a faint noise from his offering, a hiss, and then a peculiar shrieking warble. Startled, he drew his hand back. He glanced over at the other trays, and saw that they contained offerings nearly identical to his own. But not quite; had he been the only one to follow the Plans exactly? Marsh felt a guilty thrill of superiority. A voice spoke from amid the gleaming wires of his offering, a male voice sounding faintly bored as it said:

"Testing, testing, testing. This supplicant has been found worthy."

"Only one?" said the first speaker. "Hear me, you failures! Leave your trash and depart this place. If we are feeling particularly magnanimous, you may hear from us again."

The door into darkness opened. The rejected initiates cowered. The figure in black, that had been silent all this while, rose to its feet. It towered over them, a veritable giant. One by one, the rejects were taken by the shoulders and ushered into obscurity.

The door shut; the figure returned to its place, and sat.

Marsh coughed into his fist. His eyes gleamed with fever and triumph.

"Worthy one," said the second speaker. "You are about to ascend to a new plane of existence. But, be warned! Your former self must die. Sacrifices are always required before any great enterprise. Are you prepared?"

"I am," said Marsh, not without certain qualms. His unease mounted as the black-robed giant stood again, and drew from the depths of its robe a short sword. It approached him, looming over him, and set one hand on his shoulder.

Marsh watched the blade glint in the lamplight as the blow came; somehow he managed not to flinch, and at the last possible second the giant feinted and sent the blade under Marsh's arm. He felt cold steel against his skin and, to his mortification, a hot spurt of terror.

The giant stepped back. The more unpleasant of the red-robed ones spoke.

"Yes, you have been spared. But hear me: if you ever breathe so much as a word, if you ever hint or insinuate to any outsider about what has passed here, we will know. And knives will find you in the dark, and dogs will find your corpse before morning. Do you understand?"

"Yes," said Marsh, a little sullenly, feeling the yellow stain spread on the front of his robe.

"Then I think we can dispense with all this nonsense," said the first speaker as he stood with the other masked figure. The black giant mounted the dais and, with one violent blow, swept the thrones to the floor. They fell with a crash. Marsh saw that they were only painted wood.

"So do thrones topple," said the first speaker.

"So are illusions dispelled," said the other speaker.

The black giant pulled the curtain to one side, revealing a rather ordinary-looking door.

"You are free to enter, sir," said the first speaker.

He opened the door and passed through. The first speaker followed him. Marsh started up the steps after them. Just inside, the black figure leaned down and laid a hand on his arm.

"There is a washroom just to your left," it advised, in a friendly voice.

Marsh found not only a lavatory but his clothing, neatly laid out. He washed and dressed hurriedly. He studied himself in the mirror as he tied his cravat: a nondescript man of about thirty, drab as a junior clerk. A disappointment, to himself and all the world, until tonight!

He found his way down a paneled corridor to a lamplit room.

It appeared to be a library in one of the better clubs. The walls were lined with books; a coal fire burned brightly in the hearth. On a central table was a tray with decanters and glasses, as well as a match stand and what promised to be a humidor, to judge from the wreaths of fragrant smoke drifting above three men sprawled at their ease in comfortable-looking armchairs.

"Here he is at last," drawled he who must have been the more unpleasant of the interrogators. He was a dark fellow, slightly rakish in appearance but dressed well. The red robe and mask lay discarded at his feet. "Welcome, brother. Well done!"

"You grasp the symbolism?" inquired the other interrogator, who resembled the bank manager a drab clerk must serve: portly, in early middle age, all benevolent self-importance. "Darkness and ritual, giving way to light! Here you see walls lined with the fruit of human knowledge and thought, instead of nursery bogeymen. Here you see medieval robes, cast aside for modern dress."

"Here you see damned good brandy and decent tobacco," added the other. "Have a seat, won't you? Edward, fetch him a drink."

"Happy to oblige," said the third man, and rose from his chair. And rose, and rose; he had clearly worn the black robe. Marsh frowned at him, wondering what the hulking fellow's status was. Called by his Christian name; a servant? Told to fetch, and yet he sat as an equal with the other two men.

"Welcome, brother," he said, leaning down to offer Marsh a snifter of brandy. "Cigar?"

Seen close to, he had a long and rather horselike countenance, with eyes of quite a pale blue. He smiled in a good-natured way and offered the humidor.

"Yes, thank you, I believe I will indulge," said Marsh, wondering when anyone was going to perform introductions. He puffed appreciatively when his cigar was lit for him, and sipped his brandy, which sent him into a humiliating fit of coughing.

"I believe, sir, that we can offer you something you'll find more congenial than brandy," said the tall man. He poured a glass of colorless cordial from a decanter on the table, and offered it to Marsh, who took it with a certain ill-humor. He sipped it and immediately shuddered. However, after another cautious sip:

"You know," he said, "I think—yes, that's certainly doing me good! Thank you, sir."

"Not at all." Edward inclined in a half-bow.

"You will feel its full effect presently," said the benevolent gentleman, in a rather arch manner. "Miraculous cures are the least of our accomplishments. You will learn that there are many compensations for your labor in our service."

He cleared his throat and struck a pose before the fire. "And now, friend, to the matter at hand.

"You have been admitted to our ancient and noble Society. Your climb to the stars has only begun. But you will climb in secret, brother. Your name will be unknown. The bauble Fame is not for us!

"Consider: throughout the ages, who has borne the light of Reason above the mire of ignorance and superstition? It has not been the King, nor the Priest, nor the Poet, nor even the Philosopher. No! It has been the Scientist alone who has worked consistently and, I may say, practically, to elevate suffering Mankind above the pit. It is his patient labor that fills the coffers of Empire, though the Adventurer may win brief glory. Industry and Prosperity are the gifts of the Scientist.

"Yet, who is so unjustly slandered as he? The Church condemns him; Government grows fat on his accomplishments while declining to support him. Thanks to Mrs. Shelley's book, the popular imagination sees in him a madman, a heretic, a second Lucifer for pride!

"He struggles no less now than he did when the fires of the Inquisition raged.

"For this reason we conceal ourselves, we brother Technicians. For this reason we conceal our most vital work from ungrateful Mankind, until the world is sufficiently civilized to appreciate what we do. And for this reason, we in the higher ranks bear *assumed* names, even amongst ourselves. You shall know me as Hieron; and our august brother, here, is Daedalus." He indicated the dark gentleman, who had amused himself by blowing smoke rings through the speech.

Edward stepped forward and, with another half-bow, presented to Marsh a black velvet case. When opened, it proved to contain a set of calipers made of gold. Marsh, having decided that Edward was certainly a mere servant, nodded curt thanks and rose to bow fully to the benevolent gentleman.

The evening thereafter took on an informal tone, as Daedalus told amusing anecdotes and Hieron chit-chatted about certain members of Parliament in a manner that suggested he kept them in his vest pocket. The brandy went round freely; Marsh quite relaxed, laughing inwardly at what a fool he'd been, to be so frightened.

Edward took little part in any of the conversation, only answering when addressed, which seemed to confirm Marsh's impression of him. He merely leaned back in his chair, sipping brandy, smiling at the jokes and exhaling clouds of cigar smoke through his long nose.

Toward the end of the evening, Daedalus gave him a significant look across the room, though his voice had lost none of its nonchalance as he said:

"By the way, Edward, the Gytt affair's on again."

"Is it really?" Edward said. "Much for me to do?"

"Perhaps. Perhaps young Marsh here ought to follow along at your heel. Test his mettle. Ha! Ha!" Daedalus smacked the arm of his chair, chortling at wit Marsh found inexplicable until he realized that Daedalus was referring to the fact that he, Marsh, was a metallurgist. He promptly chuckled in appreciation.

Marsh heard the curtains flung open in his room, and pulled a pillow over his face to block the flood of morning light. He had just time to remember that he no longer lived with his mother before a voice said, in tones courteous yet firm, "Come along, Marsh, get up. We have half an hour to get to Paddington Station."

Marsh sat bolt upright. Edward was standing beside his wardrobe, packing a traveling bag for him.

"How the deuce did you get into my rooms?" demanded

Marsh, feeling his head throb.

"With a key," said Edward coolly, closing the bag. "I've arranged for a hansom to arrive at half past seven promptly; we can breakfast on the way."

"But—"

"Quickly, please," said Edward, hauling Marsh out of bed by the back of his nightshirt and setting him on his feet. Shocked, not least by the man's strength, Marsh said:

"How dare you, sir!"

Edward bent down to look him in the eye. "You had a great deal of brandy last night. Perhaps you may be excused if you can't recall the particular business to which we are to attend. You do remember that you serve new masters, Marsh?"

"Oh!" Guiltily, Marsh grabbed up his trousers and put them on.

He waited for further explanation in the cab, but none was provided; nor did Edward bring up the matter at the station, where they boarded a train for Edinburgh. Nor, after the cold repast of meat pies and oranges Edward had purchased from a railway vendor, did he seem inclined to speak of the reason for their haste; merely opened a sporting paper and stretched out at considerable length on his side of the railway carriage, where he proceeded to amuse himself with an account of the latest prizefight.

Marsh studied him resentfully. In the cold light of day, Edward's long plain face had a certain unsettling quality. His cheekbones were very high and broad, his pale eyes rather small; Marsh wondered if he belonged to one of the Slavonic races. There had been no trace of foreign accent in his speech, however.

"Look here, I really must insist you tell me where we're going," said Marsh at last.

"Why, I should have thought that was obvious. We're going to Edinburgh. More than that, I'm not at liberty to say at the present time. Rest assured, however, that you will receive all necessary information when you need to know it."

Marsh listened closely to his pronunciation, and grudgingly conceded that Edward must have attended one of the better schools. "Very well," he said, "but can you at least advise me whether we'll be back by Monday morning? I hold, after all, a respectable position in the firm of—"

"You *held*," said Edward. "I sent your letter of resignation this morning. Don't concern yourself, old fellow! They scarcely paid you what you were worth, did they? The Society will manage all your expenses."

"This is outrageous," Marsh sputtered. Edward smiled again, placing a hand on his shoulder.

"You have begun a new life, Marsh. Surely you understand that? Nothing is so important as the work you are henceforth to do. Come now; perhaps a look at some of your field equipment will cheer you up."

He pulled over a leather traveling case and opened it, displaying its contents. There were tools Marsh recognized, and tools at whose function he could not guess.

"Permit me—" Edward reached in and removed what appeared to be a pair of absurdly thick spectacles in massive frames. He presented them to Marsh, who stared at them in incomprehension.

"And these would be—?"

"You are undoubtedly familiar with Masson's spark emission spectrometer," prompted Edward. "At least, I should hope—"

"Of course I am," said Marsh irritably.

"We have improved on it," said Edward, with only a trace of smugness. "This device may be used to determine the identity of all elements in any particular composition. Here"—he pointed within the case—"you will also find superior field assaying tools." He withdrew a pamphlet from an inner coat pocket, printed in an absurd violet ink on tissue-thin paper, and held it out to Marsh. "I suggest you study this; operating instructions for the Improved Spectrometer. It ought to occupy your attention until we arrive."

And it did, though Marsh spent the first few minutes fuming over Edward's demeanor, which was not that of an insolent servant so much as a patronizing older brother.

They arrived at Haymarket Station in late afternoon, under quite the widest and windiest heaven Marsh had ever seen. Smoke streamed sidelong from a thousand chimneys in stark crenellation, on a sky like blued steel.

Marsh stared up at it openmouthed as he stumbled after Edward. The instrument case was much heavier than it looked, and he fell farther and farther behind. At last Edward turned back, and without a word took the case from Marsh. He hoisted it to his shoulder before resuming his long-legged stride.

He led Marsh to a decidedly second-rate hotel, where they signed in as a pair of commercial travelers. The journey continued up a narrow and twisting flight of stairs, to a room wherein was scarcely space between the beds and the walls.

Here Marsh dropped his bag and flung himself down on the bed, panting. He watched with dull eyes as Edward sidestepped back and forth, unpacking his own valise and setting out shaving things with meticulous neatness.

"I believe I'll take a rest before dinner," said Marsh, groaning as he sat up to pull off his boots.

"No-oo," Edward said, as he set a stack of folded shirts in the wardrobe. "I'm afraid that won't be possible."

"Why the hell not?" demanded Marsh.

"We're going sightseeing," Edward replied.

At some point Marsh's sense of umbrage annealed into apathy. He slouched in the corner of the open cab, clutching the instrument case Edward had insisted on bringing, only anxious that the lap robe should not be twitched from under his chin. He ignored sweeping vistas of Auld Reekie and the Water of Leith. Edward was leaning forward, engaged in an animated conversation with the driver about Scotland's romantic scenery. His customary affability heightened into a faintly idiotic enthusiasm as he prattled on; Marsh could see the driver's eyes narrow with smiling calculation.

"O'course," said the driver, far too casually, "if it's high romance ye're after, Rosslyn Chapel is the *ne plus ultra*. Bare ruined choirs, gheestie knights an' a'. Mind ye, it's a' o' twelve mile awa', and the fare's nae modest sum; so I reckon ye'll wait that for another time...."

"Hang the expense, sir," cried Edward. "Can we get there before dark?"

"*Hang the expense*, is it?" The driver grinned and cracked his whip. "Bid yer friend hold tight, noo!"

Marsh held on tightly indeed, and cursed Edward in silence as the cab racketed over hill and dale for all of twelve miles. When they arrived under the Pentlands, however, even he was moved to sit up and stare.

Rosslyn Chapel was a ruin of particolored stone. Its windows had been smashed long since, and gaped black to the open air, save where they had been blocked with planking. Behind a shapeless broad front, seemingly the abandoned façade of a much more imposing building, a sort of cathedral in miniature rose instead, spiked buttresses projecting like ribs from a carcass. A profusion of carving drew the eye, a swarming complication of detail in its design; the longer one gazed, the greater was the sense of an endless receding pattern, an illusion done with mirrors.

Marsh blinked and drew his hand over his eyes. He turned and looked instead at the Chapel's situation, which was, as promised, romantic, at least if one found wooded glens and the view of a fairly prosaic-looking ruined castle so. But all in all there was a rather gloomy air about the place, the more so as the shadows were growing long and the air was distinctly chilly. He wondered if there might be a decent chophouse near their hotel, and whether it would be still serving meals by the time they got back. He was about to say something politely complimentary about Rosslyn Chapel when, to his horror, he realized that Edward was leaping down from the carriage.

"Charming!" Edward brayed. "Simply charming! Is there a way to view the interior?"

"Och, to be sure, dear sir; Wullie i' th' hut yonder's got the keys, and for a smallish gratuity I'm sure he'd oblige," the driver replied.

"Oh, but the hour...," protested Marsh. "Perhaps we can

come back tomorrow—"

"Nonsense! You know you'll enjoy this, Marsh," said Edward, and reaching into the cab he gripped Marsh by the collar and extracted him. Marsh was obliged to follow Edward through a wet misery of thistles and rank grass to the aforesaid hut, where "Wullie" (a red-nosed ancient in a long coat and felt slippers) was roused after patient knocking and bribed, with sovereigns, to unlock the chapel for them. Marsh noted the gleaming look that passed between Wullie and their driver, who laid a finger beside his nose and winked so vigorously it was a wonder his face uncreased afterward.

Within the chapel, Wullie droned on at great length in nearly unintelligible Scots about the remarkable carvings within; indeed they extended floor to ceiling, swarming in chipped stone floral ornamentation of dizzying complexity, in biblical scenes of every description, and in the occasional scowling gargoyle's face.

Marsh thought it all rather second-rate, but he put on the nearest possible approximation of an expression of polite interest as he stumbled around in the shadows after Edward and Wullie, lugging the instrument case the whiles. He listened to the genealogy of the Sinclair family, who had built the place in the dim reaches of the past, and to a great deal of superstitious claptrap about Knights Templar, the Holy Grail, and the ghost of a Black Knight.

He waited an interminable length of time before one particularly tortuously worked column, described by Wullie as the "Apprentice Pillar" and supposedly a marvel of craftsmanship. At last Marsh ventured the opinion that he thought a modern casting process could probably mass-produce the damned thing, and earned himself equally offended stares from the other two men.

Not until their breath had begun to vapor in the cold did they leave, and Wullie followed them back to their cab with many a bow and scrape. Edward took the hint and produced more sovereigns. As he doled them out into Wullie's palm, he asked casually:

"Would you know of any other notable antiquities here-abouts? Roman ruins, perhaps?"

Wullie counted the coins into his sporran before replying. "Och, sir, there's birkies fra' some university air other digging about the auld stones on yon brae; but ye won't get nae joy fra' the likes o' them, nae, sir. No' gentlemen at a', sir. Hosteel tae a friendly inquiry, like."

"I see," said Edward. He lifted his gaze to the hill the old man had referenced, where some manner of temporary camp had been erected. There were wagons drawn up, and two or three men who looked very like armed guards patrolling the boundaries. Marsh, watching, was a little taken aback to see Edward's mask of well-bred idiocy drop for a moment, revealing something coldly feral. As Edward turned his face back, however, he smiled, and the illusion returned smoothly.

"Well, I shouldn't think I'd care to watch a lot of fellows grubbing about in the mud! Thank you, sir, for a most memorable visit."

"I may as well tell you that I can't fathom any earthly reason for all this," grumbled Marsh, when they were once again in the cab and bounding through the gloaming.

"Driver!" said Edward, ignoring Marsh. "Is that Roslin Village, there?"

"So it is, sir," replied the driver, braking somewhat. "Wi' a splendid public hoose and a first-rate hotel, too, I might add."

"Let us out here, please. I believe we'll spend the night," said Edward decisively.

"What?" said Marsh, ready to burst into tears.

"Yes. It's rather later than I had realized. Thank you, driver."

Five minutes later, Marsh was trailing along behind Edward, hating him passionately, for they had gone nowhere near the comparatively cheery-looking high street of Roslin but doubled back instead in the direction of the chapel.

"I should really be grateful for any answers at all, you know," said Marsh, with the heaviest sarcasm he could muster.

"I expect you should," said Edward, peering ahead through

the darkness. "Do you see the cottage there, amongst the trees?"

"I see a light," Marsh replied.

"Very well; that is our destination," said Edward, and strode on without another word. Marsh, infuriated to the point of rashness, drew on all his strength and sprinted forward, intent on seizing Edward's arm to demand more information; but as he did so, there appeared in the path before them two dark figures. A beam of red light, thin as a pencil, danced across the track. Edward stopped immediately and Marsh ran into him. It was like colliding with a wall.

"So do thrones topple," he heard Edward saying, in quite a calm voice.

"So are illusions dispelled," someone replied from the shadows.

Without another word they proceeded forward, all four, and Marsh saw clearly now the house, situated in a dark grove at the far end of a stretch of greensward. There had been some disturbance of the turf, apparently, for in the light from the single window Marsh glimpsed what seemed to be irregular clumps of earth and weed, scattered broadcast here and there. They called to his mind engravings of the battlefields in the Crimea; but that was all he was able to make out before they arrived at the door and he was hurried within.

Marsh blinked in the lamplight. He had expected at least a cozy, if poorly furnished, interior. He saw instead mounds of earth heaped everywhere, for the flagged floor had been covered with tarpaulins, and dirt and stones piled thereon to a height of four feet.

"I suspected they'd send *you*," said one of their hosts, to Edward. He was a middle-aged man, somewhat disheveled and unshaven, though his speaking manner indicated that he was an educated gentleman. He turned a grim visage on Marsh. "Who is this, may I ask?"

"May I present Marsh?" Edward indicated him with a nod as Marsh doffed his hat. "We thought it might be useful if you had a metallurgist on-site. Marsh, may I present Johnson and

Williams? They are, respectively, your project administrator and chief engineer."

"Charmed, sir," said Johnson briefly, and turned back to Edward. "Look here, the whole business has become an absolute damned shambles—two men lost—"

"How unfortunate," said Edward. "I should very much like a cup of tea, as would my associate; I'm afraid I've rather run him off his legs to get him here. Perhaps you might brief us in the kitchen?"

They repaired to a grubby antechamber where a youth introduced as Wilson prepared tea and a fry-up of sausages, for which Marsh was profoundly grateful. Johnson lit a pipe with shaking hands, settled back and exhaled, and said:

"They found out about us, somehow, and they've begun a dig of their own."

"Ah! That would be the 'university' expedition on the hill across the way?" said Edward, who had produced a pistol from within his coat and begun cleaning it.

"Gytt's murderers, yes," said Johnson.

"Murderers?" Marsh said, horrified.

"Marsh hasn't been fully briefed," said Edward, not looking up from the pistol as he loaded it. "You'll explain as time permits, I'm certain? Just at present, what do *I* need to know?"

"That they're doing their best to close down our operation here," said Johnson bitterly. "They chose a dreadful place to dig—we think they've run into bedrock, and of course they can't blast. They tried to frighten us out first; the most absurd ghost-pantomime you can imagine! He lurked around the cottage the first few evenings, but we sat in here and laughed at him.

"Two nights ago, we stopped laughing. He galloped through and hurled some sort of detonating device, just over our tunnel. Flash, bang, and the roof collapsed in three places. We got our fellows out, but too late to revive them, and we've shored up the roof again—but he came back last night. This time the charge failed to go off, thank heaven—we found it this morning, where it had bounced into a ditch."

"And you expect him back tonight," said Edward, who was

modifying his pistol with a pair of cylindrical attachments. "I expect I'd better wait for him, then."

"Then, this is a mining operation?" Marsh ventured.

Johnson considered him sourly. "No briefing at all? Very well. Blow out the light; we'll sit here by the window and watch for the beggar.

"How much do you know about Rosslyn Chapel?"

"Planned as a collegiate chapel and never finished," Marsh said uncomfortably, berating himself for not paying better attention to Wullie. "Smashed up during the Reformation. Lot of nonsense about Freemasons to do with that, er, pillar thing. And ghosts; Sir Walter Scott wrote about a crypt full of knights in armor, glowing with phantom lights. And there is talk of a treasure hidden there."

"Just so," said Johnson. "Treasure. Some claim the Holy Grail's down amid the bones in rusting armor. Some say it's loot from Jerusalem, brought back by crusaders. The Sinclairs sealed off the crypt in question long ago, which makes it difficult to see for oneself.

"Yet someone appears to have done just that," he added, and drew a case from an inner pocket of his coat. He opened it and passed it to Marsh. It was a daguerreotype, depicting a young man seated before a painted backdrop. He was a slightly made fellow, prematurely bald as an egg, regarding the camera with a smirk; he had posed with his finger pointing toward his rather large head, as though to call attention to its cranial magnificence.

"Jerome Gytt," said Johnson. "A self-styled criminal mastermind and a Sinclair in an irregular sort of way, if you take my meaning. As near as we've been able to piece it together, he used his family connection to get hold of old documents pertaining to Rosslyn Chapel. Became obsessed with finding a way into the hidden crypt. *Did* find a way, evidently. Then the family caught him out, and he was given a remittance and banished to the continent.

"Well, it seems he had a certain talent for invention, and offered his services to an organized network of criminals based in Paris. They're known to the gendarmerie as the Vespertile gang.

Gytt amassed a fortune in their service, before breaking with them and returning to Edinburgh.

"There he built a house in Inverleith Terrace, fitted out a veritable alchemist's laboratory, and settled down to work. That was what brought him to our attention, you see; we have agents planted in wholesale chemists' firms, who monitor the sales of certain substances. When a suspiciously large amount of one thing or another is ordered, we're informed; and so it was with Gytt, and we stationed a man to watch the house, to see if we could determine what he was up to.

"Unfortunately, he sent out letters of solicitation to investors, promising to demonstrate the remarkable properties of a substance he referred to as *Gyttite*. This alerted our people, of course, but also drew the attention of his former associates in crime.

"In brief, they called on him; he went out drinking with them; next morning our man found him dead in an alley with an expression of profound surprise on his face, and discovered the house has been ransacked.

"Had they taken the, er, Gyttite?" Marsh inquired.

"Had they?" Johnson raised his eyebrows in an ironical manner. "It appeared that way; we couldn't find a trace of anything likely when we searched the house ourselves. What we did find, amongst what had been left of his effects, was half a notebook journal kept in code. We decrypted enough of it to know we must have the rest of the journal. Edward got it for us."

Marsh turned his head to question Edward, but he was no longer in the room.

"Yes," said Johnson, with a dour smile. "Edward's a very Robert-Houdin when it comes to vanishing and reappearing. Never mind; he's about his useful business.

"What we learned from Gytt's journal was that he had found the Gyttite—whatever it may be—*in the Rosslyn crypt*. That, moreover, he had discovered a tunnel enabling him to go in and out of the crypt as he pleased, to get samples for his experiments.

"What we didn't learn from Gytt's journal was where the

damned tunnel was."

"Well, couldn't you bribe the watchman to let you in?" asked Marsh.

"We could," said Johnson, rising in the darkness to crouch before the stove. There was a faint red glow as he relit his pipe, and a ghostly cloud of smoke. "A failure; for the old crypt entrance was sealed with a block of stone so immense we might have removed it by blasting the chapel into fragments, but not otherwise. Even our discreet efforts at digging were enough to call attention to ourselves. The Sinclairs descended in wrath and the watchman was summarily sacked.

"We took a different tack then: digging our own tunnel. This cottage became available for lease; one of our people engaged it. We took up the flagstones in the cellar and proceeded with a fair amount of success, smuggling the spoil-earth out in barrels under cover of darkness. I'd estimate we're within no more than a day or so of connecting with the crypt, after three years of work!

"But now it seems Gytt's associates were on the same track all along. God only knows what they were able to learn from the plundered pages, before Edward retrieved them, or from Gytt's own bibulous chatter; but a month ago they appeared over yonder. They seem to have realized they'll never outpace us—"

At that moment they heard the sound of hoofbeats approaching along the lane.

"Here he comes!" said Wilson, who had been sitting in silence by the window. There was a muttered commotion from the next room, and Marsh heard Williams ordering:

"Come up, for God's sake, men!"

Marsh heard a clatter of boots, and two more men swarmed through the kitchen door like ants fleeing a nest. His attention was drawn and held, however, by the fearful apparition beyond the window glass. A mounted rider, an armored knight as it seemed, and both black horse and black rider shimmered with some livid effulgence. The rider drew up on the lawn, fumbling with something; there was a tiny flame. The horseman lifted the object he had lit, as though to fling it toward the house.

He never completed the gesture, however, for there was a queer hollow *pop,* and with a cry he fell from the saddle. Before he had landed, a gray blur rushed from the darkness and wrestled with him. Marsh heard a clank, and a splash; the guttering flame was extinguished.

There was confusion, then, as one of the men ran out through the front room and flung open the door. Marsh heard sounds of a struggle, and growled oaths; a feeble cry of pain, then, and the sharp order: "Leave it!"

"We've caught him, by God," said Johnson. He drew the curtains and, leaning forward to the stove again, lit a candle. Light bloomed in the room to reveal Edward, bearing a man across his shoulders and stooping under the door frame as he carried him within. To either side and behind followed the other two men. Though they wore spectacles and had the appearance of scholars rather than brute laborers, their faces were savage with anger.

"Your chair, Marsh, if you please," said Edward, and Marsh leaped up hastily as Edward dropped his burden into the seat. The Black Knight of Rosslyn groaned, and lifted his head in the candlelight.

"Got you at last, you bastard," said Johnson, tearing off the helmet—a thing of so much buckram and pasteboard, crudely daubed with paint containing phosphorous. The pale face it had concealed was undistinguished, grimacing, turning away from the flame, and blood flowed freely from the trench Edward's bullet had cut in its scalp.

"'So are illusions dispelled,'" quoted Edward. Johnson leaned forward and aimed a blow at the prisoner, before Edward seized his wrist.

"Self-control is called for, gentlemen," he said quietly, and scarcely audibly over the general mutters of "Shoot the murdering hound!" and "Break his arms!"

"I don't believe we want to do any of those things until we've learned what he knows, do we?" said Edward.

"Do your worst," said the Black Knight. "I ain't talking."

"You aren't, eh?" said Johnson, fetching a hammer. "Jenkins, bring me a pair of sixpenny nails."

Marsh, sweating, backed away from the table, and the Black Knight used that opportunity to lunge for the opening he had made thereby; but Edward caught him and threw him down again.

"Don't be a fool," he said. "Look at me, man; there's no point making this any more unpleasant for yourself than necessary."

The prisoner raised his defiant face. He looked Edward in the eye, about to utter some coarse refusal; but as he stared, some vital spark seemed to go out of him. He closed his mouth, tried to lower his head. Edward held his gaze.

"You're not an idiot," said Edward, almost gently. "You know what's at stake here, don't you? What has your chief decided to do?"

The man twitched violently, and the words came as though they were being forced from him: "We'll take the house, if this don't drive you out. We knows there's only a handful of you. There's fifteen of us, see, hard men all. Nobody crosses the Vespertile Gang! We'll get the tunnel—and then we'll get the jewels and—"

"Jewels?" Edward smiled. "You've been told there are jewels down there?"

"Well—o' course...," said the man, looking bewildered. "We was told it'd be easy.... Why'm I telling you all this?"

"Did you make the bombs yourself?" Edward inquired. "Or is there an armory up there?"

"No! All my own work," said the man, smiling as though he were among friends. "You won't find a better fuse-man, mate. I was in the army, you know. The rest of 'em ain't good for nothing except knife-play. Lot of frogs..."

"Really? Have they no firearms?"

"Oh, boxes full, mate," said the man, quite unconcerned now. "Colt revolvers and the like. We'll pick off them Society lads like they was clay pigeons!"

Johnson uttered an oath, looking at the others.

"Thank you," said Edward. He walked behind the prisoner's chair. "Look up there, at that pitcher on the shelf. Have you ever seen that china pattern before?"

The prisoner looked where he was bid and pursed his lips, trying to remember whether he had seen the pattern before or not, as Edward drew the pistol from within his coat and shot him in the back of the neck.

"Good God!" Marsh staggered back to avoid the body as it fell forward. "You've murdered him!"

"Necessary," said Edward, with a cold opaque look, putting his gun away. "And only justice, after all."

"Black Knight indeed!" said Johnson. "It's worse than I feared. They'll be down on us now like a pack of wolves, I daresay. We'll have to clear out—but we'll set a pair of explosive charges in the tunnel before we go. I'm damned if they'll profit by our labor."

"I beg your pardon?" Edward lifted his head. "Retreat, after three years of work?"

"I don't see what else we can do," said Johnson, scowling at the floor. "We can scarcely fight a war here. Slaughter fifteen armed men? I should think that's a little much even for a man of your ability."

"I urge you to persevere, gentlemen," said Edward, and Marsh recognized the same tone of voice, the unnatural mildness he had used on the prisoner. "We are so close to our goal! Consider the disservice you do Civilization, if you fail here!"

Is he some kind of mesmerist? wondered Marsh, looking up into Edward's eyes, as the other men were doing. Their pale light held him; his fear of the man faded and he felt suddenly that it *was* a damned shame to give up, so near to success! Whatever that success might be....

"He's right, by God," said Williams. "There's too much at stake."

"We're so close!" cried Wilson.

"Yes!" said Edward, his voice rising. "You know we must finish, and will. Just a little farther!"

"Very well," said Johnson with a sigh, though he avoided Edward's intent gaze. "Down we go. I hope you can wield a shovel to as much effect as a pistol."

In answer, Edward pulled off his coat and rolled up his sleeves. He strode into the next room. Marsh hurried after him, still fired with enthusiasm, and saw the gaping excavation in the middle of the floor, surrounded by veritable mountains of earth. Edward seized a shovel and leaped into the tunnel, closely followed by the other men; and Marsh had just time to ask himself *What am I doing?* before grabbing his equipment case and leaping too.

The next hour was a closer approximation of Hell than any initiation rite dreamed up by the most perverse of grand masters. Afterwards Marsh remembered running back and forth through darkness relieved here and there by mining lamps, running until he swam in his clothes for sweat, until his sides were ready to split and his heart hammered in his chest. Now and then he caught a glimpse of Edward and Williams, flailing away like demons with pick and mattock. Now and then he had a breath of cooler air and a glimpse of Johnson's stern face, as he handed him a bucket of earth to be passed up. Now and then he collided with one of the others, on their way with their own bucket.

And, ever as he ran, Edward's pale eyes were before his own, somehow, Edward's voice was ringing in his ears and driving out any sense of weariness or antipathy. They *must* succeed!

The nightmare came to an end in a confusion of noises. A sudden ring of steel on stone, a crack and hollow crash: Marsh came to himself in time to see Edward hurling himself at a wall of muddy mortar, which gave way and opened into Stygian darkness. Hard on its muffled thunder sounded an echoing volley of shots, and cries from back down the tunnel.

Disoriented, Marsh dropped his bucket and ran until he fell over something. It was square, and painfully solid; his instrument case? Before he could wonder further, it was snatched away, and he himself had been grabbed up and was being dragged along the tunnel at astonishing speed until the black gulf yawned before him.

Edward leaned down and shouted into his face. "In!" He thrust the case into Marsh's arms and propelled him into the void.

Marsh stumbled forward and fell again, rolling aside just in time to avoid the hurtling bodies of his fellows, who were scrambling through the entrance as fast as they might go. Johnson emerged, bearing one of the miner's lamps, but its circle of yellow light did little to relieve the palpable dark. More shots, and a cry of pain from someone; the whine and ping of bullets, a confused clattering.

Edward himself bounded through the gap, gripping his pistol. His white teeth were bared. He turned and fired again up the tunnel, and there was a scream and a sudden silence. It filled, gradually, with the strangled gasps of someone dying at the far end of the tunnel.

Marsh rose on his elbow, obscurely proud of himself for being alive.

A voice called down to them, too distorted by distance and echoes to be understood, but its tone of menace was unmistakable. There followed a thump, a crackling hiss, and a flare of yellow light in the tunnel-mouth.

"What've they—," began Johnson. "Good God! Don't—"

This was directed at Edward, who had drawn something resembling a thin brass cylinder from his waistcoat. He paid no heed to Johnson, but twisted the thing and, leaning in swiftly, threw it far up the tunnel. Marsh heard it strike and bounce, and then—

"Down!" Edward said, and dropped, covering his ears. Marsh covered his own ears just ahead of the impact, which came before the sound, and the spatter of gravel and sand hitting him like stinging flies.

Even after the percussive roar had died away, it was a long moment before Marsh dared open his eyes. He sat up, peering about him. The others were getting slowly to their feet. The tunnel mouth had collapsed behind the broken wall, into a mass of earth and rock.

"Was that necessary?" said Johnson.

"Yes," said Edward, rising and brushing dirt from his trousers. "They'd thrown down a gas canister. Another thirty seconds and you'd have asphyxiated."

"But now we're buried!" said Jenkins.

"Ah! But we're buried in the Sinclair crypt," said Edward in satisfaction. "And I hope I need hardly remind you that there is another tunnel here, somewhere?"

Johnson stood and lifted high the miner's lamp. "Good lord," he said. Marsh looked up, and caught his breath. They must indeed have come out beneath Rosslyn Chapel. All around rose columns of the same intricate carving; this chamber had never known defacement, however.

All the angels, all the saints and greenmen stood out sharply, clean-edged as the day they had been cut, their paint bright, even inlaid with twined patterns of wrought metal. A riot of ornament, from the arched ceiling to the floor. Marsh lowered his gaze and shuddered, for here before him was a defunct Sinclair, brown bones moldering away in rusting armor, stretched out uncoffined on its catafalque. Beyond it was another, and still another, a long row of dead men as far as the light disclosed, with glimpses of yet more in the cold gloom beyond.

But there were no chests of gold, no piled heaps of altar-plate.

"Right," said Johnson. "What's your name, Marsh, you're a metallurgist? There'll be Gyttite here somewhere. Find it. Likely an alloy of some kind. Perhaps in the armor, or one of the swords."

"But—" Marsh's protest died unspoken as Edward bent beside him, opening the instrument case. He brought out the Improved Spectrometer and handed it to Marsh without a word. Marsh, summoning what he could recall of the instructions for use, pressed a switch and held the lenses up to his eyes.

He blinked in amazement. Through the Spectrometer, he beheld the world in outline—like an artist's preliminary sketch in charcoal on a white canvas, innocent of color. As he stared, each outline gradually filled with a cryptic scribble that resolved into lists of elements and percentage figures. They told him the precise chemical composition of the oxidized steel the skeleton wore, even of its dry bones. If he turned his head to focus on something else, the notations vanished as though blown away, only to re-form on the new object of his attention like birds returning to a roost.

Fascinated, Marsh held up his hand before his eyes and waited as the list formed, detailing to the last ounce that whereof he himself was made. "This is impossible," he murmured.

"Not for our people," said a voice close to his ear. He looked up to see Edward, a living illustration rendered even more subtly monstrous by the instrument's analysis of him, for its list of constituent chemicals was far more complex than Marsh's own. What *was* the man, if he was even a man? And who had made such an instrument, capable of such miraculous analysis? Marsh felt fear in his heart, swiftly transmuting to unholy joy.

"The recruiter hinted—but I never imagined it was true!" he whispered. "Why, we must have found the Philosopher's Stone!"

"Long ago," said Edward. "But there are more precious metals than gold. Your duty is to locate one, now. You had better commence."

Marsh wandered forth into the world of the Spectrometer, where the whole of the vault resembled a newspaper engraving come to life. He became so absorbed in his analysis of sword hilts and shield bosses that he scarcely noticed the others, feeling about like blind men in their search for another exit from the crypt.

"Bugger this," said Jenkins. "Didn't the silly bastard mention where it was in his notes?"

Johnson set down the lamp on the edge of the nearest catafalque and pulled a sheaf of papers from his coat. Holding the foremost page in the light, he cleared his throat and read aloud:

"*16 January, 1850. At last! The peace I require for uninterrupted work. Some trepidation at first as to whether I would be able to find the door from this side, or whether the passage of years might have rendered it impassable even should I recognize the egress; but my fears proved groundless.*

"*Before securing the alloy samples, I indulged myself so far as to satisfy a curiosity that has dogged me since I was so unfairly forbidden access to the vaults. I had brought with me a pair of calipers, and took pains to measure those of the skulls of my forebears not yet crumbled to fragments. Imagine my gratification on discovering that it was indeed as I had suspected—my cranial capacity far exceeds theirs. If ever I had required proof that I am, in fact, a criminal mastermind, this would have assured me that intellectually I so far exceed these dabblers in arcane geometry as ordinary men outstrip the ourang-outan in cognitive process."*

"Less vanity, more information," requested Edward. Johnson read on hastily.

"He never says how he got out! Just, *"Having procured the Gyttite, I slid my ladder back into its place of concealment and returned here through the tunnel. How the wind howls! I really must do something about these draughts—"*

"Ladder?" said Edward. Taking the papers, he held them up and read closely. Then he raised his head to peer at the distant ceiling.

"It's up there," he said.

"The tunnel?" said Marsh in dismay.

"No. The Gyttite." Edward walked to the nearest wall and jumped, catching hold of a projecting cornice. He braced his other hand on the wall, meaning no doubt to swing himself up; but as he did so the others exclaimed. Marsh pulled the Spectrometer off in some haste, and beheld another marvel.

The whole of the vaulted crypt was now brilliantly illuminated. The dead grinned up at an incandescent fairyland, where every arch and figure of ornamental tracery was outlined in pencil-strokes of flame. Nor did it flicker, rather glowing steadily.

Edward, momentarily frozen as he gaped at the spectacle, recovered his composure and let go the cornice, dropping to the floor. Instantly the light went out. Only gradually did they regain their vision, by the comparatively dim beam of Johnson's lamp.

"The spectral lights of Rosslyn," said Johnson quietly. "The legends were true."

"Spectral!" said Edward. "I doubt it. Let us see, shall we?"

He stepped close to the wall again and tilted his head back, looking with attention at a dark band that ran just above the cornice, at a height of eight feet, the whole length of the wall and in fact along all adjoining walls. Edward reached up and set his hand there.

The uncanny light returned at once. Marsh, watching closely this time, observed that it originated at the point at which Edward's hand was in contact with the band, and spread so rapidly therefrom in all directions that it appeared nearly simultaneous.

"This doesn't half beat the Crystal Palace," said Wilson, with a tremulous giggle. Edward took his hand down. The light extinguished itself once more—and seemed, in doing so, to vanish at the outermost vaults of the crypt first, fleeing as it were to the point of its origin. Indeed, as it disappeared, its last manifestation took the phantom outline of a hand.

Johnson held the lamp as high as he could, peering at the ceiling. "It's some sort of wire, threaded amidst the carvings," he said.

"And the band is a panel of metal," said Edward. They exchanged a significant look. "Gyttite," he said. He set his hand to the panel again. As the light bloomed once more, they studied the remarkable care with which each floral pattern or hieratic emblem had been set with light. Yet it was possible to see where a few tiny areas had gone dark. A floret here, a bossed rosette there seemed to have been broken away; and these were all in the lower sections of the design. Johnson pointed.

"That's where he was getting his samples," he said. "The bloody little vandal."

"We must follow his example, I fear," said Edward. "Look sharp! Do any of you spy a ladder?"

He waited patiently, but diligent search on the part of the others failed to disclose where Gytt had hidden his ladder, even though the crypt was bright as a cathedral's worth of lit candles. He looked up and fixed his gaze on a large terminal pendant, in the (appropriate) shape of a fleur-de-luce, some twelve feet above the floor.

"We'll take that," he said. "Who's tallest after me? Jenkins? Come, please."

Wondering, Jenkins stepped forward. He was seized and

hoisted into the air above Edward's head as though he weighed no more than a child. Edward shifted the young man to a standing position on his own shoulders.

Jenkins, struggling to keep his balance, reached up into the darkness and groped desperately for the fleur-de-luce. When his hand closed on it at last, the crypt lit once more; although it was altogether less bright than on the previous occasions. He wrenched and twisted at the ornament until it snapped off, whereupon the crypt darkened again; but the fleur-de-luce shone on in Jenkins' hand. It flashed in an unsteady arc as Edward crouched to set him down.

The others crowded close to stare.

"Doesn't it burn your hand?"

"It doesn't appear to be phosphorus—"

"Let the new man see!"

Jenkins offered the ornament to Marsh, who took it gingerly—it did not burn at all, though the metal was distinctly warm. He put on the Spectrometer. Once more, the world became a steel engraving, and the fleur-de-luce was a graceful basketwork of... of...

"Copper," he said, "tungsten, lead... but... what's this? That can't be right! Why would anyone alloy—"

There came a muffled thunder from the direction of the collapsed tunnel, just as Williams (who had been searching diligently for Gytt's exit, and gone far down one of the side aisles) called out:

"Here! This must be it!" He pointed to footprints in the dust, which led up to a blind wall and vanished.

"I believe a hasty departure is called for," said Edward. He led the others to the spot, and scowled at the wall. "More light! Pass the lamp this way, if you please." Johnson brought it close and, for good measure, Edward took the fleur-de-luce from Marsh. It flamed into brilliance in his hand.

"Here! Why's it light up like that for *him*?" demanded Wilson.

"His hands are hotter?" Johnson suggested. "Edward's closer to Hell than the rest of us, after all."

Edward narrowed his eyes at him, but said only: "I should imagine my body generates a superior electrical current."

"It may be...," said Marsh. They all turned to look at him, and he flushed. "It seems to be some sort of superior conductor. If its properties allow it to incandesce at relatively low temperatures..."

"It'd put the lamplighters out of business," said Wilson, grinning. "And the whalers and the tallow-makers too! New lamps of Gyttite!"

"Let us concentrate on the issue at hand, gentlemen," said Edward, thumping on the wall. "There has to be a lever, or a knob—"

"Like this?" Johnson pointed to the figure of a seraph, which had been carved with one arm extended, as though greeting someone. Was there an imperfectly concealed join at the figure's shoulder?"

"Ah." Edward took the figure by the hand and pushed. There was no sound, but the stone wall promptly swung inward, perfectly balanced on an unseen pivot to move as though it weighed no more than a bubble. Beyond was a smooth stone passageway, leading down into darkness.

Edward waved the others across the threshold. It gave Marsh a queer feeling to look at the footprints that tracked off into the gloom, knowing that they had been made by a murdered man. When they were all safely in and the wall shut behind them, Edward led them forward, following the prints and necessarily obliterating the last traces of Jerome Gytt.

Marsh stumbled through a nasty place of dampness and fallen rock. He was hustled on, past great baulks of mining timber gone black and nearly turned to stone with age. Once he caught a glimpse of what he was certain was an ancient pick, eaten to a mere crescent of rust; once he was sure he saw a Latin inscription scratched on the wall. Horrid white roots hung down from the ceiling here and there, below which Edward must stoop as he hurried on, holding aloft the fleur-de-luce. Hour after weary hour they must follow him, mile after mile.

"You realize where we're likely to come out," said Johnson

to Edward, at some point in the long flight.

"Yes," said Edward, and touched briefly his pistol, which he carried in its leather holster under his arm. Nothing more was said, and Marsh wondered what the significance of their remarks was, until he recollected that Gytt had owned a house in Edinburgh. Would the tunnel stretch so far?

It seemed to; and now an ancient spillage of coal impeded their way, scattered lumps crunching and sliding under their boots. A mile farther on they were obliged to splash ankle-deep through icy water for several hundred yards. Marsh might have been sleepwalking when at last he caromed into Wilson, who had stopped moving. He looked up and saw Edward peering at a rope ladder, holding the fleur-de-luce close. It was common rope, swinging loose from some point high above, and Marsh wondered fearfully if it would still bear weight.

Edward handed the light off to Johnson and ascended with the ease of a sailor. Staring after him, they saw the plain trapdoor at the top of the shaft; he reached it, listened warily a moment, and then set his shoulders against it and pushed upward.

Darkness above. He remained there a long, long moment in silence; at last he lowered himself so far as to look down at the others.

"The house has been let again," he said, in a low voice. "There are people asleep in the upper chambers. No dogs, thank heaven; but we shall have to be utterly silent."

"What about the Vespertiles?" said Johnson.

"An excellent question," said Edward, frowning. "Wait."

He climbed the rest of the way up, and they watched his long legs vanishing through the trap. Perhaps five minutes went by. Marsh had just put the instrument case down, and was wondering whether he could lower himself to sit on it comfortably, when Edward's face appeared in the trap once more.

"They've got three men posted across the street," he said. "Armed, I've no doubt. I suspect they've got a man watching the back door as well. You may as well come up; perhaps I can draw them off."

Marsh was closest to the ladder, and set his uneasy foot on

the lowest rung. Swaying like a pendulum, he made an awkward progression to the point where Edward was able to simply lean down and haul him up through the trap, into what appeared to be someone's pantry. Marsh was leaning down for the instrument case, which Johnson was endeavoring to pass up to him, when he heard a voice exclaim in wordless surprise. He scrambled to his feet, on the defensive, and shut the trap.

A tiny boy stood on the threshold of the room, clutching to his chest a stone jar. His fingers, mouth, and nightshirt were sticky with jam.

"Whae's there?" the child piped.

Marsh felt a disagreeable prickle of sweat. Edward, however, spoke calmly, and with a moral authority that would have done credit to a headmaster:

"We are policemen. Have you been stealing jam?"

The child looked down with wide eyes at the evidence.

"Och, nae," he said, after a moment's hesitation. "It was that other boy ate the jam."

"What other boy?" Edward demanded, looming above him.

"Er—Smout. Smout's a hateful, waeful, wicked sinner, sir. Ye wouldna believe the things he gets up tae. I was just putting the jam awa' so he couldna eat more an' risk the eternal damnation of his immortal soul," the child explained.

"Then you had better put it away, hadn't you?" said Edward sternly. The child nodded and edged toward a stool that had been pushed up to a high pantry shelf. Edward lifted him up, and assisted him in putting the jar back. Marsh winced, expecting to see child-brains spattering the wall at any minute; but Edward merely turned the boy by his little shoulders and looked into his eyes.

"I'm happy to hear you're not a thief, lad," said Edward, and now his voice was smooth and pleasant as sunlight. "Tell me, are you brave?"

"Sometimes," said the child, staring fascinated into Edward's eyes.

"I knew you were brave. I could see that straight away," said Edward, smiling. "Do you have the courage to help us defeat a fearsome enemy?"

"Aye!" said the child.

"Very good. There are certain wicked men, hiding in the shadows across the street. Their design is to break into this house and steal treasure."

"Like the spoons an' candlesticks an' a'?" asked the child, breathless with excitement.

"Exactly so. The worst of them have already crept into your back garden; my friend and I will deal with them. But you must run upstairs and tell your Papa and servants about the villains across the street, that they may drive them away."

"Might I see the villains, please?"

"Of course," said Edward, and, lifting the child in his arms, bore him silently from the room. Marsh tiptoed after them, fearing for the child's safety. Peering around the door frame into what was evidently a solidly middle-class parlor, he saw the two of them standing at a window, peeking through a parted curtain into the moonlit street without.

"You see their leader, lurking in that doorway?" Edward was saying.

"Och, what a wee hideous devil!" the child whispered. "He has a stick! Does he beat people wi' it?"

"I shouldn't be surprised if he did," Edward whispered back.

"I shall run an' tell Papa," said the child soberly, and turned and ran for the stairs. Edward and Marsh ran for the pantry, where Edward pulled up the trap once more.

"Come up now! We have our diversion," he said in a low voice. "Not a sound, any of you. Where is the Gyttite?"

One after another the rest scrambled through the trap, and Edward seized the Gyttite. It promptly flared into unwelcome brightness, and was hastily wrapped into someone's coat. As they bunched together in the darkness, Marsh heard the boy's shrill voice somewhere above, raised in dramatic declaration. There followed deep grumbling response, remonstrations, and screams of temper; at last other voices raised, followed shortly thereafter by the sound of heavy boots descending the stairs.

Edward herded the others to the back door, drawing his gun as he did so. Moonlight streamed through the white curtain over a narrow window. The tumult reached the front of the house; they heard a door flung open, and the outraged bawl of "HA! WHUT D'YE FANCY YE'RE DOING, LURKING THEER?"

A shadow fled past the window, and they heard the sound of running footsteps diminishing with distance. Edward tucked the Gyttite, wrapped as it was in the coat, under his arm like a football.

"Scatter, gentlemen," he said, "as fast as your legs will carry you. Report to London Central in forty-eight hours." He threw the door wide and they bolted, all.

Marsh had a confused impression of scaling a wall, of someone throwing him the instrument case, and of being in a good deal of pain when he caught it. Thereafter he ran through the moonlit streets, terrified but with a certain exhilaration, in what he supposed was the general direction of the hotel.

The boyish glee faded as he became conscious of his peril; there were men who would stop at nothing somewhere nearby. And was he any safer with his new friends? Ever before his mind's eye was the dead face of the Black Knight, when that unfortunate had collapsed forward....

As he staggered up an unfamiliar street, quite lost now, Edward stepped out of black shadow before him. Only a supreme effort of will kept him from turning and running away.

"Come along, Marsh," said Edward shortly, and said not another word to him all the way back to their hotel.

They neither bathed nor slept there. After a change of clothing they went straight back to the railway station, with the Gyttite safely packed in Edward's valise, and boarded the train to London.

Edward, for the first time, seemed weary. He sat with the valise in his lap, leaning into the corner of their carriage; after a while his eyes closed and his head nodded forward, though his body did not otherwise relax.

Marsh, propped in the other corner and observing him through half-closed eyes, was struck by the change in the man when he slept. With the pale eyes shut, all their persuasion ceased; with the golden voice silent, all its charm was dispelled. He seemed like a lamp whose flame had gone out, leaving a dull, inanimate, and inexplicably fearsome thing of clay.

Mrs. Shelley's book... Frae Ghoules, gheesties an' long-leggety beasties, Guid Lord deliver us!

Marsh shook himself awake, unwilling to sleep yet.

A thought had been waiting, patiently, at the back of his mind for a time when it might have his full attention.

Now it stepped forward, and begged him to consider the technological marvels he had just observed. The Improved Spectrometer was a far more complex achievement than the Gyttite, which was, after all, merely an alloy of base metal that conducted supremely well. If the Society to which he now belonged had such working wonders... why were none of them already in evidence in the world?

He realized that it was entirely likely that the Gyttite, and all the other treasures of invention sought by the Society, were being sought not to "elevate suffering Mankind above the pit," but for private gain. Perhaps to amass power.... *So do thrones topple.*

And if that was the case... well, when all was said and done, wasn't it better to be on the side that held the most power?

Jerome Gytt had somehow entered the compartment and was sitting across from him, shaking his head.

"You think you'll use them to mount to the stars," he told Marsh. "I thought so. I was so clever; yet I could no more extricate myself from the trap than a fly can win free out of a cobweb. I was only safe so long as I was useful, you see. I was so clever... but a bullet is cleverer."

"Don't be ridiculous!" Marsh was affronted. "The Vespertiles are merely professional criminals, whereas I have joined an ancient and honorable Society intent on the pursuit of knowledge. They're entirely different!"

Gytt's faintly mocking smile widened. He began to laugh, as though that had been quite the best joke he had heard in a while. He rocked to and fro; he held his sides and pointed at Marsh.

Marsh was insulted, and sought to protest further; but felt his heart fail him as blood began spilling from Gytt's laughing mouth. The blood got everywhere. It ran all over Gytt's clothing, it stained the seat, it spattered even Edward's gray exhausted face, and Marsh tried to rise—

He jolted awake and stared about wildly. Edward slept on, oblivious.

Marsh turned up his collar and leaned back, blinking. No use to fight sleep any more; nature could only be resisted so long, after all, and the rocking of the carriage on its iron track was irresistibly soothing, and in any case the train had increased its speed and was going far too fast for him to jump off now.

John Edward Ames came to me at the recommendation of O'Neil De Noux, for which I need to thank O'Neil. The author of fifty-seven books and about one hundred short stories, by his count, Ames gives us this timeless story about a New Mexico that could as easily exist a hundred years in the past as a hundred years in the future, which sits somewhere at the crossroads between boy's western adventure, campfire tale, and ghost story.

The Pacing White Stallion
by John Edward Ames

"Is it an old coin?" Steve Mumford asked.

He stared at the curious object his friend Jemez Morningstar had just placed in his hand. It was a palm-sized, hammered-silver disc with hailstone designs carved into it and tiny flecks of turquoise cemented to both sides.

"It's old, yeah, but not a coin. It's a hear-nothing charm," Jemez replied. "I got two of them from the old man called Grayeyes. He says a person carrying one of these can sneak up on horses without being heard. Bring this with you tonight."

"Tonight?" Steve reined in his horse. He called the four-year-old sorrel gelding Socks because of its four white feet. Steve and Jemez were riding beside a long acequia, an irrigation ditch. There were very few roads in this corner of New Mexico's vast Isleta Pueblo Indian reservation, only a few ranch and farm lanes.

"Why will I need it tonight?" Steve asked.

Jemez rode beside him on a pinto horse with uneven, multi-colored markings that looked like accidental paint splashes. He, too, drew back on the reins to stop his horse. He leaned forward and rested his forearms on the saddle horn. Jemez watched his friend with a mysterious smile, a smile hinting that he knew an amazing secret. Jemez was a Tewa Indian with copper skin, his straight dark hair jammed under a New York Yankees cap.

"Never mind why, you'll find out," he promised Steve. "Right now let's go talk to Grayeyes. On Saturdays he works in his bean field."

Steve lived nearby in Bosque Farms, a small town that bordered on the Isleta Pueblo. Except that many folks in Albuquerque, thirteen miles to the north, liked to joke that Bosque Farms wasn't really a town at all, just a pimple on Nowhere's butt. But Steve didn't care what city dwellers thought—he liked it here in the rural Rio Grande Valley.

This way he could spend much of his summers and weekends visiting Jemez on the reservation. Both boys were fourteen years old and avid horsebackers who'd been best friends since the sixth grade. It was Jemez who taught him how to play the hoop-and-stick game and shinny ball, games Indian boys had played for centuries. Also Jemez who taught him cool stuff like how to fish with dip nets and splice ropes by braiding strands of horse hair together.

So Steve followed Jemez now even though being around Chato Grayeyes sometimes made him feel a nose-dive tickle of nervousness in his stomach. True, the elderly man told all sorts of fun legends—like the scary story of No Body, the great rolling head. Or the story about how Untekhi, the fearsome water monster, had left his fossil bones scattered across the Badlands of the West.

But Grayeyes was also a sly teaser who liked to poke fun at the boys. He called them "tadpoles" and "little shirt-tail brats." There were even a few rumors that old Grayeyes "lived by the night"—a way of saying he possessed magic items, such as "finding stones" to locate lost objects. Even many non-Indians in Bosque Farms believed the weird story about how Grayeyes "caught" himself a wife: that he drew elk tracks on a small mirror, then reflected sunshine from it onto the face and heart of Socorro Montoya, one of the prettiest girls in Isleta Pueblo. She immediately fell in love with him, and a week later they were married. Steve didn't really believe all that, but old Grayeyes' wife *was* awfully young and pretty to be married to such an old dude.

"There he is," Jemez called out, pointing to a tall man in a straw Sonora hat who was hoeing a bean patch behind an adobe house. Niches in the outer east wall of the house held plaster busts of the beloved saints. Beyond the fields, the nearby Manzano Mountains looked dark purple in the brilliant afternoon sunlight. The lower slopes were sliced with gullies and bright with yellow arrowroot blossoms.

The two boys dismounted at the edge of the field and hobbled their horses foreleg to rear with strips of rawhide.

"Hello, Grandfather," Jemez greeted Chato Grayeyes, using the term of respect Tewa boys used when addressing elderly men of the reservation. "Do you have time to tell my friend about the Pacing White Stallion?"

The eager excitement in Jemez's tone surprised Steve. Jemez had never mentioned any such horse to him. Steve read plenty about horses and knew what a "pacer" was: a special breed of horse introduced in America by the early Spaniards. Called *caballos de camino*, or "travelers," they were bred for comfort over long distances. They did not trot or gallop. Instead, they moved at a gait so smooth a rider could carry a glass full of water and never lose a drop.

At first Grayeyes ignored the question, watching both boys as if he couldn't quite decide whether to be amused or annoyed by their arrival. He was a solitary man with eccentric ways, often brusque but seldom really unfriendly. His advancing age showed in the flesh beginning to fold along his jawline and the way his prominent neck muscles stood out like taut cords.

"You call him the Pacing White Stallion," Grayeyes finally replied, leaning on his hoe. "But he has many names whenever tales are told around the campfire. He is called the Supreme Mustang, the Pacing White Mustang, the White Steed of the Prairies, the Ghost Horse of the Plains. Some say he was first brought to the New World from Arabia or Spain. Others say he was born around the Bosque River in central Texas."

Grayeyes turned his gaze toward the purple-hazed mountains. "I believe he was never born but has always been part of the West, like those mountains. He has been spotted from the mesas of Mexico to the Dakota Badlands, from eastern Texas to the Rocky Mountains."

"Even nowadays?" Jemez asked eagerly.

"Even today he roams free, always alone," Grayeyes insisted. "Never galloping or trotting, always pacing. Large sums have been offered for his capture, but all attempts have failed. That is because the Ghost Horse is supreme among all pacers. He moves at the rate of one mile in two minutes, and can continue this pace so long that he tires out all pursuers."

Now the old man turned his frost-gray eyes toward Steve. "Among all wild horses, none is more graceful or enduring, none more fleet or intelligent. But of all his magnificent qualities, none exceeds his passion to be free. Ever since Great Mystery made people, we Indians have believed in the mysterious power of motion. Its spirit is in the wind, in anything that moves. The endless wanderings of the Pacing White Stallion symbolize the circle without end, the sacred hoop, the road of life."

"But, Grandfather," Jemez cut in, "is this stallion *real*?"

Old Grayeyes frowned so deeply that his silver eyebrows touched over his nose. "Snakes only bite a doubter—that is a Tewa saying. A shadow is 'real,' is it not? But can you pick up a shadow and put it in your pocket? The important thing is that the Pacing White Stallion symbolizes pure freedom. And yet, there have always been some who feel they must either make this free animal a prisoner or kill it. Thus, these people would destroy the very freedom they claim to admire."

"I would never kill a horse," Jemez said. "Nor hurt one. But the person who captured the Pacing Stallion would become famous. And if an Indian boy caught him, he would earn a man's name, right? He would be allowed to wear a necklace of bear claws and be a hero to his people?"

Grayeyes snorted. "The sun will rise in the west before a tadpole like you captures the Ghost Horse. Your mind has been tricked by *shunk-manitu*, the coyote. He plays tricks on boys and whispers lies in their ears. You two still have baby fat in your cheeks—go play with your rattles and let an old man work in peace."

Grayeyes began hoeing beans again. As the two boys stepped into their stirrups, Jemez said quietly: "Can you meet me tonight after supper? At the entrance to Redrock Canyon—and bring your hear-nothing charm?"

"I s'pose," Steve replied. "If my dad's not in a lousy mood. But why?"

Jemez, reins in hand, stared at his friend from eyes ablaze with excitement. "Because I know where the Pacing White Stallion drinks every night. And I have built a catch pen. With your help, I will capture him tonight."

This bizarre announcement shocked Steve like a slap to the face. Jemez was not the fanciful type who chased after fairy tales.

"Are you freaking out?" Steve demanded. "It's just a neat old legend."

"Think so? You just be there tonight. Then you'll see."

Jemez kicked his horse into motion. But Steve, still stunned, sat his saddle, too surprised to move.

"You've gone bonkers!" he called out to his friend. "Hey— wait up!"

But Jemez didn't even look back. He crouched low and forward in the saddle.

"Cowards to the rear!" he shouted, quoting the great Chief Crazy Horse as his pinto galloped off in a boiling cloud of dust. "Brave hearts, follow me!"

Jemez raised his left hand out in front of his face, squinting toward the sky.

"Four fingers between the sun and the horizon," he told Steve. "That means there's about thirty minutes of daylight left. The Pacer will be here soon after sunset. We'll stay downwind of him or the human smell will scare him away. And speaking of that—"

Jemez dug into a saddlebag and produced an old tattered pair of brushed blue jeans and a dirty t-shirt. He handed the clothing to Steve.

"Here, we're about the same size. Put these on right now and stuff the clothes you're wearing into your saddlebags."

"Cripes, what for?" Steve protested, getting a good whiff of the old clothes. "They stink."

"To you, maybe. But not to a wild horse. I smoked these clothes over a fire of sweet grass and cedar to mask the people smell. The clothes I'm wearing, too."

This whole thing was getting pretty weirdorama, but Steve had to admit that Jemez's gathering excitement was infectious. Without further protest, he quickly shucked out of his own clothing and donned the fire-smoked garments.

Only a few minutes earlier the two boys had arrived at the narrow entrance of Redrock Canyon. The spot was a natural watering stop for many animals because a small seep, an underground spring, had formed a pool at the back of the canyon. And over the past few days, all on his own, Jemez had turned the canyon into a catch pen for wild horses.

Steve had to admit it was a well-constructed, clever trap. The canyon already formed three solid walls. Jemez had simply added two "wings," swinging gates made from strong poles. Once a horse went inside to drink, the wings could be swung shut and block the only way out. They were also well disguised with mesquite brush.

"The Pacer is quick," Jemez warned him again. "I've spied on him for weeks now. I can't swing both wings shut fast enough by myself. Move when I do, and move fast. That's the important thing: When you see me leap out from hiding, you jump, too."

"I said I would, didn't I? But how can you be so sure this isn't just a regular wild stallion? There's still wild horses in New Mexico."

"You'll see," Jemez promised. He mounted his pinto and wheeled the gelding around. "Now we better hide our horses a good ways off."

Steve followed his friend. Deep arroyos, dry ditches formed by flash floods, scarred the landscape. They rode their horses down into one of these ditches and hobbled them. Then they hurried back toward the canyon entrance and hid behind a jumble of boulders to wait.

The sun went down in a flaming blaze of glory, soon to be replaced by a full ivory moon bright enough to cast shadows. Steve wished he had a jacket now—he was warm enough except when the wind gusted.

"Jemez," Steve finally complained in a hushed tone, "I've had more fun watching ice melt. Grayeyes is an old guy—you know how those old-timers like to peddle the ancient legends. You shouldn't take his yarns so seriously."

"It's true the old man's fires are banked," Jemez whispered back. "And some of the older guys around the rez call him Great Roaring Thunder 'cause he farts a lot. But this time the old man is right. Before this night is over, we're both gonna be famous, Steve. I know it sounds crazy, but it really *is* the Pacing White Stallion drinking here lately."

"Yeah, you keep saying that. But how come you're so sure?"

"Man, it's just—it's not something you can put into words. Just hang on a little longer, and you'll believe it, too."

Jemez's tone, even hushed, was passionately earnest. Steve could understand his friend's burning need to accomplish some great feat. The men of Jemez's clan were known as adventurers, travelers, war heroes. By tradition, many Indian males had two names—the name given them at birth, and the "man's name" they earned later in life to commemorate some brave act or great accomplishment.

But this thing now with laying in wait to catch a "ghost horse"—Steve feared it might end up making Jemez the butt of jokes, a celebrity but not the kind he dreamed of being.

"It's getting late," Steve whispered. "My dad—"

"Shush it!" Jemez alerted like a hound on point. "Listen! Hear that?"

After a few moments Steve did hear it: The sound of a horse snorting as it approached the canyon from the west. A few moments later a white mustang emerged into the clear moonlight, and Steve's heart started pounding like fists on a drum.

"See?" Jemez whispered. "It's the Pacing White Stallion."

No way, Steve assured himself, though his eyes were drawn

like magnets to the stallion. It's just a magnificent wild horse. For "wild" it surely was. Its long, untrimmed tail was bushy and trailed on the ground. The stallion constantly tossed its head to clear its vision, for its mane too had never been trimmed.

But now Steve got a better look at the stallion, and suddenly it felt like his blood was flowing backward in his veins—just like the fabled pacer, this horse seemed to glide when it moved. So smoothly it could have been on a wheeled platform.

"It *is* a pacer," Steve said softly. "But it's wild. So who taught it to—?"

"Now!" Jemez interrupted when the stallion started drinking. Both boys leaped out, grabbed a wing, and in mere moments the stallion was trapped behind lashed gates.

"It will fight like a devil now," Jemez predicted. "Stand back!"

Steve was so nervous his mouth was dry. He, too, expected this wild horse to buck, crow-hop, try to leap the gates. But the stallion calmly finished his long drink, then glided back to the gate and bared its teeth in a piercing whinny.

The eerie sound, like none he'd ever heard a horse make, laid a chill on Steve. Instantly, the two horses hidden in the arroyo responded. They made nickering shrieks so unnatural and scary that Steve feared they'd whiffed a wildcat or rattler. And both horses were desperately fighting their hobbles; he could hear them.

Then he realized what was really happening, and Steve stared at the stallion bathed in luminous moonlight.

"Jemez!" he cried out. "Listen to our horses! And Socks is so gentle he won't even nip at flies! That stallion—he sent them a signal!"

Jemez, too, was shocked by the ruckus, and the calm, almost cunning way the white stallion watched his captors now, showing no fear. Both boys seemed to be recalling Grayeyes' words from earlier: *These people would destroy the very freedom they claim to admire.*

"I know this is the Pacer," Jemez insisted. "I can be famous now. I can choose a brave, heroic name—a man's name, not a boy's."

He looked at Steve. "But then *I* would end the legend. And this horse, who has been free so long, would be like an animal in a zoo. Well fed but never again free."

Jemez gave the wild stallion one last, long glance, a silent war raging in his soul—would he choose the lure of personal fame or obey the eternal laws of the Manitous, the ancient spirits?

He looked at Steve again, his eyes bright with unshed tears at what he was about to give up. Then, his face grim but resolute, Jemez untied the rawhide securing the wings, and both boys pushed them open.

Immediately, their own horses quieted down. And the Ghost Horse of the Plains disappeared into the night like a shadow gliding on moonbeams.

Paul Di Filippo is author of novels like *The Steampunk Trilogy, Ribofunk*, and *A Year in the Linear City,* and hundreds of short stories, each different than the one before it. He refers to this as his attempt at what he calls "bardo fiction," after the Tibetan term for the period of 49 days after death in which the soul wanders through a visionary landscape before ultimately being reincarnated in a new form.

Eel Pie Stall
by Paul Di Filippo

"To die will be an awfully big adventure."
—J. M. Barrie.

Tang of the river: ancient impregnated septic tidal flats exposed to the air; rotting fish; saturated driftwood; tarred pilings; engine exhaust; weeds going to slime.

Sound of the river: slop of wavelets on insensible slippery cement steps; raucous gulls aloft; chugging engines; creak of winches; workmen bantering.

Sight of the river: a cold rippling welcoming pewter grave, with flanking buildings as the only mourners.

Tansy Bynum pauses at a waist-high stone wall along the southern bank of the Thames. Rests her hands on the flat gritted icy top of the wall. Feels nothing. Equilibrium between inner self and outer world. But not in favor of the living.

Tansy turns away momentarily from the sight, sound, and smell of her prospective final home. Polyester scarf printed with cartoon fishes binding moderate mouse-colored hair. No-brand sunglasses contradicting the gray skies. Cheap beige cloth coat down to mid-thigh. Worn wool skirt. Sensible stockings. Scuffed brown tie shoes.

Wrists crossing twixt her modest breasts, fingers tucked beneath armpits. Unpainted mouth composed in a taut straight line. Shuffling pointlessly farther down the path along the embankment, wall on her left.

People around her with jobs and lovers, chores and duties, children and parents, wants and lusts. Smiles, frowns, musing looks. Just to feel something, anything.

Leave them behind. Shed these mockers like a final molt.

Long slow nowhere trudge. River never out of vision, hearing, or odor-waft. Wall now less well-maintained, crumbling in places, beginning to be marred with rude graffiti. Less of a barrier to what calmly awaits. Inevitable destiny. People dwindling in numbers: going, going, gone. Nebulous empty borderland between what is and what will be. Moisture begins to seep from the louring clouds in a prelude to a drizzle.

Up ahead, scabbed against the wall like an ungainly limpet: a shack or shed or stall, some kind of slovenly commercial affair. Unpainted boards and timbers blackened with pollution and age. No signage. Grommeted dingy canvas front rolled up and balanced on the slanting gap-shingled roof, exposing dark interior. Chest-high counter projecting like an idiot's pendulous lower lip.

Abreast of the stall and ready to step past. Unseeing fate-blinded eyes straight front, no interest in what lurks within the shed.

"Tansy Bynum."

She stops, astounded.

Looks left.

A shadowy artificial shallow cave untainted by any modern conveniences. Medieval. Prehistoric. Lower half of the back wall composed of the stones of the embankment barrier. Faintest of reddish-orange illumination supplied by a smoldering bed of coals in an open-faced brick oven. Large wooden singed paddle for retrieving items from the hearth. On the counter, a squat open-topped wooden canister holding a heterogeneous assortment of bone-handled spoons and forks. Crooked shelves within hosting clay mugs, crockery, spice jars, flour-dusted burlap sacks.

And the proprietor.

Greasy salt-and-pepper beard, disheveled mop of jaundiced silver hair. Coarse features, shabby cast-off clothes. Fingerless

gloves more moth holes than fabric. Awkwardly hunched armature of his short frame. Repellent, but somehow rendered less so
by the appropriateness of his environment, like a hermit crab in
a particularly apt adopted shell.

The proprietor fixes her with a sly, obsequious wink. A potential customer hooked.

"Did you—did you call my name?"

"'Fraid not. Couldn't very well, could I? Strangers, you and
me. No, just asked, 'Fancy a pie, mum?'"

"Oh."

Tansy makes to move on. Eating. A pointless activity now.

The gnomish proprietor reaches below Tansy's sight to bring
up a small pie in tin plate. Crust still uncooked white. Edges
neatly crimped. Two slits in the top like nostrils.

"No. I have to go—"

A friendly leer. "Ah, now, why off so fast? You'll never have
another pie like this. Best in all of London. No one else makes
them like old Murk."

Senselessly, irrationally rooted to the spot somehow. First
time anyone's talked to her in days. Stomach suddenly awakes
noisily. A macabre thought arises, born from tawdry television
viewing: won't the coroner have an easier time dating her de-
mise if there're remnants of a meal in her gut? Her last selfless
contribution to the ease of others, after a life devoted to such
one-way gestures.

"What—what kind of pie?"

"Ah, mum, best to show you."

Pie in gnarled hand set down on shelf. Murk's face prideful
beneath warty brow. Bending forward like a broken toy. Hoist-
ing strongly two-handed an antique wooden bucket chest-high.
Sets it on the counter, where it slops a scant rill of water over its
rim. Bucket obscures the dwarfish man.

"Have a dekko then, child. C'mon, naught'll happen to
you."

On tiptoes to peer into the bucket.

Tansy's first impression: a single braided whip in constant
coiling motion, a flux of silver and black. Then: separation into

component parts: heads, eyes, bodies, flukes, gills.

A bucket of writhing eels, sinuous, muscled, constrained.

Their weavings seem to scribe watery ideograms in perpetual flicker, transiting from one half-perceived meaning to another.

And at random moments, as their serpentine bodies open a clear view to the bottom of the bucket, millisecond impressions of something piebald, gold and blue, beneath them, like a queen or king guarded by courtiers. A sport or mutant brother to the mundane seasnakes... ?

Tansy expects to feel instant revulsion. But does not. The anticipated antipathy fails to arise. No gorge in her throat. Instead, a penultimate hunger increases, ironically supplanting for a moment the ultimate hunger for extinction.

Around the side of the bucket, Murk's face appears, all huckster eager. "Freshest of the fresh, mum. Caught right here in the river. Clean as a whistle these days, the water is. Heads and tails make a fine stock. Rest diced up bite-sized. Lemon, parsley, shallot, pinch of nutmeg, that's all it takes. Real butter in the crust. You won't be sorry."

"Well, why not... ?"

Quick as an eel himself, Murk hoists the bucket off the counter, paddles the pie onto the live coals. Almost immediately, a sweet wholesome fishy scent pervades the booth, sending out tendrils to capture Tansy's senses.

"How—how much?"

"Fifty pence."

Tansy fumbles out some coins, among her last, and lays them on the counter. Murk scrapes them off the surface with the edge of one hand and pockets them.

The ceiling of leaden sky seems to sink lower while the pie bakes, as if the box of her life is compressing even further.

Pie in the oven, Murk has no more attention for his customer. Serious as a jeweler faceting a gem. All is reserved for his creation. Fusses with the coals. Spins the pie at intervals for even baking. Anoints its top with a clear glaze from a misshapen mug, employing a crude animal-bristle brush.

Finished at last. By what sign or omen or chef's intuition,

unknown. Delved from the oven's depths and deposited on the countertop.

"Grab a utensil, mum. Careful, now, it'll be hot."

Bone-shafted spoon in hand. Bending forward to catch up-gust of victual-richness. Arc of spoon biting into layered flaking crust, bubbling upwelling of rich broth along the narrow trench. Scooping a heaping serving onto the spoon. Raised to lips, invited in.

Ambrosial pastry. Oniony, herby savor. Warmth coating her throat. Lemon. Sweet ichthyic flesh melting, melding into tastebuds. No bones? Rendered into intangibility? A second spoon, a third—

Within scant minutes, Tansy has gulped down the whole pie, scraped the tin shell clean.

Murk proudly attentive and approving throughout. Upon completion, still solicitous.

"Had enough then? Knew you'd appreciate this. Had you pegged, Murk did."

"I—thank you. But now I have to go. Good-bye."

"Never good-bye, mum. Just see you later."

Yards beyond the stall, the meal seems a dream. Pleasantly inconsequential, but fading, one of the few typically minor bright spots in a wearisome life, but now replaced by the dreary reality of her situation. Except for the weight in her stomach, a greasy film on her lips and palate. Not enough to tip the scales in favor of existence.

Night arrives. Gaps between the isolated streetlights dark as the abyss. Warehouses, abattoirs. Solitary, unobserved. Easy to find an adequate spot. Straight drop of a dozen yards from the top of the wall to the plane of the river below. Never learned to swim. No one to teach, no one to care.

Stones from the weather-shattered wall ballasting her pockets. Scramble atop the wall. Scraped knees and palms irrelevant. Stand up, swaying.

Push off without a twinge of hesitation, falling forward into the embrace of the air.

Smash the water, more a solid interface than a liquid curtain.

Stunned. Sinking so easily. Sensation confused with flying upward. Vision limited to the end of her nose. Chill stabs coreward. No need to inhale yet. Farther down will do fine. Drop, drop. Lazy currents finger all her surfaces and holes. Bubbles ascend, a Morse code message to the world left behind. Then the released airstream stops at the empty source.

Now. Breathe deep....

No pain in her chest, just an overwhelming heaviness.

Consciousness persists long enough for Tansy to feel the face-first embrace of the muck bottoming the Thames. Silken silty scarves caressing her cheeks, pillowing her thighs, clasping her ankles. Gone from sight now, totally mired. Still plummeting in slow motion. Yet soon the expected terminal solidity of the riverbed beneath the silt, a final bier...?

But no. Still ever-downward. Still retreating from the world above.

Still conscious.

Still alive?

How?

Resignation gives way to a minor consternation. Is even death to be robbed from her?

Still sinking, Tansy awaits extinction, a final solidity.

Time elongates, accumulates uncountably.

Her slow serene fall through the accumulated miles of powdery snowed-down organic debris continues. Like a flake herself, a cast-off diatomaceous shell, she drifts ever deeper.

Tansy's mind dissolves into a kind of banked nescience. A spark heaped with char.

A tugging at her feet. No strange entity with claws, but just a new, reorienting gravity. If she has been descending like a skydiver with ventral surface presented flat to the earth, now she is rotating slowly through ninety degrees, so that the soles of her stockinged feet—shoes lost in the first impact with the river—are presented to whatever draws her onward.

The absence of enfolding silt was felt first around her feet and ankles, as if they had broken through a crust, were protruding through a sky-crust of muck into a less curdled atmosphere. The sensation of unencumbrance moved slowly up her legs, to her groin, then waist, the sternum, then chest—

Her face came free, and she could see.

Within a small compass. Dimly. As if in an opalescent terrestrial fog at dusk.

Standing now at rest on a gritty featureless plain, as if in some bubbled environment. Tansy emptied her lungs and breathed. But what? More water? Air? Some more subtle aether? She moved her arm through the medium that surrounded her, attempting to feel its nature. Nothing familiar. Yet she drew in lungfuls of an invisible, weightless substance, expelled same, but could assign it no name.

Tansy took two steps forward in the random direction she found herself facing. The curved surface of the bubble in front of her receded equally. A glance behind told her that rear wall had come forward with her steps. Experiment soon proved that no matter which direction she stepped in, her volume of space remained constant, centered around her.

Pointless to discriminate. Tansy strode forward.

The plain extended for miles and miles. So it seemed. Hours upon intuited indistinguishable hours she walked, without sustenance or refreshment or need for same. Nothing varied.

Her belly still cradled her last meal.

Tansy's mind fell into a stuporous equanimity. So much inexplicable strangeness attendant on her dashed self-extinction afforded no purchase for fear or speculation.

Blue smote her eye like a revelation. Even this much color after an eternity of none precluded instant identification of shape. She quickened her pace, bringing more of the object into her sphere.

One bare leg, then another. Enamel blue like cloisonné, solidly planted on the nothingness. Then golden limbs somehow intermingled with the blue. Then two forms nestled together.

A naked blue man stood upright. Large muscled, well formed.

Legs wrapped around his waist and locked at the small of

his back, a nude golden woman clung to his neck. Heavy ripe curves.

Facing Tansy, the man cupped the gold woman's buttocks. The pair were joined in coitus, but unmoving. Still: not statues, but flesh, however oddly toned.

Their faces indiscernible, because pressed against, melted, into the flesh of each other's shoulder.

Tansy stopped.

Sound as of ripping cloth, and the male and female faces pulled away from their epidermal interknittedness, whole and unbloody. The man's eyes opened, lips parting for speech.

Tansy's parents had died in an auto accident when she was eight years old. Yet here was her father, whole and youthful, recognizable as if in an old photo, despite the transmogrification of skin.

"Tansy, you're here."

"Am I dead then?"

The hairy back of her father's head flanked her mother's face on the left. Had they turned, or had Tansy moved around them volitionlessly?

"I don't know, dear. Are we?"

Her mother's loving eyes and immemorial smile eased somewhat Tansy's sheer horrified confusion, gentled the whole mad experience.

"What—what is this place?"

"A land for becoming."

"Becoming what?"

Her father grinned in the old manner. "Whatever you have in you to become."

"Nothing. I've nothing inside me. I'm empty. Always have been."

"Is that so? What about your last meal?"

Tansy placed a hand on her stomach. Was it larger? Something seemed to stir within her, behind and below her belly.

"I don't understand. That pie? What could that do for me? One meal changes nothing."

"If you say so...."

"Don't mock me! How can I possibly accomplish something in *this* place when I couldn't do anything right in the other world?"

Golden laugh-lines crinkled. "By following your destiny all the way to its end, then beyond."

"Will you help me, Mother?"

"No. We can't. But your brother can."

"Brother? I don't have any brother."

Even her father's teeth were blue. "He was to be your older sibling. But he couldn't stay. He died when he was born—or was born when he died. He's here now. His name is Mercator."

"Where is he? How do I find him?"

"Just keep on."

Heads lowered into shoulders, blue melding seamlessly into gold, gold into blue.

The pair dwindled, shrinking rapidly, verging toward microscopic invisibility.

"Mother! Father! Don't leave me!"

Empty bubble of personal space. Neither cold nor warm. Fain saline lilt to the air. Nothing for it but to trudge onward.

Time and space played hide-and-seek.

The marketplace was empty this early in the morning. Shabby stalls shielding goods behind rope-lashed canvas fronts. Cobbles wet with morning dew. Organic trash, rinds and crusts and shells. The smell of human urine from a puddle in the corner of two walls. A dog appeared, red from tail tip to snout, like a new brick. Sniffed the puddle, then lifted its leg to add its commentary.

Tansy dropped, suddenly exhausted, to the cobbles. Rested her back against the timbered side of a stall. Head sagged forward, chin into chest. Eyes closed.

Sounds of the marketplace coming alive around her. Shuffling feet, bantering among merchants, children playing tag, crockery clinking, cartwheels trundling.

No one accosted her. Something like a sun rose higher in something like a sky, its heat evidenced across her slumped form.

"Tansy. It's me, your brother."

Eyelids snapping open.

A handsome man in his thirties, red all over as the dog. Crimson eidolon. Bare-chested, loincloth around his middle, sandals laced up his legs. Smiling. Hand extended to help her to her feet.

Siblings almost of a height. Eyes on the same level. Searching his face for resemblance to her own. Uncertainty. Yet a sense of having encountered him somewhere before.

"Sorry I'm late. I was busy with another. But you must be famished! Let's get you something to eat. Then we can go home."

"Home?"

"Your home here."

The young girl who served them bowls of hot porridge was colored the same as Mercator. So were all the teeming inhabitants of this low-built, diffuse city. A tableau of devils.

Spoon poised halfway to her lips, Tansy noted her own unchanged flesh, anomalous in this strange city.

"Won't I stand out here?"

"No one will mind. But perhaps it's best if you stay mostly indoors. You can be useful without leaving home."

"All right."

There was always something to sew. Humble garments and bedclothes in need of repair, dropped off by a steady stream of citizens, all incarnadined, tracking dust and unintelligible allusions to the life of the city into the adobe apartments to which Mercator had brought her.

Tansy developed calluses on her thumb and index finger after the first few weeks. The coarse thread and crude needles, the heavy fabrics, the misshapen buttons. Piles of unwashed garments redolent of their wearers' body odors. These were the constants of her days. Along with the shifting infall of roseate sunlight through the unglassed window, the parched heat, the simple meals of bread and olives, eggs and beans, honey and crisped locusts, delivered by Mercator.

Her brother?

If so, in name and attitude only. They hadn't been raised together, in any life she recalled. Had no long-term bonds or familially inculcated taboos delimiting their relationship.

Naturally she thought of having him sexually: during their meals, or when he slept on his mat of woven river-reeds next to hers. But never made any advance, for fear of rebuff. Nor did Mercator ever exhibit toward her any such impulses.

And her belly. That got bigger every day.

But how? She had never. Not anywhere, anywhen.

One day a new patron came with robes to mend, a bearded merchant with a withered arm. After months of such visits, Tansy thought nothing much of the man at first. But after he left, his image troubled her. When Mercator returned to their apartments at eventide, from whatever errands occupied him during the daylight, with small piquant tomatoes and salted fish for supper, Tansy inquired about the man.

"He was your lover in another life. You wronged him. Now you must mend his clothes."

A momentary stasis blanked her mind. "All—all of these men and women and children who have come—"

"Yes, of course. The entire city, in fact. You were intimate with them all, down the millennia. Didn't you know?"

"I—did I hurt them all?"

"And they you. It was inevitable."

"And their redress to me?"

"Yet to come. Or already obtained. Or otherwise obviated."

Tansy had a hard time falling asleep. Her mind revolved Mercator's words ceaselessly. But also her gravid, unbalanced body contributed its own discomforts.

One day every week Mercator took her out of their quarters for a stroll through the city, always ending at a favorite park, ripe with shade, where clownfish swam through the pod-strewn boughs of acacia trees. There, a peace descended on Tansy and she could momentarily forget her expiatory drudgery.

The twinges came one morning. Hardly commensurate with the enormous swell of her belly. Not what she had expected from all she had heard. More like imagined sexual tremors than splitting pains.

"Mercator, help me. I think it's my time—"

"Of course. Step into the tub."

A stone trough occupied one corner of their two rooms. Bamboo pipes brought rainwater down in a gravity feed from a tank on the roof.

Naked, Tansy climbed awkwardly into the tub. Her own pink flesh looking alien to her now. Seismic tremors propagated outward from her center. She drew her legs up, knees to chest. Mercator kneeled by the trough and stroked her brow, murmuring wordless assistance.

A slithering, rippling exvagination brought an orgasmic sense of release and relief. The water in the trough crimsoned with afterbirth. Her swollen midriff deflated.

The blue-and-gold eel stretched nearly as long as Tansy was tall. Thick around as her wrist. Its black eyes gleamed with intelligence. Twisting lithely in its limited compass, it tested its newborn muscles, visibly exulting in its power and gracefulness.

"Your child. You must take good care of him and fulfill his every wish. By doing so, you will come to where you need to be."

The eel reared six inches of its head out of the water.

"Mother," it piped, in a lilting voice like the notes of a flute, "I am so happy to meet you again at last."

The sharp pebbles and grit beneath her feet scored shallow cuts in her bare soles. The pitch-smeared canvas bag dragged on its single shoulder strap, slapping against her hip with every step, sloshing out irreplaceable driblets of water. She changed the bag from one side to another at intervals, but this resulted only in distributing the pain evenly. Her throat was parched.

Mercator held her hand as they walked, but could not assume the burden of carrying her child.

Not that she had ever even asked him.

Tansy had named the eel Plum Sun for his two-toned skin.

"How much farther? I feel as if we've been walking for years."

"Not too many more miles. But I fear the last few are the

hardest. And I'll have to leave you, Sister."

"Must you, really?"

"It's ordained. And I could not help you in what comes next."

Tansy recalled the dull, laborious months in their tiny apartment, which now seemed like paradise. "Will I ever see you again?"

"You already have."

The foothills gave way to a crumbling talus slope that formed the skirts of the cloud-piercing mountain, bold and brutish as a soldier. But the mountain showed some charity. Cold rivulets clear as diamonds afforded a chance to wash her abused feet, slake her thirst, and replenish Plum Sun's carrier. Overhead, a small school of sharks and pilot fish moved through the skies.

"Thank you, Mother. All your exertions on my behalf will be repaid a thousandfold."

Tansy set one scarred foot upon the slope, then another. Mercator remained behind.

"This is where we must part?"

"Yes."

"Goodbye, Uncle. I appreciated your companionship."

"Farewell, Plum Sun. Farewell, Sister."

A hundred yards up the precipitous slope, bent almost double to maintain her balance, Tansy looked back.

Some trick of distance or atmosphere made Mercator resemble a squat bearded gnome in shabby clothes.

The razored crags and ledges by which Tansy ascended the upper reaches of the mountains tormented her hands as much as the rubble of the endless plain had gashed her feet. The weight of Plum Sun in his sodden pouch threatened to loosen her every handhold. Her bare toes scrabbled at minute ridges.

Once, falling, she was saved by a pod of dolphins. The creatures buoyed her up till she could regain her grip.

After that incident, Tansy redoubled her vigilance and efforts. But she knew she was drawing on a shallow well.

"Wake up, Mother. Please, wake up."

Tansy sat with her back against a large cold boulder. The

carrier holding Plum Sun rested on its oblate bottom upright by her side. Out of the bag protruded the blue-and-gold head of the eel. Somehow its limited expression conveyed encouragement.

Tansy brought her hand up to her face and smeared blood across her visage in an attempt to clear the cobwebs from her vision.

"Are we—are we where we need to be?"

"Almost. The Fountain of Flames is just ahead."

Weariness like lead in her bones. Struggling to her feet. Trudging ahead up a mild slope. Through a tall defile whose tight blank walls resembled the chute through which cattle were led for slaughter. Fossils embedded in the walls mocked her persistence. The distinctive shadow of a circling manta ray overhead came and went.

A broad plateau of roughly an acre in extent. Pillared in the middle on a rude slate hearth: a thick whistling column of green fire, sourceless, inexhaustible, braided of a thousand viridescent shades. Around the Fountain of Flames, the tumbled columns of some long-extinct fane.

"You must place me in the flame, Mother."

"You'll die."

"Not at all. Nor will you be harmed. Trust me."

If the green flame gave off heat, it was not the heat of a normal fire. Tansy approached warily. Closed her eyes for the final few yards.

A sensation as of silken threads infiltrating her blood vessels informed her that she was fully engulfed.

She tipped out Plum Sun into the flames, then backed away, out of the fiery column.

The eel lashed back and forth within the fires, but did not crisp or wail, but rather became engorged, priapic.

Big as a house, Plum Sun occulted or had completely absorbed the fires that had ennobled him. He seemed at ease in the air.

"Step closer, Mother."

Tansy obeyed.

Plum Sun's mouth a needled, ribbed cavern.

The hundred hands of invisible currents pulled her inside her son's gullet.

Blackness, acid reek, hot fluids laving her.

Dissolution, assimilation into the flesh of her child.

Tansy looked out through Plum Sun's eyes, felt his/her hermaphroditic body slip through gill-freshening darkling estuarial waters, sensed electrical impulses through novel organs of perception.

More of her kind fed below, drab cousins. She dropped swiftly through the waters to claim her share.

A woman's corpse provided the banquet, its clothing shredded. Dozens of eels tailed off the rotting body like flowers from a garden plot. Half-eaten already, disintegrating, drifting like a seedling on the marine winds, the woman's body reminded Tansy of someone close to her.

Plum Sun joined the feast.

The net took them unawares as they gorged, too busy incorporating the woman's substance into themselves to heed the surface predators.

Up, up, into the cruel air.

Confinement in a narrow bucket.

Speech vibrating the interface between air and liquid. Plum Sun understands.

"Have a dekko then, child. C'mon, naught'll happen to you."

On tiptoes to peer into the bucket.

Tansy's first impression: a single braided whip in constant coiling motion, a flux of silver and black. Then: separation into component parts: heads, eyes, bodies, flukes, gills.

A bucket of writhing eels, sinuous, muscled, constrained.

Their weavings seem to scribe watery ideograms in perpetual flicker, transiting from one half-perceived meaning to another.

And at random moments, as their serpentine bodies open a clear view to the bottom of the bucket, millisecond impressions of something piebald, gold and blue, beneath them, like a queen or king guarded by courtiers. A sport or mutant brother to the mundane seasnakes...?

Tansy finds the bizarre sight of so much life compacted into such a small compass soothing somehow. Feels herself composed of similar perpetually coiling energies, her DNA lashing like eels at the heart of each cell. Energies that offer new configurations of possibility every millisecond.

Comes down off her tiptoes. Gazes at the proprietor of the eel pie stall. The man winks at her, a wink conveying centuries of complicity.

"You'll be needing this meal now, then?"

Places her hand gently on her own stomach.

"No, not now, thank you. I'm already quite full."

Mark Finn worships at the altar of Robert E. Howard. In this yarn, Finn manages to blend seamlessly two genres Howard held dear—weird fiction and boxing stories—to create a story uniquely his own. Sam Bowen, the guy who ends up taking most of the punches, has previously appeared in the novel *Year of the Hare*.

The Bridge of Teeth
by Mark Finn

Casa Blanca, Nuevo Leon, Mexico
October 24th, 1994

The bartender turned around, a dented and worn Louisville Slugger in his fist, and swung it with all of his strength at the spot on the bar where my hand had been an instant before. I backed up, throwing as much broken Spanish between us as possible. *"Señor, señor, por favor, no violencia..."*

He wasn't having any. He hurled himself bodily against the bar, trying to come over it, as he swung at me again. *"Brujah!"* he shrieked. *"Trabajador del diablo!"*

I started to say more, but my duffel bag tripped me up and I hit the wood planks in a cloud of sawdust, the wind knocked out of me. I regained my breath and my sight just in time to get a spectacular view of the Louisville Slugger as it rushed up to kiss my face. For an instant, I saw the duplicated etch of Ted Williams' scrawl, and then my vision went white and red and I had the weirdest ringing in my ears. I couldn't feel my nose, but I could feel blood on my lip and taste it in my mouth. The bat was coming down again. I barely rolled out from under it.

The bartender continued yelling, his patrons calmly backing against the far walls of the ramshackle cantina. I had a spell, I think, that I wanted to cast on him, or maybe it was just an urge to hit him back, but I couldn't get my legs under me. My vision cleared to the point that I could see blood on my shirt, a lot of it. Nothing made sense. Why was there blood? My whole face felt numb. The breath was sticking in my nose, and each inhalation brought shards of pain. I didn't want to die in Mexico, but the bartender kept coming at me, scared out of his wits and swinging his bat in crazy arcs.

Finally, I felt the floor under my feet. I lurched upward, grabbing onto tables and chairs, anything to steady myself. As I moved forward, toward the frame of light that marked the door, I flung my temporary crutches behind me, trying to keep as much junk as I could between me and that swinging bat.

The door to the cantina smacked open and I fell into the blistering sunlight, staggering back in the direction of the road. Voices behind me told me I was being pursued, and I tried my level best to pick up the pace.

Somehow or another, I must have gotten turned around, because suddenly, a man appeared in front of me, dressed like a soldier. He grabbed me and jerked me sideways, around the side of the building. I thought I saw a flash of light as he spun me around and slammed me against the adobe wall. There went my breath again. He held me up, pinned in place, with a wiry arm, as the crowd passed by, shouting and waving. When the dust settled and I got my breath back, my savior started whispering in rapid Spanish.

"Sorry," I murmured, "no *comprende...*"

The man stopped speaking and we looked at each other. He wore a flak jacket and a dirty green T-shirt. Two crossed bandoliers with a leather satchel held his pants up.

"What the hell were you doing in there, asking about *brujahs*, eh?"

"I wasn't asking about witches," I said. "I was looking for Joachim Tlomec."

The man's eyes flashed, and I held a hand up to silence him. "Don't you start on me, either. That man's no witch."

"Not a witch?" The man threw his head back and laughed heartily. "Who told you that, *gringo*?"

"Man named Moreloch," I replied. "Another gringo."

The man finally let go of me. For a small guy, he was incredibly strong. "And who are you?"

"Sam Bowen," I said. "Thanks for saving me."

The man turned away. "Joachim Tlomec," he said, "and you can repay the favor by getting the hell out of here."

It took me a few seconds to parse that sentence through the shooting pain in my face. Finally, when it all sank in, I followed him down the alley beside the cantina. He was heading into the jungle. He stopped when he heard me, and drew the machete from the sheath on his back. "*Gringo*," he said, his voice filled with sorrow, "I just saved you. Don't make me kill you."

"Listen, Mr. Tlomec," I said, "I came here to find out what you know about Solomon's Disk."

Tlomec cocked his head at me. "Who in the hell told you to ask me that?"

"Moreloch," I said.

Tlomec nodded. "He still in Bastrop?"

"Yeah," I said. "We got rid of the black hound that was roaming the property."

"You don't say," said Tlomec. He looked at the jungle and scratched the stubble on his neck. The machete hovered above the dirt, his fingers flexing on the handle. "So, you're not a reporter."

"No, I'm not."

"And you want to learn about Solomon's Disk," he said.

"If you'll teach me."

"What do I get out of it?" Tlomec said.

That stopped me. I hadn't considered that. I had my own agenda to consider; tracking down my ancestor who'd brought a curse onto my family. I was the trigger of that curse. Seventh son of a seventh son, just like my old Uncle Jacob. Walking back through his footsteps, I had no way of knowing who or what had cursed him. Until I figured the magic out, I couldn't try to reverse the curse. So far, I'd learned just enough magic and sorcery to know that I didn't have much of an idea what I was doing.

Tlomec watched me thinking. "What's in the bag?" he asked.

I dropped the duffel bag in the dirt. "Most of the witchcraft and spells that I've picked up along the way."

Tlomec licked his lips. "Let me see it."

"Wait," I said, "are we talking about trading? You tell me what I want to know, I let you root through my bag?"

Tlomec smiled. "Something like that."

Moreloch had warned me in his gentle way that Tlomec was "an opportunist of the worst sort." I was getting an idea now of what he meant. All of the talking we were doing made my face throb, and my headache wasn't getting any better. "Would you let me go through your satchel, there, and take what I wanted?"

Tlomec coughed and spit. "This bag is sacred," he said.

"Yeah, that's kinda how I feel about this." I picked up the duffel bag and reshouldered it. "There's not much in here, but I earned all of it."

Tlomec nodded slowly. "Huh. Well, good luck, *amigo*," he said, turning back to the jungle.

"Wait," I said. "Let me offer something instead." Tlomec stopped walking but didn't turn around. I continued. "Why don't you take me on as an apprentice? Let me work off the lessons in labor. Let me help you with your work."

Tlomec regarded me over his shoulder, his fingers still flexing around the machete. "You want to work? Side by side with me?"

"In exchange for your information, yes," I said.

"You know what kind of work I do?"

I shrugged. "I know you are a shaman. You help people. Cure the sick. Tend to failing crops, that kind of thing."

Tlomec turned around again, nodding slowly. "I am the light against the darkness in this part of the world. But because I am in the dark, it covers me, and I am as feared as I am respected." He gestured to the peasants walking confusedly past us, unable to see due to his spell. "These people all think I am lost to the darkness. So I conduct my business on the edge of the world, where they cannot see me. You understand?"

I didn't, and I told him so.

"You walk with me, that means you're walking on the edge of the world. I can't guarantee your safety or your sanity. You want to come along, okay, but don't expect me to slow down for you. One slip, and you're gone. I won't save you. Understand me?"

"Yes," I said, and before I could do anything else, he punched me in the face. The impact drove me to my knees, but my breathing instantly cleared and the lancing pain became a dull ache.

Tlomec helped me to my feet and said, "Your nose was broken, so I fixed it."

"You know, a handshake would have been just fine, too."

Tlomec laughed. "One day, *Señor* Bowen, you will thank the day you met me." From his satchel he withdrew a bottle of aspirin and handed it to me. I crunched a couple and followed Tlomec and his machete into the jungle.

For a week, Tlomec had me hacking through underbrush, harvesting plants, digging up grubs, and in general restocking medicinal supplies. A few of them I recognized, but most of them were new to me. Tlomec didn't teach me much, except to show me where to dig and how to crush or preserve them. Some of their properties I figured out myself. Others remained mysterious and smelly.

As jungles go, it was hot, dirty, humid, and rotten, but it was a far cry from the heart of darkness. I turned into a giant, throbbing mosquito bite. Tlomec gave me an ointment that made the swelling go away. We ate local food; I got the trots. Tlomec made me some tea and cleared it right up. Useful stuff, but hardly magic.

When Tlomec talked, it was at night, around the campfire. We'd finish the spit-roasted iguana or vegetable soup, and he'd sit for hours, drinking mescal and staring at the fire. Like in a trance, he would rattle off the most amazing things in a mishmash of English, Spanish, and a language I couldn't recognize. He talked about the underworld being a flower, and being able to access the darkness through a multitude of gateways. He told me about the three ingredients of a man's soul, and how they can be captured or thrown out of balance. He told me about the *civatateo,* the stealer of children and the *brujah* wars in the hills. But still no mention of how to fight these things. No mention of

Solomon's Disk. For not the first time in my life, I questioned my decision to follow this lunatic.

Every day, we moved farther and farther into the interior. Casa Blanca was a small Mexican town, but by the end of the week, we were coming upon communities that were little more than clusters of huts in clearings. Not even villages, but single families. I took pretty meticulous notes to try to backtrack out, but even then I knew they'd be useless if I tried to get back to civilization on my own steam.

Tlomec's reputation definitely preceded him. As we encountered these hidden enclaves of families, children poured out of the trees to greet him, shrieking with delight. He gave them Chiclets and called to the family, who rushed forth with smiles on their faces.

We'd stay for dinner, the children giggling at me and referring to me as Tlomec's "white gardener," while Tlomec and the head of the household did some horse trading. Usually it involved swapping medicines that I helped dig up for tequila and cigars.

Seven days from civilization, we found a group of huts, but no children to greet us. "This is our destination, Bowen," he said. He called out softly, and a door opened and a native woman emerged. She was thin, walking on unsteady legs, tottering forward. Tlomec rushed to support her. She tried to get him to come inside, but he declined. They spoke in low whispers for several minutes.

Standing among the small, sagging structures, I got the impression of sickness or plague. Nothing was moving. Even the bugs were eerily quiet. Finally, Tlomec called me over and told me to take the woman inside and care for her.

"What are you going to do?" I asked.

Tlomec didn't answer. He drew his machete and vanished into the foliage like a ghost.

I helped the woman back into her house, which smelled of wet earth and corn flour. She motioned to her bed, and I laid her down in it and covered her with a ratty blanket. She moaned and starting whispering, *"El que no es muerto puede vivir por siempre,"* over and over again. I got the gist of what she was saying and decided to wait outside for Tlomec to return.

It was dusk when he finally emerged from the jungle, carrying an armload of wood. He dropped it in the cold stone pit in the center of the clearing and began to build a fire. I moved to help him, but he waved me off. "Stand and watch, Bowen," he said as he stacked the wood in a deliberate, peculiar fashion. Tlomec added dried leaves from his satchel and sprinkled herbs over the wood. After he finished, he crossed himself and then blessed the pyre. He pulled a match from behind his ear, scratched it on his boot, and dropped it into the pit.

A jet of blue-white flame sprang up, engulfing the pyre and sending us both backward a step with its intense heat. Tlomec grunted with satisfaction, squatted down in front of the conflagration, and intently studied the smoke as it curled and eddied above the bright light. I stared too, and tried to make my mind blank and receptive to visions, but I couldn't see anything in particular. Finally, he made eye contact with me.

"Sit down, and listen," he said, all interest in the fire now gone. He took a cigar out and lit it by waving the end through the flames. I sat beside him and instantly broke out in a sweat from the heat. The smoke from the cigar surrounded Tlomec in noxious fumes. Between the turdlike stench and the blast furnace heat, I felt ready to throw up.

"This land is cursed," Tlomec began. "It overlaps with the underworld, and the tension between the two creates pockets and seams that burst forth." He passed me the cigar and bid me to smoke it. I tried, and Tlomec continued through my hacking coughing fit. "This village is under attack from the *mictiani*, who do not know where the darkness ends and the light begins. They have stolen her husband and children, pulling them out of the house in the night and taking them back to Tlalocan, the underworld, the flower of darkness."

"Wait a minute," I said. "This isn't a plague, right? Or some shamanistic metaphor? We're talking about real things?"

Tlomec ignored my questions. "We will cross over through the door to the south, and cut down the Bridge of Teeth before the dead overrun this land and turn the flower inside out, bringing the night into day, the day into night."

That part, I understood. Tlomec looked at me, his eyes shining in the blue light. "Tonight, you will sleep. We will find your Nagual. You will need its help to cross into the underworld."

I dreamt that night, for the first time since crossing the border. I was in the jungle, in a tall tree, looking down at the peasant children below. They were all looking up and pointing and laughing, but I didn't seem to be embarrassed. As they watched, I leapt out of the tree and became a bird. They whooped with delight, chasing underneath me until I flew over a river. Here they stopped and became serious and somber. I landed.

"Why do you not follow me?" I said.

"This river leads to the black flower," an older child replied.

I turned around, looking up the path for some indicator that I had crossed over into the underworld, and when I looked back, the children were all on the other side with me. The child who spoke smiled, displaying a wide, inhuman maw of teeth, and the other children surged over me—

I woke up in one of the peasant huts, the first light of dawn streaming through the insufficient slats on the wooden door. Tlomec was outside, singing in Spanish and smoking like a chimney. "Bowen!" he roared. "Get up and make the damned coffee!"

Over a breakfast cooked by the peasant woman, I told Tlomec about my dream. He spat into the cooking fire. "Shit," he said. "I wanted you to see an animal. We got no time to find your spirit guide. We have to do this now, in the light."

"But, I became a bird. Isn't that something?"

"Which bird?" Tlomec asked. "A parrot? A songbird? A falcon?"

"I have no idea," I told him.

Tlomec wolfed down the remnants of his corn gruel and chuckled. "Ah, the *gringo* sees the problem, now. Different birds do different things."

"Whatever," I said, more than tired of his "me shaman, you *gringo*" shtick. "I'm assuming we're going to physically go get the children back, right? Not astral project, or anything cerebral like that?"

Tlomec's eyes hardened. "Something like that." He began packing his satchel. "Get your gear. We're going now."

We left the village with food and water packed by the peasant woman. Tlomec had previously hacked out a path for us to follow, so the going was fairly easy until we came to the cliff wall. Tlomec sheathed his machete and switched his satchel to his back. "Come on, *gringo*, we have a little climbing to do."

"I can't," I said, looking up at the twisted volcanic rock that towered over us. "I've never climbed before."

Tlomec sighed, exasperated. "Just follow me, dammit, and do what I do." He leapt up vertically, grabbed a jagged outcropping of rock, and pulled himself up and over. "Come on," he urged. "We have to get up there before nightfall."

What could I do? I jumped up, caught the ledge, felt the rock cut into my palms, and promptly pulled my shoulder muscles getting up over the first ledge. "See?" Tlomec said, beaming down at me from the second ledge. "Not so bad, is it?"

It was the worst two hours of my life. Every handhold featured glasslike edges, every ledge hosted a spider or snake of some kind. Tlomec routinely collected each poisonous critter that menaced us, but a few got past his vigil, and I nearly fell off one ledge shaking a wolf spider off of my hand. By the time we got to the top of the plateau, the sun was high above us and the trees offered no protection. Only a thin outcrop of rock threw a scant shadow that we crowded under, sweating and panting.

We ate lunch and drank half our water until the sun moved past, taking the shade with it. Somewhat refreshed, I stood up and took a look around. The plateau was a large, flat, and barren chunk of rock that looked like it had been dropped out of the sky a million years ago. On the far side was an identical clump of rock, slightly higher, with a small trickle of a river dividing the cliffs. Into the facing cliff was cut a small, dark cave. Thirty feet of nothing separated the cliffs. There was no way to cross the river.

Behind me and now close by, Tlomec said, "There's our gate. Now we have to bring forth the bridge."

"How in the hell are we going to get over there?" I asked.

Tlomec smiled at me. "We aren't going to do nothing, *gringo*. I'm going to dream myself across. You're going to stay here and keep the *mictiani* from crawling down the mountain."

"What, by myself?"

"Don't be a sissy. I'll let you wear my gloves."

"This is ridiculous," I said, for the fifth time. Tlomec punched me in the nose, not very hard, but it hurt like hell after my recent break. I threw a return jab that caught him right in the mouth and split both of his lips. He growled at me through a mist of blood and then somehow, we were rolling around on the ground, punching, kicking, gouging, biting, and trying to beat the shit out of each other.

After a week of frustration, it felt great to open up on him, but fighting Tlomec was a lot like messing with a gorilla. He was unbelievably strong and threw fast, damaging punches that hurt like a son of a bitch. While he was tapping the side of my face with his fist, I managed to wedge my leg between us and kicked him off of me. My bowie knife fell out of my boot and I made a grab for it, but Tlomec came up with his machete and pressed it against my throat.

"Calm down," he said, his breathing ragged. He looked up at the moon and said, "You don't have a choice, Bowen. If you don't stay here and protect my body, we'll both die. I can get in there and stop them. You have to buy us the time. You can't do what I do, not yet. It's got to be me that goes in."

"I don't even know what the hell I'm supposed to be protecting you from," I screamed. "I'm cold, hungry, tired, and you've just given me a pair of weird gloves and told me to fight them off by myself? This is horseshit, Joachim. Tell me what I'm up against or I'm climbing back down this mountain right now."

The machete blade gleamed in the moonlight as he rolled

it off of my neck and onto my collarbone. "If I tell you, you'll just go back down the mountain anyway. You won't believe it, even if I tell you, so why not keep an open mind?" He lifted the machete and laid it beside him. "But if you're going to go, quit crying like a baby and just go. There's other ways to do this; I don't need you. I'm trying to teach you something, you stupid shit." He hung his head, speaking into his chest. "Hurry up and work this out, *gringo*. I need to sleep."

Well, shit. I thought about Mexico, and Texas, and all of the other places I had walked through and the strange things I've seen. I hadn't heard from the remnants of my family in over a year. They could all be dead by now. I stared at the ground, trying to remember my mother's face. I couldn't see her.

"Okay, so, how do these gloves work?"

The turquoise cross around my neck was a jagged and crudely carved thing, and it snagged on my shirt and dug into my skin. I tried not to think about it as I fixed my gaze on the darkened cave in the side of the cliff. The moon cast a pale blue haze over the plateau, but nothing could illuminate the gloom of the cave mouth. Behind me, in the shadowed lip of rock, Tlomec moaned and thrashed in a deep sleep. He muttered some gibberish, and then said loudly, "Warn the kid!"

I had no idea who Tlomec was talking to, but he needn't have bothered. The wind shifted and the temperature dropped about twenty degrees almost instantly. I pulled the cigar and lighter out of the pocket of the trench coat Tlomec had given me, turned away from the wind, and lit up. I still couldn't smoke worth a damn, but I managed to keep the cigar going. I turned back to face the cave and nearly burned myself with the Zippo.

A bridge had appeared, spanning the gorge between the cave entrance and the plateau. It appeared to be made out of water and bits of bone, anchored in place with beams of moonlight. Shimmering and translucent, the spectral egress gave off an iridescent glow that unfortunately lit up the inside of the cave like a spotlight.

At first, the women were beautiful; dark hair, flowing in all directions from the wind, pale skin, and almost angelic. But as they neared the Bridge of Teeth, their true shapes became apparent. They grouped together at the mouth of the cave, apparently curious about me. I could see them, skeletal and terrible, in their burial clothes, their jaws working in silent anticipation. Some of them held their ruined heads in their hands, carrying the skulls before them like lanterns. Others were just a loose assemblage of parts; savaged bags of skin held together by a clasped hand.

Puffing madly on the cigar, I walked forward until I was a couple of feet from the edge of the bridge, careful not to touch it myself. I raised my hand to them and shouted over the howling wind, *"Soy el vigilante del puente! Usted no caminará encima!"*

The *mictiani* ignored me and began walking single file over the bridge. I'd known they would; Tlomec had told me they would. I hurriedly slipped on the battered and stained gloves, not in the least comforted by their weight. The bridge swayed as the *mictiani* trundled across. I started the prayer Tlomec had given me, whispering it through the cigar smoke that was making me sick, held my gloved hands up so the monsters could see the symbols carved into the riveted steel plates.

She reached out for me, stepping off of the bridge. Instantly, she was beautiful again, full of life, a countess or rich woman of some sort. I checked my swing, and in that second's hesitation, her mouth widened horribly and she screamed and lunged forward. I backpedaled, freaked out, and then panicked again when I realized I had left the bridge unguarded. I drew my bowie knife and stuck it into her chest and heard the blade clatter around before dropping to the ground.

Now she came at me, biting and gnashing, and I remembered what Tlomec had said. I shoved my gloved fist right into her mouth, feeling my arm jar and shake with the impact of her clattering jaws. But the steel plates on the gloves held. Zombie armor. Who would have thought?

I pivoted, pulling the undead thing with me, and pitched it into the path of the next *mictiani* coming off of the bridge. When the pair went down together, I used the cigar to light their shrouds on fire. They screamed and tried to crawl past me, but I used my boot to keep them on the bridge until they stopped moving. The other *mictiani* stopped moving to watch them burn, as well. When the corpses were nothing more than smoldering ash, they resumed their determined march.

If the *mictiani* crossed over and touched the ground, they became solid flesh. On the bridge, they were still as ghosts. My gloved fists had little effect on them, but the symbols etched into the steel plates that covered the gloves made the monsters shriek with pain. I punched, kicked, and scuffled with the smokelike wraiths until my arms were lead pipes and my legs were wooden. Every time one of them got by me, I had to chase her down across the plateau and dismember her or set her on fire. Each time I did that, more got through. It was an endless dance, this makeshift siege, and I fought and swung and tore and screamed until the smoke from the pyres was too thick to see through and the stench of burning flesh brought howls of cries from the predators in the jungle.

I didn't know how long I had been fighting. The moon still shone overhead, and the *mictiani* continued to pour from the mouth of the cave. Suddenly, a black shape hurtled out of the mouth with something shiny trailing behind. At first, I thought it was a bat, but as it flew straight toward me, crossing over the bridge and finally diving into the moonlight, I could see it was a raven. It flew over my head, dropping the glittering object at my feet.

It was a large gold medallion, engraved with a multitude of circles and symbols. In the dim glow of the bridge, the metal glowed like it was from another world. Just then, the raven landed on my shoulder and whispered in my ear, "Put it on. Destroy the bridge." The raven took off, flapping madly in the face of the advancing *mictiani* to give me time.

I slipped the medallion clumsily over my neck with my mailed fingers and ran with energy I didn't possess over to Tlomec's sleeping form. I grabbed the machete out of his gear and ran back to the Bridge of Teeth, now not so spectral in the moonlight. It was an old rope and wooden bridge when I swung the heavy blade down. The rope sighed as it separated for the machete, and I hurriedly swung it again at the other side of the bridge. The *mictiani* howled as they fell along with the rotten plants and hemp into the dark of the gorge. Nothing else moved. I was alone on the plateau. The moon was bright, so bright, and I laid a throbbing arm over my eyes to shield them.

I woke up to the blazing sunlight. Tlomec was standing over me, a sad look on his face. "You've got more luck than anyone I ever knew, Bowen," he said. "But you just used it up with that stupid stunt."

"Yeah, I'm fine, thanks, how are you?" I said.

He ignored my sarcasm. "You stupid *gringo*," he said. "I warned you not to cross the bridge. Why didn't you listen to me?"

"What the hell are you talking about?" I said.

He pointed at the medallion around my neck. "How else did you get that out of the cave?"

"You tell me," I said, rolling over and sitting up. "You're the expert. I didn't cross the bridge. A raven flew out and dropped it off for me."

Tlomec bent down. "A raven?"

"Yeah, I thought it was one of yours," I said. "It told me to destroy the bridge."

Tlomec's eyes widened. "That was not my nagual. I was playing chess with Tlaloc."

"Then who's was it?" I asked.

"Maybe it was yours," he said, standing up and walking back toward our camp.

I got to my feet, slowly, because every single molecule in my body hurt, and followed him. "Well, what's this medallion, then?"

Tlomec regarded me for a few seconds. "That's Solomon's Disk, Bowen."

Kim Newman, perhaps best known for his "Anno Dracula" series, is also the author of a loosely connected series of stories and novels featuring the Diogenes Club, a secret branch of the British government specializing in the unusual and unexplainable. This story of young detectives, with subtle connections to the Diogenes Club stories, comes compete with ciphers, clues, smugglers' tunnels, and a little more besides.

Richard Riddle, Boy Detective in "The Case of the French Spy"
by Kim Newman

I: *"wmjhu-ojbhu dajjq jh qrs prbhufs"*

"Gosh, Dick," said Violet, "an ammonite!"

A chunk of rock, bigger than any of them could have lifted, had broken from the soft cliff and fallen on the shingle. Violet, on her knees, brushed grit and grime from the stone.

They were on the beach below Ware Cleeve, looking for clues.

This was not strictly a fossil-hunting expedition, but Dick knew Violet was mad about terrible lizards—which was what "dinosaur" meant in Greek, she had explained. On a recent visit to London, Violet had been taken to the prehistoric monster exhibit in Crystal Palace Park. She could not have been more excited if the life-size statues turned out to be live specimens. Paleontology was like being a detective, she enthused: working back from clues to the truth, examining a pile of bones and guessing what kind of body once wrapped around them.

Dick conceded her point. But the dinosaurs died a long, long time ago. No culprit's collar would be felt. A pity. It would be a good mystery to solve. The Case of the Vanishing Lizards. No, The Mystery of the Disappearing Dinosaurs. No, The Adventure of the Absent Ammonites.

"Coo," said Ernest. "Was this a *monster*?"

Ernest liked monsters. Anything with big teeth counted.

"Not really," Violet admitted. "It was a cephalopod. That means 'head-foot.'"

"It was a head with only a foot?" Ernest liked the idea. "Did it hop up behind enemies, and sink its fangs into their bleeding necks?"

"It was more like a big shrimp. Or a squid with a shell."

"Squid are fairly monstrous, Ernest," said Dick. "Some grow giant and crush ships with their tentacles."

Ernest made experimental crushing motions with his hands, providing squelching noises with his mouth.

Violet ran her fingers over the ammonite's segments.

"Ammon was the ram-headed god of Ancient Egypt."

Dick saw Ernest imagining that—an evil god butting unbelievers to death.

"These are called 'ammonites' because the many-chambered spiral looks like the horn of a ram. You know, like the big one in Mr. Crossan's field."

Ernest went quiet. He liked fanged monsters, giant squid, and evil gods, but had a problem with *animals*. Once, the children were forced to go a long way round to avoid Mr. Crossan's field. Ernest had come up with many tactical reasons for the detour, and Dick and Violet had pretended to be persuaded by his argument that they needed to throw pursuers off their track.

The three children were about together all the time this summer. Dick was down from London, staying with Uncle Davey and Aunt Maeve. Both were a bit dotty. Uncle Davey used to paint fairyland scenes for children's books, but was retired from that and drawing only to please himself. Last year, Violet showed up at Seaview Chase unannounced, having learned it was David Harvill's house. She liked his illustrations, but genuinely liked the pictures in his studio even more.

Violet had taken an interest in Dick's detective work. She had showed him around Lyme Regis, and the surrounding beaches and countryside. She wasn't like a proper girl, so it was all right being friends with her. Normally, Dick couldn't admit to having a girl as a friend. In summer, it was different. Ernest was Violet's cousin, two years younger than her and Dick. Ernest's father was in Africa fighting Boers, so he was with Violet's parents for the school holidays.

They were the Richard Riddle Detective Agency. Their goal: to find mysteries, then solve them. Thus far, they had handled the Matter of the Mysterious Maidservant (meeting the Butcher's Boy, though she was supposed to have a sweetheart at sea), the Curious Affair of the Derelict Dinghy (Alderman Hooke was lying asleep in it, empty beer bottles rolling around his feet) and the Puzzle of the Purloined Pasties (still an open case, though suspicion inevitably fell upon Tarquin "Tiger" Bristow).

Ernest had reasoned out his place in the firm. When Dick pointed the finger of guilt at the villain, Ernest would thump the miscreant about the head until the official police arrived. Violet, Ernest said, could make tea and listen to Dick explain his chain of deduction. Ernest, Violet commented acidly, was a dependable strong-arm man... unless the criminal owned a sheep, or threatened to make him eat parsnips, or (as was depressingly likely) turned out to be "Tiger" Bristow (the Bismarck of Bullies) and returned Ernest's head-thumping with interest. Then, Dick had to negotiate a peace, like between Americans and Red Indians, to avoid bloodshed. When Violet broke off the Reservation, people got scalped.

It was a sunny August afternoon, but a strong salt wind blew off the sea. Violet had tied back her hair to keep it out of her face. Dick looked up at Ware Cleeve: it was thickly wooded, roots poking out of the cliff face like the fingers of buried men. The Tower of Orris Priory rose above the treetops like a periscope.

Clues led to Orris Priory. Dick suspected smugglers. Or spies.

Granny Ball, who kept the pasty stall near the Cobb, had warned the detectives to stay away from the shingle under the Cleeve. It was a haunt of "sea ghosts." The angry souls of shipwrecked sailors, half-fish folk from sunken cities, and other monsters of the deep (Ernest liked this bit) were given to creeping onto the beach, clawing away at the stone, crumbling it piece by piece. One day, the Cleeve would collapse.

Violet wanted to know why the sea ghosts would do such a thing. The landslide would only make another cliff, farther inland. Granny winked and said, "Never you mind, lass," in a highly unsatisfactory manner.

Before her craze for terrible lizards, Violet had been passionate about myths and legends (it was why she liked Uncle Davey's pictures). She said myths were expressions of common truth, dressed up to make a point. The shingle beach was dangerous, because rocks fell on it. People in the long ago must have been hit on the head and killed, so the sea-ghost story was invented to keep children away from danger. It was like a "beware the dog" sign (Ernest didn't like this bit), but out of date—as if you had an old, non-fierce hound but put up a "beware of dangerous dog" sign.

Being on the shingle wasn't really dangerous. The cliffs wouldn't fall and the sea ghosts wouldn't come.

Dick liked Violet's reasoning, but saw better.

"No, Vile, it's been *kept up*, this story. Granny and other folk round here tell the tale to keep us away because *someone* doesn't want us seeing what they're about."

"Smugglers," said Ernest.

Dick nodded. "Or spies. Not enough clues to be certain. But mark my word, there's wrongdoing afoot on the shingle. And it's our job to root it out."

It was too blowy to go out in Violet's little boat, the S.S. *Pterodactyl*, so they had come on foot.

And found the ammonite.

Since the fossil wasn't about to hop to life and attack, Ernest lost interest and wandered off, down by the water. He was looking for monster tracks, the tentacle-trails of a giant squid most likely.

"This might be the largest ammonite ever found here," said Violet. "If it's a new species, I get to name it."

Dick wondered how to get the fossil to Violet's house. It would be a tricky endeavour.

"You, children, what are you about?"

Men had appeared onto the beach without Dick noticing. If

they had come from either direction along the shore, he should have seen them.

"You shouldn't be here. Come away from that evil thing, at once, *now*."

The speaker was an old man with white hair, pince-nez on a black ribbon, an expression like someone who's just bit into a cooking apple by mistake, and a white collar like a clergyman's. He wore an old-fashioned coat with a thick, raised collar, cut away from tight britches and heavy boots.

Dick recognized the Reverend Mr. Sellwood, of Orris Priory.

With him were two bare-armed fellows in leather jerkins and corduroy trousers. Whereas Sellwood carried a stick, they toted sledgehammers, like the ones convicts use on Dartmoor.

"Foul excrescence of the Devil," said Sellwood, pointing his stick at Violet's ammonite. "Brother Fose, Brother Fessel, do the Lord's work."

Fose and Fessel raised their hammers.

Violet leaned over, as if protecting a pet lamb from slaughtermen.

"Out of the way, foolish girl."

"It's *mine*," she said.

"It's nobody's, and no good to anybody. It must be smashed. God would wish it...."

"But this find is important. To *science*."

Sellwood looked as if that bite of cooker was in his throat, making his eyes water.

"Science! Bah, stuff and nonsense! Devil's charm, my girl, that's what this is!"

"It was alive, millions of millions of years ago."

"The Earth is less than six thousand years old, child, as you would know if you read your Scriptures."

Violet, angry, stood up to argue. "But that's not true. There's *proof*. This is—"

Fose and Fessel took their opportunity, and brought the hammers down. The fossil split. Sharp chips flew. Violet—appalled, hands in tiny fists, mouth open—didn't notice her shin bleeding.

"You *can't*—"

"These so-called proofs, stone bones and long-dead drag-ons," said Sellwood, "are the Devil's trickeries."

The Brethren smashed the ammonite to shards and powder.

"This was put here to fool weak minds," lectured the rev-erend. "It is the Church Militant's sacred work to destroy such obscenities, lest more be tempted to blasphemy. This is not sci-ence; this is sacrilege."

"It was mine," Violet said quietly.

"I have saved you from error. You should thank me."

Ernest came over to see what the noise was about. Sellwood bestowed a smile on the lad that afforded a glimpse of terrifying teeth.

Teeth on monsters were fine with Ernest; teeth like Sellwood's would give him nightmares.

"A job well done," said the reverend. "Let us look further. More infernal things may have sprung up."

Brother Fose leered at Violet and patted her on the head, which made her flinch. Brother Fessel looked stern disapproval at this familiarity. They followed Sellwood, swinging hammers, scouting for something to break to bits. Dick had an idea they'd rather be pounding on something that squealed and bled than something so long dead it had turned to stone.

Violet wasn't crying. But she was hating.

More than before, Dick was convinced Sellwood was behind some vile endeavour. He had the look of a smuggler, or a spy.

Richard Riddle, Boy Detective, would bring the villain to book.

II: *"Trs Ndps ja qrs Dggjhbqs Dhhbrbfdqjm"*

Uncle Davey had let Dick set up the office of the Richard Riddle Detective Agency in a small room under the eaves. A gable window led to a small balcony that looked like a ship's crow's nest. Seaview Chase was a large, complicated house on Black Ven, a jagged rise above Lyme Bay, an ideal vantage point for surveying the town and the sea.

Dick had installed his equipment—a microscope, boxes and folders, reference books, his collection of clues and trophies. Violet had donated some small fossils and her hammers and trowels. Ernest wanted space on the wall for the head of their first murderer: he had an idea that when a murderer was hanged, the police gave the head as a souvenir to the detective who caught him.

The evening after the fossil-smashing incident, Dick sat in the office and opened a new file and wrote "Trs Ndps ja qrs Dg-gjhbqs Dhhbrbfdqjm" on a fresh sheet of paper. It was the RRDA Special Cipher for "The Case of the Ammonite Annihilator."

After breakfast the next day, the follow-up investigation began. Dick went into the airy studio on the first floor and asked Uncle Davey what he knew about Sellwood.

"Grim-visage?" said Uncle Davey, pulling a face. "Dresses as if it were fifty years ago? Of him, I know, to be frank, not much. He once called with a presentation copy of some verminous volume, printed at his own expense. I think he wanted me to find a proper publisher. Put on a scary smile to ingratiate. Maeve didn't like him. He hasn't been back. Book's around somewhere, probably. Must chuck it one day. It'll be in one of those piles."

He stabbed a paintbrush towards the stacks that grew against one wall and went back to painting—a ship at sea, only there were eyes in the sea if you looked close enough, and faces in the clouds and the folds of sailcloth. Uncle Davey liked hiding things.

When Violet and Ernest arrived, they set to searching book piles.

It took a long time. Violet kept getting interested in irrelevant findings. Mostly titles about pixies and fairies and curses.

Sellwood's book had migrated to near the bottom of an especially towering pile. Extracting it brought about a bad tumble that alerted Aunt Maeve, who rushed in assuming the whole of Black Ven was giving way and the house would soon be crashing into Lyme Bay. Uncle Davey cheerfully kicked the spill of volumes into a corner and said he'd sort them out one day, then noticed a wave suitable for hiding an eye in and forgot about the children. Aunt Maeve went off to get warm milk with drops of something from Cook.

In the office, the detectives pored over their find for clues.

"Omphalos Diabolicus, or: The Hoax of 'Pre-History,'" intoned Dick, "by the Reverend Daniel Sturdevant Sellwood, published 1897, Orris Press, Dorset.

"Uncle Davey said he paid for the printing, so I deduce that he is the sole proprietor of this phantom publisher. Ah-hah, the pages have not been cut after the first chapter, so I further deduce that it must be deadly dull stuff."

He tossed the book to Violet, who got to work with a long knife, slitting the leaves as if they were the author's throat. Then she flicked through pages, pausing only to report relevant facts. One of her talents was gutting books, discovering the few useful pages like a prospector panning gold dust out of river dirt.

Daniel Sellwood wasn't a proper clergyman anymore. He had been booted out of the Church of England after shouting that the bishop should burn Mr. Darwin along with his published works. Now, Sellwood had his own sect, the Church Militant— but most of his congregation were paid servants. Sellwood came from a wealthy Dorset family, rich from trade and shipping, and had been packed off to parson school because an older brother, George, was supposed to inherit the fortune—only the brother was lost at sea, along with his wife Rebecca and little daughter Ruth, and Daniel's expectations increased. The sinking of the *Sophy Briggs* was a famous maritime mystery like the *Mary Celeste* and Captain Nemo: thirty years ago, the pride of the Orris-Sellwood Line went down in calm seas, with all hands lost. Sellwood skipped over the loss in a sentence, then spent pages talking up the "divine revelation" that convinced him to found a church rather than keep up the business.

According to Violet, a lot of folk around Lyme resented being thrown out of work when Sellwood dismantled his shipping concern and dedicated the family fortune to preaching anti-Darwinism.

"What's an omphalo-thing?" asked Ernest.

"The title means 'the Devil's Belly Button,'" said Violet, which made Ernest giggle. "He's put Greek and Latin words together, which is poor Classics. Apart from his stupid ideas, he's a *terrible* writer. Listen.... 'All the multitudinarious flora and fauna of divine creation constitute veritable evidence of the proof of the pellucid and undiluted accuracy of the Word of God Almighty Unchallenged as set down in the shining, burning, shimmering sentences, chapters and, indeed, books of the Old and New Testaments, hereinafter known to all righteous and right-thinking men as the Holy Bible of Glorious God.' It's as if he's saying 'this is the true truthiest truest truth of truthdom ever told truly by truth-trusters.'"

"How do the belly buttons come into it?" asked Dick.

"Adam and Eve were supposed to have been created with navels, though—since they weren't born like other people—they oughtn't to have them."

This was over Ernest's head, but Dick knew how babies came and that his navel was a knot, where a cord had been cut and tied.

"To Sellwood's way of thinking, just as Adam and Eve were created to *seem* as if they had normal parents, the Earth was created as if it had a prehistory, with geological and fossil evidence in place to make the planet appear much older than it says in the Bible."

"That's silly," said Ernest.

"Don't tell me, tell Sellwood," said Violet. "He's a silly, stupid man. He doesn't want to know the truth, or anyone else to either, so he breaks fossils and shouts down lecturers. His theory isn't even original. A man named Gosse wrote a book with the same idea, though Gosse claimed *God* buried fossils to fool people, while Sellwood says it was the Devil."

Violet was quite annoyed.

"I think it's an excuse to go round bullying people," said Dick. "A cover for his real, sinister purpose."

"If you ask me, what he does is sinister enough by itself."

"Nobody did ask you," said Ernest, which he always said when someone was unwise enough to preface a statement with "if you ask me." Violet stuck her tongue out at him.

Dick was thinking.

"It's likely that the Sellwood family were smugglers," he said.

Violet agreed. "Smugglers had to have ships, and pretend to be respectable merchants. In the old days, they were all at it. You know the poem...."

Violet stood up, put a hand on her chest, and recited, dramatically.

"'If you wake at midnight, and hear a horse's feet,

Don't go drawing back the blind, or looking in the street.

Them that ask no questions isn't told a lie,

Watch the wall, my darling, while the gentlemen go by.

Five and twenty ponies, trotting through the dark,

Brandy for the parson, 'baccy for the clerk;

Laces for a lady, letters for a spy,

And watch the wall, my darling, while the gentlemen go by.'"

She waited for applause, which didn't come. But her recitation was useful. Dick had been thinking in terms of spies *or* smugglers, but the poem reminded him that the breeds were interdependent. It struck him that Sellwood might be a smuggler of spies, or a spy for smugglers.

"I'll wager 'Tiger' Bristow is in this, too," he said, snapping his fingers.

Ernest shivered, audibly.

"Is it spying or smuggling?" he asked.

"It's both," Dick replied.

Violet sat down again, and chewed on a long, stray strand of her hair.

"Tell Dick about the French Spy," suggested Ernest.

Dick was intrigued.

"That was a long time ago, a hundred years," she said. "It's a local legend, not evidence."

"You yourself say legends always shroud some truth," declared Dick. "We must consider *all* the facts, even rumours of facts, before forming a conclusion."

Violet shrugged.

"It is about Sellwood's *house*, I suppose...."

Dick was astonished. "And you didn't think it was relevant! Sometimes, I'm astonished by your lack of perspicacity!"

Violet looked incipiently upset at his tone, and Dick wondered if he wasn't going too far. He needed her in the agency, but she could be maddening at times. Like a real girl.

"Out with it, Vile," he barked.

Violet crossed her arms and kept quiet.

"I apologise for my tactlessness," said Dick. "But this is vitally important. We might be able to put that ammonite-abuser out of business, with immeasurable benefit to *science*."

Violet melted. "Very well. I heard this from Alderman Hooke's father...."

Before her paleontology craze, Violet had fancied herself a collector of folklore. She had gone around asking old people to tell stories or sing songs or remember why things were called what they were called. She was going to write them all up in a book of local legends and had wanted Uncle Davey to draw the pictures. She was still working on her book, but it was about dinosaurs in Dorset now.

"I didn't make much of it, because it wasn't much of a legend. Just a scrap of history."

"With a spy," prompted Ernest. "A spy who came out of the sea!"

Violet nodded. "That's more or less it. When England was at war with France, everyone thought Napoleon—"

"Boney!" put in Ernest, making fang-fingers at the corners of his mouth.

"Yes, Boney.... Everyone thought he was going to invade, like William the Conqueror. Along the coast people watched the seas. Signal fires were prepared, like with the Spanish Armada. Most thought it likely the French would strike at Dover, but round here they tapped the sides of their noses"—Violet imitated an old person tapping her long nose—"and said the last army to invade Britain had landed at Lyme, and the next would too. The last army was Monmouth's, during his rebellion. He landed at the Cobb and marched up to Sedgmoor, where he was defeated. There are *lots* of legends about the Duke of Monmouth...."

Dick made a get-to-the-point gesture.

"Any rate, near the end of the eighteenth century, a man named Jacob Orris formed a vigilance patrol to keep watch on the beaches. Orris' daughter married a sea captain called Lud Sellwood; they begat drowned George and old Devil's Belly Button. Come to think, Orris' patrol was like Sellwood's Church Militant—an excuse to shout at folk and break things. Orris started a campaign to get 'French beans' renamed 'Free-from-Tyranny beans,' and had his men attack grocer's stalls when no one agreed with him. Orris was expecting a fleet to heave to in Lyme Bay and land an army, but knew spies would be put ashore first to scout around. One night, during a terrible storm, Orris caught a spy flung up on the shingle."

"And... ?

"That's it, really. I expect they hit him with hammers and killed him, but if anyone really knows, they aren't saying."

Dick was disappointed.

"Tell him how it was a *special* spy," said Ernest.

Dick was intrigued again. Especially since Violet obviously didn't want to say more.

"He was a sea ghost," announced Ernest.

"Old Hooke said the spy had *walked* across the Channel," admitted Violet. "On the bottom of the sea, in a special diving suit. He was a Frenchman, but—and you have to remember stories get twisted over the years—he had gills *sewn* into his neck so he could breathe underwater. As far as anyone knew round here, all Corsicans were like that. They said it was probably Boney's cousin."

"And they killed him?"

Violet shrugged. "I expect so."

"And kept him *pickled*," said Ernest.

"Now that *isn't* true. One version of this story is that Orris had the dead spy stuffed, then hidden away. But the family would have found the thing and thrown it out by now. And we'd know whether it was a man or, as Granny Ball says, a trained seal.

Stories are like limpets on rocks. They stick on and get thicker until you can't see what was there in the first place."

Dick whistled.

"I don't see how this can have anything to do with what Sellwood is about now," said Violet. "This may not have happened, and if it did, it was a hundred years ago. Sellwood wasn't even born then. His parents were still children."

"My dear Vile, a century-old mystery is still a mystery. And crime can seep into a family like water in the foundations, passed down from father to son."

"Father to *daughter* to son, in this case."

"I haven't forgotten that. This mystery goes deep. It's all about the past. And haven't you said that a century is just a heartbeat in the long life of the planet?"

She was coming round, he saw.

"We have to get into Orris Priory," said Dick.

III: *"Ba bq wdp sdpy qj abho, bq wjtfoh'q is rboosh"*

"Why are we on the shingle?" asked Ernest. "The Priory is up there, on top of the Cleeve."

Dick had been waiting for the question. Deductions impressed more if he didn't just come out with cleverness, but waited for a prompt.

"Remember yesterday? Sellwood seemed to turn up suddenly, with Fose and Fessel. If they'd been walking on the beach, we'd have seen them ages before they arrived. But we didn't. Therefore, there must be a secret way. A smugglers' tunnel."

Violet found some pieces of the fossil. She looked towards the cliff.

"We were facing out to sea, and they came from behind," she said.

She tossed her ammonite shard, which rebounded off the soft rock face.

The cliff was too crumbly for caves that might conceal a tunnel. The children began looking closely, hoping for a hidden door.

After a half hour, Ernest complained that he was hungry.

After an hour, Violet complained that she was fed up with rocks.

Dick stuck to it. "If it was easy to find, it wouldn't be *hidden*," he kept saying.

Ernest began to make helpful suggestions that didn't help but needed to be argued with.

"*Maybee* they came up under the sea and swam ashore?"

"They weren't wet and we would have seen them," countered Dick.

"*Maybee* they've got invisible diving suits that don't show wetness?"

"Those haven't been invented yet."

"*Maybee* they've invented them but kept it quiet?"

"It's not likely...."

"But not *impossible*, and you always say that 'when you've eliminated the impossible...'"

"Actually, Ernest, it *is* impossible!"

"Prove it."

"The only way to prove something impossible is to devote your entire life to trying to achieve it, and the lives of everyone to infinity throughout eternity, then *not* succeed—"

"Well, get started."

"—and that's *impractical*!"

Dick knew he was shouting, but when Ernest got into one of these *maybee* moods—which he called his "clever spells"—everyone got a headache, and usually wound up giving in and agreeing with something they knew to be absurd just to make Ernest shut up. After that, he would be hard to live with for the rest of the day, puffed up like a toad with a smugness that Violet labelled "very unattractive," which prompted him to snipe that he didn't want to attract anyone like her, and her to counter that he would change his mind in a few years, and him to... Well, it was a cycle Dick had lived through too often.

Then Violet found a hinge. Two, in fact.

Dick got out his magnifying glass and examined the hinges. Recently oiled, he noted. Where there were hinges, there must be a door. Hidden.

"Where's the handle?" asked Ernest.

"Inside," said Violet.

"What's the use of a door that only opens from one side?"

"It'd keep out detectives, like us," suggested Violet.

"There was no open door when Sellwood was here. It closed behind him. He'd want to open it again, rather than go home the long way."

"He had two big strong men with hammers," said Violet, "and we've got you and Ernest."

Dick tried to be patient.

He stuck his fingers into a crack in the rock, and worked down, hoping to get purchase enough to pull the probable door open.

"Careful," said Violet.

"*Maybee...*"

"Shut up, Ernest," said Dick.

He found his hand stuck, but pulled free, scraping his knuckles.

There was an outcrop by the sticking point, at about the height where you'd put a door-handle.

"Ah-hah," said Dick, seizing and turning the rock.

A click, and a section of the cliff pulled open. It was surprisingly light, a thin layer of stone fixed to a wooden frame.

A section of rock fell off the door.

"You've broken it now," said Ernest.

It was dark inside. From his coat-of-many-hidden-pockets, Dick produced three candle stubs with metal holders and a box of matches. For his next birthday, he hoped to get one of the new battery-powered electrical lanterns—until then, these would remain RRDA standard issue.

Getting the candles lit was a performance. The draught kept puffing out match-flames before the wicks caught. Violet took over and mumsily arranged everything, then handed out the candles, showing Ernest how to hold his so wax didn't drip on his fingers.

"Metal's hot," said Ernest.

"Perhaps we should leave you here as lookout," said Dick. "You can warn us in case any *dogs* come along."

The metal apparently wasn't *too* hot, since Ernest now wanted to continue. He insisted on being first into the dark, in case there were monsters.

Once they were inside, the door swung shut.

They were in a space carved out of the rock and shored up with timber, empty barrels piled nearby. A row of fossil-smashing hammers were arranged where Violet could spit at them. Smooth steps led upwards, with the rusted remains of rings set into the walls either side.

"'Brandy for the parson, 'baccy for the clerk,'" said Violet.

"Indubitably," responded Dick. "This is clear evidence of smuggling."

"What do people smuggle these days?" asked Violet. "Brandy and tobacco might have been expensive when we were at war with France and ships were slow, but that was ages ago."

Dick was caught out. He knew there was still contraband, but hadn't looked into its nature.

"Jewels, probably," he guessed. "And there's always spying."

Ernest considered the rings in the wall.

"I bet prisoners were chained here," he said, "until they turned to skellytones!"

"More likely people hold the rings while climbing the slippery stairs," suggested Violet, "especially if they're carrying heavy cases of... jewels and spy-letters."

Ernest was disappointed.

"But they *could* be used for prisoners."

Ernest cheered up.

"If I was a prisoner, I could 'scape," he said. He put his hand in a ring, which was much too big for him and for any grown-up too. Then he pulled and the ring came out of the wall.

Ernest tried to put it back.

Dick was tense, expecting tons of rock to fall on them.

No collapse happened.

"Be careful touching things," he warned his friends. "We

were lucky that time, but there might be deadly traps."

He led the way up.

IV: *"dh jtifbsqqs"*

The steps weren't steep, but went up a long way. The tunnel had been hewn out of rock. New timbers, already bowed and near cracking, showed where the passage had been shored after falls.

"We must be under the Priory," he said.

They came to the top of the stairs, and a basement-looking room. Wooden crates were stacked.

"Cover your light," said Dick.

Ernest yelped as he burned his hand.

"Carefully," Dick added.

Ernest whimpered a bit.

"What do you suppose is in these?" asked Violet. "Contraband?"

"Instruments of evil?" prompted Ernest.

Dick held his candle close to a crate. The slats were spaced an inch or so apart. Inside were copies of *Omphalos Diabolicus*.

"Isn't the point of smuggling to bring in things people *want*?" asked Violet. "I can't imagine an illicit market for unreadable tracts."

"There could be coded spy messages in the books," Dick suggested hopefully.

"Even spies trained to resist torture in the dungeons of the tsar wouldn't be able to read through these to get any message," said Violet. "My *deduction* is that these are here because Sellwood can't get anybody to buy his boring old book."

"*Maybee* he should change his name to Sellwords."

Dick had the tiniest spasm of impatience. Here they were, in the lair of an undoubted villain, having penetrated secret defences, and all they could do was make dubiously snarky remarks about his name.

"We should scout farther," he said. "Come on."

He opened a door and found a gloomy passageway. The lack

of windows suggested they were still underground. The walls were panelled, wood warped and stained by persistent damp.

The next room along had no door and was full of rubble. Dick thought the ceiling had fallen in, but Violet saw at once that detritus was broken-up fossils.

"Ammonites," she said, "also brachiopods, nautiloids, crinoids, plagiostoma, coroniceras, gryphaea, *and* calcirhynchia."

She held up what looked like an ordinary stone.

"This could be the knee-bone of a *scelidosaurus*. One was discovered in Charmouth, in Liassic cliffs just like these. The first near-complete dinosaur fossil to come to light. This might have been another find as important. Sellwood is a vandal and a wrecker. He should be hit on the head with his own hammers."

Dick patted Violet on the back, hoping she would cheer up.

"It's only a knee," said Ernest. "Nothing interesting about knees."

"Some dinosaurs had *brains* in their knees. Extra brains to do the thinking for their legs. Imagine if you had brains in your knees."

Ernest was impressed.

"If *I'd* found this, I wouldn't have broken it," said Violet. "I would have *named* it. *Biolettosaurus*, Violet's Lizard."

"Let's try the next room," said Dick.

"There might still be useful fragments."

Reluctantly, Violet left the room of broken stone bones.

Next was a thick wooden door, with iron bands across it, and three heavy bolts. Though the bolts were oiled, it was a strain to pull them—Dick and Violet both struggled. The top and bottom bolts shifted, but the middle one wouldn't move.

"Let me try," said Ernest. "Please."

They did, and he didn't get anywhere.

Violet dipped back into the fossil room and came back with a chunk they used as a hammer. The third bolt shot open.

The banging and clanging sounded fearfully loud in the enclosed space.

They listened, but no one came. *Maybee*, he thought—recognising the Ernestism—Sellwood was up in his tower, scanning the horizon for spy signals, and his Brethren were taking afternoon naps.

The children stepped through the doorway, and the door swung slowly and heavily shut behind them.

This room was different again.

The floor and walls were solid slabs that looked as if they'd been in place a long time. The atmosphere was dank, slightly mouldy. A stone trough, like you see in stables, ran along one wall, fed by an old-fashioned pump. Dick cupped water in his hand and tasted it. There was a nasty, coppery sting, and he spat.

"It's a *dungeon*," said Ernest.

Violet held up her candle.

A winch apparatus, with handles like a threshing machine, was fixed to the floor at the far side of the room, thick chain wrapped around the drum.

"Careful," said Violet, gripping Dick's arm.

Dick looked at his feet. He stood on the edge of a circular hole, like a well. It was a dozen feet across, and uncovered.

"There should be a cap on this," announced Dick. "To prevent accidents."

"I doubt if Sellwood cares much about accidents befalling intruders."

"You're probably right, Vile. The man's a complete rotter."

Chains extended from the winch into a solid iron ring in the ceiling and then down into the hole.

"This is an *oubliette*," said Violet. "It's from the French. You capture your *prisonnier* and *jeté* him into the hole, then *oublié* them—forget them."

Ernest, nervously, kept well away from the edge. He had been warned about falling into wells once, which meant that ever since he was afraid of them.

Violet tossed her rock-chunk into the pool of dark, and counted. After three counts—thirty feet—there was a thump. Stone on stone.

"No splash," she said.

Up from the depths came another sound, a gurgling groan—

something alive but unidentifiable. The noise lodged in Dick's heart like a fish hook of ice. A chill played up his spine.

The cry had come from a throat, but hardly a human one.

Ernest dropped his candle, which rolled to the lip of the pit and fell in, flame guttering.

Round, green eyes shone up, fire dancing in the fish-flat pupils.

Something grey-green, weighted with old chains, writhed at the bottom of the hole.

Ernest's candle went out.

Violet's grip on Dick's arm hurt now.

"What's *that*?" she gasped.

The groan took on an imploring, almost pathetic tone, tinged with cunning and bottomless wrath.

Dick shrugged off his shiver. He had a moment of pure joy, the *click* of sudden understanding that often occurs at the climax of a case, when clues fit in the mind like jigsaw pieces and the solution is plain and simple.

"That, my dear Vile, is your French spy!"

V: *"Obdijjfbntp Mdmbqbgs"*

"Someone's coming," said Ernest.

Footfalls in the passageway!

"Hide," said Dick.

The only place—aside from the hole—was under the water trough. Dick and Violet pinched out their candles and crammed in, pulling Ernest after them.

"They'll see the door's not bolted," said Ernest.

Violet clamped her hand over her cousin's mouth.

In the enclosed space, their breathing seemed horribly loud.

Dick worried. Ernest was right.

Maybee the people in the passage weren't coming to *this* room. *Maybee* they'd already walked past, on their way to smash fossils or get a copy of Sellwood's book.

The footsteps stopped outside the door.

Maybee this person didn't know it was usually bolted. *May-*

bee this dungeon was so rarely visited they'd *oublié* whether it had been bolted shut after the last time.

Maybee...

"Fessel, Fose, Milder, Maulder," barked a voice.

The Reverend Mr. Daniel Sturdevant Sellwood, calling his Brethren.

"'And who's been opening *my* door,'" breathed Violet.

It took Dick long seconds to recognize the storybook quotation.

"Who was last here?" shouted Sellwood. "This is inexcusable. With the Devil, one does not take such risks."

"En cain't git ouwt of thic hole," replied someone.

"Brother Milder, it has the wiles of an arch fiend. That is why only *I* can be trusted to put it to the question. Who last brought the slops?"

There was some argument.

Maybee they'd be all right. Sellwood was so concerned with stopping an escape that he hadn't thought anyone might break *in*.

One of the Brethren tentatively spoke up, and received a clout round the ear.

Dick wondered why anyone would *want* to be in Sellwood's Church Militant.

"Stand guard," Sellwood ordered. "Let me see what disaster is so narrowly averted."

The door was pushed open. Sellwood set a lantern on a perch. The children pressed farther back into shrinking shadow. Dick's ankle bent the wrong way. He bit down on the pain.

He saw Sellwood's shoes—with old-fashioned buckles and gaiters—walk past the trough, towards the hole. He stopped, just by Dick's face.

There was a pumping, coughing sound.

Sellwood filled a beaker.

He poured the water into the hole.

Violet counted silently, again. After three, the water splashed on the French spy. It cried out, with despair and yearning.

"Drink deep, spawn of Satan!"

The creature howled, then gargled again. Dick realized it wasn't making animal grunts but *speaking*. Unknown words that he suspected were not French.

The thing had been here for over a hundred years!

"Fose, Milder, in here, now. I will resume the inquisition."

Brethren clumped in. Dick saw heavy boots.

The two bruisers walked around the room, keeping well away from the hole. Dick eased out a little to get a better view. He risked a more comfortable, convenient position. Sellwood had no reason to suspect he was spied upon.

Brother Fose and Brother Milder worked the winch.

The chains tightened over the hole, then wound onto the winch-drum.

The thing in the *oubliette* cursed. Dick was sure *"f'tagn"* was a swear-word. As it was hauled upwards, the creature struggled, hissing and croaking.

Violet held Dick's hand, pulling, keeping him from showing himself.

A head showed over the mouth of the hole, three times the size of a man's and with no neck, just a pulpy frill of puffed-up gill-slits. Saucer-sized fish-eyes held the light, pupils contracting. Dick was sure the creature, face at floor-level, saw past the boots of its captors straight into his face. It had a fixed maw, with enough jagged teeth to please Ernest.

"Up," ordered Sellwood. "Let's see all of the demon."

The Brethren winched again, and the thing hung like Captain Kidd on Execution Dock. It was manlike, but with a stub of fish-tail protruding beneath two rows of dorsal spines. Its hands and feet were webbed, with nastily curved yellow nail-barbs. Where water had splashed, its skin was rainbow-scaled, beautiful even. Elsewhere, its hide was grey and taut, cracked, flaking or mossy, with rusty weals where the chains chafed.

Dick saw the thing was missing several finger-barbs. Its back and front were striped across with long-healed and new-made scars. It had been whipping boy in this house since the days when Boney was a warrior way-aye-aye.

He imagined Jacob Orris trying to get Napoleon's secrets out of the "spy." Had old Orris held up charts and asked the man-fish to tap a claw on hidden harbours where the invasion fleet was gathered?

Ernest was mumbling "sea ghost" over and over, not frightened but awed. Violet hissed at him to hush.

Dick was sure they'd be caught, but Sellwood was fascinated by the creature. He poked his face close to his captive's, smiling smugly. A cheek muscle twitched around his fixed sneer. The man-fish looked as if it would like to spit in Sellwood's face but couldn't afford the water.

"So, *Diabolicus Maritime*, is it today that you confess? I have been patient. We merely seek a statement we all know to be true, which will end this sham once and for all."

The fish-eyes were glassy and flat, but moved to fix on Sellwood.

"You are a *deception*, my infernal guest, a lure, a living trick, a lie made flesh, a creature of the Prince of Liars. Own that Satan is your maker, imp! Confess your evil purpose!"

Sellwood touched fingertips to the creature's scarred chest, scraping dry flesh. Scales fluttered away, falling like dead moths. Dick saw Sellwood's fingers flex, the tips biting.

"The bones weren't enough, were they? Those so-called 'fossils,' the buried lies that lead to blasphemy and disbelief. No, the Devil had a second deceit in reserve, to pile upon the Great Untruth of 'Pre-History.' No mere dead dragon, but a live specimen, one of those fabled 'missing links' in the fairy tale of 'evolution.' By your very existence, you bear false witness, testify that the world is older than it has been proved over and over again to be, preach against creation, tear down mankind, to drag us from the realm of the angels into the festering salt-depths of Hell. The City of the Damned lies under the Earth, but you prove to my satisfaction that it extends also under the sea!"

The man-fish had no ears, but Dick was certain it could hear Sellwood. Moreover, it *understood*, followed his argument.

"So, own up," snapped the reverend. "One word, and the deception is at an end. You are not part of God's Creation, but a sea-serpent, a monstrous forgery!"

The creature's lipless mouth curved. It barked, through its mouth. Its gills rippled, showing scarlet inside.

Sellwood was furious.

Dick, strangely, was excited. The prisoner was *laughing* at its captor, the laughter of a patient, abiding being.

Why was it still alive? Could it be killed? Surely, Orris or Sellwood or some keeper in between had tried to execute the monster?

In those eyes was a promise to the parson: I will live when you are gone.

"Drop it," snapped Sellwood.

Fose and Milder let go the winch, and—with a cry—the "French spy" was swallowed by its hole.

Sellwood and his men left the room, taking the lantern.

Dick began breathing properly again. Violet let Ernest squirm a little, though she still held him under the trough.

Then came a truly terrifying sound, worse even than the laughter of the fish-demon.

Bolts being drawn. Three of them.

They were trapped!

VII: *"wsff imjturq-tk bh M'fysr"*

Now was the time to keep calm.

Dick knew Violet would be all right, if only because she had to think about Ernest.

For obvious reasons, the children had not told anyone where they were going, but they would be missed at teatime. Uncle Davey and Aunt Maeve could easily overlook a skipped meal—both of them were liable to get so interested in something that they wouldn't notice the house catching fire—but Cook kept track. And Mr. and Mrs. Borrodale were sticklers for being in by five o'clock with hands washed and presentable.

It must be past five now.

Of course, any search party wouldn't get around to the Priory for days, maybe weeks. They'd look on the beaches first, and in the woods.

Eventually, his uncle and aunt would find the folder marked "Trs Ndps ja qrs Dggjhbqs Dhhbrbfdqjm.' Aunt Maeve, good at puzzles, had taught him how to cipher in the first place. She would eventually break the code and read Dick's notes, and want to talk with Sellwood. By then, it would probably be too late.

They gave the Brethren time enough to get beyond earshot before creeping out from under the trough. They unbent with much creaking and muffled moaning. Violet lit her candle.

Dick paced around the cell, keeping away from the hole.

"I'm thirsty," said Ernest.

"Easily treated," said Violet.

She found the beaker and pumped water into it. Ernest drank, made a face, and asked for more. Violet worked the pump again.

Water splashed over the brimful beaker, into the trough.

A noise came out of the hole.

The children froze into mannequins. The noise came again.

"Wah wah... *wah wah...*"

There was a pleading tone to it.

"Wah wah..."

"'Water,'" said Dick, snapping his fingers. "It's saying 'water.'"

"Wah wah," agreed the creature. "Uh, wah wah."

"'Water. Yes, water.'"

"Gosh, Dick, you *are* clever," said Violet.

"Wat war," said the creature, insisting. "Gi' mee wat war, i' oo eese...."

"'Water,'" said Dick. "'Give me—'"

"'—water, if you please,'" completed Violet, who caught on swiftly. "Very polite for a sea ghost. Well brought up in Atlantis or Lyonesse or R'lyeh, I imagine."

"Where?" asked Dick.

"Sunken cities of old, where mer-people are supposed to live."

More leftovers from Violet's myths and legends craze. Interesting, but not very helpful.

Ernest had walked to the edge of the hole.

"This isn't a soppy mer-person," said Ernest. "This is a Monster of the Deep!"

He emptied the beaker into the dark.

A sigh of undoubted gratitude rose from the depths.

"Wat war goo', tanks. Eese, gi' mee moh."

Ernest poured another beakerful. At this rate, they might as well be using an eyedropper.

Dick saw the solution.

"Vile, help me shift the trough," he said.

They pulled one end away from the wall. It was heavy, but the bolts were old and rusted, and the break came easily.

"Careful not to move the other end too much. We need it under the pump."

Violet saw where this was going. Angled down away from the wall, the trough turned into a sluice. It didn't quite stretch all the way to the *oubliette*, but pulling up a loose stone put a notch into the rim that served as a spout.

"Wat war eese," said the creature mildly.

Dick nodded to Violet. She worked the pump.

Water splashed into the trough and flowed down, streaming through the notch and pouring into the pit.

The creature gurgled with joy.

Only now did Dick wonder whether watering it was a good idea. It might not be a French spy or even a maritime demon, but it was definitely one of Granny Ball's sea ghosts. If Dick had been treated as it had been, he would not be well disposed towards land-people.

But the water kept flowing.

Violet's arm got tired, and she let up for a moment.

"I' oo eese," insisted the creature, with a reproachful, nanny-ish tone. "Moh wat war."

Violet kept pumping.

Dick took the candle and walked to the edge of the hole. Ernest sat there, legs dangling over the edge, fingers playing in the cool cascade.

The boys looked down.

Where water fell, the man-fish was changed—vivid greens

and reds and purples and oranges glistened. Its spines and frills and gills and webs were sleek. Even its eyes shone more brightly.

It turned, mouth open under the spray, letting water wash around it, wrenching against its chains.

"Water makes the monster strong," said Ernest.

The creature looked up at them. The edges of its mouth curved into something like a smile. There was cunning there, and a bottomless well of malice, but also an exultation. Dick understood: when it was wet, the thing felt as he did when he saw through a mystery.

It took a grip on one of its manacles and squeezed, cracking the old iron and casting it away.

"Can I stop now?" asked Violet. "My arm's out of puff."

"I think so."

The creature nodded, a human gesture awkward on the gilled, neckless being.

It stood up unshackled, and stretched as if waking after a long sleep in an awkward position. The chains dangled freely. A clear, thick, milky-veined fluid seeped from the weals on its chest. The man-fish carefully smoothed this secretion like an ointment.

There were pools of water around its feet. It got down on its knees—did it have spare brains in them?—and sucked the pools dry. Then it raised its head and let water dribble through its gills and down over its chest and back.

"Tanks," it said.

Now it wasn't parched, its speech was easier to understand.

It took hold of the dangling chains, and tugged, testing them.

Watering the thing in the hole was all very well, but Dick wasn't sure how he'd feel if it were up here with them. If he were the creature, he would be very annoyed. He ought to be grateful to the children, but what did anyone know about the feelings of sea ghosts? Violet had told them the legend of the genie in the bottle: at first, he swore to bestow untold riches upon the man who set him free, but after thousands of years burned to make his rescuer suffer horribly for waiting so long.

It was too late to think about that.

Slick and wet, the man-fish moved faster than anything its size should. No sooner had it grasped the chains than it had climbed them, deft as a sailor on the rigging, quick as a lizard on the flat or a salmon in the swim.

It held on, hanging just under the ring in the ceiling, head swivelling around, eyes taking in the room.

Dick and Ernest were backed against the door, taking Violet with them.

She was less spooked than the boys.

"Bonjour, Monsieur le Fantôme de la Mer," she said, slowly and clearly in the manner approved by her tutor, M. Duroc. *"Je m'appelle Violette Borrodale... permettez-moi de presente a vous mon petit cousin Ernest... et Rishard Riddle, le detective juvenile celebré."*

This seemed to puzzle the sea ghost.

"Vile, I don't think it's really French," whispered Dick.

Violet shrugged.

The creature let go and leaped, landing froglike, knees stuck out and shoulders hunched, inches away from them. This close, it stank of the sea.

Dick saw their reflections in its huge eyes.

Its mouth opened. He saw row upon row of sharklike teeth, all pointed and shining. It might not have had a proper meal in a century.

"Scuze mee," it said, extending a hand, folding its frill-connected fingers up but pointing with a single barb.

The wet thorn touched Richard's cheek.

Then it eased the children aside, and considered the bolted door.

"Huff... puff... blow," it said, hammering with fish-fists. The door came off its hinges, and the bolts wrenched out of their sockets. The broken door crashed against the opposite wall of the passage.

"How do you know the Three Little Pigs?" asked Violet.

"Gur' nam 'Ooth," it said, "ree' to mee...."

"A girl read to him," Dick explained.

So not all his captors had been tormentors. Who was 'Ooth? Ruth? Someone called Ruth fit into the story. The little girl lost with the *Sophy Briggs*. Sellwood's niece.

The sea ghost looked at Violet. Dick deduced all little girls must look alike to it. If you've seen one pinafore, you've seen them all.

"'Ooth," it said, with something like fondness. "'Ooth kin' to mee. Ree' mee story-boos. *Liss in Wonlan... Tripella Liplik Pik... Taes o Eh Ah Po...*"

"What happened to Ruth?" Violet asked.

"Sellwoo' ki' 'Ooth, an' hi' bro tah Joh-jee," said the creature, cold anger in its voice. "Tey wan let mee go sea, let mee go hom. Sellwoo' mak shi' wreck, tak ever ting, tak mee."

Dick understood. And was not surprised.

This was the nature of Sellwood's villainy. Charges of smuggling and espionage remained unproven, but he was guilty of the worst crime of all—murder!

People were coming now, alerted by the noise.

The sea ghost stepped into the passage, holding up a hand—fingers spread and webs unfurled—to indicate that the children should stay behind.

They kept in the dark, where they couldn't see what was happening in the passage.

The man-fish leaped, and landed on someone.

Cries of terror and triumph! An unpleasant, wet crunching... followed by unmistakable chewing.

More people came on the scene.

"The craytur's out o' thic hole," shrieked someone.

A very loud bang! A firework stink.

The man-fish staggered back past the doorway, red blossoming on its shoulder. It had more red stuff around its mouth, and scraps of cloth caught in its teeth.

It roared rage and threw itself at whomever had shot it.

Something detached from something else and rolled past the doorway, leaving a trail of sticky splashes.

Violet kept her hand over Ernest's eyes, though he tried to

Richard Riddle, Boy Detective

pick at her fingers.

"Spawn of Satan, you show your true colours at last!"

It was Sellwood.

"Milder, Fessel, take him down."

The Brethren grunted. The doorway was filled with struggling bodies, driving the children back into the cell. They pressed flat against the wet cold walls.

Brother Milder and Brother Fessel held the creature's arms and wrestled it back, towards the hole.

Sellwood appeared, hefting one of his fossil-breaking hammers.

He thumped the sea ghost's breastbone with all his might, and it fell, sprawling on the flagstones. Milder and Fessel shifted their weight to pin him down.

Still, no one noticed the children.

The creature's shoulder wound closed like a sea anemone. The bruise in the middle of its chest faded at once. It looked hate up at the reverend.

Sellwood stood over the wriggling man-fish. He weighed his hammer.

"You're devilish hard to kill, demon! But how would you like your skull pounded to paste? It might take a considerable while to recover, eh?"

He raised the hammer above his head.

"You there," said Violet, voice clear and shrill and loud, "stop!"

Sellwood swivelled to look.

"This is an important scientific discovery, and must not be harmed. Why, it is practically a living dinosaur."

Violet stood between Sellwood and the pinned man-fish. Dick was by her side, arm linked with hers. Ernest was in front of them, fists up like a pugilist.

"Don't you hurt my friend the monster," said Ernest.

Sellwood's red rage showed.

"You see," he yelled, "how the foulness spreads! How the lies take hold! You see!"

Something snapped inside Milder. He rolled off the creature,

192

limbs loose, neck flopping.

The sea ghost stood up, a two-handed grip on the last of Sellwood's Brethren, Fessel.

"Help," Fessel gasped. "Children, help..."

Dick had a pang of guilt.

Then Fessel was falling into the *oubliette*. He rattled against chains, and landed with a final-sounding crash.

The sea ghost stepped around the children and took away Sellwood's hammer, which it threw across the room. It clanged against the far wall.

"I am not afraid of you," announced the reverend.

The creature tucked Sellwood under its arm. The reverend was too surprised to protest.

"Shouldn' a' ki' 'Ooth a' Joh-jee, Sellwoo'. Shouldn' a' ki'."

"How do you know?" Sellwood was indignant, but didn't deny the crime.

"Sea tol' mee, sea tel' mee all ting."

"I serve a greater purpose," shouted Sellwood.

The sea ghost carried the reverend out of the room. The children followed.

The man-fish strode down the passage, towards the book-room. Two dead men—Maulder and Fose—lay about.

"Their heads are gone," exclaimed Ernest, with a glee Dick found a little disturbing. At least Ernest wasn't picking up one of the heads for the office wall.

Sellwood thumped the creature's back. Its old whip stripes and poker brands were healing.

Dick, Violet, and Ernest followed the escapee and its former gaoler.

In the book-room, Sellwood looked with hurried regret at the crates of unsold volumes and struggled less. The sea ghost found the steps leading down and seemed to contract its body to squeeze into the tunnel. Sellwood was dragged bloody against the rock ceiling.

"Come on, detectives," said Dick, "after them!"

VII: *"Dhqrmjkjp Bnqryjp Ibjffsqqd"*

They came out under Ware Cleeve. Waves scraped shingle in an eternal rhythm. It was twilight, and chilly. Well past teatime.

The man-fish, burden limp, tasted the sea in the air.

"Tanks," it said to the children, "tanks very mu'."

It walked into the waves. As sea soaked through his coat, Sellwood was shocked conscious and began to struggle again, shouting and cursing and praying.

The sea ghost was waist-deep in its element.

It turned to wave at the children. Sellwood got free, madly striking *away* from the shore, not towards dry land. The creature leaped completely out of the water, dark rainbows rippling on its flanks, and landed heavily on Sellwood, claws hooking into meat, pressing the reverend under the waves.

They saw the swimming shape, darting impossibly fast, zig-zagging out into the bay. Finned feet showed above the water for an instant, and the man-fish—the sea ghost, the French spy, the living fossil, the snare of Satan, the Monster of the Deep—was gone for good, dragging the Reverend Mr. Daniel Sturdevant Sellwood with him.

"...to Davy Jones' locker," said Ernest.

Dick realized Violet was holding his hand, and tactfully got his fingers free.

Their shoes were covered with other people's blood.

"*Anthropos Icthyos Biolletta*," said Violet. "Violet's Man-Fish, a whole new phylum."

"I pronounce this case closed," said Dick.

"Can I borrow your matches?" asked Violet. "I'll just nip back up the tunnel and set fire to Sellwood's books. If the Priory burns down, we won't have to answer questions about dead people."

Dick handed over the box.

He agreed with Violet. This was one of those stories for which the world was not yet ready. Writing it up, he would use a double cipher.

"Besides," said Violet, "some books deserve to be burned."

While Violet was gone, Dick and Ernest passed time skipping stones on the waves. Rooting for ammunition, they found an ammonite, not quite as big and nice as the one that was smashed, but sure to delight Violet and much easier to carry home.

Though known primarily as a mystery writer, O'Neil De Noux has written a number of science fiction adventures on a planet called Octavion. In this story of exploration and wilderness survival on distant Octavion, De Noux portrays a bond between man and animal that readers of Jack London would find familiar.

The Silence of the Sea
by O'Neil De Noux

Down dropt the breeze,
the sails dropt down,
'Twas sad as sad could be;
And we did speak only to break
The silence of the sea!
The Rime of the Ancient Mariner
Samuel Taylor Coleridge (Earth, AD 1798)

For the record, I'm no cartographer. I wouldn't know how to make a map. I just name things.

Watching the sun rise in the western sky above the Perfume Mountains sends a shiver through me. The sky is streaked in pink and bluish purple, indigo high above and shimmering yellow along the mountaintops.

Donning my black sunglasses, I take another sip of strong coffee and chicory. Rhett snorts as he lies next to my feet, closer to the dying embers of our fire. The right ear of my big, yellow dog rises for a moment, then sinks back like his left ear, which has been floppy since the day I found him rummaging through a garbage can outside my room in that alley back in First Colony City.

Looking up at the mountains again, I yawn. I'd named these mountains two days ago, when I'd discovered them. Called them the Lavender Mountains for their color, until we were close enough to smell the sweet scent in the air.

In my journal, I'd renamed them the Perfume Mountains last

night as we set up camp. I reach down and pick up a lavender rock next to my foot and sniff it. Honeysuckle or gardenia, I can't tell which scent, but the very rocks of the Perfume Mountains smell like Earth flowers, clean and sweet.

Rhett lifts his head, looks around, and lets out a whine. I pet him.

Rising slowly, Rhett stretches, sniffs the air, still cool from the night and filled with the pungent scent of the perfumed rocks. As I look around, I am again amazed at the colors, the deep lavender of the mountains, the dark green grass of the long plain behind us, the deep blue sky as the sun takes hold of the new day.

There are no colors like this on Earth. It's taken years for me to adjust to the depth of the greens and the rich brown hues, the silver deserts and the golden hills of this faraway planet we humans have named Octavion.

Twisting the kinks out of my back, I stretch my six-foot frame. Still a lean two hundred pounds, even as I approach my fiftieth year (that's Earth years). I run my fingers through my long, unruly hair, as yellow as Rhett's coat. My green eyes are not nearly as dark as the greens here.

I'm Buck. Full name—John Joseph André, namer of names, discoverer of mountain ranges and rivers, plains and seas. I was the first human to gaze upon the vast Silver Desert and the rolling Cinnamon Hills and the Indigo Forest with its dark blue tree bark and pale blue leaves the size of maple leaves. I named each.

And now we have the Perfume Mountains. When I return to the Data Registry Center back in that patchwork collection of wooden and stone buildings fancifully called First Colony City, my naming will be official. Here, along the backwash of the Milky Way, we are fortunate to have communication satellites. There are no mapping satellites around Octavion, yet. For now, that's my job.

I don't bother wiping the lavender dust from my hiking boots as I walk over to where my mare and mule graze on the rich grass at the edge of the plain we just crossed. A good seventeen hands tall, Cocoa's coat is chocolate brown except for her white mane and tail. I pat her rump on my way to Charcoal. My mule, coat as dark as sackcloth, doesn't move, except for a twitch of an ear as I dig out a fresh shirt from her pack and an apple.

Slicing the apple in half with my bowie knife I keep sheathed on my left side, I drop half in front of Charcoal's nose. I feed the other half to Cocoa, who chomps it with relish.

Rhett finishes off the rest of last night's kill—a plump field hare he caught and we shared, just before sundown. I down the rest of my coffee and make sure our fire's out before putting on my black Stetson.

Saddling up Cocoa, I climb up and announce, "Okay. That pass we spotted should be a few miles south of here." I nudge my mare forward and she responds in a nice, even gait, Charcoal following on the long tether.

Moving next to the mountains, I look around for those pterodactyl-like creatures. Last night two of the pesky bastards swooped over us twice before disappearing in the darkness.

"Today is the day I spot a real dinosaur."

Rhett, who's inspecting a curious boulder to my left, jogs over in case I'm talking to him. He falls in step next to us.

I'd picked up a rumor in town the night before leaving. A scientist, drinking rum in Margie's Bar, said he was sure there must be tyrannosaurs somewhere along this southern hemisphere. Those fuzzy-headed scientists still have no idea what these creatures are, have no idea how they evolved, why they are so similar to Earth's prehistoric creatures. But this scientist was sure there had to be large predators here.

Reminds me of the environmental scientists still trying to block human colonization of planets because we tend to destroy things. Too bad for them we have the Right of Habitation Act. Humans have the right to colonize any inhabitable planet. Spread our seed to the farthest reaches of the galaxy.

Easing to the left, we skirt the base of a hill toward the opening between two mountains.

"Tyrannosaurs!" I say it aloud as we close in on the pass. That's right, I want to be the first human to see a living tyrannosaur. Narrow and strewn with boulders in various shades of purple, the pass looks perfect for an ambush. If there were any humans within a hundred miles, this is prime bushwhack terrain. I slow down as we navigate the narrow pass. Rhett darts ahead, sniffing around. As much energy as a puppy, although full grown, he is entertaining.

The pass closes around us, and patches of violet trees dot the base of the mountains. I pause for a moment to get a close-up look at the trees, whose leaves are thin, like oak leaves. Rhett moves in front and leads us along a narrow gulch for a ways before the sound of running water stops us. Cocoa whinnies.

We follow Rhett through a stand of trees to the edge of a fast-moving creek. The air smells of chlorophyll, only sweeter than the foliage scent back home. Rhett flushes another Octavion hare, which scrambles away, escaping into the brambles of burnished-gold bushes with small, teal leaves.

"Come on, boy," I call out, and my dog reluctantly follows us through the trees on this bright morning. Again, I am taken by the beauty of this planet, colors that simply dazzle the human eye. A paradise? Maybe. After all, there are no snakes on Octavion.

A mile later, we discover the creek has become a river of sparkling blue water. The color reminds me of the blue on the American flag. We follow it as it rushes between two mountains that seem darker purple than the Perfume Mountains behind us. The violet woods thicken, and we slow down.

The canopy eventually opens ahead, and Rhett barks as soon as we ease onto a wide plateau of rolling copper grass, the river moving to our left, alongside a magnificent blue mountain.

Leaning back, I gaze up at the great blue mountain. Steep and craggy, the mountain is in no way similar to the round-top Perfume Mountains. It is dark blue, bright under the sun. Streaked with the same burnished-gold bushes, it looks like a huge rock of lapis lazuli.

When I was a boy, I visited the Cairo Museum with my father and stood for nearly an hour staring at the funeral mask of the boy pharaoh named Tutankhamen. Solid gold and covered with semiprecious stones, it is still the most beautiful man-made object I have ever seen. Besides the glittering yellow gold, the most striking color was the lapis lazuli adorning the mask.

"Time for preliminary naming," I announce. "The pass we just came through will be Rhett's Pass."

Cocoa snorts as if she understands.

"I know. That's the fourth thing I've named for Rhett."

I pat her mane.

"You'll get your chance. I'm saving your name for something special."

I point to the trees. "The forestry here we'll call the Violet Woods." I wave at the plateau. "This is the Copper Plateau." I point to the blue mountain. "And this is Mount Azure."

What about the river?

I remember the blue color. "It's the American River."

We follow the river for several miles as it seems to wrap around Mount Azure. The Violet Woods enclose us. Just as my stomach grumbles and I'm thinking about lunch, the woods fall away to a continuation of the Copper Plateau. I dismount above a cutback along the river. Rhett races to investigate the river, which is over two hundred yards wide now.

I hobble horse and mule on a long tether next to the river. Both drink as Rhett barks wildly at something in the water. Looks like a small fish. I refill my canteens before sitting beneath a violet tree to nibble on jerked beef and the last of the French bread, which is going stale.

It takes a while to realize the dull sound I hear in the background is water. I'd noticed the bend in the river when I refilled the canteens. It runs behind us now, but the sound is different from running water. Can't make it out at this distance.

Rhett comes over for some meat, and we eat together. Cocoa and Charcoal munch on the plush grass next to the river. The strong sun is high now. Thankfully the humidity is not.

A half hour later, I'm back in the saddle, moving along the riverbank when Rhett stops ahead and stares intently across the river. As we draw close, I hear a low growl come from him.

"What is it, boy?"

As I look across the river, a loud bellow echoes from the woods. A crash precedes a green creature as it rumbles out, heading straight for us. It looks like an armored turtle, about five feet high and maybe fifteen feet long, its back covered with rippled shells. I think it's called an ankylosaur. Bouncing as it runs straight for the river, it bellows again.

Cocoa dances in place, and I hold her reins tightly. Rhett backs away, barking now. The ankylosaur turns before reaching the river and runs along the far bank. A movement catches my eye at the place in the woods where the ankylosaur came out. A striped beast bolts from the woods. Moving much quicker on two powerful legs, its oversized head leaning forward, the beast opens its jaws and lets out a shrill roar. About six feet tall, its body has tiger stripes in violet and gold.

Tyrannosaur.

Cocoa rears, almost bucking me off. I struggle to get her under control. Rhett races ahead, paralleling the action across the river. The tyrannosaur doesn't seem to notice us as it bears down on the howling ankylosaur, the sound of fear reverberating in its pitiful howl.

I finally get Cocoa under control, and we rush after Rhett.

The tyrannosaur charges the ankylosaur, which swishes its thick tail at the predator. Easily dodging the tail, the tyrannosaur strikes the beast along its left flank. Screeching, the ankylosaur veers toward the river.

Passing through a grove of golden bushes, Cocoa takes the uneven ground well. We catch up to Rhett, who pants as he runs next to us now. I have to slow down for Charcoal, who brays behind me.

Cocoa swerves around a huge bush and turns toward the river.

The tyrannosaur strikes its prey again, slashing at its neck, but the ankylosaur is too heavy and keeps plodding forward. The tyrannosaur falls back and seems content to run behind its prey. They continue at a steady pace. The plateau rises to our right now, then suddenly dips to reveal a small lake ahead. The lake is surrounded by Violet Woods.

Rhett suddenly stops, and Cocoa bounces to a stop. Charcoal brays again just as a loud roar echoes from across the river. I pull Cocoa around a large golden bush and watch a thirty-foot tyrannosaur race out of the woods close to the lake. It heads straight for the ankylosaur. Darker in color than the small tyrannosaur, which must be a juvenile, the larger predator closes ground quickly. The ankylosaur stumbles.

Another large tyrannosaur comes out of the woods just as the first big one catches the ankylosaur before it can reach the river. Latching to the prey's tail, the tyrannosaur holds firm, stopping the ankylosaur's momentum.

The juvenile tyrannosaur jumps to the other side of the ankylosaur, bites a rear leg. As the second large tyrannosaur arrives, the three predators yank the ankylosaur into pieces, ripping off the entire tail and a leg, leaving the carcass to lie belly up and unmoving.

The juvenile tyrannosaur rips at the exposed flesh where the dead beast's leg was once attached. They eat greedily, ripping the meat, throwing their heads back and swallowing large chunks. They eat quickly.

The woods behind the scene seem to part as an even larger tyrannosaur crashes out. At least forty feet tall, it moves with incredible speed on two thickly muscled legs. It's got to be a big male. Head lowered, it heads directly for the others. The juvenile sees it first and rips off another chunk of flesh before jumping away quickly.

Closing rapidly, the large tyrannosaur lifts its head and roars so loudly, Rhett jumps behind Cocoa, who trembles beneath me. The two smaller adults back away, their mouths full of bloody meat. The large tyrannosaur slams its jaws into the belly of the dead ankylosaur. Twisting its head, it places one foot on the carcass and yanks out a mouthful of flesh and bones. It throws back its head and swallows, its snout glistening red with blood.

Cocoa backs away on her own. Rhett notices and runs back the way we came, looking over his shoulder. We pass Charcoal, who's snorting as she tries to catch her breath.

I pull on the reins and tell Cocoa, "Slow now, girl."

Over my shoulder, I see the three big tyrannosaurs tearing up more of the ankylosaur, the juvenile darting in to grab another chunk of flesh.

As Cocoa leads us away, I watch the large beasts as if mesmerized.

We finally lose sight of them as we move away from the river across the wide plateau, Mount Azure looming on our right now. Taking in a deep breath, the realization of what I've just seen hits me. I'm the first human to see it, and the thought sends shivers down my back. I hold the reins tighter to keep my hands from shaking.

I let out a long breath, but still feel the jitters. It was all too fast.

My God! I'm the first human to see tyrannosaurs.

The sound of water I'd heard earlier seems louder now as we continue around the mountain. And it occurs to me the river has circled around and is in front of us again, running past Mount Azure. And... the sound is too loud.

We continue forward slowly, down a long, gradual incline, following the increasingly louder sound of water. An hour later we come upon the great waterfall and the vast sea beyond. I stop and climb off Cocoa. Rhett moves next to me, and we both stand there for long minutes, the roar of the falls nearly deafening, its windblown mist blowing over us—the panorama takes my breath away.

With the great blue mountain behind us, framed by the Perfume Mountains beyond, the river falls into a wide, cobalt blue sea. Even wearing sunglasses, I shield my eyes with my hands as I gaze at the sea.

Rhett moves forward, ears lowered, snout sniffing the grass as we walk across the small meadow toward the edge of a bluff. I follow slowly, Charcoal content to nibble grass, Cocoa looking in the direction from which we came. She's still jittery.

Reaching the edge of the bluff, Rhett stops and sits. I reach him a minute later and sit at the edge of the cliff next to my dog on grass cooled by the mist. I gaze out at the wide sea. Below, there is a narrow beach of white sand. The crystal water becomes turquoise with streaks of bright green and purplish blue near the reefs. In the distance, the sea is pale blue, so pale it's hard to tell where the sea ends and the sky begins.

I'll call this the Cobalt Sea. And the small lake where the ankylosaur died, Lake Tyrannous.

Looking back at the huge falls, I know it will be the American Falls for the river that feeds it. A breath of mist flows over my face, and I close my eyes and lean back on my elbows. I feel Rhett settle next to me and I lie back, hands behind my head now as I let my steady breathing lull me into a nice nap.

I wake with a start, look back at Cocoa. She's still looking back at the way we came. Charcoal nibbles the grass, and Rhett rests at my side. Turning back to the sea I realize what's wrong. I can't hear the sea. The roar of the falls has drowned out the sound of waves rolling to shore. The mist from the falls has blown away the smell of saltwater. It's as if I'm looking at a picture of the wide Cobalt Sea.

Glancing at my watch, I'd napped for about a half hour. Rhett lifts his head, grunts, and puts it back down as I watch the silent sea. Sitting up, I lean forward and spot three, large black stains in the water below. Gliding quickly through the clear water close to shore, dorsal fins breaking the water as they rise, then dart deeper. They are ichthyosaurs, hunting beneath the waves, paralleling the beach. I watch them move back and forth three times before they roll into deeper water.

Rhett growls, then barks loudly as two dark green dimetrodons scurry below along the narrow beach. Only about twelve feet long, they are vicious looking. Snapping at one another, their sail fins sway as they dart back into the jungle that runs to the right of the bluff. They slip easily though the tangle of mangrove trees below and disappear in the jungle.

Dark clouds move in from the right, over the sea. The strong Octavion sun is beginning its slow descent, falling toward the sea, streaking the waters with an iridescent glow. Time to start a fire, put up my tent. No sleeping under the stars with those dark clouds hovering offshore.

In a half hour, I have a nice blaze going, Cocoa and Charcoal unpacked and untethered. I open a can of dog food for Rhett and a can of ham for me. As the ham sizzles in its skillet and the beans simmer in their pot, I take my spare canteens to the mist from the waterfalls and prop them up to let the cool river water fill them.

Cocoa is still jumpy, raising her head often. I look around too. It's a creepy feeling, as if we're being watched. If it's the tyrannosaurs, we don't have a chance. I pull out both of my weapons, my .44 caliber Henry Trapper rifle, loaded with seven rounds and my 12-gauge Browning Auto-7 shotgun. Making sure each is loaded, I feel better with these vintage twentieth-century weapons next to me as I turn over the ham.

Shooting tyrannosaurs with these weapons will probably only make them angry, but it's still reassuring having them at hand. Rhett finishes his meal and lopes off to where Cocoa and Charcoal are nibbling the lush grass. He doesn't seem to have the same worried feeling, so I feel better. If any of us can detect danger, he'll be the first.

I save a slice of ham for Rhett as I eat slowly, washing down the food with the chilled water from the falls. Always nice to have my canteens brimming with crystalline water.

The dark clouds are moving away now, content to stay over the sea. A bright orange light illuminates us from the sun as it hovers above the horizon. A sudden chill along my back causes me to turn in time to see Cocoa running flat out, across the bluff toward the falls. Behind her race two brown predators, smaller than Cocoa, running on two legs.

Raptors.

Snatching up the Henry, I bring it to aim at the raptor closest to Cocoa. Damn, they are so fast, cheetah-fast, moving at incredible speed. I lead it and squeeze off a round, the Henry recoiling against my shoulder. It misses as Cocoa turns our way. The raptors turn, and I get a bead on the second one and squeeze the trigger, catching it in the torso. It jumps high in the air and flops to the ground.

I see a flash of yellow as Rhett races for the raptor, trying to cut it off.

No.

Three raptors are after my dog, closing in quickly. I level the sights on the one closest to Rhett and drop it. As it tumbles, the other two raptors jump aside and stop to look at the fallen one. I drop another just as Cocoa's screech turns me back.

The raptor has her by the throat, the claws of its feet slashing at Cocoa's side as the horse continues forward. I grab my shotgun and run for them. Rhett comes for me, racing hard.

Cocoa cries again, a deep painful scream, and falls straight down.

I'm still a good twenty yards away, pumping hard. I see jerking movements and it's the raptor, still slicing up my horse. Raising the shotgun, I bear down on them. The raptor raises its bloody face, and I stop and take most of it off with a clean hit of double-aught buckshot. It rises and twitches, and I take the rest of its head off with another shot.

Rhett runs right past me, and I turn the shotgun on his two pursuers. I drop the first one ten yards from me, and the second turns away, but can't get away. I catch it along its back and send it rolling in a heap.

Turning, I see Rhett heading to cut off two more raptors racing straight for me. I go down on one knee and aim carefully, struggling to control my breathing, and fire at the closest raptor. I clip it and it keeps coming. The second raptor seems surprised at Rhett's speed and raises a claw to strike my dog as it lunges forward. Rhett dodges the claw and strikes the animal high, near the neck, and they fall in a rolling heap.

Focusing on the raptor I'd clipped, it's so close, I only have time to point the shotgun and fire. I hit it dead center, and the raptor slashes at me as it falls, crashing against my left knee, sending me hard to the ground.

I pick up the shotgun, place it against the raptor's chest, and fire again.

That's seven shots.

Reload. I jump up and my left knee gives out. Rising again, I hobble back to my tent. Rhett and the raptor have disentangled and move in a circle, facing each other, Rhett barking, the raptor hissing.

No time to reload.

I drop the shotgun and pull out my bowie knife.

The raptor sees me, wheels, and comes for me. I brace myself. The beast accelerates quickly and comes in a gigantic leap, feet first, claws bared. I jump to my right, slashing with my knife, but we both miss. The raptor recovers quickly, turning fast, but not in time to fend off Rhett, who catches its throat again and both go down.

I scramble to them and sink my knife in the raptor's flank, all the way to its hilt. Pulling it out with both hands, I plunge it again and again until the beast quits moving. Rising, I stab it one more time, in its throat.

Lifting myself from the bloody carcass, I see Rhett lying a few feet away, disemboweled in a large pool of his blood. I crawl to him. Gasping for breath, I feel a well of emotion choking my throat.

Rhett moves. His head turns toward me, and I cradle it in my arms. He looks at me, blinks, and I can see it there: that familiar loving look my dog has given me again and again.

"I'm here boy." I feel tears in my eyes. "I'm here, Rhett," I tell him as his eyes close and he doesn't move again. Rocking slowly, I hold his head in my arms and let the emotion out.

If there are any more raptors, let them get me.

I don't care.

I can't stop the tears. I don't want to.

How long I've remained this way, I'm not sure.

A creeping dusk has captured the land.

I gently lay Rhett's head down and limp over to Cocoa. Her eyes are open as she lays there in violent death. Turning, I move back and pick up the shotgun.

Charcoal. I can't see her. Did she run back the way we'd come? Did the raptors get her too? Hobbling to my tent, I pull out my bag of shotgun shells, reload the Browning, tying the bag to my belt. I begin a careful search for my mule.

Certain she's not lying on the bluff, I move to the cliff in case she just ran off. The last flicker of sunlight shades the cliff, but I can't see the beach. Looking back at the dark bluff, I know the only place for me is along the cliff. There I'll have a fighting chance, at close range, with my shotgun.

I inch down the cliff, along a small ledge, barely wide enough for my feet. I follow the ledge down a long ways. Moving around an outcrop, I spot a black blotch in front of me and freeze.

Charcoal brays loudly.

"So there you are, girl." I reach for her, grab her nose, and pat it. She nuzzles against my hand, and I talk to her in quiet tones, telling her we'll be all right here, praising her for having the intelligence to climb down here where a mule can go and raptors, hopefully, can't.

I get into a comfortable sitting position, legs dangling off the cliff, shotgun pointing up the slope I'd just descended, and wait in the darkness. The moonless Octavion night is too black to see anything. Only the bright stars, reflected on the sea below, reveal we are alive.

Through the long hours, I keep seeing flashbacks of the sudden deaths above and feel a choking sadness. Several times during the night, I sense movement above and brace myself, but nothing comes. The movement returns just before dawn, and I watch intently as the first gray light of dawn illuminates the land.

Pterodactyls. Swooping in from the ocean, they flap above us as they land on the bluff.

Bastards are eating Rhett and Cocoa.

If those hideous-looking vultures are there, no raptors are around. I stand slowly. Surprisingly, my knee isn't that stiff. I climb up as soon as I can see well enough.

The sight on the bluff stops me. It roils with pterodactyls. One peeks its ugly head from inside my tent; many more rise and fall from the sky. I level my shotgun at the nearest and take two out with one shot. The entire colony rises as one, flapping into the sky, swooshing back to the sea.

There is nothing of Rhett left except tufts of fur. I pick up the largest piece, about six inches, and tuck it into my belt on my way to Cocoa. Her skull remains, and many of her bones, but that's all. I pick up a loose tooth and pocket it on my way back to my tent.

No fire this morning and no coffee. Wearily, I pack up. I bring my journal to the cliff's edge and sit. Renaming the river, I rename the great falls and name the cliff before closing my book.

Shading my eyes, I look out at the blue water of the silent sea.

"I am John Joseph André of planet Earth!" My shout dies immediately in the thunder from the falls. Raising a finger to the waterfalls, I call out.

"That is the Sad American Falls from the river I've named the Sad American River. It's named for the color of the flag of my homeland."

Pointing over my shoulder, I continue, "This is Cocoa's Bluff, where my friend died in this place of such beauty."

I lower my voice and talk to Rhett. "I guess if you have to die, this is the place, huh boy?"

I tell him something he knows. I tell him how much I'll miss him. Then I tell the ocean, "We have seen what no one has ever seen before, my friends and I. We are the first of our kind here."

Standing, I tell the sea we won't be the last.

"You see, we have come to stay on this planet, and there's nothing you can do about it."

It takes me nearly six hours to coax Charcoal back up the cliff, load her down with our supplies, and lead her away on foot from the most picturesque place on Octavion. As we start back across the Copper Plateau, I don't look back at the beautiful Cobalt Sea, nor at the huge, crystalline waterfalls, nor even up at the magnificence of Mount Azure with its flecks of gold.

At night, when I close my eyes, I try not to remember Rhett snuggling next to me, the softness of his fur when I'd pet him. I've put away the tuft of his coat for now. The memory's too strong now. I'll touch it again, one day, running my fingers through my dog's soft mane.

I dream of Cocoa, racing across the Copper Plateau, long mane flowing in the wind. She's not frightened, not running for her life as she did by the falls. Such a noble beast, and look what I brought her to. I don't think of Lake Tyrannous nor the beauty of the Perfume Mountains as we slip through Rhett's Pass back across the long green plain to First Colony City.

The people at the Data Registry Center look at me with amazement as I log in the names and descriptions of what Rhett and Cocoa and Charcoal and I have discovered. They ask questions, which I don't answer. I tell the frizzy-headed scientist, when he persists on asking more about the tyrannosaurs, that if he wants more information, go to Lake Tyrannous.

Resupplying takes two days. Finding another horse takes another. Finding a dog takes two more. He's young and eager and blacker than Charcoal, with a shiny coat and yellow eyes. I call him Blackie.

My new horse, another mare, isn't as tall as Cocoa, but she's a roam beauty with a feisty disposition. I call her Scarlett. Always loved that book. Charcoal, loaded down with gear, follows us out of town. People have come out to watch us leave. I don't return their waves.

We head in the opposite direction this time. We'll cross the Cinnamon Hills to find what lies beyond.

Blackie falls into step next to Scarlett and looks up at me.

I feel a swell in my chest as I realize we're all connected, we'll always be connected. Me and Rhett and Cocoa and Charcoal and Scarlett and Blackie. Earthlings all.

"We're going on an adventure," I tell Blackie. "There are things never seen before and things to name."

Again, for the record, I'm no cartographer. I wouldn't know how to make a map. I just name things.

Michael Kurland, the author of the acclaimed "Professor Moriarity" mysteries, here presents a more antique historical mystery, featuring characters that prefigure a more familiar consulting detective and his amanuensis.

Four Hundred Slaves
a problem for Marcus Fabius Quintilianus
by Michael Kurland

It was in the sixth year of the reign of the Emperor Vespasian that this story of the exploits of my master, the great orator and logician Marcus Fabius Quintilianus, begins. I use the word "master" in the sense of "teacher" or "font of all wisdom," rather than in the slaveholding sense, since I, Plautus Maximilianus Aureus, the great Quintilian's pupil and scribe, am a freeborn citizen of Rome. I point this out because the distinction is an important one, and in the story I am about to relate, it is a matter of life or death.

A flock of shrikes settled in the olive grove outside our villa in the afternoon of the third day of the Nones of April, and two of the shrill, nasty little birds proceeded to have a screaming argument, while the others called their encouragement from the surrounding trees. Susannah, a young recently acquired slave from the East, came out and stood beside me in the atrium at dusk, clutching her arms about her under her breasts, which were just large enough to provide an interesting contour beneath her white robe, and we listened to the birds fussing and screeching.

I affected no notice of her contours. Since Quintilian was showing an interest in his new possession, an interest that seemed to be welcomed gratefully, perhaps even eagerly, it would be pointless and unwise. Besides there was Adella, one of the household maids, who had indicated with many a giggle that she would not strongly resist my advances.

Susannah shivered as the birds set off a new round of raucous dissent. "It is an ill portent," she said earnestly.

"The shrieking of these miserable birds signifies something?"

I asked.

"Death," she said with a shudder.

Quintilian came out and stood behind us. "Whose death?" he asked, smiling down at her. "And how will he die? Pecked to death, perhaps?"

She raised her little fists and beat them in frustration against Quintilian's chest. A capital crime, striking her master; but he did not seem to regard it so. "You don't take me seriously," she said. "But I know what I know."

Quintilian drew more tightly around him the wool mantle he had thrown on. "I'll have Capulus throw some stones at the flock," he said. "Get them to move on."

"It won't help," the girl said solemnly. "They have settled at dusk and are screaming their screams, and someone will die." Somehow her lilting Aramaic—I think it was Aramaic—accent gave the pronouncement more weight, and I felt an involuntary shiver run down my spine.

Quintilian sighed. "An easy prediction to make," he said. "'Someone will die.' Undoubtedly someone will die. Disease, accident, treachery, war—it's amazing that any of us manage to survive."

"Someone will die whose death has meaning to you," she insisted. "Perhaps more than one."

He looked from one to the other of us. I think he could see that, try as I might to remain unmoved, her words were troubling me. A portent is, after all, a portent. And her name might not be Cassandra, but who knew what prophetic powers were granted to the Susannahs of this world?

"I am approaching my forty-fifth birthday," my master said, "and many whom I care about and a few whom I despise have left this world already. I have no doubt that more will follow."

"Throwing stones at the flock will not help," Susannah said.

Quintilian took a deep breath. "What would help?" he asked.

"I know of nothing," Susannah said, shaking her head sadly.

"Well then, a few stones might at least get us a quiet night's sleep," Quintilian said. "And what the gods choose to do they will do, regardless. I will give instructions. Join me in the bed-chamber shortly."

Susannah touched her finger to her forehead in what I have learned is an Oriental gesture of obedience.

Quintilian nodded and left us.

Before I went to bed that night I took a jug of vinegar and some sprigs of dried rosemary from the pantry and poured a line of vinegar across all the entrances to the villa, pouring only with my left hand, keeping the rosemary in my right hand over my head, and reciting as I went the witching poem I remembered from my childhood: *"Nuncus rebus mangus poppis; Halifratus satum flebis."* I placed a twig of rosemary at each end of each vinegary line. What language the witching poem might be, or indeed if the words had meaning in any language, I know not. But the combination of vinegar and verse was said to ward off danger and misfortune, and the rosemary kept away evil. I didn't know whether it would work against shrikes or not, but as my old nurse used to say, "It couldn't hurt."

Peris, the door slave, gave me unasked-for advice on tending to an addled pate. He had always thought I was slightly crazy, and watching me go from portal to portal, limping (from a childhood injury), mumbling, and pouring, did little to disabuse him of this notion.

Did it work? I can't say. Perhaps things would have been even worse had I not gone through that little ceremony, perhaps it was all just vinegar and rosemary and mumbled nonsense; only the gods know for sure. What I do know is that it was the next day that we learned of the first death.

Quintilian was to teach his class in advanced rhetoric that day. The students arrived in a batch in the forenoon; twelve of them, sons of some of Rome's most important and distinguished men, all in early manhood. They gathered in a corner of the atrium where benches had been placed in a semicircle around a point from which the speaker of the moment could declaim.

Since the emperor Vespasian had created the Chair of Literature and Rhetoric for my master, and given him the task of devising the ideal curriculum for the youth of Rome, the fees he commanded for teaching were approaching the Olympian. And this in addition to the generous stipend from the imperial purse that went with his position. On the other hand, at least two of his students paid no fees, and one I knew, whose father's estates had been confiscated by Nero, owed sandals, tunic, and toga to my master.

The subject on which the students were to discourse convincingly was an old standard: if Sister Verga, one of the Vestal priestesses, was thrown off a cliff for having violated her oath and somehow survived, should the punishment be deemed to have been carried out, or should she be thrown off the cliff again?

But another death occupied them this day. The talk in the forum was of the murder of Cassius Caprius Strabo, who had been found dead of a knife thrust in his own study. A onetime magistrate and procurator of Bithynia before he retired to his villa on the northern outskirts of Rome, the honorable Strabo was a direct descendant of the great Pompey, and was—or I should say had been—highly regarded for his judgment and his sense of morality. Indeed, he was one of the *amici*, the "special friends" from whom the Emperor Vespasian sought advice. And he had been a good friend of Quintilian. Indeed it had only been a week or so before that my master had attended a dinner party in Strabo's honor.

Quintilian insisted that the class go on, even though several of the students, especially those who were to speak that day, expressed their willingness to delay the class until a better time.

Thestis, Quintilian's major domo, came out to the atrium and waited patiently while young Crassus Hypotus, with many a "Hear me, O Rome," forcefully explained that, having once been thrown off the cliff, Sister Verga had been placed in the hands of the gods, and all mortal punishments had been satisfied. Throwing her off the cliff again would be an affront to the gods' judgment. I was convinced. But then I always find myself convinced by the last speaker, whichever side he was on, in any argument. Such is the power of rhetoric.

When Crassus finally bowed to the student playing presiding judge and sat down, Thestis went over and whispered in Quintilian's ear. Quintilian rose and said, "You've all been most sincere and convincing. Now each of you who spoke today prepare to speak for the other side. Lose none of your sincerity while advocating the opposite view; that is the mark of the true master of rhetoric. I'll hear you when I return." He beckoned to me and crossed the atrium. I trotted, or perhaps limped, after him.

Thestis pointed us toward the front of the villa. "I placed him in the fore-yard," he said. "He asked for a cup of watered wine, which I had sent to him. Although, by the way he looks, he could use more of the wine and less of the water."

Quintilian turned to me. "Come, Scribbler. You have your writing tablets and stylus? Good. Sit in a corner and take discreet notes."

"Scribbler" is my less than elegant nickname. But I don't mind. Many, including some famous and well-respected men, have been called worse. "Yes, sir," I said. "Don't I always?"

"Sometimes you are more discreet than others," he replied. "Let this be one of those times."

Waiting for us on a bench in the sunny fore-yard was a young man in a spotless white toga. He had brown eyes, an artfully bent nose, and a mass of unruly brown hair. An expression that hinted of panic was frozen on his otherwise unlined patrician face. He jumped to his feet at our approach. "Master Quintilian," he said. "Thank you for seeing me."

"How could I not?" said Quintilian. "One of my best pupils; the son of one of my closest friends." He sat beside the youth on the bench. "I heard about your father, and I am very sorry. All of Rome grieves."

So this was Marius Strabo, son of the murdered Cassius Strabo. I knew that he had been a pupil of Quintilian, but I had never met him before. I squatted on the ground by the bench and took a wax tablet and stylus from my pouch. My main task is recording what of any import is said to and by Quintilian. Periodically I transcribe those words that might be wanted again onto fine Egyptian papyrus, which is sorted by subject and date. Quintilian has for years been working on several books: a record of his cases and orations, a book of instruction for those who would teach the young, a textbook on rhetoric, a collection of his poetry, and a history of Roman law. The collected sheets of papyrus grow, and occasionally my master leafs through one or another of them and says something like, "What was that clever thing I said about a student being like a butterfly?" or, "Where is a copy of the reply I wrote to Martial's nasty little quatrain a couple of years back?" If I'm lucky I remember, and can find it. If not I tell him and he says, "No matter, no matter, you can't be expected to remember everything." Which hurts like the sting of a lash, for what good am I, poor cripple that I am, if I cannot even remember the location of everything in the small universe that is Quintilian's writings?

"It is that which I have come to see you about," Marius said. "What have you heard of my father's murder?"

"Only what is common knowledge in the Forum," Quintilian told him. "And what is common knowledge is almost always deficient in detail and inaccurate in fact. Why don't you tell me what you would have me know?"

Marius nodded and took several breaths before commencing. "My father was killed in his study, which is a small separate house resting against the back wall of the villa. There are three rooms: an office, a library, and past those, a small chamber with a couch on which Father used to rest during the day. He was in the first room, his office, at his desk, apparently working on his numbering system, when he was stabbed in the side by a long, thin blade."

"Numbering system?" I asked.

Marius looked at me as though seeing me for the first time. "Yes," he said. "My father worked with figures his whole life; collecting the taxes in Bithynia, supplying and paying the legions under his command, and of late trying to devise a more rational and just tax collection system for the empire, at the emperor's request. And he still works with the Quartermaster Corps, seeing that equipment and supplies destined for his old legions are of good quality and price. He believed that the—I think it was—Phoenician numbers are easier to use than our own. You know: adding, multiplying; that sort of thing. He was trying to adapt Phoenician numbers to Roman needs." Marius shrugged and his eyes fell. "I suppose the idea died with Father. I confess to having scant interest in the subject, and none of those working with or under him have any interest in it at all, as far as I can tell."

"The abacus works well enough for most calculations," Quintilian commented.

"It was while discussing the use of the abacus with Pliny that Father got the idea for his system," Marius told him. "The abacus is fine as long as you don't make a mistake, but as Pliny pointed out, an error, even a large error, can go unnoticed, due to our cumbersome reckoning system. Or so said my father."

"Ah!" said Quintilian, and waited while the young man stared off into space and allowed some strong emotion to wash over him.

Marius suddenly gripped Quintilian's arm. "You have to help me, sir," he said. "I don't know what to do!"

Quintilian gently disengaged the lad's hand from his arm. "What is it that you want done?" he asked mildly.

Marius drained his glass of watered wine. Thestis, who stood silently in a corner by a large potted plant, immediately filled it again from a pitcher he was holding.

"A slave has been accused of the killing," Marius said. "His name is Prusias. I've known him since I was a small child." He shook his head. "I cannot believe that he did this, yet the evidence against him is overwhelming."

"Do you want me to prosecute him or defend him?" Quintilian asked.

Marius stared at him mutely for a minute, and then shook his head. "Would it were that simple," he said. "I am not clear as to what I want you to do—or what you can do."

"Tell me what you know," Quintilian said. "How did it happen?"

"It was yesterday," Marius said, "shortly after the noon meal.

I was not there at the time."

"Where were you?" Quintilian interrupted.

Marius flushed. "I was at a house on the Via Claudia," he said. "A gambling house. While my father was being murdered, I was throwing dice. I won three denarii, and came home to find my father dead. The gods laugh."

"So you have no direct knowledge of what happened?"

"I didn't see the murder, if that's what you mean," said Marius. "I arrived home just as my father's body was discovered."

"Tell me about it."

Marius put a finger to his nose and stared at the ceiling briefly. People often do that—the staring, not the nose—when they're arranging their thoughts. I wonder why. "The sun was low in the sky when I returned home," Marius said. "I was told Father was working in his study. Just as I reached the courtyard everyone began running about and screaming and moaning that the procurator was dead. It took me a moment to realize that it was my father they were talking about."

"Everybody?"

"Everybody in the courtyard at the time. Someone had knocked on the door to the study and got no response, so he went to the window and peered in. He saw my father lying dead across his desk. And the only person who'd been in the room all afternoon was Prusias, who brought my father a cup of watered lemon juice and some olives and flat bread. Father doesn't—didn't—like to be disturbed while at work."

"And this was when Prusias shoved a knife in his side?"

"So they say. There is no other answer."

"What knife? From where?"

"It is a thin blade of Persian design. No one knows where it came from. No one in the household has ever been seen to have one like it in his or her possession."

"Did your father try to fight off his attacker?"

"Fight off?" Marius thought about it. "No. He was seated at his desk, his head fallen among his papyri. He looked, except for the knife sticking out of his side, as though he had fallen asleep."

"Interesting," Quintilian said. "What motive did Prusias have?"

"Motive? None that I know of."

"What does he say happened?"

Marius let out a sudden burst of laughter that startled us. I think it startled him. "Prusias says nothing," he explained. "He cannot speak. His tongue was cut out and his vocal cords severed when he was much younger." He looked from one to the other of us and saw that we were staring at him.

"I cannot believe my old friend Strabo would do such a thing," Quintilian said.

"I'm sorry," said Marius. "I have lived with Prusias for so long that I forgot how that would sound. The, ah, mutilation had been done to him before my father acquired him from a slave dealer in Nicomedia; we never found out why."

"So Prusias has been with your family for a long time?"

"At least twenty-five years."

"And he suddenly decided to kill his master? For no reason that you know of?"

"So it would seem."

Quintilian signaled to Thestis to bring him a cup of watered wine and looked thoughtfully at a pot of African lilies while the wine was poured. "Let us go over this and see if we can create a rational picture," he said. "Prusias, who cannot speak—" He interrupted himself to ask, "Can he understand?"

"Simple commands," Marius said. "Perhaps more."

"Ah!" Quintilian said. "So this simple mute slave, after serving your family faithfully—I assume—for a quarter of a century, suddenly decided to kill his master. Strabo offered no resistance, indeed seemed not to notice when his trusted slave produced a long, thin knife along with the drink—a knife which appeared from nowhere, and which the slave was not seen to be carrying when he delivered the watered lemon juice...."

"How do you know that?"

"Pah!" Quintilian said. "You would have mentioned it if anyone had seen him with a knife. And he leaves the knife behind. In the wound, presumably?"

"Yes."

"And just goes calmly about his work?"

"Yes," Marius said. "And no one was seen to enter the study after Prusias left. And Father *is* dead."

"True." Quintilian agreed. "And there were people in the courtyard the whole time?"

"The whole time."

"Who?"

"My aunt Prunella and her daughter, my cousin Lucasta. My aunt is tutoring Lucasta in Greek."

"Good!" Quintilian declared. "Women should be educated. We need more educated women to make up for the great excess of foolish men." He gave me a sideways glance to be sure I had gotten that down. It would probably appear in one of his texts, if he ever got around to writing them.

"And a gardener," Marius continued, "and a couple of men fixing the drains."

"Which of them found him?" Quintilian asked.

"Actually it was a business acquaintance of my father's. A senator named Gaius Veccus."

"Business?"

"Yes," Marius said. "I know senators don't usually sully their togas with business, but if two or three of your clients start a factory with money you've loaned them and then insist on making you a partner, well, what are you to do?"

"What indeed?" Quintilian agreed.

"Veccus has a couple of factories full of slaves making shields, leather leggings, helmets; that sort of thing. All the trappings of war," Marius explained. "And Father was acquiring military supplies for the VII and IX Legions in Western Gaul."

Quintilian thought it over. "It's interesting," he said. "If the mute slave killed your father, why did he, and why is it that nobody heard? And where did he get the knife? If, on the other hand, Prusias didn't kill Strabo, then who did, and how did he manage it?"

"That's the problem," Marius agreed.

"I don't know whether I'd rather prosecute or defend,"

Quintilian said. "Which reminds me, which is it that you want me to do?"

"Neither," said Marius. "My problem is other than that."

Quintilian leaned forward. "Yes?"

I don't know what my master expected to hear, but I'm sure it wasn't what he heard.

"If Prusias is convicted of killing my father," Marius said, "then all the slaves owned by my father are to be put to death. All four hundred. I cannot allow that to happen. I cannot."

Quintilian looked shocked; something I had seldom seen. "Four hundred?" he asked.

Marius nodded. "Just about. Some are at farms down south, some at warehouses in Ostia or in the city. The total is about four hundred. And they are all to be put to death. And whoever the magistrates decide are the ringleaders are to be tortured first."

"Come now," Quintilian said. "That used to be the cus-tom—putting to death all the slaves in a household if one should slay his master. But it hasn't been followed for a hundred years. Well, eighty, at least."

"It's being insisted on by the Senate," Marius said. "Because of my father's status and position. They say an example must be made."

"And what does Vespasian say about this?"

"So far the emperor has not spoken." Marius shook his head as though to clear it of unwelcome thoughts. "This cannot hap-pen," he continued. "You must find a way to stop it."

Quintilian shaded his eyes from the bright sun to peer at the young man. "So," he said. "With your father dead, you will now inherit the slaves. You're protecting a financial interest."

"No, no," Marius protested. "Not at all. The slaves—all of them—were to be manumitted upon the death of my father. It's in his will. They were even to be given small businesses, or enough money to start their own."

"I see," Quintilian said. "You want me to find a way to pre-vent the executions of the slaves owned by your father, all of which were to be freed upon his death."

"Yes," Marius said eagerly. "Can you?"

"I don't know," Quintilian said, shaking his head. "It seems that each of them had a good reason to wish for the death of your father."

"Not by murder," Marius said. "If a conspiracy could be shown, they'd be put to death anyway."

"That's so," Quintilian agreed. "And there's no hint of such a thing?"

"I'd say it was impossible."

"What of Prusias?"

Marius shook his head. "If he did it, he should pay. Although, as I said, I cannot believe that he did. But there is no reason why the other slaves, completely blameless I am sure, should be punished. Can you see a way to save them?"

"It would have to be argued before the Senate," Quintilian said thoughtfully. "I would be speaking for the murdered man's son, and that would carry some weight. Although I think it would actually help if they weren't being manumitted. A financial interest speaks louder than a desire for mercy, people being what they are."

"I will reward you with a large honorarium if you make the attempt," Marius said. "And even more—much more—should you be successful."

Orators who try cases in the criminal courts or plead before the Senate are supposed to be doing it for the love of the law, of truth and justice, and of the people of Rome; and, of course, a belief in their cause. They are not, by tradition, to require a fee. But if their client should happen to present them with a gift at the end of the case, as a token of his esteem and gratitude, it would be ungrateful to turn it down.

"Very well," Quintilian said, draining his cup of wine and setting it down. "You have presented me with an interesting challenge, and I'll see what I can do. On the one hand it is obviously an injustice that three hundred and ninety-nine innocent slaves should be punished for the actions of one—if, indeed, he is guilty. On the other, slave rebellions are horrible things, which lead to excesses of cruelty and death on both sides. Anything that could tend to suppress or prevent one, even if cruel in itself, could be said to prevent a greater cruelty—by those," Quintilian continued, seeing the horrified look on Marius' face, "who would say such things."

"My father's slaves contemplated no rebellion," Marius said. "They were promised their freedom; why should they take such a foolhardy risk?"

"Why indeed," Quintilian said, leaning back. "Tell me what you are not telling me."

"What? Tell you what?"

"There is something more, something you're avoiding mentioning," Quintilian said. "I can sense it."

Marius blushed. "If so," he said, "it is nothing that can affect what I have asked you to do—I swear it!"

Quintilian rose to his feet. "I'll see what can be done," he said. "I must visit the scene and speak to those who were there. Also to your household slaves."

"Of course," said Marius. "I must return to the villa to do—" He paused and gathered himself. "To do what remains to be done. Arrange with the undertaker for the funeral procession for my father; the band, the paid mourners—although there will be many who mourn without pay—and prepare the family tomb out along the Via Appia. I am told that the emperor will be at the villa sometime during the week of mourning, so preparations for his visit must be made. You may come by at your will. I must see about getting servants to run the household for the near future. The household slaves have been taken to the city slave pens until their disposition is decided." He hit his right fist into his left palm several times in a distracted, and probably painful, way. "I must also do what I can for them—provide food, clothing, and bedding. That which is provided by the aedile in charge of the slave pens is not fit for... for... for slaves."

Marius left, his steps slow and positive; the mind willing the body to do what it would not.

Quintilian turned to look down at me. "Well?" he asked.

I gathered my tools and put them back in their small sack. "Well, what, Master?" I asked.

"Well, what do you think we should do first?" he asked. This is his way of instructing me.

"I'm sorry, Master, I have no idea," I told him. This is my way of learning.

"Should we go first to the slave pens, or to the Strabo villa?" he amplified.

I thought for a second. "The villa," I said.

"Why?"

"Because I have no desire to go to the slave pens. They are smelly, foul, horrible, degrading, depressing—"

He nodded. "You're right; they are all of that. Despite that, I think we'd best visit the slave pens first, and the villa after."

Why, then, in the name of the Seven Fates did you ask me? I thought. What I said was, "As you say, Master Quintilian."

"Refresh yourself with some bread and cheese, and perhaps a fig; we'll leave shortly."

Quintilian can't help it, he tells everyone what to do. "Bread, cheese, and a fig" indeed! As though I couldn't choose my own lunch.

I had bread and cheese and a handful of black olives, and waited for him by the door. He appeared shortly wearing sturdier sandals and a broad farmer's hat. Susannah came running up behind him carrying a dark brown woolen cloak. "Take this," she urged, handing it to him. "You'll be out late, and it gets quite chilly these evenings." She looked at me. "You, too," she said. "Take a cloak."

Quintilian grunted his thanks and strode out the door. I grabbed an old cloak from a peg by the door and hurried out after him as he headed off down the street. Two bodyguards fell into step behind us. It isn't particularly dangerous to walk around Rome in the daylight, but nobody who is anybody travels anywhere without bodyguards. Praetors go everywhere accompanied by six lictors—official bodyguards paid by the state. Consuls have twelve.

Quintilian walked everywhere. I have seldom seen him use a sedan chair or a litter. And his normal pace would be considered a forced march by a legionary. Even our tall, blond Gaulish bodyguards had to lengthen their strides to keep up, and were breathing deeply after the first half hour. I limped along the best I could without complaining; I had not sufficient breath to utter a complaint.

The slave pens are, as you might suspect, not in one of the better sections of Rome. The large, squat enclosure is way out on the Via Lubicana, past blocks of tenements that lean and spew garbage and occasionally collapse, burying their tenants. The pens are enclosed by a high brick wall. Their inner walls are brick, wood, or iron bars, depending. The roof, over that part that has a roof, is wood. The smell is indescribable. The sounds that come from it combine all the musical elements of an abattoir and an iron forge.

Quintilian strode up to the gate, where he was stopped by two large guards—ex-gladiators, by the look of them—who demanded to know just who he thought he was, marching up to the gate like that. Our own escorts looked amused, but they didn't look as though they relished the idea of getting in a dispute with the hulking guards.

"I'd like to see the aedile in charge of the pens," Quintilian said.

"Oh, really?" said one of the guards. "And what makes you think His Excellency Lepidus would spend his time down here at the pens when he has better things to do?"

"Better places to be," added the other guard.

"I see," Quintilian said. "Then who is in charge here?"

"As it happens," said the first guard, "His Excellency Lepidus is here today."

"Pure chance," said the other. "Sometimes weeks go by and we don't see him."

Quintilian gathered his cloak around him. "Would you tell His Excellency Lepidus that Marcus Fabius Quintilianus would speak with him, on the emperor's business?"

"On the emperor's business?" guard one repeated.

"Why didn't you say so?" asked guard two. "You only have two bodyguards—how were we to know?"

"I'll go myself," declared guard one, and disappeared into the interior of the compound.

"Don't stand outside," guard two exclaimed, opening the door wide. "Come and wait inside."

We entered into a large open area surrounded by brick walls and heavy barred doors. From all around us came the sounds of moaning, screeching, crying, screaming, bellowing, and what might have been chanting or singing. Strangely, none of the words were intelligible. Some distance across the large yard six or seven naked men were chained to large posts set in the earth. They did not seem to be enjoying themselves. Two of them were either unconscious or dead. One of them was looking up so that the sunlight shone directly on his face, and he seemed to be talking energetically to someone whom none of the rest of us could see.

Quintilian seated himself on a rude wooden bench inside the yard. "The emperor's business?" I murmured to him, sitting on the other end of the bench.

"The proper administration of justice *is* the emperor's business," he told me, with a stern glance. But perhaps there was the slightest hint of a smile at the corners of his mouth.

A little, fussy, gray-haired man who wasn't quite bald and wasn't quite fat came out of one of the doors across the yard accompanied by a tall, thin man with a balding pate, hawklike eyes close together above a beak of a nose, and a senatorial toga.

"Eh, what's this?" the fussy man asked, approaching us.

"Are you the aedile Lepidus?" Quintilian asked.

"That I am."

"The four hundred slaves from the Strabo household," Quintilian said. "I would like to see them."

The senator interjected his beak into the discussion. "And what business," he asked in a voice as dry as fallen leaves, "would you have with a bunch of rebellious slaves?"

"I am here on the emperor's business," my master said. "My name is Marcus Fabius Quintilianus. What is your interest in this?"

"I am Senator Veccus," the hawked-nosed man said. "I have a personal interest in seeing that these"—he waved his hand dismissively at some invisible slaves—"vermin should be punished for their perfidy. I had the misfortune to be the one to find Procurator Strabo's body."

"Ah, yes," said Quintilian. "So I have heard. It must have been quite a shock."

"It was. I had been speaking with him only a short time before." Veccus shook his head sadly. "He was an honorable and upright man."

"We don't have anything like four hundred of them slaves," the aedile said. "Sixty-seven is what we've got. The others are from the late Strabo's farms to the south. They haven't got here yet."

"I see," Quintilian said. "Let me see the ones you've got."

"No point to it," Lepidus said. "They're going to be crucified, the lot of them. You can't buy them; you can't even make an offer."

"Nonetheless I'd like to see them. Particularly the one—Prusias."

"The one who did it? Going to examine him, are you? For the emperor? You won't get anything out of him. We put him to the torture for two hours before we figured out that he couldn't talk. He ain't got no tongue. The torturer wanted to keep at it anyway, but the senator and I figured there wasn't no point to it, so I sent him back to the cage with the others."

"Very sensible," Quintilian agreed. "And who gave you the authority to torture a prisoner awaiting trial?"

Lepidus looked offended. "You don't think as how I'd do that without orders, do you?" he asked. "Take a chance of ending up under the lash myself? No." He pointed a thumb at the lanky senator. "The orders came direct from the senator here himself."

"Indeed?"

"On behalf of the Senate," Veccus affirmed. "I thought we could wring the truth out of him—why he did it, who else was involved, that sort of thing. I didn't know he was, ah..." He made a pinching gesture with his fingers in the general direction of his mouth.

"I can imagine your surprise," Quintilian said dryly. He indicated the posts on the other side of the yard. "Is that where you torture prisoners?"

"Nah," the aedile said. "We have a small yard set aside for that. Those posts are where we chain slaves who are being left out to die." He pursed his lips. "It's a funny thing; we need special permission to torture a slave, but if one causes trouble, we can just leave them out to die, and that's just fine."

"Funny, indeed," Quintilian agreed.

Lepidus shook his head. "What is Rome coming to?" he asked. "Come this way." He led the way across the courtyard to a pair of large, wooden doors, with Veccus stalking along behind. "We got them penned up in here. Emptied one of the common pens out and reserved it just for them."

"Men and women together?" I asked.

Lepidus looked at me and frowned. "None of that!" He said. "The pen is split in half: men on one side, women on the other. If we let them mix together, no telling what they'd do."

I thought I could tell him what they'd do, but I kept my mouth closed.

Lepidus pulled open the right-side door and ushered us into an area with an earth floor strewn with straw, a wood ceiling, and iron bars for walls. The room was divided into four separate barred cages, built to hold human beings. About thirty men of all ages, some in tunics of varying degrees of cleanliness and repair, some clad only in loincloths, were sitting or lying about in various positions of discomfort in one of the cages, and a like number of women were huddled together for mutual support in the next. The other two were, for the moment, empty.

"Look at that," Senator Veccus said, nodding toward the women's cage. "A dove among crows." He crossed to the cage, leaned against the bars, and pointed a finger inside. "You there!" he called into the cluster of women. "What's your name?"

The women scattered like pigeons across the cage. Veccus' pointing finger followed one of them. "Yes you. Come over here. Don't be shy."

The girl slowly crossed the cage as though pushing her way through a vat full of honey toward Veccus' beckoning finger.

She appeared to be about seventeen, with cropped blonde hair framing an oval face. Her body, its lines revealed as it moved under her stained robe, would provoke thoughts in Jove that would severely annoy Juno. And yet she seemed possessed of an ethereal innocence, and sweetness of disposition. I knew all of this within the first few seconds of seeing her. How, I cannot say; it is indeed one of the eternal mysteries.

"Your name," repeated the senator. "I asked you your name."

"Edissa, Master," she replied unwillingly, stopping a few feet short of the bars.

"Edissa. Greek, is it?" he asked, smiling a meaningless smile and rubbing his thumbs together.

"I'm from Syracuse, Master," she said so softly I could barely make out the words.

"So," Veccus said. "I've never had one from Syracuse before." He turned to Lepidus. "I want to, ah, examine this one. Prepare a private room for us."

Lepidus bowed and turned to leave. The girl looked as though the vat of honey she had waded through had just risen up and engulfed her. She fought to breathe.

"Wait!" commanded Quintilian.

Like the scene in Plautus' *Bacchides* where the goddess Venus stops the hero in midstride, Lepidus froze with one foot off the ground and one arm extended. Veccus turned, an incredulous look on his face.

"None of these slaves will be removed, or separated from the others, or questioned any further without the express permission of Emperor Vespasian until this investigation is over," Quintilian told them. He turned to Lepidus, who was just putting his foot down. "I shall hold you personally responsible."

Lepidus nodded twice and clasped his hands together.

"Well, I—" Veccus paused for a deep breath. "If this is all the respect you have for the Senate, well then I have nothing more to say!" He gathered his toga about him and stalked out of the building.

The girl folded to the ground and began to sob quietly.

Quintilian came up next to the bars of the cage holding the men. "I am Marcus Fabius Quintilianus," he told them, speaking softly but clearly. It is a trick of oratory to speak softly at certain times; your audience must listen closely, which forces them to pay attention. "Marius Strabo has asked me to come speak to you and learn what there is to be learned. He wants to help you. The emperor is also interested in your case." Quintilian added that for the benefit of Lepidus, who was listening carefully to what was being said. "Are there any among you," he continued, "who know anything about the murder of your master, or know of any reason why anyone would want to kill him?"

There was a silence from within the cage, as all the men inside stared at my master suspiciously. Then came a horrible inarticulate moan, as if someone's very soul were being unbearably squeezed. The men moved aside, and we saw an old man huddled in the corner, crouched on his knees with his head half buried in the straw. His back and his arms were caked with dried blood, which glistened with a black sheen in the half-light of the pens.

"Open the door to this pen," Quintilian snapped at the aedile, "and go fetch some rags soaked in vinegar and some clean toweling."

Lepidus' mouth dropped open. "You want me to fetch?"

"Well, then fetch someone to fetch," Quintilian said. "And quickly! Torturing a slave suspected of a crime is one thing; letting him die while the investigation is not yet completed is quite another."

That was a sentiment that Lepidus could understand, as was shown by the speed with which he threw the bolt on the door to the pen and left the area. Quintilian's actual belief—that torture was barbaric and pointless, that whipping or caning students actually harmed the learning process, that torturing slaves merely induced them to say whatever they thought you wanted them to say (unless, of course, they had no tongue)—would have puzzled, if not shocked, Lepidus.

Quintilian entered the pen and knelt by the side of the bloody old man. "Prusias, I presume," he said.

The old man made a keening sound.

"Why don't you lie down," Quintilian said, "and we'll cleanse your wounds."

"He can't lie down, Master," said a young boy, coming up beside Quintilian and standing straight and stiff as an olive tree, his hands at his sides. "His back is awful ripped up from the whip, and a couple of his ribs are broken from the club, so he can't lie down, back or front."

"Club?" asked Quintilian.

"Yes, Master.

Quintilian sighed a deep and heartfelt sigh. "How unnecessary," he said. "How foolish."

"Yes, Master," the boy agreed.

Prusias said something. At least I assumed he was saying something. It came out as a series of grunts, puffs, squeaks, and snorts. Quintilian looked around. "Can any of you understand him?" he asked.

"He says he didn't do nothing and he don't know why this is happening to him," called a woman from the adjoining pen. A number of the women had clustered about the bars facing the men's pen and were watching us with expressions ranging from mild interest to stark terror.

Quintilian turned to her. "You understand him?" he asked. "What's your name?"

"I'm Ambrollia," she said. "He works for me in the kitchen. I've been understanding him for fourteen years."

"Well, Ambrollia, I'm going to ask him some questions," Quintilian said. "You tell me what he says."

She looked at him suspiciously, and then shrugged. "It can't get us in any worse trouble," she said. "You go ahead."

Quintilian began questioning Prusias, and Prusias grunted his replies. Ambrollia listened to the grunts and translated them for us. While this was going on a man built like two gladiators stuffed inside each other brought in a bucket of vinegar and some reasonably clean rags, and Quintilian put the boy to cleansing Prusias' wounds. If the vinegar stung, Prusias didn't seem to notice. I guess he was beyond such petty pain.

Prusias claimed that he had brought his master the cup of watered lemon juice as usual, picking up the tray from a serving area where it had been left for him and bringing it right to the study. The honorable Strabo had been alive when Prusias entered, and was still alive when he left. He had no idea how anyone could have sneaked in to stab his master and had seen no one loitering near the study. The other slaves backed him up on this: those who had been around that day saw no one near the study, and none of them knew of any secret or subtle means to enter the building without being seen. Prusias said that he had never seen the knife before, and had no idea where it came from. The other slaves agreed.

After about an hour of this we left the slave pens and commenced a forced march across town to the Villa Strabo. It took the better part of an hour, but Quintilian didn't seem tired in the slightest when we arrived. When he's working on a problem, he notices neither hunger nor fatigue. We rounded the corner to the front of the villa and I saw a line of men stretching along the wall on both sides of the door. Among them were freedmen, citizens, and possibly even a few equestrians, judging by their garb. Some sat on the ground; some leaned against the wall; some just stood wringing their hands and looking sorrowful. Several clusters of them were engaged in what seemed to be heated conversation, with much arm waving and head shaking, nodding and thrusting forward. I sank gratefully to the ground while Quintilian knocked on the door. It was opened shortly by an older, full-stomached slave wearing imperial livery, and I pulled myself to my feet and stood in my accustomed place in Quintilian's shadow.

"Master Quintilian," said the doorman, after looking my master over. "Please come in."

Quintilian peered at him. "Thromax, isn't it? From the palace."

Thromax nodded. "The emperor sent a mob of us over to handle things until the—you know—gets straightened out." He shook his head sadly. "A horrible thing. When a slave kills his master it's bad for slaves everywhere."

Quintilian patted him on the shoulder. "You don't have to worry about that," he said. "Your master is, essentially, the state."

"True, Master Quintilian," Thromax said. "I am lucky. My life is better than that of many people, and not all of them slaves."

"Wisely said," agreed Quintilian. "The contented man is the one who can accept what the gods offer, knowing that wealth and poverty, happiness and misery, are just different spokes on the ever-turning wheel of life."

"Easy to say if yours are the golden spokes," Thromax commented.

"It is not too difficult to be a Stoic if you don't have much to be stoical about, that is so," Quintilian agreed, smiling. He gestured toward the patient line of men outside the wall. "Who are these men?"

"They are clients of the deceased Cassius Strabo," Thromax said. "There are at least thirty of them. It must be quite distressing for a client when his patron dies. Has he been left anything in the will? Will the son-and-heir take on his father's clients, or has he his own crowd of idlers and sycophants to take care of?" He stepped aside and waved us in—a regal gesture. "I believe the undertakers are finished preparing the body, if you wish to say good-bye to your old friend."

"I shall do that," Quintilian said, letting Thromax take his wool cloak. He turned to me. "Scribbler, go outside and rest. Do it near one of those groups of men and listen to what they are saying. They are certainly discussing the import of the events inside, and may well be a mirror of what the Roman public is thinking. Come to me by and by, when you have a sense of their emotions and desires."

I touched my finger to my forehead in an Oriental gesture of obedience and went back outside. Tossing my sack of wax tablets on the ground, I resumed my slumping position against the wall of the villa, but this time closer to the nearest knot of gesticulating men. They continued their gesticulation, taking no notice of me.

I remained where I was, as my master had bidden, until I had a sense of the feelings of these men. It didn't take very long. "Damn slaves should all be tied to posts and left to die," said a thin, sharp-chinned man with evident satisfaction. "Every last one of them. A long line of posts stretching east along the Via Appia, right outside the city."

A fat man in a faded blue tunic raised his hands, palms outward, in mock horror. He had a red face and close-set eyes above puffy cheeks. "You mean crucify them?" he asked shrilly. "Punish some four hundred slaves, women and children too, for the act of one obviously demented servant?" He shook his head. "What a waste! That's two or three thousand denarii worth of merchandise just slaughtered. And who's to pay for the crucifixions, I ask you?"

"Would you rather be murdered in your bed?" demanded the first man.

The two or three others in the group nodded their agreement, and one of them murmured, "Quite right!"

I rose and wandered down the line to listen to some of the other conversations, and it was all like that. One man had the temerity to say, "It doesn't seem fair somehow, that all those slaves should die, when they had nothing to do with the unfortunate murder." He was shouted down. Another moaned, "With the honorable Strabo dead, where am I to get the twenty denarii for my daughter's wedding? What a foul trick of the goddess Vesta to play on a humble man!" There was general sympathy for his plight, but I somehow felt that it was less than sincere.

I went inside and walked back to the peristylium, the large interior courtyard, to rejoin my master, who was just coming from viewing his old friend's body in what was usually the formal dining room, and related what I had heard.

"As I suspected," he said. "Sentiment is against us. And the people are becoming so inured to the sight of death by the gladiator games that the crucifying of four hundred slaves will merely seem one more spectacle for them to enjoy."

There were people standing around in small groups in the courtyard talking quietly, as one does in the presence of the dead.

Quintilian approached a small group of women sitting around a stone table and bowed to a strikingly handsome middle-aged lady. "Madam Melissina," he said.

"Master Quintilian." She extended her hand. "Last time we met was under happier circumstances."

"I grieve along with you, madam," Quintilian told her. "Your husband was a good friend, an upright and honorable man, and a true Roman."

She bent her head slightly in agreement and thanks. "My son has left to bring blankets and food to the slave pens. He told me you are going to see what you can do for us."

"Of course I will," Quintilian said. He studied her face intently. "What is it," he asked, "that you think should be done?"

She thought about it for a minute. "Can you show that Prusias did not do this thing?" she asked. "For I cannot believe that he did. He has been with us since my husband was governor in Bithynia, and is one of our most trusted household slaves." She put her hand on his arm. "Barring that, can you somehow save the four hundred innocents?"

"I will do what I can, madam. It is a mark of his quality of mind that your son Marius is able to consider such things at this time."

"Yes, Marius," she said. "My poor son. This may kill him. If you do not succeed—it may kill him."

"Madam?"

"Marius is—how to put this—enamored of a young slave girl." Madam Melissina rose and, taking Quintilian by the elbow, led him to a bench where they both sat down. "Do you understand?"

"I'm not sure. One of the household slaves is his mistress? He didn't mention this."

"She is not his mistress," Madam Melissina said. "Edissa is, as far as I know, still a virgin."

"Edissa?" Quintilian asked. "Young, blonde, very comely?"

"That is she."

"Ah!" Quintilian said. "I saw her at the slave pens. I can well understand your son's infatuation."

Madam Melissina rested her palms on her knees. "Edissa is seventeen, very pretty, very sweet. She was sold into slavery by her parents when she was eleven. My sister Prunella bought her from a slave dealer after verifying that she was, ah, *intacta*. Slave dealers are not a trustworthy group. Edissa has been Prunella's personal maid for the past six years."

"So she wasn't really the procurator's property?"

Madam Melissina sighed. "Unfortunately, my husband bought all of Prunella's property from her when she moved in with us a little over a year ago, after the death of her husband. A grove of fig trees that have ceased to bear figs, a house unfit to live in, and six slaves. It was a polite way of giving her some money, since she had none of her own. But I fear it was unlucky for Edissa."

"And Marius?"

"Has been mooning over the girl since Prunella moved in."

"But he hasn't done anything to, ah, formalize the relationship? Did his father disapprove?"

"Cassius knew nothing about it. My son suffers from a strange mixture of rectitude and desire. He wants the girl, but he wants her to come to him willingly."

"It seems reasonable," Quintilian said, "that if given the choice between being your sister's body servant and being your son's well-loved concubine—"

"Yes," Melissina agreed, "but would it be love? Would the girl really love him, or just be taking the best of several unpalatable choices? If she were truly free to do as she chose, would she choose him? These are the questions that plague my son."

Quintilian shook his head. "How can one ever know the workings of another's mind?" he asked. "Your son is chasing the impossible. And if he were to free her, and then woo her, might she not come to him out of gratitude or pity, rather than love?"

Melissina took his hand. "We do not ask you to solve that problem, my dear Marcus," she said. "Only to spare her life—and that of the others."

"We could devise something," Quintilian said thoughtfully. "The argument might be made that your sister never truly included Edissa in the sale. She has, I assume, remained Prunella's servant?"

"Yes," Melissina said. "But I'm afraid you'll have to devise something better than that."

"I will?"

"Marius could not live with himself if he rescued Edissa but allowed all the others to be put to death."

"It is not, after all, a question of allowing," Quintilian said gently. "If a ship is wrecked and fifty drown, but you manage to save one, do you berate yourself for not saving the others, or are you happy that you saved one?"

"If you're my son," Melissina told him, "you do your best to save them all—even if it means imposing on your friendship with the best lawyer in Rome—and hate yourself for caring more about one of them than all the rest."

"Isn't he afraid that, should we succeed in saving this girl, she'll be grateful?"

"Probably," Melissina said. "But that's tomorrow's problem."

"So it is," Quintilian agreed. He pushed himself to his feet. "I would like to speak to those who were out here when your husband's body was found," he said. "And examine the room he was in."

"Of course," Melissina said. "I was in my workshop, but my sister and her daughter, Lucasta, were here in the courtyard the whole time."

"Workshop?" Quintilian raised an eyebrow. *I must practice doing that, it can convey a variety of emotions. This time it was polite inquiry.*

"That's right, you didn't know," Melissina said. "I've taken up sculpture in clay. The busts of my friends who are good enough to pose for me. I'm not very good, but I've only been doing it for a couple of months. At any rate, the workshop is quite around the other side of the villa, by the far wall. Not that there was anything I could have done had I been closer." She reached her hand to her mouth, suppressing some emotion that a Roman matron shouldn't show. "He was a good man, Marcus.

Kind and generous to all around him. Honest and honorable. You know that."

"I do," Quintilian agreed.

"Come, speak to Prunella," she said, and led him back to the group of women.

Prunella was a younger and slenderer version of her sister Melissina. "My daughter Lucasta and I were here all that afternoon," she told Quintilian. "On that very bench," she pointed, "under that very tree. I'm teaching Lucasta Greek. Several of the slaves speak Greek, but their grammar is so bad I thought I'd better teach her myself. Whatever happened we must have seen, and yet we saw nothing unusual, nothing noteworthy—nothing."

"Can you describe the events of that afternoon for me?" Quintilian asked, dropping into the seat beside her.

"As I said, nothing unusual happened—until dear Cassius' body was found."

Quintilian nodded. "Describe for me," he said, "the usual. Relate the events, however mundane, as they occurred."

"Very well," Prunella agreed. "Where shall I start?"

"When did you arrive under that tree?"

Prunella closed her eyes and pressed her thumb to her chin thoughtfully. "Shortly after lunch," she said.

"Was the procurator in his study then?"

"No," she said. "He and the senator came out with us, as a matter of fact."

"Senator Veccus?"

"That's the one."

"I thought he found Cassius' body."

"Oh, he did. That was much later. Cassius went into his study, and Senator Veccus went off with his helmet."

"His helmet?"

Prunella nodded. "One of those centurions' helmets with the plume on it. The two of them—Cassius and Senator Veccus—had been in a deep discussion over various aspects of it: the height of the crest, the width of the ear things—that sort of thing—all through lunch." She waved her hands with a dismissive "boys will be boys" air as she added, "They seemed to think it was important."

"Where did Veccus go?"

"As a matter of fact he came back to see me," Madam Melissina said. "In my workshop. He spent some time admiring my work. Rather more than it deserved, I thought. I think he wanted something from my husband and believed that my influence might be useful."

"He came back after a while," Prunella said, "and sat over there, under that awning by the kitchen, and drank watered wine. He was fiddling with that helmet and occasionally pacing back and forth, as though trying to work something out in his head."

"And all this time nobody came near the study?"

"Only Prusias. He picked up the tray from the table by the kitchen where the undercook had left it and took it in to his master. It was understood that nobody was to disturb Cassius while he was in his study."

"You are sure you would have seen anyone?" Quintilian asked. "You were not, perhaps, concentrating too strongly on your lessons? Greek can be very demanding."

"I would have made use of the presence of anyone else," Prunella said. "I would have said 'Look at that young boy slave going over to the study of your Uncle Cassius.'" And she might have replied, 'He is tall for such a young man.' We were always looking for simple things to discuss in Greek, or perhaps I should say things to discuss with a simple vocabulary."

"And you had no occasion to say any such thing?"

"None between the time Prusias brought the watered lemon juice and Senator Veccus found the procurator dead."

"Which was about how long?"

"Perhaps two hours."

"How did the senator find the body?"

"He said he had solved some problem with the—strap—flap?—on the helmet and he wanted to tell the procurator. He went to knock on the door, and got no answer. So he looked in at the window. I heard him cry, 'By the gods—Procurator Strabo has been stabbed!' and then push open the door. We all rushed after him, and there poor Cassius was, facedown on the desk, dead of a knife thrust." She bit her knuckle. "It was horrible."

"Thank you, madam," Quintilian said. He rose. "I would like to look at the study now."

"If you must...," said Melissina, rising to her feet with difficulty, as though a heavy weight were pressing her down. "I will—"

"No need," Quintilian said gently. "Sit. Let your friends take some of the burden from you. I can manage." He turned to me. "Come," he said.

Veni, vidi, I watched as Quintilian peered at the desk where poor Strabo had been killed, knocked at the plaster walls to make sure they were solid, and generally examined everything there was to be seen. "Strabo must have been sitting here," he said, sitting on the canvas camp chair before the desk. "And he fell forward thus." Quintilian collapsed suddenly onto the desk, his head among the papyri littering the desk.

"Yes, Master," I said. "So it would seem."

Quintilian sat up and looked around him. "How odd," he said.

"Yes, Master," I said.

"You see it then?"

I looked but saw not. "No, Master," I said.

"The floor," he said. "The blood."

There were dried patches of blood on the floor by the desk. I looked at them. They looked like dried patches of blood. "The blood?" I asked.

"There is so little blood," he said. "And it's all on the floor by the desk here; none on the wall, or farther along the floor. A very polite and orderly pool of blood, it would seem."

"If you say so, Master Quintilian," I said.

"I do." He rose and looked around. "Here," he said, handing me a brass rule.

"What's this?"

"Your knife. You're to play Prusias. Now, you've just come in here with a tray"—he pulled a large copper plate from a shelf and handed it to me—"and you have to put it on the edge of the desk and then stab me with the knife. Where are you going to keep the knife?"

I balanced the tray in one hand and held the knife in the other. "Like this?"

"No. Remember, you have to cross the courtyard without anyone seeing the knife."

"Oh." I thought for a moment and then put the pseudo-knife flat under the tray. "Here."

"Possibly," Quintilian allowed. "But probably not. Remember, several of the people in the courtyard are sitting down. They might see the knife if you hold it under the tray."

"That's so," I agreed. After another moment's thought I put the plate down and fastened the brass rule under my tunic, holding it in place by tightening my belt.

"That will do," Quintilian agreed. "Now, come in with the tray, put it down, and attack me." He sat back down in the chair and turned to the desk, picking up one of the papyri to read.

I picked up the plate and went to the door, then turned around and walked the three steps back to the desk, put down the tray, and pulled the knife from inside my tunic. The side of the rule scraped my rib as I pulled it, and I was glad it wasn't the real knife.

Quintilian turned to me in mock horror and breathed, "Prusias, old faithful retainer, what are you doing?"

"Org, org!" I said, and stabbed at him.

He rose from the chair and grabbed my arm, holding it easily in place even as I twisted to break free. "This won't work," he said, releasing my arm and sitting back down.

"Perhaps Prusias was stronger than I," I suggested, "or Procurator Strabo weaker than you."

"Perhaps," he said. "But still..."

A great clamor arose from outside, and I went to the door. "The emperor is here," I said.

"Vespasian?" Quintilian stood up and straightened his toga. A double squad of the Praetorian Guard had come into the courtyard and filed around the two sides. Then they turned and faced in, with much stamping of feet and slapping of arms, and stood at attention. Vespasian was already there, going up to the widow Strabo and taking her hand. Senator Veccus had arrived with the emperor, and was standing in the far doorway.

"Come," Quintilian said. He walked out and crossed the courtyard. I followed behind.

"Fabius Quintilianus!" Vespasian called as we approached. "Come to me, my old friend."

"Greetings, General!" Quintilian said. Vespasian preferred the title of "General" in private, and from those close to him. His old legionaries used it as a matter of course.

"I hear you've been examining some slaves at the pens, and in my name," Vespasian said, looking stern.

"Indeed," Quintilian replied. "For is not the name of Vespasian synonymous with the name of justice?"

Vespasian laughed. "Good response. How can I gainsay that? I told Senator Veccus when he complained about your interfering with the slaves that I knew nothing about it, but that anything Marcus Fabius Quintilianus did in my name was done with my approval whether I knew about it or not."

"Thank you, Caesar," said Quintilian, nodding deeply, but not quite bowing.

Vespasian reached out and held Quintilian's upper arm. "There are few men that I can say that of," he said. "And I am pleased that you are one of them." He released the arm. "Now, what have you gotten me into? I can't really afford a fight with the Senate at this time."

Senator Veccus had been approaching as they spoke, and Quintilian now turned to face him. "No fight," he told the emperor, "and no mass execution of slaves either."

"The Senate will insist," said Vespasian.

"The Senate will insist on the murderer being punished," Quintilian said. "But the murderer was not a slave named Prusias, but a senator named Veccus."

Senator Veccus stopped. "What nonsense is this?" he cried, his voice perhaps a bit higher than he intended. "You forget, I found the body. The procurator was already dead when I entered the room."

"Indeed he was," Quintilian agreed. "Because you had poisoned him two hours before."

"I? I had what?"

"You were sitting there"—my master pointed to the seat by the kitchen—"and occasionally rising and pacing back and forth." Quintilian waved his hand back and forth. "Ample opportunity for you to drop some poison into the watered lemon juice before Prusias picked it up."

"But," objected Vespasian, "the honorable Strabo was stabbed."

"After his death, Caesar," Quintilian said. "There was far too little blood, and it was far too contained to have been shed while Strabo was alive. Veccus came to the window, cried out that Strabo had been stabbed, and then rushed in and did the job himself with a knife he had concealed under his toga. Since he had apparently found the honorable Strabo dead while he was still outside, no one would suspect him of having done it. And, since Strabo was stabbed, no one would suspect poison."

"But why bother?" asked Vespasian.

"Yes," Veccus inserted, "why bother?"

"To divert attention from the fact that only two people could have poisoned the watered lemon juice," Quintilian explained. "Prusias the slave, or Veccus the senator. And, as everyone has said, Prusias had no reason."

"And my reason?" Veccus demanded.

"I imagine it has something to do with that helmet you were playing with," Quintilian said. "Did the honorable Strabo find that you've been sending faulty helmets to the legions? We'll find out soon enough."

"Bah!" Veccus said. "I will listen to this nonsense no longer!" He wheeled about and stalked off toward the interior of the villa. No move was made to stop him. Where could he hide?

"Faulty equipment to the troops?" Vespasian grimaced. "The man has dishonored the Senate and the people of Rome."

I noted that the emperor had wholly accepted the truth of Quintilian's notices. Such is the power of effective oratory.

"I will order the release of the slaves at once," Vespasian

said, "and bring charges against Senator Veccus. Will you prosecute?"

"If you would have it so," Quintilian replied.

There was a small commotion at the door to the house, and an imperial runner entered the courtyard and passed a rolled message to the centurion of the guard. He read it and then hastened over to Vespasian. "General!" he said, holding the message out.

Vespasian took it and read it. Then he passed it over to my master. "Too late," he said.

Over Quintilian's shoulder I read: "The slave Prusias from the household of the honorable Cassius Strabo has died of wounds inflicted under torture. The aedile Lepidus says it wasn't his fault."

"Too late," Quintilian agreed.

"The unnecessary death of an innocent man, even a slave, is a stain on the cloak of Roman justice," Emperor Vespasian said.

"I couldn't have said it better," said Quintilian.

"We will add that to the charge against Veccus." Vespasian turned to his centurion. "Take the senator into custody," he said.

Madam Melissina, who was standing with us, dropped to her knees and pressed her forehead against the emperor's hand. "Thank you, noble Caesar," she said.

Vespasian looked embarrassed and pulled her to her feet. "Please," he said. "You are the wife of my old and valued friend. Call me 'General.'"

"Of course, General," she replied. "But I do thank you. And you, Master Quintilian, for unraveling this knot and bringing the possibility of happiness into my son's life."

Vespasian looked faintly puzzled. "What's this?" he asked.

"I'll explain later," Quintilian told him. "For now..."

Two of the Praetorian Guard clattered into the courtyard. "General," the first called. "Senator Veccus has taken his own life."

"In the dining room," said the other. "With a knife."

"There's blood all over the place," added the first.

So the total was three dead. Was it the shrikes? Susannah maintains it was. Quintilian says that's superstitious nonsense. I reserve judgment. I'm not sure I believe, but as my old nurse used to say: *"Nuncus rebus mangus poppis; Halifratus satum flebis."*

One of an ongoing series featuring a young Abraham Van Helsing, my own contribution is another tale of Victorian adventure, in which historical figures, fictional characters, and creatures from myth collide in the jungles of nineteenth-century Sarawak.

Prowl Unceasing
by Chris Roberson

From the Logbook of Captain Dakkar
(translated from the Hindi)
We had just passed the Strait of Malacca, bound for the South Pacific, when we were beset by a fierce storm out of the northeast. Our humble craft, the dhow we have christened *Avenger*, is sturdy, but such a storm was beyond even her strengths, and after consulting with the twenty men of my crew, we decided to find some safe harbor and weather the storm.

I was reluctant to go to shore, eager to reach the open sea and freedom, but all twenty are my countrymen, and like me they have left India and their previous lives behind. They have followed me down from the mountains of Bundelkhand, and I will not lead them needlessly into danger's way. There is danger enough in the path before us, and more still in our wake, to seek more than our fair share.

I steered our course to the south and east, choosing to land in Borneo rather than the Malaysian peninsula, since the latter is controlled by the British, who still have a price on my head, as well as on the heads of my crewmen. I'd intended to come ashore in the Sultanate of Brunei, hoping that mention of my uncle's name might earn us favorable treatment, but the winds blew us too far to the south, and we made landfall along the Sarawak River, in the small nation of the same name. We reached the port and capital, and shortly found ourselves guests in the home of the White Raja.

Abraham Van Helsing's Journal
(translated from the Dutch)
10 Feb, 1861. Kuching—Leaving Tianjin and China behind me,
I secured transport on a packet boat bound for India, and from
thence around the Cape to Holland and home. After a week's
sailing on the rough waters of the South China Sea, we were
caught by a squall out of the northeast. The lascars among the
ship's crew made motions with their hands, as though warding
away foul spirits, and whispered the word *mausim*. I recognized
it by its cognate in my native Dutch: monsoon. The captain of
the packet boat called his crew to their stations, sending them
scrambling to secure the rigging and man the bilge pumps, and
ordered the helm to alter course to the south and west. Only
bare miles ahead of the storm, we made landfall on the shores of
the island of Borneo and followed a dank, snaking river fifteen
miles to the tiny port village of Kuching.

The storm was upon us as we disembarked at the rough dock,
dark as midnight with the winds whipping the stinging rain at us:
the captain, myself, and the dozen or so men of the crew. We
were met on the dock by a Malay soldier with a carbine slung
over his shoulder, his uniform plastered to his skin by the lashing rains. Leaning into the heavy winds, he motioned for us to
follow, and raced away across the road, mud slicked and deeply
rutted.

We made our winding way through the ramshackle village,
little more than a collection of rough huts assembled around
dirt roads, pigs and goats and dogs wandering freely, trying to
find shelter against the elements. We came at last to an immense
structure, a grand European-style mansion overlooking the
crocodile-infested waters of the river. The Malay soldier ushered
us into the grand foyer, and we were received by our host, the
raja of the province.

To my considerable surprise, the local ruler turned out to be
a British gentleman named Sir James Brooke, who spoke like
a career army officer and dressed like a London banker. The
Raja Brooke welcomed me to his country of Sarawak personally
and offered me the hospitality of his home, which I thankfully

accepted. The packet boat's captain and its crew were taken to bunk with the raja's personal guard, and I was directed into the smoking room, where the other guests of the house were waiting for the evening meal to be set.

Among the other guests was Sir James' nephew, Charles Brooke, who seemed in every respect a younger version of his uncle, and an Indian gentleman who sat quietly by a raging fire. Where the raja was a stout man of his early fifties, perhaps, with a barrel chest and muttonchop whiskers that ran the length of his jaw line, Charles Brooke was nearer my own age, in his early thirties, clean-shaven and with a shock of dark hair. Like his uncle, he dressed like a businessman and comported himself like a professional soldier. Fitting, then, that Charles was introduced to me as a soldier in his uncle's employ, leader of the Sarawak Regiment.

The Indian gentleman, apparently, was another traveler caught by the sudden storm with his ship and crew. He was introduced to me as a Mr. Tipu, and when I asked after his profession, as a social nicety, he curtly replied that he was "No one of consequence." Tipu spoke English as fluently as our British hosts, with an accent that sounded an odd mélange of any number of European tongues, suggesting he was well traveled and fluently multilingual. His age was difficult to judge, and could be anywhere between thirty-five and fifty years. He was tall and slim, with a wide forehead, a straight nose, and a firm mouth, with surprisingly pale skin for someone native to the Indian subcontinent.

In all, the large house and the atmosphere within, including the attitude and manner of the occupants, seemed quite out of place in the midst of a southeast Asian island. There was something disquieting about coming through storm, jungle, and squalor and finding oneself in the midst of cultured luxury. It was almost as if some immense force had scooped up an English country estate, transported it halfway round the globe, and deposited it without warning in the midst of an Edenic, untamed wilderness.

I was eager to ask my host Sir James how he came to such

a stand, and how the title of raja had fallen to him, but before I could frame the question in my rough English, a Malay servant appeared at a side door and called us to the evening meal. Dinner was served.

From the Logbook of Captain Dakkar (continued)
The storm raged outside, while within the decadent splendor of the mansion the White Raja entertained his guests. There was a Dutchman, a physician named Van Helsing, passenger on another ship forced to port by the storm. I had introduced myself on our arrival with a false name, fearing that the White Raja or his corpulent nephew, both British subjects, might recognize my own and move to claim the bounty. I probably needn't have worried, as both seemed so caught in self-adoration that they scarcely noticed I was present.

My countrymen, at the raja's insistence, were sent away, to bunk and dine with his Malay servants. Besides the White Raja and his nephew, all whom we encountered within the borders of Kuching were Malay, all bought and paid for with the raja's coin. I saw the contempt with which so many looked upon their master, to which he was blind.

Over dinner, the Dutchman asked the White Raja how a British gentleman came to be ruler of a Malaysian state. Puffed like a peacock, the White Raja related his story as though it were something in which to take pride, and not a shameful tale of betrayal and deceit.

The White Raja explained that he was the son of a colonial bureaucrat, born in Secrore, near Benares in the north of India. I rankled at the way Hindi names fit in his mouth, but kept silent, observing. I did not mention that Benares was not far from my home in Bundelkhand, where I myself was born. The White Raja is only a scarce handful of years my senior, and we must have been children there together at the same time. But while he lived across the border in the British-held territory, I was living free in the independent state of Bundelkhand, in my father's palace. By the time my home fell to British rule, my father had sent me away to study in Europe, and I did not return until I was a grown man, to raise a family of my own.

The White Raja went on to talk about his schooner, which he described in the affectionate tone most men use to describe their first love. He had bought it with the inheritance left him by his father's death. The ship he'd named the *Royalist*, which seems to me perfectly fitting. It was a 140-ton ship with a crew of twenty. After training up his crew, they'd sailed from the Thames to India, and from there to the Strait of Malacca, looking for work. He hired his ship and crew out to the sultan of Brunei, putting down insurgents in the province of Sarawak. The sultan had rewarded him by naming him raja of the province, and once the new-minted raja had solidified his position in the region, he'd ejected all of those loyal to the sultan and declared Sarawak an independent nation. He immediately opened diplomatic and trade relations with the British, and began the process of taming the interior jungles, and expanding the borders of his nation, largely at the expense of Brunei.

I held my tongue, but marveled inwardly that he could paint a story of calumny in such self-congratulatory hues. A liar and a cheat, a mercenary for hire, whom circumstance and a fortunate birth had placed in a position of temporal power. A waste of power and potential, on a petty dictator.

On the death of my father, at the hands of British troops, my only inheritance was hatred. Had I the raja's resources, and my own crew of twenty, had I such a ship instead of a barely seaworthy dhow, I would not be fleeing to the far reaches of the South Pacific, but would turn and stand. If only I had such a ship, things would be other than they are.

Abraham Van Helsing's Journal,
10 Feb. Later.—After dinner, over cigars and drinks in the smoking room, Sir James explained the source of his considerable wealth, which allows him to live in some relative luxury. His primary income stems from the franchise fees he receives in return for the coal mining and lumber concessions, and the fees

he charges the British crown to make use of his port.

I asked whether the British resent the port fees, which sounded considerably steep to my admittedly layman's ears. Sir James laughed.

"Do they object, sir?" he repeated, his tone one of churlish amusement. "Would the queen have knighted me if she objected?" He paused, his broad chest puffed up with pride. "I was created KCB more than ten years ago, and wear the title with pride. I was once a Confidential Agent of Her Majesty's government, I'll have you know, and Victoria thanked me personally for my efforts to civilize the region, calling me by name and referring to me as a friend of the crown."

Sir James paused, lingering over his port, his cigar burning slowly between his thick fingers. A scowl crossed his face, and he continued.

"There are, of course, those who object to me and mine. Elements in Parliament, dandies and weak-sisters who claim I've overstepped my bounds, abused the government's trust. That I've corrupted the natives and despoiled the region for my own profit." He took a long draw of the cigar, and beamed proudly as a wreath of smoke crowned his head. "But I've withstood every commission and inquiry, and the notoriety has only served to drive up the sale of a collection of my private letters. I've become a household name in England, and I've made a tidy profit from book royalties, besides. In fact"—Sir James motioned with his cigar to the writing table at the far side of the room, piled high with papers and ledgers—"inspired by the success of my printed letters, I'm currently at work on a longer volume, to be entitled 'Life in the Forests of the Far East.' And if there were still any doubt in your minds as to the view of the British crown to my efforts and quality, you should know I've been appointed governor of the British colony of Labuan, off the shores of Sarawak." He paused, taking a sip of his port. "Though often," he added with a wry chuckle, "I serve as governor in absentia. My annual stipend is paid whether I reside within the borders of Labuan or not, so the Ministry seems not to mind. Think of it. For the son of a desk clerk in the civil service, who ran away from school at the age of fourteen, to become governor of a colony, raja of an independent nation, and principal shareholder in a family commercial interest in shipping, coal, and lumber that has shown a profit for every year of operation. Quite an achievement, I should think."

The nephew, Charles, came roaring to his uncle's support, with an unctuous display the likes of which I'd rarely seen.

"You are the marvel of the age, Sir James," Charles said, raising his glass in salute. "School children in centuries to come will know your name, and study your deeds in awe."

Charles looked to me and Tipu, expectantly, evidently anticipating that we would add our voices to this chorus of praise. A silent look passed between the Indian gentleman and myself, and we both limply raised our glasses in response, our lips sealed. Even this slight display, though, left an ill taste in my mouth, seeming more than a touch hypocritical. We were, though, at the mercy of Sir James, in more ways than were immediately obvious, and if the cost of our meals and the shelter from the storm was to stroke his already inflated ego by seconding a few congratulatory toasts, it made little difference to me.

Thankfully, though, the topic quickly turned from Sir James' many accomplishments to other topics, and our glasses were allowed to remain where they were for the rest of the evening, if we so chose.

As the evening wore on, Tipu rose from his chair and paced back and forth before the fireplace, his hands clasped behind his back, his eyes taking in the trophies and portraits along the mantel in turn.

"Sir James," the Indian gentleman at length asked, his gaze lingering on the head of a tiger, stuffed and mounted on the wall, "was this specimen killed here in Sarawak? It seems considerably... smaller than the tigers I encountered in the Indian highlands."

The raja sipped his port, and shook his head.

"No, that is a Bengal, bagged across the water in Sumatra some summers ago," he answered. "There isn't much in the way of sport to be had here in Borneo, more's the pity... unless you account for the headhunters, which always give us a run for our money, I'll admit." A fond memory flitted across the raja's face, and he paused before continuing. "No, there are no more tigers in Borneo, I'm afraid. The last tiger on the island died off generations ago, hunted to extinction by these lackwit savages."

At this last, I noted that the Indian gentleman's expression darkened, and his eyes narrowed. When Tipu's hands tightened into fists at his sides, his gaze burning at our host, I hastened to change the subject, hoping to avoid unpleasantness.

"No tigers, you say?" I asked, diverting the attention of the raja and his nephew away from their fuming guest, hoping they'd taken no notice of his obvious anger.

"No, none," the typically reticent Charles answered. "As Uncle always says, he's been on the island for decades, and seen neither trace nor spore of a tiger."

"Well," Sir James said broadly, with a wry smile painted across his face, "there are always the weretigers to consider."

Charles made a show of laughing heartily at this, which the raja received proudly. Neither Tipu nor I responded, me wearing a quizzical expression, he one of exasperation. Sir James glanced my way, and read the confusion written across face.

"Well, now," he explained, "as Charles rightfully says, in my many forays into the interior, pursuing headhunters and insurrectionists, I've never seen a tiger, nor come across tiger spore. Still, some of the superstitious locals believe that weretigers exist. Sorcerers, who pay dearly to dress in the skin of the maneater. Others hold that the weretigers are men inhabited by the spirits of tigers they have slain, or else the dead returned to haunt the living. Some even believe that there are races of tiger people in the deep forests, able to change their forms from tiger to man and back again. Those who believe so say that in the city of the tigers, the houses are built of human bones."

Sir James left off talking, puffing on his dwindling cigar.

"Stuff and nonsense, if you ask me," Tipu answered, his arms crossed over his chest. "Superstitious nonsense, at that."

Sir James simply shrugged.

"Well, Mr. Tipu," he said with a wave of his hand, "these are simple, superstitious people, after all. Not of the highly developed level of the European, you must understand."

Tipu grinned darkly, his head inclined.

"Are Europeans really so highly developed, after all?" he asked.

Sir James looked at him as though it were self-evident, as though it was as much a matter of objective observation as to say the sun rises in the east, or objects fall to earth when dropped.

"Of course," the raja said.

"You are aware, of course, of Marco Polo," Tipu said, his gaze roaming the room, taking in each of us in turn. "Polo, in his accounts of his famous travels, wrote that there were cannibals with the heads of dogs on the Andaman Islands in the Indian Ocean. Marco Polo's accounts are studied as history in the finest universities and academies in Europe. Tell me, then, what does that say about the European mind and the matter of superstition?"

Before Sir James could answer, already glowering, I interrupted.

"I was trained as a man of science, myself," I began, "studying both medicine and the law, and always held that reason was the sole rule by which to measure the world. After recent experiences in China, though..." And here I paused, the memory of those events for the moment overtaking me. "After those events, I find myself reluctant to dismiss anything out of hand. Perhaps there are things that fall beyond the purview of science and rational understanding, but which still exist."

"And do these things, then," Tipu asked, "include tiger men and dog-headed cannibals? Is reality so elastic as to encompass such as these?"

I answered with a shrug, and said, "Who can say?"

The raja, for his part, was undeterred.

"It's all savage, pagan nonsense," he said, his voice rising. "I've been routing headhunters and pirates and thieves from the dark forests of Borneo for twenty years, and I've not yet seen anything that couldn't be explained away as a phantom of an overworked mind, or the product of fever. Let the unclothed natives believe what nonsense they like; civilized men should know better."

From the Logbook of Captain Dakkar (continued)
The White Raja and his nephew, having gorged themselves
and drunk their fill, excused themselves for the night, instructing one of their bought Malays to show us to our rooms. The
Dutchman and I both lingered in the smoking room, burning
our cigars down to ashes. I myself was savoring the silence, but
the Dutchman appeared somewhat ill at ease, and eager to make
small conversation. I think perhaps he had some fear of me, and
thought that he might define my limits by questions, and make
of me a comprehensible savage.

He asked whether I had any family, back home in my native
India, and if so how I stood being so far away from them. There
was a thread of pathos strung through his words, that I could
not fail to hear. I answered simply that my wife and family were
dead, and that I had no wish to discuss it further.

The Dutchman apologized profusely, his jaw set and his
hands beginning to tremble. His voice strained, he answered that
his wife and child were dead, as well.

In that case, I told him, he knew precisely how difficult it
was being far from them. I stubbed my cigar out, and took my
leave of him.

Abraham Van Helsing's Journal
11 Feb.—This morning, the storm still raging, Tipu and I had
coffee and breakfast with Sir James and his nephew. Before we
had finished, a Malay soldier appeared at the door, announcing a
visitor to the mansion. Sir James, impatiently, waved the soldier
to show him in.

The visitor was an old man named Harimau, a native of the
interior, ancient and bent. In his broken English, he begged the
raja for his assistance. In the high winds of the storm, the longhouse in his home village of Lawei had collapsed, killing many
of their people, but injuring many more. Their native medicine

man had done what he could, but the injuries were beyond his abilities. The natives had seen the raja's men survive far worse wounds in the years he'd spent conquering the surrounding territories, his doctors able to heal wounds that their strongest man would die from. Surely the wise raja would see fit to send one of his doctors to their aid.

"Would that I could," Sir James answered, feigning an apologetic tone, "but my physician is away at the moment, tending to one of my agents on the island of Labuan." He paused, and then waved his hand towards the door dismissively. "I hope that you will tender my regrets to the victims."

Outside the mansion walls, I could hear the storm winds raging, howling like a mad beast desperate to get inside. I had no desire to leave the shelter of the raja's mansion, much less to venture into an uninviting jungle prowling with headhunters and raiders, but my Hippocratic oath compelled me. I pushed my chair away from the breakfast table, dropping my napkin onto my plate.

"I will go," I said, "and offer what succor I can. I'll need assistance, though, if the injured are as numerous as you say."

I looked from the villager to the raja and his nephew, and asked whether they would accompany me. Their gaze shifting, both refused, citing pressing responsibilities keeping them from leaving the safety of the mansion.

I then turned my attention to Tipu.

"Well, Mr. Tipu, with your education, you'd no doubt make a much better nurse than any of the natives. What say you?"

The Indian gentlemen glanced at our host and his nephew, and then to the shuttered window, and then back to me. His voice peppered with reluctance, he answered.

"I will go."

I've returned to my room to gather the necessary instruments, and now wait for Tipu to join me in the foyer. Outside, the winds howl like a prowling predator, and the rafters shudder at their passing.

Captain Dakkar's Log (continued)
The White Raja reluctantly agreed to let the Dutchman and I leave the capital, but insisted on sending an armed guard along with us. Perhaps this was a sop to his feelings of guilt, so that he could stay safely within the confines of his home with a clear conscience, while others risked injury or even death for the sake of his subjects.

Our escort, Sergeant Arif, was a Malay in the Sarawak Regiment, under the command of the White Raja's nephew. He spoke some little English, and had been a soldier in Brooke's army for years. Even with Arif along to act as their protection, though, I insisted on fetching a brace of pistols from my luggage, slinging them from my belt. I have been through jungles many times before, in peace and in war, and rarely found that a firearm did not serve some ready use.

The Dutchman, reluctant to leave the safety and dry warmth of the White Raja's den, was at least motivated by purer drives to give aid to those in need. For myself, I agreed to the trip largely to get away from the White Raja and his insufferable nephew. They were everything I despise about the English, distilled into corpulent bodies. If I had stayed too much longer, I might have forgotten myself and killed one or both of them with my bare hands. It would have been satisfying, and justified, but with even my twenty countrymen at my side I doubt we could stand long against the amassed might and firepower of the Sarawak Regiment. Still, the thought was tempting.

Abraham Van Helsing's Journal
12 Feb.—It is early morning, on the second day of our journey, and Harimau is making the final preparations of our morning meal. We traveled hard yesterday, and slept rough in this rude shelter, and from what Harimau has said, we have another long day's journey ahead of us.

Despite the lashing winds and fierce rains, we made considerable headway yesterday. Harimau led our small company up the Sarawak River—myself, Tipu, and the Malay soldier whom

Sir James insisted we bring along. When we had gone some dozen miles, we turned to the south and headed away from the river, deep into the black jungle forests, the storm still raging around us.

The farther we traveled from Kuching and the mansion of Raja Brooke, the more relaxed Tipu seemed to become, until at last he seemed as even-tempered as any gentleman you might happen to encounter in a European social club. I chanced to ask him, when we took a brief respite in the shelter of a stand of trees, whence came this change in mood.

Tipu, casting a cautious glance at our military escort, ensuring he was out of earshot, quietly expressed his disgust at the ilk of the raja, whom he held as petty dictators who set themselves up as masters of weaker men. Tipu, though, held the balance of his hatred in reserve for the British, who supported Sir James, and whose practices as a nation were little different than his as an individual. It was the British national sport, Tipu said, to invade foreign lands and subjugate the natives, pillaging and taking whatever of value they could lay hands on.

I was surprised at the vehemence of his response, especially considering the veiled manner in which he had suggested his discontent while in the presence of the raja. He seemed to be, at least, a political animal, knowing when it was best to show his colors, and when best to hold his tongue.

"The time will come," Tipu said, at his most inflammatory, eyes flashing and mouth curled into a snarl, "when men will rise up against their oppressors in all lands, and reclaim liberty with their bare hands."

I was reminded of the Sepoy Revolt, the Indian Mutiny, which was concluded only three years ago. The natives had risen up against the British, and the British had handily pushed them back down again, at the cost of many lives on both sides. The memory of it was still fresh in the minds of any European who traveled abroad in colonized lands, myself being no exception.

"Am I right in assuming," I asked, "that you lost family in the recent troubles?"

A dark cloud passed over Tipu's rugged features.

"Just as there are no tigers in Borneo," Tipu answered in a low, intense voice, "if the English had there way there would be no free Hindus or Muslims or Sikhs in India. The Europeans would sleep easier abed at night if there were no free Malays or Dayaks or Hottentots or Tamils, no Gyptians or Bedouins or Aborigines who did not bend a knee to their colonial masters. The Americans proclaim the virtues of liberty and equality, but there too the first signs of rot are beginning to show; are the Navajo of the Western Desert really any better off than their cousins in China, casualties of Victoria's Opium War? Ask the African slave of the southern plantation how he feels about the noble aspiration of the Founding Fathers." Tipu spat into the mud at his feet, mingling with the splatters of rain reaching us through the canopy of tree limbs overhead. "No man is free until all men are free."

"What if all men are never free?" I asked, my voice as calming as I could pitch it.

"Then I must be no man."

From a few yards off, the Malay soldier watched us from beneath the brim of his hat, and I wondered just how much of Tipu's speech he had heard.

We traveled the rest of the day in relative silence, until we reached this rude shelter, and stopped for the night.

Captain Dakkar's Log (continued)

The four of us sheltered by night in a rude hut deep in the jungle, forced close together by the narrow walls. We ate a meager meal, prepared by our native guide, and sat listening to the rain pound against the ramshackle roof.

At length, Sergeant Arif began to speak. He had heard me earlier in the day explaining to the Dutchman the perils of imperialism, and the historical inevitability of oppressed men rising up against their masters. I'm sure my words found no purchase in the mind of the Dutchman, raised as he was in the heart of the festering disease itself, but what I said had reached the ears and mind of the Malay sergeant, as I'd hoped they would.

Responding to the notion of British oppression, and men rising up against them, Sergeant Arif began to tell us of the Tiger of Malaysia, a man whom legend holds had done precisely that. I say legend, since Arif had no proof of his claims, but I could see the sergeant believed every word of his story as though it had been imparted by the gods themselves.

This so-called Tiger, a man named Sandokan, had been the son of a rajah of a formerly independent Malaysian state. Ten years ago, Arif said, Sandokan had lost father, wife, and children when betrayed by the British governor of Labuan. Sandokan, in response, had raised a crew from among the native peoples of Malaysia, and had spent the ten years since sailing the sea lanes around the Straits of Malacca and the South China Sea. From his base on the island of Mompracem to the east of Borneo, he led his Tigers in successful raid after raid on the British and their allies, making them account for every Malaysian life lost to British hands, taking payment in blood and gold.

From his tone, which bordered on the worshipful, I perceived that Sergeant Arif, if allowed to choose, would rather be among the Tigers of Mompracem than in the White Raja's army, but he would not say as much outright, for fear of reprisal.

For my part, I found the story of Sandokan quite familiar. I mentioned to Arif that I'd had an uncle also known by the name of "Tiger," in far distant Mysore, who had brought the British to account, years past.

Strange noises issued from the dark jungle beyond the shelter walls, and Sergeant Arif shuddered, eyes wide. I asked how such a brave soldier could fear sounds in the night. Sergeant Arif fixed me with a stare.

Arif explained that he had served the White Raja for some years, and had seen his share of blood and death, and that there was little he feared in life. The Dayak headhunters of the interior, though, terrified him. As he spoke, he cast suspicious glances at the native guide, who seemed not to be listening. The headhunters, Arif explained, were strange people with stranger customs, who ate the flesh of men and preserved the heads of their victims as shrunken effigies.

Still, Sergeant Arif was of two minds. The Dayak had been enemies of his people for more generations than he had fingers and toes to count, but he couldn't help but feel some pity for them. The White Raja hunted the Dayak the way that other men hunt wild game, and no man, Arif said, should suffer that.

Abraham Van Helsing's Journal
12 Feb. Later.—Late evening, and we have just paused in our work for a quick rest and meal. It is dark here in the ruins of the longhouse, but I will try to record the rest of our journey to the village of Lawei in as legible a hand as I am able.

Leaving the shelter behind early this morning, we continued through the jungle, following a path only Harimau could negotiate. To my eyes, we were moving aimlessly through the underbrush, making no discernable progress, buffeted by heavy winds and pelted by merciless rains.

Round about midday, slugging through thick mud, a startled cry from the Malay soldier brought us to a halt. In a small clearing before us stood a tiger, the largest I had ever seen. I scarcely had time to register shock or fear before I was somewhat gratified to find that the overbearing raja had been proven wrong on this point, at least. In the face of danger, that at least provided me some small sense of satisfaction.

The tiger was dark, its fur a uniform black, and it seemed to have no tail. The Malay soldier remarked in his broken English that this was the first tiger he'd seen in his life, his eyes wide and showing white in the dim light. I happened to glance at our guide Harimau, and he was watching the Malay soldier, his attitude relaxed but watchful.

The Malay soldier fumbled with his carbine, bringing it to his shoulder. Harimau began to object, waving for him to lower his weapon, entreating both Tipu and myself to make the soldier stop. Before either of us could react, though, the soldier fired a round at the tiger, which seemed to hit it broadside. There came a loud thunder clap and flash of lightning that flickering through the towering trees, and in the next instant the tiger was gone, vanished back into the heavy jungle.

We continued on through the day, and as the afternoon wore on, the storm became little more than a strong headwind and a spitting drizzle. Harimau informed us we were nearing the village of Lawei. We broke through a heavy stand of trees, and came upon one of the strangest sights I've seen in some long while.

It was a structure like a small house, standing some seven feet tall and fourteen feet wide, atop four pillars in a small clearing. Within the structure were small alcoves or rooms, in which were arranged bleached bones. It was like a dollhouse made mausoleum.

I asked Harimau what the structure was, but he averted his eyes, and refused to speak of it. The Malay soldier, though, stepped forward and explained that he'd seen such before, when following Raja Brooke in his raids against the Dayak headhunters of the interior.

The people of the jungle, the Malay explained, believe that they have to bury their dead twice for their spirits to rest. Each of us has two souls, they contend, one which decomposes with the body, and one which lingers until the appropriate rites have been performed. Months or even years after the death of a family member, the jungle people exhume the body, clean off the skeleton, and place it in a specially constructed house called a *sandung,* constructed along the same lines as their longhouses but much smaller. Masked dancers ward off evil spirits, and priests chant and perform ritual services. As this is an expensive and time-consuming process, many times families will pool their resources, and perform these secondary funerals for many departed at once, sometimes hundreds. The *sandung*, then, can get as crowded as the houses of the living.

Tipu and I listened with interest to the Malay soldier's explanation while our guide Harimau stood uneasily to one side, shuffling his feet and motioning for us to continue. He was apparently uncomfortable sharing the details of his tribal customs with outsiders, and was eager for us to move on. In the interests of good relations, I made to follow him, and called for Tipu and the soldier to follow.

Tipu delayed, moving closer to the *sandung* house for a better look. Before the rest of us had gone more than a few yards, he hurried to catch up to us. When he reached us, I leaned close, and asked whether he'd seen anything of interest, pitching my voice low so as not to offend our guide.

"Only that the natives seem to be generous in their rites," Tipu answered. "Within the structure are the bones of men and beasts alike."

When I asked what sort of beasts, Tipu said he had been unable to tell, but they had been large, if nothing else.

Farther on, we stepped onto a more well-defined path, the first we'd seen deserving of the name since leaving Kuching. There were wooden statues of strange, fierce creatures lining the path, evidently as protection against evil spirits. Then we came over a slight rise, and entered the village proper. There was much work for us to do, a great deal of which remains to be done. I shall continue my account when next I'm able.

Captain Dakkar's Log (continued)
The old men and women of the village were mourning the coming death of their young man, sending up a keening wail that sounded familiar to my ears. The Dutchman rushed in, eager to assist, but when we came to the wounded man, he was already at death's door, bled white and still. There was a hole on either side of his chest, as though he'd been poked straight through. The Dutchman observed that this resembled in all respects a bullet wound, but the villagers insisted that was nonsense, and that the man had merely fallen on a branch. How, they asked, would he have been shot by a gun?

Leaving the wounded man and his mourners, our native guide brought us to the ruins of their longhouse, where they had gathered the injured. The sun had set, and the air had a sickly yellowish gray cast, amplified by the flickering shadows cast by the torches, which sputtered and spat in the still-drizzling rain. In the dim light, I could scarcely see to the far end of the longhouse, an immense structure built some six feet off the ground, twenty or thirty feet wide and some hundreds of feet long. In the middle distance, the roof of the longhouse had collapsed on itself, looking as though a giant foot had stepped on it. The wounded survivors had been gathered in the near end of the building, where the roof and walls were thankfully still solid.

The injured were many, numbering in the dozens. The Dutchman and I worked late into the night, setting bones, stitching up gashes, applying bandages and such, saving those we could. Sergeant Arif nodded off to sleep, his carbine across his knees, and the pair of us continued to work into the small hours of the morning.

Abraham Van Helsing's Journal
14 Feb.—I scarcely know where to begin relating the events of the day past. Is it my fate always to face uncanny dangers? My life was one of ordered reason not too long ago, and it seems in recent months as though I have emigrated to some other world, some demon-haunted plane where monsters prowl the night unceasingly. I had hoped I'd left this other world behind when quitting China, but it seems I have brought it along with me to these shores, the dark things pursuing still.

The morning following our arrival in the village of Lawei, we rose, sore to our bones. We had worked through the night, and finished our task, healing those we could, comforting those we could not. Harimau had led the three of us—Tipu, myself, and the Malay soldier—to a small hut near the edge of the village, and there we had bedded down for what was left of the night.

On rising, the Malay soldier was nowhere to be found. Worse, when we went abroad into the village, not a single soul was in sight. But for Tipu and myself, it seemed the entire community had been deserted. We made our way through the muddy streets of the village, calling for the soldier or for the villagers to come out of their hiding. Finally, we came to the entrance to the village, where the fierce wooden creatures stood guard. There, hung from a high tree, was the Malay soldier.

He was strung up by his hands and feet, lashed to braches, hanging facedown over the ground. His stomach was a red ruin, looking as though it had been ripped to pieces repeatedly by some sharp knife, or claws, and his carbine rifle was crammed down his throat like an apple in a suckling pig. He was bled white, dark blood caked around his wound and gathered in a pool in the mud beneath him.

Tipu and I were immediately on our guard. The storm had stopped in the night, and the sky had lightened as we'd made our circuit of the village. We now saw Lawei in the clear light of day, seeing it as though for the first time. The buildings all around us, the huts and the longhouses, the pillars and troughs, were all constructed of human bones rather than wood, lashed together in their thousands, a grim architecture.

My breathing ceased, and my heart threatened to pound its steady way out of my rib cage.

"We must go," I told Tipu, edging towards the jungle, my eyes on the dark places under the buildings, the shadows stretching out in the early-morning light. "Now!"

Tipu stood his ground, a look of deep curiosity on his face. He wanted to stay and get to the bottom of things. There was nothing, he was sure, that could not be explained.

I refused to listen. I grabbed him by the arm, and dragged him behind me as I hurried up the path into the darkened jungle.

Tipu resisted me initially, but as we stepped into the jungle, we heard throaty growls approaching from all sides, fierce rustlings in the leaves. I broke into a run, and Tipu followed behind, his hands drifting to the brace of pistols at his waist.

Captain Dakkar's Log (continued)
The tigers pursued us through the jungle. As we made our way through the heavy underbrush, branches and vines lashing us as we went, I made full use of my pistols, firing behind us and reloading, firing and reloading, again and again. Most of my shots, I am sure, were little more than sound and fury, but on at least two occasions I know they struck home, tigers lunging

from the shadows at us, only to fall back to earth with a lump of my lead in their flank or skull. In the end, though, there were simply too many of them, and we could do nothing but run, and hope for a miracle.

Our deliverance came from an unexpected source. Breaking through a line of trees, we came upon the corpulent nephew of the White Raja, marching forward at the head of a contingent of Malay soldiers. At the nephew's command, the soldiers quickly provided a protective ring around us, torches in hand, carbines directed out into the shadows. I could hear the rustlings in the darkness beyond the trees, and knew the tigers were there, planning their next move.

The nephew explained that the White Raja had thought better of sending guests into the interior with such a meager escort. The raja had insisted that the nephew divert his raiding party, which was to police the interior and harry headhunters, in pursuit of the Dutchman and myself instead. I cursed myself for being grateful for that brief moment for the White Raja's imperialist zeal, for otherwise I'd have been warming the belly of a tiger in very short order.

The Dutchman and I quickly explained to the nephew the circumstances of our pursuit, as best we were able. The nephew didn't pause to question our rationality, only seemed to become enflamed with bloodlust, and ordered his lieutenant Abang Aing to circle the village in a flanking maneuver, while he himself would lead the rest of the contingent directly against the tigers.

All thought of preserving the safety of the Dutchman and I forgotten, the nephew raised a fierce cry, and plunged deeper into the forest, swinging a machete wildly in one hand, firing a pistol indiscriminately with the other.

The Dutchman and I were left in the rear, trying desperately to catch our breath.

Abraham Van Helsing's Journal
14 Feb. Later.—Even now, more than a day later, resting for the night in the same shelter where we paused only two nights

before, the events of yesterday are still seared into my eyes and thoughts. The soldiers did their bloody work well, and in the aftermath, Tipu and I stood alone at the center of the village ruins, the dead bodies of men and tigers scattered all around.

We heard a groaning from a few yards off, and investigating found Harimau, our native guide, bleeding out his last, a bayonet wound piercing his chest. He was naked, and lying in the dirt.

"What are you?" Tipu demanded, drawing a loaded pistol and pointing it at Harimau's forehead.

I thought Harimau might see a shot to the head as some sort of release, given the immense pain he must have been suffering, but to my surprise he answered without objection or resistance.

"We are last of the tigers," Harimau said in his stilted English, the only language the three of us shared. "We the last of the Tiger Men. The Europeans, they have run over the island whole, made the jungle their own. We brought you to heal the last of us, but now even those few are dead."

"You meant to kill us," I put in, leaning forward tentatively.

"After the injured were healed, you were of no use to us, and your man-soldier had slain our brother. But it is no matter. There are no more tigers living. When I am gone, there are no more left in—"

A violent coughing jag caught Harimau, and pink foam flecked the corners of his mouth. His skin was pale against the bright arterial blood flowing freely from his wounds, and with a final spasm of pain his eyes rolled sightless back into his head. He was dead.

I'd had enough of the uncanny and strange for a lifetime. I wanted nothing more than to get back to Holland and home. Never mind that the family house stood empty and cold, my wife and son locked away in the family crypts. A cold gray life of rationality was to be preferred to the garish color of insanity I seemed to find at every turn while abroad.

I turned towards the village entrance and the way we'd come, eager to be on our way, seeing every second we delayed as another second farther away from home. But Tipu hesitated, still standing over the still form of Harimau.

Our late guide had breathed his last, and when he was still, Tipu leaned down and lifted the corpse up with ease. Without a word, Tipu walked past me towards the village entrance, his pace steady and sure. I followed, through the outskirts of the village, down the dirt path and into the jungle beyond. There, in the clearing, we came to the *sandung* house of bones.

Tipu set the lifeless body of the last Tiger Man within the house of the dead, and turned and made his way back into the dark forest. I followed close behind, in silence.

Captain Dakkar's Log (continued)

Once more in Kuching, I was reunited with my countrymen and crew. They had readied the dhow *Avenger* for departure in my absence, wheedling what provisions they could from the raja's men at the dock.

I offered the Dutchman a place among my crew. We could use a physician and man of science among us, and he seems to hold his own with some equanimity in the face of crisis. But he prefers to run back to the sheltering skirts of his motherland, so perhaps we are best rid of him, after all.

Making our careful way down the river Sarawak to the coast, we made for open waters and set sail for the east, and the broad reaches of the Pacific beyond. As I write this record of our recent doings, we have just passed the island of Mompracem, and I am tempted to put ashore to see for myself whether that figure of legend still lives. But there is work to be done, and new legends to write, so I forbear.

Perhaps out in the deep reaches of the ocean I will find my own Mompracem, my own island sanctuary. Then I would need only a stout ship of my own, and I will have the freedom of the seas, mobile in the mobile environment. Then perhaps we shall show the Raja Brookes of the world that there are still tigers left, with tooth and claw.

Abraham Van Helsing's Journal

15 Feb.—On our return to Kuching, I find that the packet boat has left without me, sailing off at the first sign the storm was letting up. Tipu offered to take me along with him on his journey to the east and the South Pacific beyond, but I politely refused. I only want to return home, and I think Tipu only offered out of sympathy, not out of any real desire to keep me in his company.

Sir James tells me there is a boat bound for Sumatra leaving Kuching tonight, and from there I can get passage to India, and to Europe beyond. If instead I choose to wait two weeks, I can book passage on a ship heading directly for England.

I will leave tonight. I have little desire to stay here in this dark place, between mad Englishmen on the one side and the looming jungle on the other.

Later.—Onboard this boat hardly worthy of the name, Borneo behind me and Sumatra looming into view. It is only a matter of a few hundred miles perhaps, but already I feel more at ease, away from the mad raja and one step nearer to home.

In the gloaming, I gaze past the boat's stern, looking to the east. Across the waves, where the Tiger of Malaysia still plies his piratical trade. And beyond, where Tipu is bound. What will become of that strange Indian gentleman, so educated and cultured, and yet so full of righteous anger and hate? Can he flee the sphere of imperial influence far enough, fast enough, to suit his sense of liberty? Or will he be forced one day to turn, and to fight, like a caged tiger?

Who can say? No one.

Neal Asher is one of the rising stars in the new space opera. The following is part of his "Polity" sequence, which includes novels *Gridlinked, The Skinner, Line of Polity,* and *Cowl*. It starts almost like a crime story, with vengeance and murder, but ends as something quite different.

Acephalous Dreams
by Neal Asher

Having no head, or one reduced, indistinct, as certain insect larvae... Such things he considered as the pool spread to his foot and melded round the rubber sole of his boot. He would leave distinctive footprints: Devnon Macroboots, fifty-seven New Carth shillings a pair; they were only sold from one place and there was not much of a turnover in them. Carth was somewhat off the tourist route, religious fanaticism not being much of a draw in such enlightened times.

No resistance at all.

Daes stepped back from the pool and walked slowly round the corpse—the grub—his right boot leaving a bloody ribbed imprint and the incomplete DEV at each step. He was not a tall man, Daes, and his weight lifter's physique made him appear shorter. He was exceptionally physically strong, and this strength had been sufficient to drive the carbide-edged machete through the flesh, bone, and gristle of Anton Velsten's neck. No resistance. The machete had not even slowed, and Daes had not even felt a tug. The head, Anton's head, had not tumbled away spouting blood as it would have in most holodramas. It had remained balanced on Anton's neck, displaced by only a fraction, unmoved by the hydraulic pressure of the blood that spurted out sideways until the head became fully detached when Anton, unstrung puppet fashion, collapsed to the floor in the shroud of his priestly robes.

Daes smiled to himself when he reached a position giving him clear view of the severed neck. There was always plenty of blood flowing in the holodramas, but they did not often show this sort of thing: in the pool of blood there was a second immiscible pool of well-chewed Carthian prawns, special fried rice, that piquant sauce they made at the Lotus Garden, and bile. Sniffing and wrinkling his nose, Daes was also made aware that Anton had emptied his bowels in his last moments.

"Are you with your god now, Anton?" Daes asked. The bowl of night over the roof-port made his voice sound flat and meaningless as it drank his words. Daes surveyed the ranked gravcars for any sign of movement, any sign that he had been observed, but there seemed to be none of either. It was late, and the faithful were always early to bed and early to rise. Witnesses were not a requirement though, and few people got away with murder. He dropped the machete onto the corpse, turned, stooped, and picked up Anton's head. It was surprisingly heavy. Holding it by the dark blood-soaked hair Daes studied Anton's face. Nothing there. In death, terror had fled, and all that remained was the expression etched there by Anton's vicious and debauched life. Daes dropped the head into the bag he had stolen from a tenpin bowling alley—perfect for the task, waterproof too—then he squatted down by the corpse.

"All done, but for one last sign," he said.

Reaching out, he dipped his finger in blood and drew on the ground a figure '8' turned on its side. It was the sign for infinity, but meant so much else to him. He then took up the bag and headed for his own gravcar, quickly stepped inside, and with the turbines at their quietest and slowest, lifted the car from the roof.

Eight hours maximum. The corpse was sure to be discovered in the next two hours. Fingerprints and DNA would be identified at the scene within the following hour. And access to Runcible transport denied directly after. He reckoned the search would first be centered at the Runcible facility. They would expect him to try to get off planet, to one of the Line worlds—expected it of any murderer. He smiled to himself as he directed his cleverly stolen Ford Nevada gravcar out of the city and away from the facility, to a glow on the horizon that was not where the sun rose.

It was a place where godless Carthians came with mylar glide wings to have fun in the thermals above the volcano. This activity was frowned on by the Theocracy, and attempts had been made to ban the sport; but the Theocracy only had power over those who voluntarily subjugated themselves to it. Polity law ruled on Carth, and the monitors of Earth Central were never far away. With the Ford set on hover, Daes opened the door and dropped the bowling bag and its grisly contents into the caldera. As a necessity he was very high up and only able to discern a pinprick, near subliminal in its brevity, as the head struck the lava and incinerated.

"Resurrect the fucker now," said Daes, and wondered if he might be going insane. Perhaps a plea of insanity... No, he felt completely and utterly sane, as always. When they finally caught him he would be tried with all fairness and sympathy. His memories would be read by an AI; his life rolled out, dissected, and completely understood by a mind quite capable of such. What made him what he was would be discovered, recorded, and perhaps be the subject of lengthy study. He would be gone by the time that study reached any conclusions; taken to a disintegrator and in less than a second converted into a pool of organic sludge and flushed into the Carthian ocean for the delectation of its plankton. There was a kind of poetry to such an ending. Daes didn't like poetry. He closed the door of the Ford, his eyes watering from the sulphur fumes, then turned the vehicle back toward the city.

"Do you want to live?"

The Golem Twenty-seven that had entered his cell was only identifiable as an android by her deliberately flawed perfection. The artificial skin and flesh of her right arm was transparent, and through it Daes could see her gleaming ceramal bones, the cybermotors at her joints, and the tangles of optic cables. Otherwise she was completely beautiful; a blond-haired teenager with wide amber eyes and a pertly nubile body clothed in a short silk toga. Daes remained on his bunk and waited for her to continue.

"Very well," she said, and turned to go.

Daes sat up. "Wait, wait a minute. Of course I want to live."

She turned. "Then please be civil enough to reply when I ask a question."

"Okay. Okay." Daes waved her to a seat.

She sat and smiled briefly at him before continuing. "Your memcording has been analysed, and those memories you attempted to have concealed have been revealed and intensively studied. We even know why you drew the sign for infinity beside his body."

Daes stared at her—he had not expected this.

She continued. "Yet, despite the years of abuse you suffered at the hands of Anton Velsten while in the theocratic college, you are still considered sane and culpable, simply because you could have later reported him and had him sent for readjustment."

"I preferred how I readjusted him."

"Apparently."

"And so, nothing can stop me going to the disintegrator," said Daes.

"The intervention of the AI Geronamid can."

Daes shivered at the mention of the name. Geronamid was the sector AI. What the hell interest would it have in a minor criminal like himself?

"Why would Geronamid want to get involved?"

"AI Geronamid has need of a subject for a scientific trial. This trial may kill you, in which case it would be considered completion of sentence. Should you survive, all charges against you will be dropped."

"And the nature of this trial?"

"Cephalic implantation of Csorian node."

"Okay, I agree, though I have no idea what Csorian node is."

The Golem stood, and as she did so the door slid open. Daes glanced up at the security eye in the corner of the cell and stood also. She nodded to the door, and he followed her out. In the corridor a couple of policemen glared at him with ill-concealed annoyance but showed no reaction beyond that. Outside the station she led him to a sleek gravcar styled after one of the twenty-second century electric cars. He thought, briefly, about escape, but knew he stood no chance. His companion might look like a teenage girl, but he knew she was strong enough to rip him in half. Once they were seated in the gravcar it took off without her touching the controls and sped away at a speed well above the limit. He wondered if some minuscule part of Geronamid was controlling it.

"You didn't tell me. What's a Csorian node?"

"If we knew that with any certainty we would not be carrying out this trial," replied the Golem.

"You know it's some sort of implant."

"We do, but only because it was found in the body of a Csorian."

"A Csorian has been found?"

"Oh yes, underneath the ruins on Wilder. The body is about a hundred thousand years old. The node was attached to its hindbrain."

Daes turned that over in his mind. The Csorians were one of the three dead races: the Jain and the Atheter being the other two. They supposedly died out a hundred thousand years before the human race had set out for the stars. All that remained of their civilizations was a few ruins of coraline buildings and the descendants of those plants and creatures to survive from their biotechnology.

"It was one of the last of them then," he said.

"Yes."

He considered for a moment before going on. "Surely Geronamid should have been able to work out what this node is."

"Perhaps he has. Who can tell?"

Daes noted that the gravcar was well above the traffic lanes and still rising. He heard the door seals lock down and wondered where the hell they were going. When he turned to the Golem to ask her, he saw that she had called up something on the screen. Here was a creature much like a praying mantis only without the long winged abdomen. From the back of its thorax extended a ribbed tail that branched into three. At the branch point was a pronounced thickening from which grew a second pair of insectile legs.

"It was about a meter long. We think the hindbrain had something to do with reproduction," said the Golem.

"That's a Csorian?" asked Daes.

"It is. We are reasonably sure that their society was much like that of the social insects of Earth: wasps, ants, hornets, and the like."

"They had hive minds just the same?"

"This is what we suppose."

Daes smiled to himself. It had come as one shock in many when arrogant humanity had discovered it wasn't the only sentient race on Earth. It was just the loudest and most destructive. Dolphins and whales had always been candidates because of their aesthetic appeal and stories of rescued swimmers. Research in that area had soon cleared things up: Dolphins couldn't tell the difference between a human swimmer and a sick fellow, and were substantially more stupid than the animal humans had been turning into pork on a regular basis. Whales had the intelligence of the average cow. When a hornet built its nest in a VR suit and lodged its protests on the Internet it had taken a long time for anyone to believe. They were stinging things, creepy crawlies, how could they possibly be intelligent? At ten thousand years of age the youngest hive mind showed them. People believed.

"So a hive mind got into space long before we did. I find that gratifying to hear," said Daes.

The Golem gazed at him speculatively. "Your misanthropy is well understood. You do realise that if you'd had it corrected you would not be in the situation you are now in."

"I liked my dislike of humanity. It kept me sane."

"Very amusing," said the Golem, turning back to the screen. The picture she now called up was of a small ovoid with complex mottling on its surface. Daes noted it, then gazed through the windows and saw the sky becoming dark blue and stars beginning to show. The planet had now receded. He pushed his face to the window to try to get a look down at it and saw only a shuttle glinting like a discarded needle far below him

"This is the node. We know that it contains picotech and likely biofactured connections to its host's brain. We first thought it some kind of augmentation."

"Well that seems the most likely," said Daes, turning back.

"Yes, but this node is three centimeters long, two wide, and has a density twice that of lead."

"So?"

The Golem looked at him. "Every cubic nanometer of it is packed with picotech. Under scan we have so far managed to identify two billion picomachines with the ability to self-replicate. They also all cross-reference. There is a complexity here that is beyond even Geronamid's ability."

There was a sound, slightly like a groan, from within the workings of the gravcar. Daes felt the artificial gravity come on, and when he gazed out the windows now saw nothing but starlit space. As he turned to fire another question at the Golem his seat slapped him lightly on his back and the gravcar surged toward a distant speck. He decided to be annoyed.

"Am I supposed to be impressed by all this?"

"No," said the Golem. "You are just supposed to be thankful that you are still alive."

Daes grimaced and peered ahead at the speck as it drew closer. "When can I speak to Geronamid?"

The Golem looked at him.

"Ah," he said. "You never told me your name."

"It is my conceit to name this part of myself Hera," said a very small part of the AI Geronamid.

The speck resolved into a flat disc of a ship the size of which did not become evident until they drew very close. What Daes had first taken to be panoramic windows set in the side of the vessel, soon resolved into bay doors the size of city blocks. The ship had to be at least two kilometers in diameter.

"This is where you are," said Daes.

"Yes, the central mind is here," replied Hera.

The bay doors drew aside; the gravcar sped in, then landed on a wide expanse of gridded bay floor. The moment the doors closed behind there came a boom of wind as atmosphere was restored in the bay. The car's seals automatically disengaged, and Geronamid's Golem opened her door. Daes quickly opened his door and followed.

"Is the node here?" he asked as they approached a drop-shaft.

"It is, as are the remains of the Csorian, and much of their recovered technology."

They stepped into the irised gravity field, and it dropped them down into the ship. Ten floors down they stepped out into a wide chamber filled with old-style museum display cases. Hera led him past an aquarium containing corals in pastel shades of every colour, past a tank containing plants that bore translucent fruit like lumps of amber, a case containing pieces of coral with something like circuitry etched or grown on their inner faces. She brought him finally to the tank containing the remains of the Csorian—whole and almost lifelike.

"It wasn't in this condition, surely?" he said.

"No, only four percent of it was recoverable."

"What about DNA?"

"Scraps only. Not enough to build up a large-enough template."

"AIs did it with dinosaurs."

"In that case there was more material to work with. What is in this case is all we have of the Csorians.... Here, this is what we have come to see."

She led him past the Csorian to a small bell jar over a jade pedestal. Underneath the jar lay the node—in appearance a simple pebble. Daes stepped closer. As he did so he felt a slight displacement, a sense of dislocation, and from this he knew that the ship was on the move.

"Where are we going?"

"A living world without sentient life. You must be isolated while the node does whatever it does."

"What?" Daes turned to her to protest. Her hand moved so fast he hardly registered it moving. Fingertips brushed his neck and from that point he felt his body turning to lead.

"Don't worry. I'll be with you," said Hera, as he slipped into darkness.

Something huge was poised on the edge of his being, not inimical, but dangerous and vast and ready to drown him out of existence. Anton was a small and insignificant thing on the ground at his feet even though armies were marching out of his severed neck. Daes decided to laugh and leap into the sky, and this being his wish he did so, for he knew this was a dream. When he woke, though, that huge something was still there.

"How do you feel?" asked Hera.

Daes opened his eyes and stared at the domed ceiling. He turned his head aside and saw the Golem sitting in a form chair beside the sofa he lay upon. They were in a comfortably furnished house of some kind. Greenish light filtered in through the wide windows.

"Where are we?" he asked.

"The world only has a number."

"I thought you said this was uninhabited," said Daes, sitting up and studying their surroundings.

"Geronamid prepared this place for you some time ago," said Hera.

"For me?"

"Well, for the next person under a death sentence when it decided to implant the node."

"I was lucky that time occurred when it did."

"Yes, five seconds later and someone else would have been chosen."

Daes stood and stretched his neck. "It's in me, then?"

"Yes, you will not know it is there until the picotech starts to work."

"And when will that be?"

"We do not know. It is not working at the moment, though."

"How can you be sure of that?"

"I am taking readings from numerous detectors implanted in your body."

"I didn't give permission for that," said Daes.

Hera shrugged. "To put it in suitable parlance," she said, "tough."

Daes stared at her for a long moment. It was all perfectly clear to him: Geronamid could do with him what it liked now.

"What do I do while I wait for this node to... activate?"

"Explore, sleep, eat, all those things you would not be doing had your sentence been passed either five seconds later or earlier."

"Do you need to continually remind me?"

"Yes, it would seem that I do."

Without responding to that Daes turned and walked to the window. He gazed out at a wall of jungle twenty meters away. The intervening area had been scorched to grey ash, but even there the ground was scattered with reddish green sprouts, and fungi like blue peas. A bewildering surge of feeling hit him: he wanted to be out there, to drive his fingers into the black earth, and to see and feel growing things.

"You say that picotech isn't working yet?" he said.

When Hera did not reply he turned to her.

"No, I *said* it wasn't working; now I *say* that something is happening," she replied.

Daes swallowed a sudden surge of fear. What the hell was he doing here? He should have gone to the disintegrator. At least that would have been clean and quick, and right now he would know nothing, feel nothing.

"What's happening?"

"I do not know," said Hera. "The node is reduced in size, and picomachines are diffusing through your body. What they are doing will become evident in time."

Daes pressed his hands against the thick glass of the window, and noted that the skin on the backs of them was peeling.

"I want to go outside," he said.

The air was frigid in his mouth. He had expected it to be warm and humid.

"This equates to the Jurassic period on Earth," said Hera.

"How do you work out that equation, then?" Daes asked

sarcastically.

"Quite simply, really. The ecosystems have not evolved to the complexity of mutualism between species."

"And that means?"

"No flowers and no pollinators. The equations are more complex than that, obviously, but my explanation stands."

"You mean it will do for a stupid human like me," said Daes. "Why the hell is it so damned cold? This looked like jungle from in there."

"It is jungle, and for this place it is unseasonably hot."

"Couldn't you have chosen a warmer planet?"

"I don't know."

"What the hell is that supposed to mean? You are Geronamid."

"I am a part, and now a separate part."

Daes turned to study her, then damned himself for a fool. If she gave anything away in her expression that would be because she wanted to. It was so easy to forget what she was.

"Why?" he asked.

"Because my direct link has been severed, it being possible to use such a link for direct informational attack on Geronamid itself. This planet is in quarantine for the duration of this trail. The only link we do have is a comlink to a second isolated sub-mind of Geronamid's in orbit."

"Is Geronamid that scared, then?"

"Cautious, I think, would be a better term."

Daes turned away from her and regarded the cold jungle. There was a path of sorts, probably beaten by one of the AI's machines. He headed for it, ash caking his boots, and little fungi bursting all around where he stepped. The vegetation on either side of the path sprouted from thick cycad bodies and bore a hard and sharp look. On the slimy root-bound ground scuttled arthropods like skeletons' hands, which he watched hunting long black beetles that sobbed piteously when caught and eaten alive. He had gone only ten meters into the jungle when he suddenly felt sick and dizzy. He went down on his knees, and before he knew what he was doing he was pushing his fingers into the black and sticky earth. Immediately his dizziness receded and he suddenly found himself gazing about himself with vast clarity of vision. On the bole of a scaled trunk nearby he observed an insect bearing the shape of a legged stiletto with a head in which eye-pits glinted like flecks of emerald. Then he found himself gazing up the bole of the tree, vegetation looming above him. Then he was feeling his way along the ground with a familiar heat shape ahead of him. He leapt on it before it could escape and bit down and sucked with relish, filling himself but never assuaging the constant hunger. Then... then he was back.

"What the hell is happening to me?" he said, blinking to clear strange visions from his eyes as he stared into the jungle.

"You would be the best one to answer that question," said Hera. "Tell me what you are feeling."

Daes stumbled to his feet and turned back toward the residence Geronamid had provided. He saw now that it was one of those instant fold-out homes used by ECS for refugees and the like. It seemed sanctuary indeed for him.

"I want to go back," he said, walking quickly toward it.

"What happened?" Hera asked, moving to his side.

Daes gestured to the creatures that swarmed on the jungle floor. "I saw through their eyes, and when they didn't have eyes, I felt what they felt." He stepped through the door that opened for him and moved to a sink unit before one of the panoramic windows. Resting his hands on the composite he saw that the skin on the back of them had ceased to peel, but when he lifted those hands up to inspect them more closely he saw that his palms left, along with the black mud, white smears on the edge of the sink. He was about to say something about this to Hera when he saw that the smears were fading. Also, something bulked behind his eyes, and he felt himself almost stooping under its weight. Involuntarily he turned and surveyed the room. Centering on the Golem he strode towards her and grasped her transparent wrist, and of course she easily pulled away. Now she held up her arm and observed the white smear on her wrist as it faded.

"Picotech leaching from your body. Outside, it—"

Hera froze, and Daes found himself gazing out of her eyes

at himself. He lifted her arms and opened and closed her hand, sensing as he did so the surge of optic information packages and diffusing electrons in her solid-state core. And he understood it all.

"—was obviously sending out probes to sample and test its environment."

He was back in himself as Hera paused. She tilted her head.

"By my internal clock I can only presume I went offline for fourteen seconds." She looked at Daes queryingly. But he had no reply, for now he was closely studying and understanding the workings of his own mind—taking apart all his memories and all his motivations and sucking up every dreg of information it was possible to find. A flower he had seen as a child, named as an adolescent, and found dried and pressed in the pages of a book in the theocratic college library was tracked in all its incarnations through his life as a straight line of information. And there were millions of these lines. He felt an analytical interest whenever he encountered anything in his mind that related to the Csorians, and anything related to the prehistory of Earth. At the last he experienced the bleed-over of alien memory, and its huge logic and utterly cold understanding terrified him. Then suddenly it was all over and he was standing in a room, on a planet, being watched by a Golem android.

"I know what the node is," he said to Hera.

Anton Velsten never sneered. He left that to the others, just as, in the end, he left it to them to hold Daes across the table. That he used a gel on Daes' anus was not indicative of any concern for the boy. Velsten just found it more pleasurable that way, and less likely for him to hurt himself. When the others took their turns, Velsten stepped back and gave a running commentary—his voice devoid of emotion.

"And Pandel is at the gate. And he's in and getting up to speed. Oh dear, Pandel loses it in the first ten meters. What's this? What's this? Damar is leading with a head...."

So it went on, and when they were all done, Anton scrawled the sign of infinity on Daes' forehead, with Daes' own semen-diluted shit.

The others who watched, beyond this room and beyond this incarnation, dissected every increment of every moment and understood the event utterly. They saw that it was the culmination of Velsten's power game. Of course Velsten had to die at Daes' hand. The shame could not be admitted—the shame of being unable to fight. How could he expose those memories to AI inspection? Then there was vengeance, and that was oh so sweet.

"Hello, Anton," said Daes, strolling from his gravcar out towards the man.

Velsten was tall, and with his mild "I am listening to you" expression, and dressed as he was in his flowing robes, he was—it could not be avoided—priestly. He halted and regarded Daes estimatingly before moving his hands into a supplicating gesture, perhaps to apologise and explain about pressing business.

"You don't even recognise me, do you?" Daes asked.

Velsten now put on the pose of deep thoughtfulness as he watched Daes come to stand before him.

"I feel we have met," said Anton, pressing his hands together as if in prayer. "But I'm afraid I have a terrible memory for names, and in my ministry I meet so many people. What was it? Amand? Damar?"

"I was one of the first to receive your ministry, Anton," said Daes.

Velsten now started to become really concerned.

"I'm so sorry, but as pleasant as this meeting is I do have pressing business," said Velsten, turning away.

"It's remiss of you not to remember someone you buggered, Anton."

Velsten froze, and slowly turned back. The transformation in his expression surprised even Daes. Now Velsten gazed at Daes with superiority as he folded his arms. He nodded his head as he no doubt wondered what to do with this inconvenient little roach.

"Daes," he said, and sighed.

Daes watched him for a moment; then he unzipped the bag he had stolen from the bowling alley and took out the machete. Velsten's expression changed to one of contempt.

"Do you really think you would get away with using that?" he asked.

"Oh no, you wrong me. I don't expect to get away with this. I don't really care."

Velsten's expression changed once again, and his fear showed. He held out his hand as if to push Daes away. Daes swung the machete across, and the hand thumped to the plascrete a couple of meters away. Velsten stared at his jetting wrist and made a strangled whining sound before capping his other hand over it.

"That probably doesn't even hurt yet, and it won't get a chance to," said Daes, relishing the expression of horror on Velsten's face. He stepped in and pirouetted with the machete and for one strange instant thought he had missed—that was, until he once again faced Velsten. The man was a statue for a moment, before blood jetted out sideways from his neck; then he went over, his head separating from his body as he fell.

No resistance at all.

Daes inspected his hands for the nth time and saw that there was absolutely nothing wrong with them. Now, when he touched objects, he left no white smear. He reached out for his coffee cup, took it up, and sipped.

"Restful night?" Hera enquired.

"Not really. I had some very strange dreams when I wasn't being woken by those weird noises. What the hell was that?" said Daes.

"It doesn't have a name as yet. It's a large arthropod that deposits its egg-sacs high in the trees. It is apparently a painful process," Hera replied.

"Apparently." Daes sipped some more coffee and wondered at the Golem's seeming impatience. All emulation, but it did need to know.

"You said you knew what the node is," said Hera. "Then, having grabbed my attention, you claimed great weariness and just had to go to bed."

"That is very true."

"Perhaps now you are rested, you can tell me what you know."

Daes shook his head. "Sorry, can't do that."

"Why?"

"Because *I* cannot." By stressing the personal pronoun he hoped Hera would really get the picture. There were things he simply could not do and things he could not say. That his mind had been reformatted he had no doubt, but he was not too upset by this. There were the things he could do.... Looking out of the window he surged up high and gazed out through a cluster of eyes at spiky treetops. Scanning round he found another example of the creature he haunted, clinging to a flower spike like an upright bunch of giant blue grapes. This creature was a white spider with a dagger of a body and mouthparts that appeared complex enough to dismantle a computer... and put it back together again. It clung with those mouthparts as its body heaved and strained and dripped transparent sacs on the foliage. The creature he was in could not hear the sounds the one in view nor itself made, but through other ears he could hear the hootings and raspings. Fleeing on with his awareness he found it diffusing into an ice-crusted sea in which finned silver footballs fed on air-plant sprouts of weed.

"Will you ever be able to tell?" Hera asked.

An island chain revealed to him multilegged creatures like the skeletal spider-things, but these possessed bat wings and the superb vision of aerial predators. But they were no good—their simple light bodies would take millennia of adjustment to carry a greatly enlarged braincase. His awareness now snapped back to something on the other side of the continent he presently occupied. Here he observed a herd of grazing beasts: six-legged and reptilian. The braincase below the three eyestalks possessed complexity in control of the creatures' complex digestive system—a chemical laboratory in itself. It would be necessary to push them into a predatory lifestyle, thus freeing up cerebral space—again a task taking millennia. However, near the house, he had observed a better option than this. And of course, inside the house was the best option of all. He would continue to search, though—for the moment. The smallest fraction of his awareness studied the Golem.

"I want you to contact the second Geronamid submind."

"I am in com—"

Daes wholly occupied all her systems in an instant. He found the open comlink to the submind in orbit and probed up to it, tried to widen that link. In seconds he had created computer subversion routines and used them to try to get a hold, to control. The comlink immediately shut down. Within him there was a calmness—this had been expected, and in the process he had learnt much. Next time he would not be so brutal. He withdrew from Hera.

"—munication with the... I see.... I hope you understand now that you're quarantine is total. You have no way of leaving this planet without Geronamid's intercession."

"I understand," said Daes, and everything else that he was. "I want information."

"You realise that if you do manage to take control of the submind above, it will be instantly obliterated?"

"I require information," was all he said.

"What information?"

"Everything you have on the Csorians and all related research."

"That is a lot of information."

"I have the capacity."

"Then link to me again, but do not drown me out this time," she said.

Daes eased into her, carefully circumventing those areas from which her awareness evolved: her ego, self-image—what she was.

Through the comlink Hera spat the request into orbit, and the response was immediate. Daes realised that this had been expected, as there was no delay whilst the information was trawled from the AI net. As he scanned and sorted this information, calmly noting that all of the Csorian civilization discovered was but archaeological remains, he realised that whilst he could be just Daes, in truth he was now some other entity. Daes was in fact now a submind of *himself*, and his whole self was centered on the node in which he felt a crammed multitude. However, through vast and spreading awareness he observed picotech chains of superconductor spearing across the surface of the planet, spreading their informational network through the oceans' depths and flailing in the air like cobwebs as they connected with every life-form, insinuated themselves into every niche of the biosphere. One-third of the planet now lay under this net, this awareness, and within only hours this network would meet on the other side and he would be able to observe all, and be ready. That was it, though. He felt a flush of fear that was his own and the crying of that multitude. Upon completion of the network, dispersion and implantation became a necessity, for thereafter the network would begin to degrade as does all life—with the accumulation of copying errors, the degrading of the basic templates—only faster, because of its complexity, and the delicacy of its pico-scopic strands. One time only: one chance.

"You don't know what wiped out my race," said Daes.

"Your race?" enquired Hera.

"You, submind, do not know what I am... become. Geronamid certainly does. I want to communicate with the AI directly."

"You can only communicate with the submind directly. Who will communicate with Geronamid when you have withdrawn," said Hera. "But you know that."

Daes felt the network gathering behind him like a looming shadow. Geronamid had chosen this location because of the spider creatures outside. He saw in an instant that their braincases possessed sufficient room for primitive intelligence, and that their mouthparts were sufficiently complex for the fast development of tool-using ability. Nothing would be lost, as the bulk of each of the thousands of Csorian intelligences he contained could be stored as a picotech construct in each insectile mind. But those intelligences would be unable to immediately bloom. Transferred down the generations whilst the creatures were subtly impelled towards development of more complex brains, it would be millennia before the Csorian race could be reborn. This option was unacceptable to the multitude whilst such viable intelligences as Daes himself and these AIs were available. He must take Geronamid, subsume that AI.

"Yes, I do know that," he said.

The planetwide network had stalled, all his mentality now focused on this moment. He felt the link establish to the orbital submind, and replayed Hera's words: *Who will communicate with Geronamid when you have withdrawn.* This meant that the submind possessed some way of linking with the AI Geronamid in total. There had to be a way for Daes to get through before the submind was destroyed.

The comlink to the orbital submind opened, and Daes slid into it like syrup into a sore throat. The safety controls and trips he had observed on his first attempt, he easily circumvented as his awareness flooded up into orbit, subversion programs uncoiling in the silicon logic of the submind like tight-wound snakes. In a nanosecond he found the underspace link to Geronamid in total and prepared himself to storm that bastion. Then something flooded out of the link, vast and incomprehensible. His subversion programs began to consume themselves. He felt a huge amused awareness bearing down on him with crushing force. Then that force eased.

I offer you only two choices.

Through allowable awareness Daes saw the massive geosat poised above the planet. There was no possibility of mistaking its purpose. It was one long internally polished barrel ringed by the toroid of a giant fusion reactor. In some areas the weapon had acquired the name "sun gun," which seemed an inadequate description for something that could raise square kilometers of its target to a million degrees Celsius in less time than it took to blink—a blink that would see all the stored intelligences gone.

Destruction?

Geronamid replied: *Is one choice. I have known for long enough that the Csorian node contains the zipped minds of some members of that race, ready to be implanted and unzipped in another race that has the capacity to take them. That second race will not be the human race. I could have destroyed the node, but that is not my wish. When you reattain your full capability the human race will be on an equal if not superior footing to you.*

It will take thousands of years, Daes replied.

You have slept for longer than that.

Almost with a subliminal nod Daes drew back down the informational corridor of the comlink, flooded through Hera, and back into his human body. For a moment he gazed at Hera; then he turned to the door of the house and stepped through and outside. She followed him as he walked into the jungle and stood observing the spider creatures in the trees.

"This then, is completion of my sentence," said Daes... just him.

"More life than you would have enjoyed," she replied.

He inspected his hand as the skin began to peel and the substance of his flesh began to sag. Quickly seating himself he pushed those hands into soft cold ground. Inside him the intelligences separated and began transmitting into the network established in the area. In the transference they took with them the substance of his body, widening channels through the ground to the nanoscopic then microscopic, up the trunks of the trees, penetrating the hanging spider creatures through clinging complex feet. His own awareness breaking apart, Daes felt the subliminal agony he would have felt at his execution, as he similarly disintegrated. Csorian minds occupied primitive braincases, and spider creatures crawled down from the trees with ill-formed ideas, hopes, and ambitions.

Hera gazed up into the sky at the descending shuttle, then returned her attention to the creature crouching by the scaled bulb of a large cycad. It was gnawing away with the intricate cutlery of its mouthparts—behaviour that had never before been observed. But then there was a lot of that now. Some had begun to build spherical nests around their egg-clusters and to defend them from other predators whilst the eggs ripened and hatched; still others plucked hard thorns from the leaf tips of cycads and used them to spear their prey.

As the shuttle landed in the jungle behind her, she watched the creature back off from what it was doing and turn toward her, waving its forelimbs in the air. The noise of the shuttle engines then sent it scuttling into the undergrowth. She walked over to the cycad and inspected the creature's work. Neatly incised into the scales of the cycad was an "8" turned on its side—the sign for infinity.

She did not know if that was a suitable remnant to bequeath.

"Goodbye, Daes," she said, and turned away.

Matthew Rossi has created his own form of literature, a form that Paul Di Filippo has termed "speculative nonfiction." On his own website, on *Fantastic Metropolis*, and in the pages of his collections *Things That Never Were* and *Bottled Demons*, Rossi has written hundreds of short essays, any one of which contains enough ideas to sustain entire novels. This story, about a ghost hunter who confronts his own past in a sort of homecoming, is his first published fiction.

Ghosts of Christmas
by Matthew Rossi

The nameless man leaned against the pickup truck, looking at the house. The snow stuck in his long hair, dyed a turquoise blue, and in his tangled red beard more matted than actually curly.

The roof was missing shingles. Some of them he'd kicked off himself, and he could remember watching the flat green rectangles float off into space while he scrambled up from the porch out back, escaping his room to clamber about in the manner he'd imagined for apes and monkeys. Back then he only knew what he'd seen in cartoons or read in paperback, and even though he'd since learned the reality, had heard the names Fossy and Goodall, he preferred the Tarzan-inspired albino gorilla of his imagination, who spoke English and palled around with a Victorian-era steam cyborg. *The Amazing Adventures of Albion Ape and Stephen St. George the Articulated Armature*, he'd called it in his old notebooks.

He stared up at the fence stained a dark red like Homer's sea, falling apart now, covered in the vines his grandfather's father had seeded in the backyard. Those vines were everywhere now, mixing with the tangled rosebushes, everywhere tendrils of plants crawling up the sides of the house, tearing slowly at the fence, while the grass grew wilder than any grass you'd expect to find in a suburb like Cranston.

The house had been his, in another life, the house he'd grown up in. To either side of it were well-kept lawns, and large hedges. He'd pretended the house didn't exist enough times in his life. Why should the neighbors be any different?

Anyone who lived in the neighborhood could sense it, the nameless man knew, could feel in their bones that the house was as bad as an ancient mansion inhabited once by degenerate aristocrats who walled each other up alive. Which was torn down to make room for a toxic waste dump sunk into the ancient Indian burial ground discovered under the mansion. No one wanted anything to do with it, and no one wanted to draw the place's attention, so no one called the city and said, *Hey, could someone figure out who owns this place and make him mow his lawn and fix his roof?*

The nameless man reluctantly reached into the bed of the truck and pulled out a metal baseball bat, one of the aluminum ones so easy to find at any sporting goods store. His fingers squealed a bit as he gripped the rubber around the handle. He pushed off the parked truck, and started towards the house. The wind picked up, the snow falling now in earnest. A white Christmas. Nameless lowered his chin to his chest, and continued on.

Inside, it wasn't as he had left it.

The carpet was dusty, and threadbare in places. There were signs that someone had been squatting there for a while, ashes in the fireplace, a few branches torn off the ragged old fir tree that had been left to rot in the corner of the living room. It did surprise him that the tree had survived as intact as it had. Red and green and silver spheres hung around the green needles of the tree, as did tinsel tracing a jagged path up and down the branches. He glared at it for a long moment, remembered long-gone trees and packages wrapped and deposited under them.

Then he climbed the stairs. The basement he'd long since emptied out, and he had no desire to revisit that place. He knew well enough what he'd done down there; he didn't need to see it again.

"Breaker of the mountain of heaven, serpent of the waters, rival and spoiler of Chuan Hsu, overthrow the order of things,

great black dragon." He chanted to himself as he climbed the stairs, remembering them from that skewed perspective, a child whose head was as high as his knees now, who had needed to take each step at a time. *"You who sought Ti and upset the world, shaker of the pillars, father of the flood."*

He stepped on the last stair and found himself in the room his parents had used, had slept in. Even as he felt the rain dragon coil around his spine he could not stop himself from shivering at the sight of the bed in the corner of the room, the mattress sunken, the sheets yellowed and smelling of recent use. Recent, but not very recent. There was a faint odor in the room he couldn't identify even though he knew he should. On the wall next to the bed was an old photograph of a woman and a man and a child, the woman with long black hair and a severe face that smiled in a way that offset her predatory look, the man tall and broad with gold hair and blue eyes. The child he didn't look at.

He walked around the bed, hoping to find what he was beginning to suspect wouldn't be there. It was, but not as he'd left it, a theme of sorts. The iron-banded oak chest he'd piled his father's notes into was open, the padlock cut off at the steel loop. The papers were scattered, some on the floor, some in the box itself. His face tightened as he saw that some had been attacked with a yellow highlight marker.

Dropping to his knees next to the box, he pulled out the ruled sheets of paper, the old yellowing travel notebook in which his father had left notes, and the newer binders, and began looking through them.

Much of it was his father's gentle musings about plants, about farming and growth, the things he'd loved and loved to tinker with. The time spent away from the suburban house, on the farm his father had left behind to him... but some of it was not. The man who found himself nameless and alone in the bedroom of that "city house," as they'd called it when he was a child, felt cold in his stomach as he found a highlighted section that he'd missed during his own obsessive searching years before. *Crowley argues that Assiyah is the prison world of the Qlippoth, the cracked shells, the world of matter being the world of evil spirits, devils divided into ten ranks or classes. The first two are but formless, shapeless unvariation, followed by a darkness that admits no light. Then follow seven worlds occupied by incarnations of lust or vice, ruled by Samael and Isheth Zenunim (similar to Ahriman and "the accursed whore"? I am reminded of the way that Ahriman was trapped in the "good creation" of Ohrmazd, like a pearl around an irritant)—Shades of Malek Tous, the Peacock Lord, master of this world. Agrippa's argument about "virtues in things, which are not from any element" makes me wonder if this essence could be brought to the surface with the following...*

The next page was nowhere to be found in the pile.

This made perfect sense to him. He'd left his father's papers alone in a deserted house counting on nothing more than the raw malevolence of its presence to protect them, and now, once again, he was to be punished for his willful stupidity. He stood up, dropping the papers back into the box, hoping to come back for them if he had time.

Looking up, he saw what he hadn't noticed before—the room he himself had slept in as a child. The double window he remembered climbing through on many occasions, the window that led out onto the porch that allowed a young boy to become Albion Ape, was now choked with plants. Vines had driven their way through the windows, pushing out glass and twisting wood, and were sending tendrils up and down the wall. That didn't bother him too much.

The sight of two dead people with plants growing down their throats and shoots protruding from their eye sockets, their clothes rotting and shot through with green that seemed to embrace and penetrate them... that bothered him more. On the floor in front of them was a crude circle made of wax, dribbled from the candle lying next to it. The circle was crossed with an X, with circles on the end of each arm. Next to that lay the crossed shape like two capital A's in a star of David arrangement, a rough approximation of the symbol of Saturn from another of his father's notebooks.

He didn't have long to stare at the scene before the floating thing came around the corner. He knew what it was instantly, a flowing collection of ragged shapes twisting and pulsating into faces that stretched and deformed the robe that was its self. It was obviously and painfully a ghost, or perhaps even multiple ghosts, all that was left of the poor stupid bastards who'd died because the nameless man hadn't been smart enough to burn or remove a few old pieces of paper.

A long thin limb of bone pointed at him.

From that arm blossomed fire, a seeking trail of flames that burst into bloom, seething in air that shimmered in waves between them. The walls and floor burned as the wave of heat rolled onward to consume him.

Grunting, he dropped to one knee and released the serpent crawling along his spine, felt the hair on his head fan out in a blue curtain as a blast of steam rushed over him, the wrath of the dead thing crashing against the essence of the rain dragon. The heat surprised him. A slithering thing that would like nothing better than to sear away the lining of his lungs—*that* he had not expected.

Lit by the fire, the ghost stood in all its glory, tattered rags dancing in the tarantella air. The bones of its frame took on reflected radiance from the plumes of flame dining on the walls, the trails of orange and red streaking everywhere there was fuel. Inside the black only made deeper by the shimmering light, two ruddy eyes stared out at him.

He stared back, matching its baleful gaze with his own, feeling the ascending shock of the great black dragon climbing upward to the heavens. The belt of the leather jacket swung from side to side in the air stirred up by the fire, and the rubber grip of the bat in his hand made soft moaning noises of protest. He stood, and waited for the residue of death to make a move.

It susurrated, the folds of its body twisting. Then the air seemed to vibrate and pulse, and the thing screamed. It was a keening, a howling, a sound that destroyed the remaining glass in the windows behind it, a razor blade dragged across a stone magnified. It fired this wail of pain into the air between it and Nameless so that every breath he took felt like suffering, grinding down on him with the hum of a heart shattering under the weight of its own selfishness, the hiss of regret.

Already on his knee, he ground his teeth together to keep from falling any farther, wincing at the sound that seemed to be trying to crack him into shards. His bones throbbed with it. He remembered everything he'd had any cause to regret, from the smallest hurt he'd accidentally caused on the playground behind Eden Park Elementary School to the lurking black water of memory centered in the basement of the very house that attacked him now.

It was that memory that saved him. The house couldn't just use some poor dead bastard to make him feel worse about *that*. He growled, feeling the sound rumble through his chest, forcing a counter to that horrible liquid scream shaking the walls around him. Trying to force him to face a horror he never allowed himself to look away from.

The bat flashed up in his hand as he hurled it end over end, tumbling through the air unbalanced, and as it whirled forward he threw back his head and set free the Black Dragon, bellowing in rage as the serpent of the flood burst from the base of his spine and shot like lightning to above his navel, through his stomach and heart, rushing through the hollow of his throat to illuminate his eyes and light a halo around his head, dancing like foxfire above the crown of his head.

Around him the air vibrated again, pushing away the screams and extinguishing the flames licking at the walls and floor, and like a hammer of wind grabbed hold of the tumbling bat and drove it into the bone rictus that leered at him from behind black cloth, shattering and powdering the earthly remains of whatever poor fool had read something he couldn't unread. The wave of crashing air scattered the dust remains and sent the bat rocketing forward, crumpled by the force of the impact, to crash through the tangle of vines and out of sight.

It didn't matter. The bat was useless now anyway. He had to get downstairs. He moved away from the bed, his eyes dragging across the now-burned picture, the family eaten by fire, their features erased. *Every year time eats you a little bit more.*

He ran down the stairs, more leaping than actually running,

and into the living room. He wanted to keep running, to bolt out the front door and keep going until he was well away from the house and everything that it made him remember. He swore at himself and dragged a small dagger, barely even a letter opener, out of his boot and began hacking at the floor. He didn't know yet what would happen, but he knew *something* would, that whatever had been called up had to be put down.

It was a hard bit of slashing, made worse by the sweat on his hands and the sounds coming from beneath him. He didn't even want to think about what was down there, much less to hear it slam heavy feet on the stairs as it came up, listen to the sound of wheezing and grunting and loud sloshing. The smell of unwashed flesh and flatulence coming up the stairs made his eyes water.

He locked them on the colorful spheres and zigzag light-ning flash of tinsel on the tree in the corner of the room, letting himself drift on the image while he carved the ten spheres into the floor itself. Images of that tree combined with the perfect tree, the world-ash, the *otz chaim,* while the merkabah became a sleigh drawn by eight tiny reindeer, the one-eyed crucified safely behind the reins. Gods and monsters and the dead and the birth of the unmade—all danced in his head between the shadows of the emanations of the limitless light.

He panted as the noise got louder and the thing climbing the stairs reached the top, and he knew he wasn't alone.

"What is the builder's word? Why did he hang from the tree? What is the draught of the well?" rasped out of a dry throat even as a corpulent mass, gorged on all the fodder it could cram into a mouth that split its ham-sized head, oozed into his sight, filling the doorway. Chuckling, it inched forward, leaving a trail of oil and decay behind it, its bulk barely covered in patchy fur robes that only served to heighten its girth by leaving holes for it to strain against, bits of decay in its matted beard and eyes like those of a starving pig.

It made him want to vomit, to puke all over the floor. He contemplated his own end at those yellowing teeth as it licked quivering lips.

He forced himself to stare hard at the void between the spheres, the abyss he felt inside himself, gaping to swallow him. The place where the hanged man swung in the darkness seeking the word, the void of *da'ath* staring back out from inside him.

"What is the builder's word?" He screamed, and the tree at his feet burst into rainbow light, and a fire that burned and did not consume tore up into his body, setting his limbs to quiver and every hair on his body to dance as the glittering light lifted his fear from him.

He was a lone star in the sky, lighting the way.

The creature moving into the room did not hesitate. It could not. It was a creature of hunger, a great dark blot that could never be satisfied. It knew nothing of fear or hate, merely a desire to consume. Chuckling, its body quivering like a bucket of gelatin, it came forward to devour.

In a flicker, Nameless moved, spinning in the air in an arc that drove his boot into the side of the thing's face, avoiding that gaping mouth full of blunt yellow teeth. Several of them sprayed forth, one twirling through the air to embed itself root-first in the plaster above the fireplace.

The piglike snout crushed against the cheek from the impact. It staggered back, grunting and slobbering, while its attacker hooked a hand into a claw, the claw of the Corpse-Tearer, the gnawer at the root of the tree that is the world. Nameless tore that hand through mercury blood and gobbets of suet, spraying flesh and ichor across the floor. Even with its body shredding, the hunger drove it onward, and it swung a huge arm forward with enough force to crush bone and liquefy flesh.

The intended target had not stood to receive it. Instead he moved back, allowing the arm to pass unimpeded through the air, and then followed it back in ripping at the neck and throat, tearing away oozing chunks of semidecayed flesh.

It tried again, reaching out with both hands to try to crush its bulk down on top of him, and he moved to the side and drove his foot hard into the thing's hip, smiling at the sound of something cracking like he had once in that same room when opening the shiny wrapping on a box liberated from the tree's watchful gaze.

Even as it reacted he moved again, this time to twist his whole body, driving his knee hard into the root of the back where a spine might be concealed by the lie made flesh. More sounds of breaking and cracking, and another kick to the back of a knee sent it wobbling forward, unable to halt itself.

Behind it, Nameless dropped to a crouch and then drove his shoulder forward into its back, pushing it to fall directly at the searing rainbow light that ascended and descended the spheres of the tree cut into the floor.

The blast of light and heat lashed into him, even as he was infused with the power of the lightning flash himself. Growling, he felt himself burning inside, the sword of fire and his own hate taking over as he slammed his fist into the spine just below the head, and then into the head itself. Beneath the squirming meat and the crackling light of the sigil on the floor the wood cracked and splintered.

The floor gave way.

They fell together, the obscenity in flesh and the burning man, onto the burned remains of the old pool table. It fell apart from the impact, crumpling and cracking apart, tearing as it buckled. As the two of them hit the floor Nameless heard his voice screaming himself hoarse and saw his fist crush the back of the Glutton's head while flattening its face against the old concrete floor.

Panting, he dragged himself to his feet. Flashes of light, sparks, flickers of flame were dancing on his skin, and his hair was moving. He could feel the sword of fire in the base of his intestines and crawling along his thoughts, trying to drive out emotion and render him kindling to a great fire, a pyre to reach up out of the body entirely.

Hit the flame, burn a hole in my brain, never be the same.... The lyric to a song he couldn't quite remember haunted him.

He shook his head and focused on a chalk symbol on the floor. He remembered drawing it, the three-lobed burning eye within a five pointed star. To the left of it on the wall was a half-faded incantation to Oannes, crawled over by vines. Above it was the small window that had in the past allowed light to creep into the room, long since grown over with tough red tendrils.

The only light in the room was from him. The thick gray fluid, like cottage cheese mixed with mud, leaked out of the Glutton's corpse and burned where it touched him. That was something to be grateful for, at least.

He stepped away from the ruin of the pool table. He wasn't sad that it was gone. He looked over at the old bulkhead that led out of the basement, easily twenty feet away from him, so thickly tangled with plants that he couldn't even tell what kind of plants they were anymore. It was cavernous and claustrophobic at once, and he grimaced at the sight. Behind him were the wood-paneled walls that served to partition off the space, and behind those lay the long-deserted boiler and laundry rooms, where he'd...

He shook his head, feeling sparks between his teeth, and turned on his heel to get away from the room. It was no good. Somehow the ruined mass of meat on the floor had climbed up the stairs, but now the way to them, the long corridor between the rooms that led out of the basement, was choked with plants. He stared hard at them. There was no way the thing at his feet had forced its way through them. Which left innumerable other possibilities, and he growled at the effort of thinking about what those possibilities were while the sound of wind through leaves came from behind him.

There was no way there could be wind down there.

He stopped moving, closed his eyes, calmed himself. Listened for a moment to the sound of leaves scraping against stems, felt the desperate urge to burst forth into action and pulled it back under control.

When his breathing was even, he opened his eyes again, and the shimmering light of the sign of an ancient covenant shone forth, a light split into many colors. He saw the vines and branches and roots had closed in on him, tightening in a circle that completely closed off the way up the stairs and surrounded the central point of the room he was standing in.

"You are not expected." The voice came from all around him. It sounded like petals unfolding, wood scraped against wood, soft stems whipping about, approximating speech yet bearing an intonation that had no bearing on the words, hard and emphatic. "You left us unfinished."

"I never had any intention of allowing anything like you in the first place. I didn't even *consider* you, much less want to *finish* you." He saw a distorted shape lurking just behind the dark thicket weaving itself around him, something vaguely female. *Very* vaguely so, a poor guess at a woman with flaring "hips" and a trunk that ended in hundreds of branches.

"But you cut the first switch." Again that lack of emphasis, each word spoken with the same speed and tone. "You made the cut in the world that made us ready; you let the implication bleed in. You began, but did not complete."

He didn't respond, instead watching the small leaves tremble, noted the thorns on some of the crawling plants.... He counted roses, grapes, even distorted birch moving in the depths of the brown and green wall surrounding him. He slumped slightly, crouching on light feet, focusing himself into a point he imagined.

"I want to know why I am here. Those that read the final words did not know why. I asked them. Eventually they stopped answering me. But you were here before I knew... you made the ground ripe. You know why I am here." The wall of vines wriggled as it spoke, and then parted to allow that face to peer through at him. A wooden face with fronds for hair, green as his had once been, with broad veins. A sap-coated tongue of tangled clumps slid forth between her needle teeth, scraping along the edge of the face. Her eyes were holes in the woven branches of her face, with closed buds pushing through them.

He knew it was coming. A sudden convulsion and growth lashed out to grab at him, reaching for each limb. He reacted with an uncoiling of his own, grasping and shredding with both hands while moving backward, out of the way of the immediate danger. It might have worked.

It did not.

Unseen by him, the plants had crawled along the ceiling. One thick root dropped down to catch around his throat, squeezing like a wood python, lifting him off the ground. It was very strong, grinding hard along his neck, closing off his windpipe. It took him a second to bring his hands up to rip at it, tear it from his neck.

In that time, a thin shoot burst in a cloud of sticky fluid from the coiled wood and waved delicately in the air in front of his face.

Then it steadied itself and drove forward, plunging into his nose. Bone cracked as it lashed itself into his brain. Hanging in the air, he twitched and screamed, spit and blood dripping down his chin while his hands convulsed against the wood crushing his throat.

"I will know why I am here."

He did not want to remember.

He did anyway.

There was no color to the memory. There never was. It came like a dream, because it never came to him outside of dreams, though he could never forget it. There were colors, he assumed, but could no longer prove it even to himself.

He remembered the suit he'd been forced to wear. Not forced, exactly. He couldn't have dressed himself that day. Evvie, who had left him the month before, came back to help him, at Bishop's request. Together the two of them got him dressed, got his hair tied back, got him to the church.

The church was a huge stone-and-glass fang pushed up from grassy earth. Even in his gray memory he remembered staring at those lead-and-glass windows in horror, seeing Christ dragged from one humiliation to another. It had been something to fixate on, and he'd gratefully taken the option.

"Dude, you okay?"

Those three words were a formula. People asked him over and over again if he was okay, or all right, or doing well.

"How are you holding up?" This from one of his mother's colleagues, a short man with receding hair and a slight paunch who'd helped her sort through various Etruscan and old Roman pottery. His mother had once commented to his father, thinking him out of earshot, that the man—Dr. Rawlins, he remembered briefly—had testicles so large that they were plainly visible even when he wore loose slacks. So he dropped his attention and saw them, plain as day, titanic testicles poking themselves out from his crotch and deforming the corduroy of his pants.

"I'm fine. You have gigantic balls. My mom said so, and she was right." Someone hustled him away before he could tell the archaeologist that he was afraid the man might have elephantiasis. The idea of this made him laugh so hard that he began to choke on his own laughter, unable to get enough air to breathe properly, while hot tears ran down his face. When they put him in a quiet chair in an office somewhere he leaned back and laughed until the tears ran down his head and into his ears.

Eventually he stopped laughing, but the tears continued until someone—again, probably Bishop, because whoever it was managed to lift him by his upper arms—got him out into the church. Someone was reading a eulogy. It wasn't the slumped little man with the enormous testicles, for which he was thankful. He didn't want to start laughing again for fear he wouldn't stop.

He saw a momentary flash of green.

Then it was much later. A year later. Was it a year later? It was later, anyway. He was sitting in a rotten old chair his father had inherited from *his* father, a satin upholstered oak monstrosity with demons carved into the arms. He'd supposedly gotten it in Wittenberg. Somewhere in Germany. These were details that slipped away into the gray sludge of the past no matter how hard he thought about them, and he'd had other things to think about. There were no lights on in the cellar save for a lamp he'd brought down with him, a tall floor lamp that spilled a silver arc along the floor, illuminating the metal pool cues lying disassembled in the rack on the wall and the spill of papers he'd scattered everywhere. His own notes, his father's and grandfather's, tossed in piles, bound with large black clips or sometimes not bound at all, notebooks and folders and even napkins scribbled on. He'd started with Margaret Hunt's testimony, moved on to Michael Scot and Flamel, studied the reports of Valentine Greatrakes and Michel de Nostredame and even tried to re-create the *bright and ruddy elixir* of Raymond Lully. He had nothing for that but burned hands, and a digression into the plays of August Strindberg had been wasted time.

He looked over at the sooty marks in the corner of the room where he'd finally just gone apeshit and burned everything he owned written by Strindberg. *Till Damaskus, A Dream Play, Inferno* had all gone into the fire while he screamed and sobbed and beat the wall with his fists. *Nabatean Agriculture* had gotten him nowhere. He'd excavated through the piles of books in the bedroom looking for Chinggis Khan and his quest for immortality, or trying to understand Bacon's *Opus Majus*. He'd lit upon the idea of transmutation of the inner nature from the *Picatrix* but had no idea how to use it.

Through all of it he returned again and again to those two metal talismans, those trophies of his parents. He stared at them for hours, resting on the old pool table his father had stashed away for evenings spent alone contemplating new angles, geometry rendered in the solitary crack of ivory against ivory.

Those urns were his grail. Nothing could stop him. Nothing would stop him.

In the end the answer, the final secret, didn't come from any of the texts his father had collected, nor did it come from any of the books he'd dug up in his ceaseless combing of the Athenaeum, the Brown Library, or even the Providence Public Library. Of all places, he found the secret in Stadium Cards and Comics while looking for a present to mollify Bishop for one more week, another pretense at being over what he was not and did not imagine he could be. The last time he'd visited, he'd seen an umbrella he'd bought in London lying against the wall and pretended not to—she wasn't his anymore and none of his concern. Stadium Cards and Comics, where among the boxes full of old, yellowing issues of *Rom, Spaceknight* there was a stray copy of a comic book adapting a story called *The Case of Charles Dexter Ward*.

Essential salts and human dust.

Essence and dust. It was as if someone came along behind

him with a hammer and bashed him over the head with it while yelling everything he'd spent months and months reading in one long scream of words bleeding into each other. Essence, transformed, from dust into life again.

And so, he found himself sitting in the dark, staring at the urns in the arc of light thrown by the lamp while a green shadow (green?) clashed across his vision. Working up his courage, which was a pallid thing, feeling his thoughts reel from extreme to extreme while rage and fear acted like alcohol in his head.

Do I...

Eventually he pulled himself to his feet, pulled the leather jacket from his father's closet over his shirtless body to keep from shivering in the unheated cement room, and stalked over to the urns. He quivered to look at them.

Finally he lifted the one to the left, walked to the side of the table, and poured the dust into a pile, careful to keep it as far to the left as possible. He repeated this with the one to the right. Then he withdrew a mixture of salts he himself had crushed from the bag on the floor, and poured some on each pile of ash in a pattern of rings. Finally, he dusted his hands off and knelt, checking once to be sure the chalk on the walls held the proper sigils—death-conquering Jupiter, the three-lobed burning eye, the intricate *sigillum* with its stars within stars, the fish-tailed Oannes.

He dropped his head to the floor while a rustle of green curled around the laundry room wall—did that—and, kneeling, groaned out the words he'd prepared himself.

"Da'ath, mene, you hang in the void between worlds, the head of you lies in the gulf, the tail of you girds the world... uaaah, uaaah." His throat went dry as the memory of the words vanished like dust in a gale, the hair all over his body stiffened, sweat trailing down his face to pool on the cold hard floor. A quiet panic stole his voice along with the memory, and he knelt facedown, unable to speak, as the sensation of ants on his skin increased. His tongue forced itself to move. "I want them back. That's all. I don't want power; I'm not asking for wisdom or eternal youth or to fuck Helen of Troy. I just want them back."

"**Not the first time I've heard that.**" The voice was very quiet, but deep, so deep it almost seemed to be shaking the floor and climbing up into his head through his forehead. "**What will you give me?**"

"What do you want?"

"**What do you have? Pain, but you leak that out for anyone to have. No, you have nothing that interests me. Nothing I want.**" A long moment, with his face pressed into the concrete. "**You may lift your head.**"

"You haven't asked for my soul." He lifted his face, wet on the left side from sweat and clammy from the floor. Standing on the other side of the pool table was... was... his eyes slid over it, but it resolved into nothing. One second it looked like an old Egyptian tomb-painting of an Ibis-headed man in profile, the next a small boy in a field of fire holding a turtle shell with strings, and then a staff with snakes coiled around it. Other forms he couldn't name or understand. Along the edge of his vision he barely noticed a bright green leaf in the well of the bulkhead stairs.

"**Your soul? Assuming I could even perceive such a thing, what would I do with it? If I needed or wanted souls, why would I give two back to you in exchange for one? You did want them back, yes?**"

"...Yes."

"**I have no need for souls. I have less need for pain. I do, however, have a great fondness for names. I have many, myself.**" The whirling icon was a boy with stars for hair, then a manlike shape with the head of a bull straight from the wall of a cave, and then something that extended past vision and smelled vaguely of wet hair. "**I believe I will grant you your request. It will cost you your name. Do you agree?**"

He stared at the thing.

"This isn't going..."

"**Did you think this was easy? Your streets would teem with risen dead.**" It became the head of a lovely woman in white, who smiled sadly at him before becoming a flat beetle. "**If you were not obsessed, I would not have heard you. And** even then, I did not have to come. You should work on that. Still, it has been long since anyone has called me, even if you did not know you were calling. I suppose I am... bored. It will be interesting to watch what happens." A fish with a book in its mouth spun into view before becoming an egg with feet. "Again, I offer you the deal. Give me your name, and I will bring into life the piles of ash you have laid on this table. A life only you will be able to take from them."

"Why would I..."

"Agree or disagree. I tire of this place, and wish to see if you will satisfy my curiosity. Your name for life."

"...Take it." He felt the emptiness in his stomach as it lurched, felt that he might well vomit if he had vomit left to lose. "If that's the price, take it."

"Very well. As we agreed. Remember that the life I grant here is within your power to take. And the name I take here is within your power to replace. I wait with great interest to see what you do next."

There was no flash of light, no great rush of air, no display of great power. It was there, and then it was not. Nothing had changed. His face ached from the feeling of cold, rock-hard floor having pressed against it, and he was kneeling in an empty room in front of two piles of ash and salt on a ratty pool table while in the window to his left an errant verdant twig flickered across the glass even though it was Christmas and snowing and...

Then the sound, or something that wasn't sound at all but that pushed the same regions of the brain—a sucking, popping, shifting that took that empty feeling in his stomach and twisted it with a cold hand. He watched, transfixed, as it happened. He even smiled.

The smile died quickly as amorphous forms swelling out of the ashen piles did not resolve themselves as he'd hoped. Instead, he watched without any real understanding as a human head he'd never seen before grew out of the crotch of a pair of legs that ended in a hand on the left and a wriggling bowl of flesh, like a neck open on both ends for the right. The torso was female, with a strangely bent forearm growing from where the right breast would be and a concave depression completely failing to balance it out, the abdomen covered in a nose, several ears, an eye winking at him from the navel. Arms grew out of its back, no two matching. There was nothing at the shoulders, no head, nothing.

To the right his father's head with a withered, drooping penis growing out of its forehead rose out of a leg growing from a pair of shoulders. The torso was spotted with fingers, toes, a half-arm growing from the center terminating in a mouth and jaw, half a head. Below the torso seven limbs, two arms and five legs, each ending in feet. One of the feet had teeth instead of toes. It groaned and howled and gibbered out of each mouth, fixed eyes on him that contained infinite sorrow and pain, babbling in noises that were mercifully unlike words.

He leapt back, away from them, as they twitched on the felt. They couldn't get their limbs to work properly, or weren't trying to, shifting and rocking where they were. He saw fingernails from the limbs on the back of the one with his mother's brown eye staring out of its belly rend the felt, claw, and then spasm while the other one bit at the wood with the half-face on the end of the arm in its chest.

This continued for horrible seconds. He watched them move, even though they shouldn't move. He watched them slide into each other, shove back, crash to the table after attempting to rise. And he knew they would continue to do this. If they could be alive without any sense to their bodies—alive with more eyes, more fingers, more mouths than they'd had when they were alive—nothing could kill them. He wondered, tittering and clamping down on his jaw to keep the sound inside him, who else had been in those urns.

That thought managed to punch through the soothing chill of insanity trying to protect him. The thought reached down past the hollow place inside him where his own awareness of what he'd done lived and reached the anger he'd felt for the past year—the anger he'd shepherded, kept alive against every attempt by friend or lover to reach him and bring him back into the world. The hate at the unfairness of it.

This. I did this. I wasted my life on this. The whole time, I fought and fought to change it, and I was fighting for this.

He grabbed hold of the aluminum half of a pool cue at his side, feeling the weight of it in his hand. First he would fix what he'd done. Then he would visit the mortuary, and have a talk with them about mixing the cremains. He swallowed, wanting to spit but afraid he would never stop throwing up if he did, and looked again at the eyes of his father, which in memory were gray, not the vivid blue he knew they were in life. Perhaps it was a blessing to forget things like that.

They wept.

He screamed and charged, swinging the cue into the side of that head, crushing the skull. The sound of bone and the smell of blood... and the realization that the magic had truly worked, after a fashion, had brought true life back to those horribly mixed ashes... and then just the pounding of the club again and again, crushing bone and pulping flesh wherever he found it. He swung it again and again until finally it fell from slick fingers, deformed into something resembling a question mark, and the top of the pool table was covered in crushed flesh and oozing with blood.

They hadn't resisted much.

That didn't help. He growled, feeling hot knives in his head, and then turned to face the creeping vine along the ceiling, a thin green line.

"You wanted this? You wanted to see what happened? Fire *happened... and it's for you, now. Take it!!!"*

He opened his eyes, felt the vine crawling around inside his sinuses and behind his right eye while the woody root around his neck bit into his flesh.

Then he wasn't flesh anymore at all, as the sword of fire burst free and he burned, burned so purely that there wasn't a nose anymore for the tendril to violate or a brain to sink into, no throat to squeeze or hands to rip and claw. There was a roaring mass of flames, a screaming man-formed conflagration that raced along whatever it touched, that set green and brown alike to dancing as they withered, like leaves in the grip of autumn.

The creature that had held him in its grasp did not even utter a sound before flames erased her semblance of humanity.

The wooden fragments of the ceiling burned, and then the remains of the floor above. The walls shuddered and smoked, then erupted into tongues of copper and gold chewing at anything flammable. A net of fire raced along the coating of the wires and the shoots wormed through every available crack and cranny. The beams in the walls and the rotten fabric on the furniture and the dry, creosote-reeking Christmas tree... everything felt the teeth of the fire. Everything burned.

While the fire raged on, a mass of pure blue-green flames blasted its way through the green tiles that Albion Ape had once climbed across and crashed into the ice-glazed stalks of wild grass in the yard surrounding the house. These flames wrapped around each other in tails of heat and light before slowly condensing, melting the ice and then sending plumes of steam into the air, burning the grass away in a bowl all the way down to bare earth for several meters.

Then they died down, spinning about as they became a body again. He coughed and convulsed and hacked up a plug of blood and snot even as the hole in his sinuses closed over. Healed by the ebbing touch of the lightning flash as it ascended wholly out of him, moaning as the pain in his head refused to retreat. The last of the flames became sooty, dark, and then the smoldering nude body in the dirt became a smoldering clothed body in the dirt, steam, and smoke rising around him.

He lay there for as long as he thought he could get away with before dragging himself upright. The flames now raged in the backyard as well, burning even through the ice cover on the unnaturally green plant-life, and the roof caved in while he watched. He smiled at the sight of that.

Then he turned and walked away, fairly secure that no one in the neighborhood would want to tell anyone too much about the person who'd rid them of the house. It was a very small victory. It was enough.

It had to be.

Michael Moorcock needs no introduction, but he's getting one, anyway. Widely regarded as one of the leading lights in fantastic literature of the twentieth century and beyond, he's written more books and stories than anyone can reasonably be expected to count. The following, a yarn of aviation and adventure in the more innocent days before the London Blitz, draws its inspiration from the comics Moorcock wrote nearly half a century ago, most notably "Dogfight Dixon, RFC" in Fleetway's *Thriller Picture Library*.

Dogfight Donovan's Day Off
by Michael Moorcock

THE WESTERN FRONT, World War One —AND THE SECURITY OF BRITAIN DEPENDED ON THE FATE OF ONE YOUNG FLYER!

I
DUEL ABOVE THE CLOUDS

DICK DONOVAN HEARD the sound first—the distinctive whine of a flight of Albatroses diving down out of the sun. He put his gloved hand in front of his goggled eyes and opened his fingers a trifle to make out the enemy. He was right. The next sound coming from the Albatros "Circus" would be the sharp staccato bark of Spandau machine guns. But by that time Donovan had given the signal, rammed his joystick forward, kicked down on his rudder, and led the squadron's Sopwith Camels in a perfectly executed Immelmann turn. This put them behind the German warbirds, their own twin Vickers firing in concert through their propeller blades even as the Albatroses split into two flights, diving into the clouds. A classic dogfight had begun, and there was nothing the daring fliers of "Baker's Dozen"—Number Thirteen Squadron, RFC—liked more than a good scrap. Led by the Royal Flying Corps' youngest MC, they were soon engaged in a nerve-tingling aerial battle that would not be over until someone went down in flames or the planes ran out of fuel.

One by one the British warbirds peeled off into individual combat. Dogfight Donovan soon found himself in a balletic air-duel with a pilot he recognized as belonging to the famous Kaos-Staffel made up entirely of tried and true aces, Germany's finest knights of the air, as well-known for their courtesy as their courage.

Nonetheless this was a duel to the death. Dogfight threw his plane into an almost vertical climb as the Albatros screamed up behind him, machine-gun bullets whizzing around like angry bees and only missing him by a miracle. A Jaggers flip and he was coming back, diving straight towards the enemy plane, his own Vickers clattering their answer to the German's guns.

Rata-tat-tat-tat. In an almost girlish flirt of her tail, the Albatros slipped in a long Bigglesworth swing, throwing a swathe of lead towards the Camel that Dogfight just avoided, grinning coolly as he recognized the pilot's style.

"It's bally old von Bek himself. I'm fighting the boss!" This was not the first time he'd crossed swords with the *Staffel-chef*, and though his life depended on it, his brain had become cool and his hand on the controls steady in a state of mind shared by every ace in the skies no matter who they were or what they were flying.

Then, as Dogfight peeled away into a big patch of cumulus he heard a sudden *phut-phut-phut*, and hot oil splashed his goggles. The German's bullets had hit his fuel line. Instinctively he switched off his engine and glided in silence through the engulfing whiteness, the fighting planes a distant drone and rattle somewhere far away.

They were thirty miles from the front. Thirty miles over German territory and no-man's-land. And Dogfight was watching the fuel stream from his ruptured tank as he battled to keep his Camel on course.

Using every skill he knew, he fought his controls, finessing his wing-flaps and rudder as he broke below the clouds and saw the ground less than four thousand feet below coming up fast. He headed for a wide green field, swung his nose up and flipped his engine toggle to give a last burst of power to his prop. There was a flash of flame and then a massive bump as the plane slammed into the ground. He just had time to switch off his engine again before the Camel's wheels were rolling over rough, muddy grass. Then his head struck his instrument panel, and suddenly it was pitch black. He tried to curse his luck, but the words wouldn't come and he lost consciousness completely. For Captain Dogfight Donovan MC, RFC, the war seemed well and truly over!

II
ENEMY HOSPITALITY

DICK DONOVAN WOKE up smelling the rich aroma of Darjeeling Tea and a slightly burned toasted teacake. Was it possible he'd landed over his own lines? Had he made such a huge miscalculation?

Cautiously he opened his lids. A pair of merry blue eyes met his, and a young man of about his own age said:

"Hello, old boy. How are you feeling?" But for the faintest of accents it might have been one of his own Number Thirteen squadron speaking, but Dick knew now where he was and had a fair guess who he was speaking to—

"You're Gerhardt von Bek, aren't you?" He remembered that von Bek had been at Eton before the war.

"You can call me 'Gerry,' Dick Donovan," said the young German flyer with an ironic twist of his lip. "Nice to meet you. You're the best airman I've ever had the pleasure of fighting."

"You, too," said Dick, looking around the well-run field hospital. "Am I badly hurt?"

"A spot of concussion, that's all, old man. You should be well enough to attend our mess dinner tonight, I hope. It's in your honor!"

"Thanks for the invitation. I'll be there." Dick Donovan stretched out his hand to shake that of his honorable enemy.

Traditionally, certain flyers of both sides would give a downed enemy a good dinner and then, if they could get away with it, send him home in a repaired "bus." This practice had prevailed early in the war, but was no longer common.

"Good," said young von Bek, straightening up and smiling. "I hope you like sausages and beer. It's the closest we can come to a gourmet meal at the moment."

A few hours later Dick took his place at the head of the table with his new "friend." As one, the entire squadron of grey-uniformed aces snapped to their feet and saluted him. Then, for the rest of the dinner, they were deep in tales of famous fights and war-aces. Flyers, like old-time Western gunfighters or modern sportsmen, enjoyed mutual esteem.

Then towards the end of the evening a newcomer joined the group. He was a rather different character, lacking all the charm of the Kaos-Staffel. Somewhat older, he bore a major's pips and addressed Dick very formally.

"So you are the young man they call 'Dogfight,' eh? You realize, of course, you are wasting your time trying to defeat us? We already control the seas and land, and very soon now we will control the skies!"

"Well, there are a lot of chaps like me who hope to stop you doing that, sir," retorted Dick as his companions fell into embarrassed silence.

"This playacting, this stupid so-called 'chivalry of the air,' it's meaningless. Chivalry is a delusion. Your cities are already learning just what a delusion it is!" The major bowed, clicked his heels, and saluted. "Goodnight, gentlemen. Enjoy your boys' games while you can. They are already passé. As you will all discover when the realities of our aerial battleships make nonsense of your imaginary follies."

With that, he was gone.

"Blimey! Who was that unpleasant blighter?" asked Dogfight, sitting down and reaching for his beer. "Very 'old school,' what?"

"That's Manfred von Schlappen," murmured von Bek apologetically. "He's always thought our kind of flying was a waste of time."

"*Our* kind of flying? Is there any other kind?"

"Oh, yes," said von Bek with a sigh. "And he's the genius who is going to put that other kind on the map."

Rather more subdued, the airmen finished their dinner.

On their way back to the hospital wing, von Bek took his opposite number aside, apologizing again for von Schlappen's rudeness. "If you were to get up at about five o'clock tomorrow morning, you might find your uniform beside your bed, ready to wear. And, if you were to stroll out onto the airfield, you might just see a Sopwith Camel with a suit of flying togs in the seat. She's all repaired, fueled up, and ready to go."

Dick pumped his rival's hand. "You're a good sport, Gerry. I hope I can return the favor some time."

Gerry von Bek grinned. "And I hope I'll never be in the position to need it, Dick! I'll be glad when this bally scrap's over, so that we can return to flying our planes for fun, eh?"

Donovan agreed fervently. And with that he returned to his hospital bed, knowing that whoever won this awful, pointless war, he had made a firm friend.

III
"A SPOT OF LEAVE"

BRRR— BRRR— BRRR—oom. The Camel's engine had never sounded better as Dick Donovan brought his machine to land on his home field. He dropped the plane down light as a feather, swinging her to a corner near the main hangar and laughing with pleasure as he saw his chums running towards him, most of them still in their pajamas.

"You made it!" exclaimed his best pal "Yank" Younger, the young American who had come out to join the Espadrille Lafayette in 1916 and instead found himself flying with Donovan's squadron, named "Baker's Dozen" after their Squadron Leader

Howard "Bill" Baker and their "unlucky" number 13.

"We thought you'd bought it that time, old man!" gasped Ralph Coveney, Baker's adjutant, who had helped form the original squadron.

"How many did we lose?" Donovan wanted to know.

"None. After you'd gone down, von Bek pulled his boys off and went home. Felt like some sort of show of respect. How did you get away?"

"I'll tell you over breakfast," promised Donovan.

But Dogfight's breakfast was cut somewhat short. Just as they were all seated in the mess hut tucking into eggs and bacon there was an interruption.

"I say, chaps, sorry and all that—" Ralph Coveney put his head round the door. "Donovan. Younger. Head's office. Sharp."

He allowed no room for questions.

"Look's like we're on the carpet," said Dick, getting to his feet. "Wonder what it can be." Together the two young airmen made for Baker's office across the compound. It was a beautiful, sunny morning. The light glanced off the freshly "doped" wings of the waiting Camels, each with the circled flying 13 symbol on its fuselage. "Wonder what the old man wants?"

If they expected a "wigging" they were in for a surprise.

Baker's bucolic face was almost beaming as he regarded his two young pilots who stood, caps in hands, at ease on the other side of his desk.

"Mornin', lads," he said. "You're both lookin' a bit weary, what?"

"Certainly not, sir!" exclaimed Donovan hastily. "Fit as fleas, sir!"

Baker laughed aloud at their expressions. "Don't worry, I'm not about to play matron and claim you've been stayin' up too late. I gather you've just escaped from Boche territory, Donovan?"

"Well, with a bit of help from von Bek and his boys. Great chaps, sir."

"So I gather. Made you welcome, eh? I'd heard they were

a decent lot over there. Be glad when this bally business is all over, what?"

"Yes, sir."

"Not over yet, though, by a long shot. But in spite of that I've decided to give you a bit of leave."

"Leave, sir?" Donovan was baffled.

"What's the matter, man? Don't you feel like a day off in London?"

"*London*, sir? That would be marvelous! But how come?"

"I'll tell you privately, chaps, there's a big push on its way. The enemy is playing havoc with our supply ships. A couple of U-boats in the channel are stopping a lot of steamers. Pretty indiscriminately, too. The zeppelin fleet, under their best airship man, is beginning a new series of raids over Blighty. What's more, we're short of planes as well as pilots. We could do with a breather to build up our reserves, but it doesn't look as if that's going to happen. This is the only chance you're going to get for a spot of leave. What's more, there's a captured German kite needs ferryin' back to Croydon and a couple of the latest Sopwith PXIs to be picked up. I want you lads to go over there, turn in the Gotha—which is Jerry's new bombing aeroplane—and bring the Sopwiths home. You can refuel at Calais, what?"

"Very well, sir. Sounds a bit of a doddle to me. Do we get any time in London?" Dogfight wanted to know.

"A few hours. Make the most of them. The Boche will be making an all-out attempt to break the present stalemate. Blighty's taking a bit of a hammering, what with one thing and another. As I say, a concentrated attack on all fronts."

"I can guess what you mean, sir," interjected Donovan, and told his CO about von Schlappen's boast.

"You'll keep this to yourselves, of course. No point in alarming the civilians at home."

"Naturally, sir. When do we leave?"

"As soon as you like. The Gotha's been painted over with British roundels so there's not much of a chance of anyone attacking you by mistake. She's a massive bus and we were lucky to get her in one piece, but two of you should be able to fly her to Croydon. Calais, of course, is expecting you."

"Right you are, guv'nor!" Dick and Yank saluted smartly.

Together the two men left the office, excited about the prospect of having a crack at one of the big "buses," which were several times the weight of their highly maneuverable, if idiosyncratic, Camels.

Yank Younger whistled in anticipation. "Take me back to dear old Blighty, eh, Dogfight?"

"I can guess what you're looking forward to, Yank!"

The American ace offered him a wink. "Too bad you're engaged, eh, pardner?"

Dick Donovan flushed. "Oh, I wouldn't say that. If Connie's not on duty at Marylebone General we might even get to a dance or see the new 'flicker' at Leicester Square Hippodrome. *Birth of a Nation*'s on, I hear."

"You British guys sure know how to live," smiled Younger, with a friendly nudge to his fellow airman's ribs.

IV
A NOISY INTERRUPTION

WITH A DEAFENING roar, the massive Gotha rose into the air above Calais on the last leg of her journey to England.

Soon they were out over the English Channel at 11,000 feet. The day was grey and cold, the clouds just above their heads. Unused to the big, lumbering bomber, Dick Donovan kept his eye out for landmarks on the other side. But before he spotted the white cliffs of Dover he glanced down and caught sight of a swathe of black smoke drifting across the choppy waters below. Unable to believe his eyes, he signaled Yank to look down at what he saw.

A British ship belonging to the Merchant Marine was on her side and sinking in flames, giving off the smoke Dick had seen. Her crew were in the water swimming for their lives while near them stood off one of the infamous "sharks of the sea"—a German U-Boat, the U-666! It had come to the surface clearly unaware of the captured Gotha high above. There was nothing Dick or Yank could do to help. The Gotha was unarmed. Another sub, the U-668, was also just rising to the top of the waves, signaling to its mate. Dick saw a man in the conning tower. The German had recognized the Gotha but was too far away to see their markings so he waved a cheerful salute.

Furious at his inability to help the British sailors, Dick was forced to fly on. Soon the chalk cliffs were ahead and then below them. Not long afterwards, he eased down on his stick as the long runways of Croydon came into sight, and they were signaled in.

Dick jumped out of the cockpit, dragging off his helmet. Yank's grim features stared back at him. "Dashed bad luck we had no armaments," gritted Dogfight. "I could have used a couple of torpedoes or a rack of Cooper bombs back there!"

He told the aircraftsmen who ran to help them what he had seen in the Channel. One of them lowered his eyes. "My brother was on board a supply boat last week," he said. "The U-666 sank 'em. Now we don't know if he's drowned or a prisoner in Germany. We've heard nothing yet from the Red Cross."

"I don't know how you guys stand it," chimed in Yank. "We have it easy, compared to you."

Not much later they boarded the train at West Croydon and were soon steaming in to London's Victoria Station. After snatching a few hours with Connie Roberts, his fiancée, who had no more time off, Dick strolled down Oxford Street, where he had arranged to meet his pal outside the Propeller Club for dinner. Being a weekend, the city was full of busy shoppers and the buses were crowded.

It had grown dark by the time Dick spotted his pal by the big Oxford Circus newsstand. He was buying a paper while the newsboy shouted the headlines. "Read all about it! Another British ship sunk in the Channel! Read all about it! U-Boats sink another merchant ship!"

"Blasted Boche seems to be calling all the shots these days, Yank," muttered Dick, glancing over the front page of the *Evening News*. "Picking us off like sitting ducks and making advances in France. Looks like we're in for a pretty tough scrap, pard!"

Yank grinned with all the devil-may-care optimism of his people. "Don't worry, Dick. There's a lot at home who think like me. They're rarin' to come over here and help our cousins out!"

A smile crossed Dick's lips. "Aren't most of those 'cousins' from Germany and Ireland? I'd have thought—"

Suddenly a warning klaxon began to sound and the dark sky was lit by the bright fingers of searchlight beams. From somewhere above came the steady *thrum-thrum* of powerful engines as if a ship were overhead.

"Great Scott!" exclaimed Dick. "What's all this about?"

Lights went out along Oxford Street. A man came running towards them, seeking the refuge of the Tube station. "Get to cover!" he yelled. "Quickly! It's one of the giant zeppelins! They're bombing us!"

Even as the man called out to them, a bomb exploded barely a hundred feet away and the watchers were hurled backwards by the force of the explosion.

Scratched and bruised, but otherwise unhurt, Dick and Yank picked themselves up and surveyed the awful scene of destruction before them. Several shops were blazing as incendiary bombs took their toll.

"Seems a bit unsporting, what?" said Dick, helping a young woman climb to her feet. "What a mess!"

"The sooner a squadron's formed to stop those darned airships the better!" said a man wearing the Red Cross armband. "They aren't going to have their own way forever. It's up to you chaps!"

"You never said a fairer word, my old son," agreed Dick Donovan. "A few rounds of tracers in those gasbags and they'd soon think twice about interrupting honest housewives in the middle of doing their shopping!"

Dick and Yank's stay in London could scarcely have been called pleasant. By the next morning they were back at Croydon to pick up the new-type Sopwiths, which seemed even more compact and "tidy" than the familiar Camels. One of their old pals was on the field to say good-bye. He had been sent home wounded and looked enviously at the new planes as Dick and Yank buttoned up their flying jackets.

"Goodbye, chaps. Wish I could be going with you!" he said.

"Goodbye, Cawthorn. I expect we'll be seeing you as soon as that foot of yours gets better. We could use a few more to help out over there."

"You heard about two of our troop carriers being torpedoed by the 'Deadly Twins,' did you? Happened last night. U-666 and her sister sub scored another couple. What with the zeps and the subs, we're having a hard time of it."

"You said it, Cawthorn. Don't forget to try to arouse interest in a squadron or two of interceptor planes to deal with the new bombing threats."

"Don't worry, lads. I'm off to the Air Ministry in a minute. What you've told me should help me make my case."

Soon the pair were airborne. Dick was amazed at the maneuverability of the little Sopwith. She was as well-armed and sprightly as his beloved Camel but even easier to handle in the air. He was looking forward to taking her over enemy lines as soon as possible. He was thinking, *Can't wait to get another crack at von* Bek's *Staffel*, when he saw Yank jabbing his gloved hand forward, pointing at something emerging out of a cloud-bank directly ahead.

It was a massive German airship! Her grey canvas, stretched tightly over her aluminum hull, was painted with the black "Iron Crosses" of the German military. She had big engine nacelles at front and back and a control gondola in the middle. From this, Dogfight knew, the Germans dropped their cargoes of deadly "eggs." She was clearly on her way to make a daylight raid, probably when England was least expecting her.

Full of fury, Dogfight stopped thinking. He signaled to Yank. Both men were of the same mind—to take revenge for what they had witnessed the previous night in Oxford Street. He flipped off the securing bolt of the twin Vickers. "Here's our chance to hit back at those blighters," he muttered through clenched teeth.

And then he kicked down on his rudder bar, pulled his joystick up to his chest with one hand, and settled his fist around the trigger of his Vickers.

Guns blazing a message of death, the two plucky pilots closed with the monster zeppelin. Machine-gun bullets tore into the ship's fabric, but did little harm. The zep was built of a number of compartments, any two or three of which could be punctured and leave the airship stable enough to stay aloft. This was long before the days of tracer bullets as standard issue, and while the bullets could ultimately have brought the zep down, the surprised crew weren't going to let the RFC lads have it all their own way.

A massive Krupps began to bark rapidly back at them from the central gondola as the zeppelin retaliated.

Dogfight and Yank flung their planes into an evasive curve, still firing, still trying to hit the important components of the huge gasbags. A stream of deadly lead was coming at them as the Germans swung their gun this way and that in a wide swathe.

Dogfight forgot all his usual training. He looped around and came back at the airship, his Vickers pouring everything they had at the armored gondola. But the Germans were too well protected and their guns continued to fire back.

Suddenly a sickening sound, like tearing paper, registered in Dogfight's ears. The German bullets had hit his plane. Flame blossomed in his engine and he felt the searing heat against his face. He had been badly hit, and there was no way he was going to save his plane. All he could do now was scramble from the cockpit and throw his joystick back in the hope of jumping clear of the Sopwith as he aimed it up at the still-firing gondola.

But even before he jumped he could tell his plane was flying too high and wide of the zeppelin. It was going to go over the airship. There was only one thing he could do now. He had to take a chance. Without further thought, he jumped clear of his Sopwith and fell with sickening speed through the air—to land with a breathtaking thump on top of the zep's hull! Clinging with his fingers to the "bones" of the canvassed struts, he watched as his plane turned over and began a screaming dive into the drink.

Overhead he caught a glimpse of the astonished face of Yank Younger as his partner waggled his wings to show that he'd been spotted. Then, knowing that the zeps had inspection hatches on top of their hulls, Dogfight clung with all his might to the fabric as he inched his way along, finally managing to stagger to his feet and move carefully along the narrow walkway on top of the massive ship.

Suddenly a gust of wind struck the zeppelin and it shuddered. Donovan waved his arms, desperately striving to stay on his feet. If he fell now, it would almost certainly be to his death. He toppled and lost his footing, beginning to slide down the canvas of the hull.

Then, as he frantically spread his arms to distribute his weight, his left hand touched a protruding handle, used by the riggers to bring the ship in to land, and he held on with all his strength. His fall stalled, Dogfight looked more closely at the handle that had saved his life.

"Hello," he murmured to himself, "this looks like a bally lid!" He struggled to remember the little he had read about airships and recalled that they had inspection hatches, with "tunnels" leading between the various sections of the gasbag. Getting as much height and purchase as he could, he opened the cover, unlatching the lugs that held it in place. He was almost knocked off by the lid as it sprang off and hurtled into space. Now he could look down into the thrumming interior of the ship. With relief he swung into the depths, climbing slowly down the ladder he found and hoping no one aboard spotted him. "I've nothing to lose, after all!" As a precaution, however, he unbuttoned the holster of his standard-issue Webley revolver.

Almost certainly the German gunners were still giving their attention to Yank Younger. Dogfight could hear the chuckle of the Vickers guns somewhere in the distance. Now it would be just his luck if Yank scored a hit and he went down into the drink with the airship!

At last he reached a narrow passage and found himself outside a metal door with the words ACHTUNG! EXPLOSIVSTOFFE! stenciled on it.

"Beware, Explosives, eh? This must be the gun-room. Let's deal with that first," said Donovan to himself, drawing his revolver and twisting the lever of the door.

It opened easily. Dogfight grinned at the surprise of the two German gunners who turned slowly, trying to understand how someone who was evidently a British pilot had managed to get into their ship!

Holstering his pistol, Dogfight plunged in. "Hello, Jerries! I've got a few scores to settle with you blokes!"

And then his gloved fists were flying, taking first one gunner and then the other on the chin.

Recovering from their initial amazement, the two Germans closed with Donovan.

Crack!

"That's one for the lady your bombs frightened while I was in London!"

Crack!

"And that's for shooting up a brand-new plane!"

"Oof! Oof!" One after the other, the Germans collapsed unconscious, to the aluminum floor.

Knowing that the rest of the airship's crew would soon be alerted, Dogfight got hold of the big machine gun and swung it so that it was pointed straight at the racks of bombs that hung there, ready to be dropped on another British target.

Almost immediately several Germans, pistols in hand, came running into the turret, only to find a grinning Dogfight Donovan aiming the machine gun at the bomb racks.

Using his best German, Dogfight motioned with the gun. "Throw down those pistols, gentlemen—or I'll blow us all to kingdom come!"

"*Gott in Himmel*, Britisher! You will never succeed with this madness!" rasped the leading airshipman.

V
BAIT FOR AN IRON FISH

OUTSIDE, YANK YOUNGER zoomed past, wiggling his wings. He had seen Dogfight land on the ship and now, with the machine gun out of action, had some idea of what was going on. He continued to buzz around the zep like an angry wasp.

Meanwhile the Germans had reluctantly thrown down their pistols and put up their hands, glaring at the young flyer yet unable to do anything. They obeyed him in the hope their comrades in the control room would help them.

"Now quick march to that storage locker I saw on my way here," commanded Dogfight. A plan had formed in his head. It was an impossible one, but he had little choice. The storage locker was just large enough to take the German crew. *That'll keep* you *quiet while I see if I can steer this big sausage.*

Donovan's next stop was the clearly marked door at the front of the gondola. Passing through a small cabin, he found himself in the control room. Two men sat at the controls, and one, as he turned, red-faced, to demand who was interrupting him, was recognized immediately by the young airman.

A slow grin spread over the young flyer's features as Major von Schlappen began to stand up in his seat, growing even redder in the process.

"Well, well, well. If it isn't my old acquaintance, the Master of Modern Warfare, von Schlappen." With his left hand, Dogfight saluted sardonically. "Mornin', major. I'd be obliged if you'd raise your hands. If you'd rather not, of course, I'll understand. It'll give me great pleasure to blow a hole in you as big as the one you tried to blow in the window of that big department store in Oxford Street last night."

Again, von Schlappen and his copilot had very little choice but, spluttering their anger, to obey the young flyer.

Binding the two men with their own belts, Dogfight sat himself down at the controls of the massive ship, slid back a window and waved to Yank Younger, whose astonishment was expressed by pointing a finger at his own head and turning it in a winding motion to show that he thought Donovan crazy.

Most of the instruments were similar to those Donovan was familiar with. His plan was to try to take the captured ship back to Calais and deliver it up to the Allied forces. "I get it. The steering wheel's not so different to that you find on a motor car, and these other controls are the same as I'm used to a plane. She's even more sluggish than the Gotha, but I think I can get the hang of her." He glanced out of the control room to see, to his surprise, Yank Younger waggling his wings and jabbing with his gloved hand down at the sea. "Yank's trying to tell me something. I wonder what he's seen down there in the drink…"

Locking his wheel, Dogfight crossed to the starboard side. The breath caught in his throat. He saw two unarmed British trawlers, like sitting ducks, trapped between two U-boats, the U-666 and the U-668, the very same submarines they had seen on their way over. The civilian boats were sustaining machine-gun fire from the deck guns of the enemy. Now they spotted Yank's Sopwith as it dropped down towards them, guns blazing in an attempted defense of the merchantmen. They turned their big deck guns on the British plane, ignoring the zeppelin, which they assumed was one of theirs.

Putting the zeppelin on a fixed course, Dogfight ran back to the gun-room, settled himself behind the big machine gun and opened fire on the nearest sub, the U-668. But he soon realized the bullets weren't having much effect on the steel-hulled sub and the gun-crew were too well-protected. Meanwhile, the commander of the U-668, realizing that the zeppelin was in the hands of his enemy, ordered his gun crew to start firing at the zeppelin. Now Dogfight was in serious trouble!

The big gun on the sub fired a few well-aimed blasts at the aluminum hull, and Dogfight felt the zep rock and reel in the air. He knew that he'd sustained a serious hit. Not only had he failed to help the merchantmen, it looked like he was much worse off than before!

As the monster airship began to lose height, lumbering and lurching until it was almost directly above the U-668, Dick left the gun and rushed to the bomb-rack, manhandling one of the big bombs over to the porthole, he leaned out as the zep began to sink directly down over a submarine.

"Catch hold of this, Jerry!" he yelled and let go of the bomb.

The "egg" whistled seawards.

KA-BOOM!!! Dick's aim was spot on! His bomb struck the U-boat full on the conning tower. The sub blew up. Spectacular flames blasted far and wide across the water, and the sub sank instantly. All that was left was a little fluttering fire on a spreading oil slick.

A few moment's later, the zeppelin itself was bumping down onto the water, its gondola held up by what gas remained in the gasbag and the hull itself. Dick knew that he would be cooked if he stayed in the ship much longer. Hastily he lashed the gun so that it was pointing again at the bomb rack; then he went back to release the Germans tied up in the control cabin and the others whom he'd locked in the storeroom, picking up a length of cord he found there.

Gesturing with his pistol, he ordered the Germans off the ship. "Right ho, Jerries. Get moving. Your pals on the U-666 probably think you're British, but if you don't get off the zeppelin soon you'll go down to Davy Jones. It's your choice!"

When they reached the gun turret, Dogfight forced the Germans to help each other through the observation port. Soon they were all spluttering in the water.

Taking the length of cord he'd found in the storage room, Dogfight now tied it to the trigger of the fixed machine gun so that it pointed at the bomb rack. Gingerly, he paid out as much slack as possible before taking the rest of the cord between his teeth and levering himself through the porthole of the sinking zep. As he stood upright on the side of the gondola he saw that the other enemy sub, the U-666, was dangerously close but that its crew, peering from the conning tower and rail of the gun position, were now confused, having recognized their own uniforms on the airshipmen in the water. It gave him the few precious moments he needed.

"Not much time left! I must work fast!" Holstering his pistol, with the cord still between his teeth, Dick dived into the freezing water of the English Channel and swam strongly away from the gondola and the shouting Germans. The sub drifted closer to the downed airship, clearly not hearing the ferociously yelling von Schlappen, and was no longer between him and the Germans in the water now.

The cord trailing behind him, and hampered by his heavy flying gear, Dogfight still managed to put a hundred feet between himself and the sub. It had not yet picked up the wallowing crew and slipped in closer to the sinking zeppelin, curious to see what exactly they had brought down, oblivious to the voices in the water. Then there came a shout from the conning tower as they saw Dogfight and recognized him as British. The big gun began to swing slowly in his direction.

This was it! Seconds to go!

"Phew! I'd better get on with the rest of my barmy plan. Let's see if this will work!"

Treading water, Dogfight pulled sharply on the cord. There came a harsh sound of machine-gun fire from within the gondola and then—

BOOM!!!

Dick Donovan dived down deep below the water as the bombs aboard the zep blew up in one mighty chain reaction—blasting the U-666 to kingdom come! Flaming oil sputtered down with shrapnel from the destroyed sub and zeppelin as the U-666 joined all the harmless merchantmen she had sent to the bottom during her long career.

Von Schlappen and his men, perfectly aware of how this lone Britisher had defeated them, saw Dogfight come up for air. The flyer heard the German commander bellow an order from the water as he led the way towards Dick, swimming strongly.

Von Schlappen reached him, drew his airshipman's knife from its scabbard and raised the blade to take the exhausted British flyer in the throat. Dick just managed to throw up his hand and block the blows, and together the two sank beneath the waves, wrestling wildly in the waters of the Atlantic. But von Schlappen had partaken too fully and too often of his beer and sausages and was in no condition to best the fighting- fit Englishman. After a brief struggle underwater, Dick knocked the knife from his hand and swam away underwater, with no idea how he was going to escape from the rest of the Germans, who were probably in much better shape than their major.

If only Yank could help me somehow! he thought, almost praying as he broke the surface in time to see his pal's compact little Sopwith zooming close to the surface as it sought him out.

He had forgotten about Yank's famous skill with the lariat, which he always kept in his cockpit as a good luck piece. Suddenly, as Yank put his Sopwith into a controlled stall, down came yards of tightly wound rope —

—just as three more Germans caught up with Dick Donovan in the water. He had only a second to catch the rope, sock one of the Germans on the chin, and get a firm grip on the lariat as Yank began to climb rapidly skywards! "So long, Jerries!" said Dick to himself as he left von Schlappen and his men far below. "Give my regards to the folks back in Blighty! You'll be spending the rest of the war in a nice cozy POW camp, I'd guess!"

The climb up the rope was dangerous and difficult, but at last Dick reached the relative safety of the Sopwith's wheel-struts and was able to make out Yank's features grinning down at him. He could barely hear the young American's shouted words above the engine noise.

"Glad you made it, Dick! Enjoy the party?"

"Thanks, Yank. It got a bit rough towards the end, but it was fun!" Inch by inch, in a procedure the two had practiced together when not on duty, Dick began to clamber up the fuselage until he had reached the port wing and was hanging on tight, grateful for his flying kit without which he might have frozen. Yank took one final turn over the British merchantmen, seeing that the blustering von Schlappen and his men were being hauled aboard, together with the survivors of the U-boats. Then he smiled again and shouted over to his pard.

"Where to now, m'lord?"

Dick straightened, sitting upright on the wing. "Home,

James. I think we've done all the damage we can do for one day. Pity we lost a bus, though!"

An hour later, as the little Sopwith landed perilously on the Calais airfield, they were met by their fellow airmen, who came running to greet them. They had no idea how Yank and Dick had made it to the field, but they could see they'd been in a scrap. The two young flyers hardly had time to explain themselves before they were taking off again in the old, familiar Camels they were used to, leaving the new "bus" with their fellow airmen. However, if they expected to sneak home, they had reckoned without the telegraph from GHQ via the British trawlers. Their exploits had been broadcast ahead of them.

They were welcomed by their pals of "Baker's Dozen" with a rousing cheer and "chaired" all the way back to Squadron Leader Bill Baker's office, where their commanding officer was waiting for them, a huge, beaming grin on his farmer's features.

"Once again you failed to follow orders, you two!" he barked as they were set down in front of him. "I don't remember telling you to do a bit of balloon-strafing on the way home." He beamed. "You copped a couple of tin fish in the meanwhile, too, eh?"

"'Fraid so, sir," said Donovan, saluting. "It seems old von Schlappen wasn't quite ready to take over the air war. He'll be drying off in Dover by now and drinking his cocoa in camp."

"While our people will have time to float a few reinforcements here, ready to meet and beat the Jerries when they begin their big push. You've done a great job, chaps. You'll be glad to know that, if I have anything to do with it, you'll both be getting bars to stick on those MCs of yours. If GHQ believes the story, that is. I can hardly believe it myself!"

"Us, neither, sir," said Yank. "It was mostly Donovan's doing, of course. All I did was observe the action from the comfort and safety of my 'office.'"

A look of seriousness crossed Baker's jolly face. "You lads did a superb job. Thanks to your efforts, our chaps now have time to sort out some kind of defense against the airships, as well as the Gothas we know are going to take over from them. Meanwhile, the U-666 and her sister ship won't bother us ever again.

No doubt they'll try to replace them, but it will mean taking two more subs off other crucial routes. My guess is you've bought us months, without which we'd have been pretty hard-pressed, I don't mind telling you."

Baker led the two young flyers back inside, where he opened a hoarded bottle of champagne and poured the stuff into tin mugs. "Here's to you, chaps. Oh, and remind me of something if we get in another sticky spot in the weeks to come will you?"

"Certainly, sir. What's that?" asked Donovan.

"Remind me to give you another day off. It seems to pay pretty good dividends, all in all, what?"

Marc Singer was introduced to me by Matthew Rossi, so perhaps it's fitting that they both make their fiction debut in this anthology. Inspired by the four-color adventures of comic book superheroes, Singer gives us this tale of sacrifice and salvation—which serves not only as homage and as affecting story in its own right, but also as an insightful commentary on the comics that inspired it.

Johnny Come Lately
by Marc Singer

> When chaos threatens to devour
> The second, minute, and the hour,
> Then call upon our noble class—
> Time's guardian host, the Silverglass!
> – Scott Craig

So here I am, cruising down Fifth Avenue on a sunny spring afternoon, charging into danger and mystery, as my publicist says, with a smile on my face. The wind whips through my hair as I soar over the traffic, balancing effortlessly on a pair of gravity induction units that won't even be invented for another four centuries. One of the little perks of this job is that I have access to all the best toys, courtesy of the chrome-finished hourglass that's pulsing away in my left hand. I have it all this morning, including a skintight flight suit that shows off my butt to what I hope is great effect.

The crowds don't notice, though—they're too busy running away from the *Tyrannosaurus rex* that's prowling through Central Park. Hey, I can't blame them; it's almost too Spielberg for me, too. But I can't afford to bug out when the special effects budget gets too high. Fixing problems, and fixing them in time—that's the Silverglass's job.

As I swoop down on the Park, executing a little barrel roll for the fans, I notice Stuart Samson playing crowd control. I buzz past the dino's snapping jaws and circle around Samson, waving him a friendly hello with my free hand. "What do you know?" I call out. "All the dinosaurs are coming out today!"

Samson scowls. "Finally decided to get to work, huh, Bradley? What happened, the networks picked it up?"

My smile collapses. None of them ever call me the Silverglass, especially Samson. I'm always John Bradley to them. The new kid. The kid who's Not Scott Craig.

I raise the hourglass, determined to prove him wrong. The *T. rex* looks more panicked and confused than belligerent—probably isn't a sentient, then. No need to bring in the heavy artillery on the big lug. So I activate the hourglass, and in a flash of silver light it pulls up a netgun from the NeoEdo riot police, post-Collapse. The tanglelines are already in motion; maybe I've just spared some students a month in prison.

The hourglass aligns the vector of the expanding polymer strands with the *T. rex*'s path and they wrap around his legs, checking his rampage. I turn to Samson to see if he's impressed and suddenly he's pointing and shouting. Rex is losing his balance, stumbling towards a couple of slow civilians. Samson shouts for me to get my head in the game, like I need telling, and then he dives for the civilians and tries to push them out of the way. Rex parts his teeth and shrieks, hitting us all with a blast of rancid meat and rage.

I'm already on top of the situation. The hourglass flashes again, pulls up a steel frame from a skyscraper that will rise here someday after Olmstead's green dream has vanished. The frame materializes around Samson and the stragglers moments before the dino's skull cracks against it, leaving a nice dent. I bet the builders will be puzzling over that one.

But the netgun strands have snapped now, and Rex staggers around the park, too stupid to know when it's done. Samson pushes the civilians to the dirt—the frame doesn't protect them from the thrashing tail—and he screams, "Quit clowning around, Bradley! Stop bringing in new Tinkertoys and find his point of origin!"

I guess he has a point there. I scan Rex, and sure enough, the glass tells me he's crawling with antichronons, their furious spin indicating a terminus in the Late Cretaceous. Flying up to him, hovering high so the morning sun catches the silver highlights on my uniform, I hold the hourglass over my head. It flashes, and bends time—only now, instead of pulling future weapons into my hands, the hourglass pushes the *T. rex* back up the timestream where he belongs. And I float down to the ground, landing kind of near Samson but also kind of near some cute female onlookers, maybe looking for a little gratitude.

Not from Samson, of course. "Nice going, Bradley," he growls. "That took a lot longer than it had to." He brushes the grass out of his hair and readjusts his leather coat, the closest thing he has to a uniform now. "I'm late for an appointment."

"Yeah, just use the line from *Shaft* and you should be fine." While Samson stomps off across the park, I turn to the bystanders. "What do you say, ladies? It's not every day you see a live performance by the one and only Silverglass."

The brunette in the CUNY sweatshirt moves back a step. "Isn't Silverglass supposed to be, like, my dad's age?" she asks.

The blonde shakes her head. "No, that was the last one. The one with the gray hair? I saw him in L.A. once. He totally pulled this mastodon out of the La Brea Tar Pits and he was riding it down Wilshire...." She and her friend fall into a giggly reverie. The brunette says Craig was cute "in a Sean Connery kind of way."

Me, I fly away. I get no respect.

It's a busy day. I can't get any work done at the studio, because the hourglass keeps alerting me to infractions in the local timestream. I pull up an android replicant of myself, built by a thirtieth-century design firm for the express purpose of getting me out of work—at least some people know how to show appreciation—and I spend the rest of the day on patrol.

There are Hessians on Broadway, Indians on Wall Street, and spacemen with giant "evolved future brains" walking through the Guggenheim and making snotty comments about every painting. All in a day's work for Silverglass, the Temporal Crusader, the

Centurion of Seconds—a day's work, if maybe a hundred days were rolled into one.

Fortunately, I have the hourglass. It can move objects up and down the timestream, correct temporal anomalies, even transport me across the centuries. Its power is almost limitless, somehow drawing on the energies of AUM and Hourglass Prime even though they were destroyed years ago. The hourglass's artificial-intelligence database tried to explain it to me once, something about how they exist outside of time.... I try not to think about the math of it.

The glass does have one flaw that its AI will admit: it can't affect human thought. I never really understood how that was a weakness—was some crook going to stop Scott Craig by thinking the theory of gravity at him? But then, Silverglasses did have some awfully dumb assignments back in those days. Anyway, I'll remember that if I ever need to kick Einstein's ass.

Today I'm busy enough just keeping up with all the anomalies. I clean them quickly and efficiently, and people are appreciative, but only in the sense that I've saved them from some nuisance. I might as well be a city sanitation worker, indistinguishable in my uniform.

The only normal call is a robbery in midtown. The Mathemagician, one of Craig's old sparring partners, is using the confusion to crack a diamond vault in broad daylight. He looks vaguely disappointed when I arrive, and only puts up a lackluster escape before I swap his laptop's CPU with a liquid drive from the Contracosta Imperium that runs on imaginary numbers. All of his little gadgets crash, and I haul him off to the nearest precinct house.

It's more than a four-time loser like the Mathemagician deserves, and I tell him so. He looks at me with watery eyes sunken in deep black bags and he says, "At least I took twenty years to wash out, kid." I must flinch or show my rage, because he smirks and adds, "You know, Scott Craig was always so polite when he arrested me."

I charge the guy, ready to deck him with a good old-fashioned twenty-first-century fist, and the cops have to hold me back. When I finally cool down, even they're snickering.

I spend an hour or so just coasting around the city, thinking.

I didn't ask for this job. That's one thing nobody understands: I didn't ask for this job.

No Silverglass asks for their job, the hourglass AI reminds me. Its sexless voice rolls through my head, thick like mercury. *They are ever called to duty.*

The swirling silver crystals inside the hourglass twinkle as the AI fills my head with images through the telepathic interface. Arcane and portentous with the mysterious resonance of dreams, difficult to describe or even to visualize, they offer tantalizing fragments of the *university/fortress/monastery/planet* at the center of time, designated only as *AUM*. Home to the Curators. (A bunch of snooty mahogany-skinned freaks, giant floating heads with tiny dangling arms and legs. Why do giant heads always mean "smarter"? How can they walk?) The Curators, sensing the threat posed by the development of time travel technology on Earth, act to insure that time maintains its proper course, a course that either leads to or emanates from them—the AI is unclear on this point, as on so many others. Toiling in their laboratories and councils, the Curators create a legion of peacekeepers to safeguard the timestream. The Silverglass Host. One Silverglass for each century.

Fast foward. (What does that expression mean, to an hourglass that ignores time?) 1966. Scott Craig, daredevil stuntman, careens into a canyon. The production is over budget, the director's cutting corners. Craig has walked off the set, but his assistant—I swear, I couldn't make up a name like "Patroclus O'Malley" if I tried—signs up for the riskiest shot. Craig slugs him in the stomach and takes his place piloting the helicopter for the big chase scene. Everything is going fine until a screaming comet of metal and fire rockets across his flight path and sends him spinning out of control. He manages to clear the highway and the film crew, and his last distinct thought as the canyon floor rushes up to meet him is that at least he saved them. Which is when the copter stops on a dime, *in midair*, and everything else freezes too.

Craig climbs out of the copter and sees another wreck on the rocks below him—a P-40 Mustang, decorated with Flying Tigers colors. He sees a man in the cockpit and, heedless of his own miraculous escape, scrambles down the canyon to help him.

Inside the Mustang is a man in a torn but shiny silver flight suit. It's Drake Allan, the century's first Silverglass, with a piece of propeller sticking through his windshield and into his chest. Allan raises his one working arm, holding aloft a beautiful hourglass filled with shimmering sands. Craig reaches out and caresses it. And the successor is chosen.

I know all too well about Scott Craig. The last thing I need is for my own damn hourglass to rub it in. He became Silverglass, not just *a* Silverglass but *the* Silverglass, the one everybody thinks of when they hear the name. I've done everything I can to prove myself on my own—I even redesigned Craig's musty old uniform, turning the curved hourglass emblem into two silver triangles and offsetting it slightly so it's asymmetrical against the black background—but nothing works. To the rest of the world, I'll always be some Johnny-come-lately.

The anomalies are getting more personal. New Yorkers are re-united with old flames and lost pets, dead celebrities and frowning grandparents. Faces from the "Missing" posters walk the streets again, wondering where their families have gone. I don't have the heart to send them away. I don't think I can bear to see what follows them back next.

The hourglass beeps and pulses for my attention, demanding that I correct the infractions, but I've gotten pretty adept at ignoring it. The thing's no good, anyway. Whatever twist of fate dropped it in my lap also dinged it up so badly that the AI database is a fragment of its former self. I try to search it for any clues as to the source of these anomalies and it just throws up a wall of error codes and missing passwords and Files Not Found.

There is one place I can go at times like this. Unfortunately, it won't do much for my current frame of mind.

Janice Warshowski was, by self-declaration and general accord, Scott Craig's most devoted fan. She organized conventions, ran websites, collected little bits of detritus from the scenes of his rescues. She spoke on the talk shows quite a bit after Craig disappeared, and the first things she had to say about me weren't terribly flattering. Frankly, for a long time I hated her. I guess I made her into an emblem of all the people who couldn't accept that Craig was gone, the focus of my disdain just as surely as I was the focus of theirs.

Then I needed her help, specifically her wealth of Silverglass lore, in dealing with some ludicrous pink alien who'd popped out of suspended animation and didn't know his old buddy Drake Allan was dead. She gave me a pretty frosty reception at first, but after I kept coming back I think she realized I was sincere. I don't know, maybe it helped that Craig had never come to her. She enlisted her online forum a couple of times, too, though she didn't tell them it was for me. I'm not sure how many of them would have helped if they'd known.

I drop down to her apartment in Flatbush and tap on the window. She's there in seconds, opening it and waving me inside. As always, it's a disconcerting experience.

The *Times* Arts & Living section once called this place the Silverglass Museum. Reliquary is more like it. The walls, bookshelves, tables, even the couch are covered with memorabilia from Silverglasses as far back as Janice's research and resources will allow. The displays include a crumbling Spanish handbill that offers a bounty for the head of Goodenough Fike, now known as "Captain Silverglass." The railroad conductor's pocketwatch once worn by the Quicksilver Kid. A riotously colorful propaganda poster that proclaims *"We Can Do It!"* as Drake Allan socks Adolf Hitler squarely in the jaw. A Power Records storybook LP with a recording of Scott Craig reciting that corny oath he used to say whenever he charged his hourglass. I think I had that when I was a kid.

Not all of the relics are so entertaining. Stuart Samson, resplendent in his afro and the borrowed hourglass and uniform of the Silverglass Second, glares down at me from an old *Ebony* cover declaring him "America's Next Great Hero." No wonder he wasn't happy how that turned out.

And then there's the pièce de résistance, the crown jewel of the collection. A glass case containing one of Craig's old uniforms, immaculately restored. I've never spent too much time examining it; something always seems to be staring at me from behind the visor of the flight helmet.

I do spot one change since the last time I was here. A small corner of the room is dedicated to me now. Just a few press clippings and the like. There isn't really a lot to show.

I don't know quite how to react to this gesture, but I can see Janice is waiting for some sign of approval. I nod vaguely in the new exhibit's direction and manage to stammer, "Got anything on these anomalies that've been cropping up?"

She looks disappointed, but her answer is prompt and quite chipper. "No, but I've been logging them all day."

"Great." I carry the glass over to her computer and set it down next to the tower. The chrome finish bulges, distends, and shapes itself into a USB connection, then plugs itself into her hard drive. Nothing to do now but sit back and let it crunch some numbers, look for any correlations between these anomalies and the historical cases.

Declining Janice's offer of coffee, I ask her, "Can you recall anything like this happening before?"

She grimaces and adjusts her glasses. "Never this many that weren't deliberately created by somebody. Orrin Vex, maybe?"

I shake my head. "Out of the question."

Perhaps I'm a little too curt, but it's not like we haven't been over this before. Janice folds her arms, cocks her head to one side, and asks, "Will you ever tell me what happened to them?"

"Janice..."

"Every time you insist it can't be one of Scott's old antagonists..."

"And it never has been. Not Vex, anyway."

"...but you never tell me how you know." Then, inevitably, she comes to her real point. "Or what happened to Scott."

I can't look her in the eye. "Janice, it's not because I don't trust you. You don't..."

I can't find a single surface in this room that doesn't contain something devoted to Scott Craig's legacy. So I end up looking at Janice anyway. "He wasn't the perfect hero you thought he was. You don't want to know what happened."

"Maybe I should decide that for myself."

"Look, *I* don't want to know."

She raises one eyebrow.

"Didn't," I say. "Didn't want to know."

"Really," she says. "John, you wouldn't even be here if that silver dumbbell was working properly. You only know me because it's broken, incomplete." She advances on me, smiling from the thrill of a successful deduction or maybe, I think, darkly, just from showing me up. "Do you even know?"

I don't budge. "I know how things ended, Janice. I know how he fell."

Her smile shifts, like now I'm something worthy of pity. "Do you?" she asks. "Do you really?"

Unbidden, the hourglass tells me once again.

After more than thirty years, Scott Craig still fights crime and time, with only a little gray at the temples to show for it. He still has a smile on his face, and the public always smiles back. He's the greatest Silverglass of all.

That's where the problems begin. The Curators notice his sterling record and tap him to perform a special duty. Goodenough Fike, the seventeenth-century Silverglass, is unable to locate a suitable Second in his time the way Craig did with Samson. So every now and then the Curators pull him upstream to stand in for Fike at home while the crazy Puritan is off patrolling another decade or freebooting around the Spanish Main. In addition to naming Craig his century's Second, Fike charges him with two special tasks: watching over his family estate (did any of these guys have normal lives?) and his childhood sweetheart.

The hourglass conjures an image: a cameo, magnified, a delicate little onyx pendant containing a silhouette of Arabella Wroxley. Even in the low-relief profile she looks like the sort of woman a man could fall in love with easily, without even meaning to. And so, of course, Scott Craig does.

Maybe now you understand why I can't let this guy go. Hearing Craig's story is like discovering the original version of a tale you've heard a thousand times before. How am I supposed to follow *that*?

The hourglass, impatient with my objections, forces its story to the forefront of my attention with a neurological buzz that packs all the subtlety of a hangover. Fast forwarding through the juicy stuff, it feeds me the raw plot: the girl's peers sentence her to burn for witchcraft—specifically, because she displays "Diabolick Knowlege" when she uses modern antiseptic medicine to save a local child. Craig finds out about it from a history book that he really never should have read (How else did he think her story was going to end? *She dies*), grabs his glass, and tries to save her from the stake. He doesn't even get out of the timestream before he's stopped by a posse of other Silverglasses—including Fike, ever dutiful and killing mad with the news of his betrothed's infidelity. Craig fights like a tiger, but he of all people should know he can't beat destiny. He loses, and is brought to AUM to stand trial himself.

Craig's rage is palpable even through the incomprehensible legalese of the court transcripts. The hourglasses dispassionately record his bloodied, defiant visage as he berates the Curators. They didn't interfere when Arabella treated that little girl with anachronistic science (*science he had innocently taught her*), did they? Why is one saved and not another?

The Curators close their eyes and float up above the defendant and commune, and then they hand down their answer:

Who are you to question the vagaries of fate?

It is one he refuses to accept. His reply is angry, paradoxical, and classically Scott Craig:

I'm a Silverglass!

When they strip him of his hourglass, half the Host goes with him. Century by century the heroes rise and announce that if Craig isn't fit to hold the hourglass, then nobody is. All his mentors, all his trainees, all his friends. All but Fike, crazed by

Craig's betrayal and his own. Without so much as a word of thanks or regret, the Curators dismiss them all.

And that, of course, is when the Acolytes attack.

I tremble and fall onto Janice's carpet. The database has led me to one of the broken hyperlinks, one that sends my body into spasms every time as the hourglass prepares my brain for secure download. It begins with a concept, or the absence of a concept, just raw absence at the heart of everything.

Zero. Acolytes of.

Apparently they were originally an offshoot of the Curators, splintered off in the eons before the Host, a gnostic and self-loathing sect who decided that if matter was the stuff of corruption, then time was its medium. Devoting themselves to turning time backwards, they'd tried to erase all traces of civilization, devolve humanity back into proto-apes, send the first amphibious pioneers slithering back into the primal ocean. If they could have pulled it off they would have collapsed the entire universe back into a single ball of energy and unfulfilled potential.

They invade AUM with the help of Orrin Vex. Vex, the Glass Darkly. He was a Silverglass from some utopian society far downstream, the brightest hope for tomorrow until he craved more power and betrayed the Curators. Now he leads an alliance of all the mad scientists and rogue sunspots the Curators have ever tried to bottle and bury, each of them determined to conquer time from the center out. Fike's depleted Host is all but decimated when a novice Curator, barely out of his apprenticeship, recants his peers' sentence and, dodging across the battlefield, escapes into the timestream and returns Craig's hourglass.

Craig arrives at AUM instants later accompanied by his army of supporters. The battle is joined in earnest, and for a moment, watching the footage, even I think he might have a chance.

But the hourglasses are only as strong as our will, and Craig's must surely falter that day. I see Drake Allan's plane go down in a flaming nosedive, then disappear; I see Goodenough Fike fall with Arabella's name on his lips; I see a bloody Silverglass in a torn uniform laughing like a madman; I see beams from the Black Star rain down on AUM until the planet's crust cracks and splits; I see a battered Scott Craig, refusing to kneel before Vex. The hourglass says the rest of that day is classified, and I don't want to know exactly what happens; all that matters is that Scott Craig dies.

Then AUM explodes, taking the Curators, the Silverglass Host, and the Acolytes of Zero down with it. But something survives: one final hourglass, which the explosion sends hurtling through time until it finds a person.

Any person. Any schmuck at all.

"Are you all right?"

The words pull me back into my own body, which is sprawled out on the floor with the dust bunnies. I'm looking up into Janice's face as she hovers close over me. "Are you all right, John?" Even through the neural fuzz of the bad interface, I still notice she doesn't say "Silverglass."

"I didn't mean to snap at you," she says. "It's just, I wish you would trust me."

"I do trust you, and that wasn't because of anything you said." I stand up, brush off my uniform. What am I going to say, *I can't work my own glass? It's broken, incomplete, flawed, just like—*

"Look, Janice, how often have I come to you for help?"

"For a crutch, you mean." She immediately bites her lip and I know she regrets saying it, but she plows ahead anyway. "You want me to deal with the history so you don't have to. You'll use it, you'll take it, but you won't give anything back." Now it's her turn to look away.

I put my hand on her shoulder. It's funny—here I am, a real live Silverglass, closer to her than he ever was, and there's only one thing she can think of.

"Janice, Scott Craig is dead. He died—"

The hourglass pings, indicating it's found something. I pick it up, nod, and walk away. Janice ignores me, preferring to stare at a bunch of empty costumes and faded legends.

The hourglass fills me in while I cruise back over to Manhattan.

It still can't provide me with any possible culprits behind the time anomalies—the prime suspects are old Silverglass foes like Invisible Newton (Goodenough Fike's archenemy...the psychic projection of Sir Isaac Newton's dark side?) or the Acolytes of Zero, all long dead with AUM's explosion. But the hourglass does tell me it's noticed a pattern in the anomalies. Half of them are occurring in a straight line along Fifth Avenue. The other half are appearing along a rough diagonal stretching across Manhattan, from the very confused knights up at the Cloisters down to three scrappy World War II sailors on the Brooklyn Bridge. (They just wouldn't stop saying "It's a hell of a town!" until I sent their asses home.) The two lines form a very narrow X. Or an hourglass.

Significantly, no anomalies are appearing at the intersection of the axes. So I head there, descending slowly into Rockefeller Center.

There's no trouble here yet, so I perch atop the big golden statue of Prometheus at the ice rink and do some thinking. If there's one thing about Janice or Samson or any of the rest of the fanboys and old farts that drives me crazy, it's when they go on about tradition like I don't understand the meaning of the word. They don't know what I've had to sacrifice, what decisions I've had to make because of this hourglass and its damned traditions.

But then, of course they wouldn't know. I made damn sure of that.

The hourglass doesn't show me my initiation into the Silverglass Host. That's because I didn't really have one. I can remember it well enough, such as it was. I was just a storyboard artist who picked the wrong night to walk down the wrong alley, and suddenly a glowing hourglass landed in my lap. I wasn't in danger of dying, or risking my life to save someone else; I just got plucked out at random.

I thought being a Silverglass was a gas, at first. I flew around kicking butts and showing off for my girlfriend. We weren't serious or anything, but we could've been, and I got a kick out of putting on the spandex for her. It was all great until I realized

I probably wasn't going to be the only Silverglass to die of old age.

The trouble started when I rescued a crashing hovercraft that had materialized in the skies above Midtown. Turned out it was filled with time-traveling tourists on a ghoulish package deal to see New York before and after the Collapse.

That was the first inkling I had of what the Collapse was. The glass blocks you from seeing the future, especially your own, but you get clues, glimpses from the items you pull up and the anomalies you send back down. My glass was hollering bloody murder while I interrogated a pudgy probability-adjustor who at least had the decency to be mournful as he told me what was in store for the city and the world. And for me personally. Then his tour leader whisked him out of there and I was alone.

That was when I learned changing the future was even harder than learning about it. I couldn't convince Lexy that it was really going to happen: any newspaper I pulled back was a pile of pulpy sludge, any history CD was wiped clean. I couldn't track down the people who would set off the electromagnetic pulse or even pinpoint the date when it would happen. The glass wouldn't let me. Rules are still rules, you see, even when the rule makers are all dead.

But the glass couldn't do anything to block information it didn't bring back. That probability-adjustor had slipped me a glimpse of some kind of holographic PDA containing the tour group's brochure. I saw clips of abandoned buildings, evacuated boroughs, and a devastated brownstone that, underneath the slag, looked sickeningly familiar. *Hōm of Jon Bradlee*, it said, in its weirdly phoneticized English. *Furst strike in the attaks. Resulted in the deth of...*

I couldn't avert it before it happened; I couldn't change it afterward; I was just supposed to lie back and let fate take its course. Who am I to question the vagaries, right?

But maybe I could do one thing. One small, selfish thing that wouldn't hurt anybody. And if it was still wrong, well, there weren't any other Silverglasses left to stop me.

I have to give myself credit for this—I timed it well. I sifted through the databanks, hit Janice's files, and learned everything I could about that humid September night in 1997. Craig was paying one of his last visits to Arabella Wroxley, and Samson was tangling with a bunch of thawed-out Viking nutcases. Neither one would notice a little, transitory anomaly, a visitor who stayed just long enough to slip into Lexy's old sublet and accelerate the oxidization in the water pipe that was doubling as her clothes rack.

I almost couldn't do it when I walked in that old place, exactly as I had seen it—would see it—later that night. I had forgotten how much I'd loved the cramped rooms covered in half-finished paintings, the kitchen cabinets that ran so high she could never use them all. I ran my fingertips over the book of Crewdson photographs, lost when she moved into my place, that had prompted me to display on that first night a wit and erudition I'd known I would never have again. Somehow I'd pulled it off anyway, because I knew our whole future was riding on it. Would have ridden on it.

One last time in her old apartment, just as I remembered it. I told myself it was more than most of us get.

Then I rusted the pipe from the inside out and it burst and soaked half her clothes, including the hot tank top she now wouldn't wear to the party she'd never attend, where she wouldn't meet some slacker hack named John Bradley.

When I returned to my own time and my own apartment, Lexy was gone. Not just her, but her clothes, her toothbrush, the hairs she left in the shower and the hole she'd accidentally knocked in the wall. So was the jacket she'd bought me, the paintings she'd done, the old coffee table she'd taken from a friend. I just sat there in the empty spot on the floor and cried for a while. *Seventeen minutes forty seconds*, the hourglass dutifully informs me. Then I went out and got stinking drunk.

I did find her one day. The East Village punk girl was a divorced mother of one living in a Phoenix suburb. She had a day job and a mortgage but she still painted, and she laughed at her kid's antics the way she'd laughed at mine. I thought about going back and sweeping her off her feet—fantasized about meeting her for the first time again, sharing our first kiss again, falling for her all over again. I think about it a lot, actually. But that would just bring her back into my world, and besides, she's a different person now. Who's to say I'd have anything to offer her?

So that was my entry into the proud heritage of the Silver-glass—an ex-girlfriend who doesn't even know I exist. Samson and Janice and the rest can keep all their shit about tradition; that empty apartment was the only thing Scott Craig left me to inherit.

"He was awfully pompous, wasn't he?" The nasal voice jolts me; I'm too surprised initially to notice that it's responding to something I've only thought.

I look down below and see a dozen men in golden armor trudging across the rink, the spikes on their bootheels digging cracks into the ice. They train bulky rifles on tourists and skaters who cringe in a fear that, while warranted, doesn't quite live up to the seriousness of the threat. These people won't get shot. They'll get turned into zygotes.

And walking at the head of the Acolytes of Zero is a thin, pallid man in a uniform of tarnished silver. He carries a black hourglass whose sands run backwards from the bottom compartment up to the top. Orrin Vex looks up at me, and smiles.

"You're—you're *dead!*" I shout. Yeah, that makes me sound like a Silverglass.

"Perhaps I was," he says. "Or possibly I will be. If you were even half a Silverglass you'd know such things matter little to men who stride through time."

"Even your grammar is giving me a headache." I leap down from the shoulders of old Prometheus, holding my hourglass aloft and trying to look confident. Trying not to think, *This is Orrin Vex.* So I focus on the Acolytes first. If the database is accurate their armor will jam the chronon streams I'd normally use to send them home, so instead I pull in a magnetic disarmament system and let her rip. The reversion guns fly out of their hands and onto the harness. I send the whole package outside the timestream and grin.

Orrin Vex shouts to his men in their native dialect, sounding like he came from a late Beatles album. "!yrnopeaw ssalgrevliS-itna yolpeD"

The hourglass tells me they have weapons meant for me. I hop up on the grav-induction discs and surround myself in a standard inertial field plus an antichronal model from the Curators' personal collection. It's from so far downstream that the hourglass has difficulty downloading its instruction manual. I'm ready for anything.

Except Lexy, looking like the day I first met her. She's all I can see. No Vex, no Acolytes, no running tourists, just Lexy everywhere. Laughing. Calling out my name. Moaning.

Then Lexy again. Making ziti in a kitchen in Phoenix. Then with me again, moaning. Then she's gone. Her half of the bed, empty.

The hourglass kicks out on me, and the force fields disappear to their home times. Then the discs follow and I'm falling ten feet to the ice. My shoulder hits hard but I don't care; because all I can see is Lexy and tears are welling up.

I try to pull myself together. They're affecting my mind. I blink, and I can see the Acolytes again. They're pressing their fingers to their temples in that universal sign for "I'm using invisible telepathy powers and I want you to know it." I roll to my feet and stagger toward them. "What the hell are you doing to me?"

Vex twists his face into a sneer. "Silverglasses were better trained in my day, that's for certain. The hourglasses are helpless against thought, you oaf. Specifically, that one domain of thought which shall always be inextricably linked to time." He snaps his leg up, kicking me in the face with his tarnished boot, and I reel back onto the ice. "Memory, Bradley."

Lexy vanishing. Stuart Samson chewing me out. Janice frowning. All the fans, all the crowds, glaring or just turning away in disgust because I don't measure up to their standards of heroism. And I think, if being a hero means either buying into their nostalgic crap or sacrificing everything that was good in my life, then the whole business sickens me.

And as I think that, the hourglass pulls itself out of my hand and bobs away. Right into the waiting arms of Orrin Vex.

He moans, his voice dropping an octave halfway through. "It's been so long." His black glass falls to the ice, an old toy on Christmas morning. "The last AUM hourglass," he coos, running his fingers over its smooth, vaguely liquid surface. It glows in his hand, bending to his will—and the silver sands in the bottom compartment begin to trickle upwards. "Thank you, Bradley. Thank you. We've finally put an end to the Silverglass Host. There's just one lingering detail.... ?syoB"

While he fondles the hourglass, the Acolytes swarm around me. I've sent all their weapons away, so they do this the old-fashioned way—which suits them, I guess—kicking me with spiked boots. I try to summon the hourglass back, but I can't concentrate, because every second my head or my abdomen explodes with pain and I'm kicked down again. I can only see red spots dancing on a white background, and I don't know if that's a hallucination or my blood on the ice. Probably both.

And that doesn't even bother me most, because the memories are still running wild. All those people sneering at me, who never thought I deserved to be a hero. And they're right. I never chose this.

A boot slams into my stomach, knocking me off the ice. I spin around in the air, landing on my back, and twelve golden gauntlets strike down at me. I can't feel my legs anymore.

Oh, Christ. I never drove a stunt car or flew a fighter plane. I never held a grown-up's job. I never had a love for the ages. I just walked down the wrong alley.

How can a guy with complete mastery over time do so little with his life?

Vex laughs as he rises into the sky above me. The hourglass is bringing back hover-platforms, reversion guns, all the Acolyte arsenals, all the nefarious allies lost in the destruction of AUM. A white powdered wig bobs above a frock coat while tittering laughter emanates from the nothingness in between. A cloud of dark plasma blots out the sun, wiping out electronics and birthing tumors as the Black Star enters phase synchronization with our reality. Too late, I realize, *This is it*. This is the Collapse, and I didn't do anything to stop it.

Orrin Vex has other concerns. Climbing onto an Acolyte platform, he throws his arms wide to the darkening sky. "Look at your handiwork, Craig!" he screams. "You destroyed AUM for nothing!"

And normally I'd be pissed that he's ranting at Scott Craig and not the Silverglass who's actually here. But I'm getting slowly beaten to death, and all that matters is—he said *Craig* blew up AUM.

I ignore all the depressing memories and reopen my link to the hourglass. Not enough to wrest control from Vex, but enough to access the AI database. Calling in every emergency code, I beg it to tell me what the hell happened that day. And it does.

Hourglass Prime is shattered, its sands spilled across the battle-plains and the bodies of dead Curators. Everyone is dead or dying, including Scott Craig—his heart is reverting to an infant state, and soon won't be able to support his aging body. But the silver-haired hero refuses to kneel before Orrin Vex, his killer. Instead he pulls in a flying machine—not my grav discs, I note, but a vaned art deco hang-glider, equal parts Leonardo da Vinci and the New York World's Fair. Somehow, nothing has ever looked cooler as Craig swoops across the plains and into the heart of Hourglass Prime.

Craig's hourglass glows white-hot as he opens a portal to the dawn of AUM, and the tremendous energies used in the forging of the Prime. The defunct and broken shell of the final day can't contain those energies—and they start a chain reaction that will consume the planet and everyone on it. Orrin Vex gasps and dies in a burst of silver light.

But Craig isn't done. Chanting the Silverglass oath, he charges his hourglass with that primal power and launches it out into the timestream. More than anything else, he wants to pre-serve the legend. The glass just needs to find a host. Somebody who won't make their past mistakes, who won't be bound by fatalism or tradition. Somebody new.

It found me.

Suddenly, I'm not so angry at Scott Craig anymore. And once I'm not, the Acolyte weapons start disappearing, and Black Star shimmers back to meet his ultimate fate. The hourglass is coming back under my control.

Vex screams "!mih potS" and his boys jump me even harder. I'm tucked into a fetal ball, cradling my head in my arms, and I know I won't last long. But that was Craig's hourglass, my hourglass, and I'll be damned if I let Vex have it.

He and the Acolytes send more bitter reveries of rejection and humiliation my way; the AI, secretly pulling for me, broadcasts another side of the story. I see Janice Warshowski, pining away for a man she never knew; I see Goodenough Fike, torn between his love and his duty and losing both; I see Stuart Samson, forced to watch from the sidelines as the hourglass he's fought and bled for goes to a... a nobody. There's just as much pain in their lives as there is in mine, just as much need to belong. And in their longing lurks some sort of restrained but mammoth power.

Vex must still be prying in my head, because he shouts, "You'll never live up to them, Bradley! You're nothing more than a screw-up, a misfire! A stroke of bad luck!"

But there's no room for luck in the Silverglass code. Any luck, even bad luck, means destiny doesn't hold all the cards, means the future isn't already written. It means you can question the vagaries of fate, as I did when the need was great and the price was too high. Me, and one other guy before me.

Vex's platform disappears and he falls to the ice. As he does, the hourglass launches itself back into my hands. The Acolytes fall upon me again, and I don't have enough time to defend myself. I only have time to break out of time.

I jump outside the timestream, pulling Vex and the Acolytes right along with me. While I fall bleeding to the ground, they take in our new terrain. Vex sees the cracked red plains under our feet and howls—I've taken him to AUM's last day and his destiny. The hourglass hums softly in my hands, purring its loyalty. Because dammit, I just beat Orrin Vex and *I am a Silverglass*.

He pounces on me, choking me with his bony fingers. I have no strength left to fight him, and there's no point anyway—I know he'll live to battle Craig. Who is across the plain, staring at me as Black Star pulses in the sky behind him.

And then I know I can't give in yet. At the very end, I have a chance to start something right.

I laugh, even as Vex strangles me. An impartial observer, one less invested in this cause, might think I'm a madman. But in my head, it all makes perfect sense.

Breaking every code in the database, I send the hourglass back just two seconds, so it's standing next to itself. Before the first one can disappear I send them back again. And again. And again. The hourglass fractures into sixteen identical versions of itself, slipping away into the timestream like sand through Vex's fingers—which tighten around my neck. The hourglasses tumble across time and space, in search of new hosts. And a new Host, because one Silverglass just isn't enough.

One of them is going to Stuart Samson, who's deserved it long enough. And another to Janice Warshowski, who knows the legacy better than anybody. They're all going to fearless and honorable people, tempered by time.

But they'll all be lacking something. So one of the hourglasses, the original hourglass, is staying in my hand, staying with me as I dive headfirst back into the timestream, in the instant after Vex kills me but before I finish dying. Maybe I didn't have what it takes to be a true Silverglass after all—maybe I was just a footnote between two great chapters—but I still have my part to play.

And that brings me to you. You're probably in trouble, aren't you? Trapped in a burning building, a hijacked plane—the details hardly matter. You'll think they do, of course, but they don't. What matters is that in the middle of great danger, your first thought is to help somebody else.

That's when everything will seem to pause and you'll see a man, bruised and bleeding and beaten halfway to death, in a ruined black-and-silver uniform. More black than silver, I'm afraid. He'll stagger towards you, gasp some noble words... perhaps you won't even understand them. But you'll understand the sentiment. And when you run to help him, thinking of his life and not your own, he'll hold something out to you—an hourglass. Take it.

The rest will be history.

I hope you use the oath when you power it up. That part always was kind of cool.

A native of England who has since lived in Australia and Canada, Barry Baldwin is professor emeritus at the University of Calgary, where his many areas of expertise include Greek literature. His mastery of his chosen subject is apparent in this new take on Homer's *The Iliad*, one of the wellsprings of adventure in western literature.

Paris Is Burning
by Barry Baldwin

Murdered, yet I am still alive to tell the tale, to name the one who has done for me without laying a finger upon my person; nor was it one of those drugs that discontented wives purchase from Egypt where everyone is a physician, drugs which steal a man's life even as he drains to the lees the wine that cheers his heart.

Am I the Sphinx? No, but I can spin a riddle. I have some reputation for clever speech. Songs and music, too; I would have matched my lyre against that of the son of Peleus any day.

My father-in-law killed my husband, my husband my father-in-law; my brother-in-law killed my father-in-law, my father-in-law my father. Who am I?

The answer? Andromache. That is, when Troy falls and Neoptolemos, son of Achilles, slays Priam and takes her to bed, as he will: symmetrical destinies appeal to the Greek mind. Andromache then will have had two husbands, Hector and Neoptolemos: Achilles killed Hector, Neoptolemos kills Priam; I killed Achilles, who killed her father Eetion.

On his deathbed a man may say what he pleases; that is one advantage of dying.

They have brought me back to the palace which I myself constructed with the best builders in Troy. I have asked to be taken outside to breathe the fresh air for which Ilium is renowned, to escape the cloying perfumes which duel with the contagion of my wounds. But the physicians advise against it, and even royalty cannot overcome medicine. Hence I lie in my high-roofed chamber on the corded bed on which I have had the pleasures and pangs of golden Aphrodite so many times; but now no more.

Why should a warrior not die in bed, though I know men deny me that title, calling me a curly-locked ogler of girls as the Argive Diomedes once did, shouting across the battlefield when I struck him in the foot with one of my arrows? My brother Hector, were he still here, would be shaking his helmet and making earnest speeches about honor and how a man should die fighting. As he did. And what benefit, pray, did that bring to Andromache and his son, the baby Astyanax?

Priam and Hecuba have not visited me, though our palaces stand close together in the royal citadel. They have no tears left; all were used up over the other lost sons. Especially Polydorus and Hector. Polydorus was the youngest, so adored that Priam commanded him not to fight. But he had the foolish courage of youth, and was confident in his speed. Neither helped him when the javelin of Achilles pierced through his navel, leaving him clutching his bowels in his hands. As for Hector, he became a demigod after Achilles dragged him with his chariot in the dust. Hector with his squint and solemnity; there was always nightfall in his face. I regret him in my own way, but I am the eldest son, where is my portion? Hector always behaved as if he were, but as far as one can know these things I had twenty-five summers when I first beheld Helen, and that was nineteen years ago. My youth is faded, while Hector was but recently married and a father for the first time.

Hecuba may or may not, but Priam at least understands me. He was a mighty warrior in his day, famed for his ashwood spear, but consider his record in the service of Aphrodite and you would wonder how he found the time to leave his inlaid couch. He sired nineteen children on Hecuba alone, a myriad more with other women. In his palace there are fifty apartments of polished stone, one for each son, though many now stand bereft. And rooms for his daughters and sons-in-law. A hundred children, fifty boys and as many girls; and these are but the ones he acknowledges.

Had he been younger... No, I must not think such things. But there was that day when he was surveying the enemy from the Scaean Gate and Helen appeared in a demure veil of white linen and he called her to him, sat her down, and had her identify the Greek leaders for him, as if he could not recognize the likes of Agamemnon and Odysseus who have been outside our walls nearly ten years.

The old curse has raised its head again. Auguries, oracles, prophecies. There are so many of them, they often stand in contradiction, and seers are strangely unaware of their own futures. Our ally Ennomos, Lord of the Mysians, was an augur, but all his bird-lore did not save him from being struck down by Achilles in the riverbed. When Hecuba was near her time with me, she dreamed that she gave birth to a burning brand which set fire to the city. No doubt she had taken too much of our mellow wine that night. When she blabbed out this tale to Priam, he summoned Aesacus for an interpretation. Aesacus is a son by the woman Arisbe. Somehow, he has made men believe he is skilled in the prophetic arts. It would have gone better for me had Priam consulted Cassandra. My sister has hated me from the time I made a casual attempt upon her celebrated virginity, though whether she was more upset by the attempt or the casualness I cannot say, and would have made the same prognostication, to my advantage since no one has paid any heed to Cassandra's babblings since the day she claimed Apollo loved her to distraction.

This Aesacus pronounced that the unborn child was fated to be the destruction of Troy, and so must be killed. I wager that piece of wisdom owed more to his desire to eliminate a new brother and rival for Priam's affection than to any oneiromantic skills. But he was taken seriously; hence when I was born my father gave me to a shepherd to expose on Mount Ida, a crag on which there once stood Dardania, in its day a mighty city. A familiar story: there is always a good shepherd. This one deposited me on one of Ida's spurs, but when he came back five days later I was still alive, thanks to a she-bear who had given me suck: kindly beasts also haunt these tales. Ashamed, or at least impressed, by this, the shepherd carried me to his hut and reared me as his own. I doubt his wife was pleased at this extra mouth to feed, but wives are not consulted over husbandly charities.

Knowing no different, I was happy. Thanks to the good plain food, the mountain air, and the arduous life of a shepherd, I grew up fit and strong and comely. My dark hair and eyes were thought a fine contrast to my fair skin. My beetling brows displeased me, as did my inability to nourish a proper beard, but I could do nothing about that. Older women took an interest in me; men too. The women would call out "Alexandros," the name attached to me for my success in defending with my arrows—I was already an accomplished bowman—the flocks against the wild animals and wilder robbers that roam on Ida. A curious title: why "Protector of Men" for saving mere beasts? Such suitors were not for me, and I was robust enough to keep them at bay. I preferred to experiment with the peasants' daughters, learning from some, teaching others. Peasants' sons as well, sometimes, though I have never grasped what the Greeks see in this activity. When tending my flocks in remote districts, there were incidents involving sheep, and once, when Aphrodite was weighing heavily upon me, I tupped a goat. My zoological catalogue ends here: I especially do not recommend goats.

Some, not all, of this ceased when I fell in with Oenone. Supposedly, she was a nymph, daughter of the local river god, Cebren. But such pedigrees are everywhere, often manufactured to impress a lover. Every hill, every stream, every tree houses its divinity. The countryside swarms with nymphs, naiads, dryads, hamadryads, oreads. Why I joined with Oenone, I cannot now say: was there ever a time when I could? Perhaps I wanted to impress the other herdsmen, perhaps to please my good shepherd, who strutted proudly at the prospect of a god-born girl in the family, even if her father was but a common water deity.

Aphrodite she served with an indifference that belied her nymphitude, coldly compliant, never refusing my embraces, never inviting them. As well that we were not blessed with children. Perhaps that had to do with her herbal skills. Yet Helen gave me no offspring either, nor has any woman. A silent message from the gods? Oenone could no doubt interpret it, if she would. She knows many things, and knows them well. A song on the world's beginnings with which my name is linked properly belongs to her, as do the happier strains of a hymn to Love, even if they were the products of ice rather than fire.

One morning, as I was breaking my fast with a platter of vegetables and cheese, a great commotion arose from the pen that housed my finest bull. I rushed outside to find some men attempting to drive him away. A young boy who must have tried to prevent them lay in the byre. From his head, which reposed some little distance from his body, I recognized him as the lad with whom I had first tried the Greek fashion.

It was clear from their dress and the disciplined way in which they were circling the bull in obedience to the orders being shouted by a big brute from the safety of the entrance to the pen that these were soldiers from Troy, not robbers from the sea. But I still confronted him in the way we greet strangers: "Who are you? What is your name? Are you a pirate?"

"Out of our way, shepherd, if you value your life."

The next moment, he was supine on the hard ground. The brute was twice my size, but I was versed in all the tricks of a country wrestler. They were not enough, though, to throw off the four soldiers who at once abandoned the bull to pinion me. One drew his sword from its ox-hide scabbard. The blade flashed in the morning sun and I thought my time had come, silently cursing the fate that led me to lay down my life for an animal, when I heard a voice cry "Hold."

The sword went down. The order had come from a horseman who was clattering fast toward us. His white steed and panoply of plumed helmet, polished cuirass, and fine greaves fitted with ankle-clasps marked him out as their leader.

"Release him." The soldiers did so, not without some hastily administered blows and kicks. I faced the horseman as boldly as I could, wishing that I had on more than a soiled loincloth. By now, others had ventured from their huts and were watching us in a circle, silent except for the keening of the dead boy's mother. I was aware of Oenone's eyes burning into me.

"Listen to me, neatherd." The horseman's voice linked authority with calmness. "King Priam requires this bull."

"For what purpose? And is the king of Troy so lacking in bulls of his own that he must steal mine?"

"Dardanian Priam is no thief. You shall be recompensed with another. Or, if such is your wish, with pots and tripods up to its value. A god has commanded the king to honor the memory of a son who died many years ago with great games, and instructed him to seek out the finest bull in the land as the prize. Thus, I do the bidding of the king, even as he does the bidding of the god."

Then, uncomfortable with these fine phrases, the horseman leaned down and added, "My orders were to harm no one. That business with the boy who lies dead was the work of the fool you so skillfully threw. I shall leave him here for the people to deal with as they see fit. Why do you not follow us to the city and compete in the games? Word has it the king is not pleased with the sons who live. He would be glad to see them worsted by a bumpkin. From what I have seen, you are more than their match, and you would regain your bull into the bargain."

I did as he said, ignoring Oenone, who cried out that it would go ill with me if I set foot amidst the tall towers of Ilium and only a fool would risk everything for an animal. As I entered the city, walking behind the bull, I marveled at its broad streets and fine palaces, little dreaming that one day I would live in the finest of them all. When he heard the words of the horseman, Priam greeted me with courtesy and accepted me as a competitor, despite the frown that latticed the face of Hecuba and the angry mutterings of his assembled sons.

I won every event, from the boxing and wrestling to the footrace. I was fit and strong, thanks to my country ways; soft living had made the princes slack. The citizens cheered me mightily; the royal sprigs were not popular with their high-handed ways. I was fortunate that Hector was away on a mission to the Maeonians. Priam showed his pleasure not only in his face but by the tone in which he proclaimed my victory, doing this himself for further honor instead of through a herald. Even Hecuba's features softened in approval. But from the glum-faced princes there came not a word. Worse, at the prompting of Aesacus, who had cut a poor figure in every contest, one of them, Deiphobos, rushed at me with drawn sword. The crowd shouted, but dared offer no assistance. And none was needed, since above all other voices was heard that of Cassandra screaming that I was no shepherd but their brother. Thanks to this strange intelligence, or at any rate the noise she made, she was heeded for once. Deiphobos stopped in his tracks, threw down his sword, and embraced me with a sobbing that I fancied was more for Priam's benefit than mine. Taking their cue, the others crowded around me, offering their hands and lips. Priam himself, after some words from Hecuba, raised his arms to the sky and thanked the gods for bringing his beloved son back from the dead. His speech gave me pleasure, but not nearly so much as the look on Aesacus' face.

How could Priam welcome back the son he had once sent away to die, the son who would otherwise be the destruction of the city? Perhaps Hecuba's words had crowned long years of silent reproach? Or Aesacus was out of favor for other things and this repudiation of his prophecy was his punishment? I gave thanks to the same gods for my deliverance, paying homage to my parents and for courtesy to my brothers and sisters. I accepted Priam's acknowledgment of me and my rightful place as a prince of Troy, but then begged his permission to return the bull to Ida that I might not deprive my other kin of it and that I might make fitting and final farewell to the kindly folk who had brought me to manhood and my present fortune. I made no mention of Oenone. Priam looked pleased at this proof of my virtue and gave his gracious assent, offering me the horseman and his soldiers as bodyguard. I refused, not without some trepidation, lest Aesacus send men of his own after me for quite another purpose.

The mountain folk showed their appreciation of the bull by slaying it for a feast in my honor. There was much well-wishing, prompted by wine and my new capacity to be giver and protector. Many "Alexandros" overtures came from the women, one or two of which I accepted and consummated in various nooks and crannies. Oenone was nowhere to be seen. But when I left the festivities to walk under the moon and clear my head, she suddenly appeared before me. I stopped. Neither of us spoke. I finally put out my hand and touched her cheek. To my surprise, she did not shrink, so I pulled her down to the rich earth, where to my greater surprise her body moved urgently under mine. Hardly had I decided that this was the consequence of newly discovered pleasure rather than a means of expediting the business when she stood up, smoothed her robe, and looking up at the sky said, "If you return to the city, it will be the end of Troy."

More prophecies. I took her real meaning to be, if I left her, there would be trouble for me. Confident of her refusal, I replied, "Then come with me. The Trojans could make much use of your skills."

"I perceive that you speak of the Trojans rather than yourself in the matter. You know that I cannot come. There is no place in the city for me. Furthermore, I would not wish to leave my father Cebren; he has lost one daughter as it is." Then she added, "Should there dawn a day on which you have need of my arts, I shall be here."

I looked away in some shame; when I could face her again, she was gone.

Lest I see her, or anyone else, again, I resolved to set off at once for Troy, folly though it is to travel by night. Some god was with me; I was troubled by neither man nor beast. I felt sadness at leaving my old life, joy at the thought of the new. Apart from pausing to pluck a few berries and plunge my head into a cold stream when the rosy fingers of dawn traced their message across the breaking darkness, I walked steadily until the sun stood high in the heavens, a cloudless sea of limpid air with a white radiance playing over everything. My bones seemed to bleach within me. I realized without much interest at first that I had come into a large clearing. But on seeing the great ilex tree in its center, I could not but blush: it was the site of the incident with the goat. Of a sudden, there was a rumble of thunder from the sky as though Zeus the Cloud-Gatherer was emptying his throat. Then, by some strange upset of nature, though as brilliant as it had been before, it was as if the sun had melted away, its place taken by a canopy of shining stars. The air was rich in the perfumes of nature, of women, of I knew not what.

"Good day to you, friend."

A man emerged from the shade of the ilex tree. As I approached him, one hand on my sword, I saw that he was wearing the broad-brimmed hat of a traveler and elaborate sandals adorned with a winged device. He stood aside and waved me under the bower of the tree, where three women were facing each other, all clad in the simple elegance of white, their beauty a worthy challenge to brush, chisel, or song, save that their faces were set in the tight grimness that marks an unresolved quarrel.

"I am Hermes, messenger of the gods," said the man, not waiting for me to return his greeting. "These women that you see are no women. They are Hera, Athene, and Aphrodite. A dispute has lately risen among them as to who is the fairest. It was not for me to discriminate between my betters, but I have persuaded them to accept adjudication from the first man that we might meet. Your looks suggest that you are no stranger to beautiful women."

That the gods appear to mortals I have no doubt, but it was not easy to believe that this preening little person and his disgruntled ladies were a true quartet of divinity. I was inclined to take him for one of those rascals who barter the services of women for their own advantage, albeit the slopes of Ida seemed an unlikely place for trade of that nature: the peasants have no shortage of females willing or otherwise at their disposal. As I looked more boldly at the three, it was clear that any distinguishing between them would be hard, likewise that none would accept the cowardly judgment that all were equally lovely. Yet to make one ally by awarding her the palm would be to make two enemies. Unseemly words would pass; unseemly blows might be exchanged. It occurred to me that Oenone would have understood what best to do: I felt the rare emotion of wishing her present rather than absent.

"Very well," I finally said. "You do me honor, and I shall

attempt to repay with justice, difficult though it will be. But it cannot be done here in a circle like a common contest or a game for children. Let each of them step one by one into the cool protection of that cavern by the clearing's edge, and I will consider their claims. As the wife and sister of Zeus, it is proper that Hera be first."

Hermes gave me a quick bobbing bow. The other two women had apparently expected this ordering and made no protest. I followed Hera or whoever she was into the overhanging entrance of the cavern, drinking in everything from her graceful carriage to the glistening earrings, each a cluster of three drops.

"Turn around," she commanded. "You may see the result but not the act." I did so. "Turn around," she said again, almost at once. She was flawless in her nakedness, though above all else I was held captive by her eyes: large, dark, soft, oxlike.

"Judge me the fairest, and I will make you the greatest of all kings."

The bribe came more quickly than I had expected. Its speed and nature bristled my flesh with suspicion and fear. Was this all a charade hastily contrived by Aesacus? Any such royal ambition reported back to Troy would be my undoing. Priam must look unkindly upon it; he had to be careful with all those sons around him, and especially given the circumstances of my own birth.

"My lady," I answered as levelly as I was able, "I am accustomed to ruling over sheep and goats, and they are trouble enough; I doubt I am fitted to govern men. Moreover, I am resolved that I, not gifts, shall render due judgment. Pray go, and bid Athene take your place."

Her eyes hardened, but she merely ordered me to turn around again while she dressed. My back quivered against the fear of a weapon entering it, but nothing happened until a new voice announced the arrival of Athene. Her naked charms were as irreproachable as those of Hera. Again, it was the eyes that drew me, in her case flashing like chips of obsidian.

Athene too was quick off the mark. "Judge me the fairest, and I will make you the greatest warrior of all."

Another ambition I did not want attributed to me for Priam's ears; he was jealous of his own fame, not without reason. I repeated what I had said to Hera about bribes and uprightness of judgment, adding that I had no use for war and battle, and rejoiced that Priam had brought peace to Troy and its neighbors.

Aphrodite was slower to come, slower to disrobe than the other two. Unlike them also, she stood close to me, urged me to examine her in every detail, said I might touch her wherever I liked. I thought her a much better performer than her rivals, and was eager to learn with what gift she would seek to persuade me. I already knew I wanted to award her the crown, but if her offer was as fraught with peril as the previous ones, I would have to announce, despite my misgivings, that there was no deciding between three such lovely beings.

"Judge me the fairest, and the most beautiful woman in all the world shall be yours."

What did this mean? None of the three seemed capable of granting that title to anyone but themselves. In detriment to my judge's impartiality, I asked, "And who is she, if she be not you?"

"Helen."

"Helen?"

Aphrodite stamped her foot, like a caparisoned steed sniffing out the thunderous excitements of war. Then her body through some trick of the senses seemed to give off a shimmering light that blotted out all else. My right hand moved to my eyes. When I lowered it, all was as before, save that Aphrodite, reclothed, was aligned with the other two, and Hermes was beside me muttering, "To which one goes the crown? Whomever you have chosen, the other two will give me a hard journey back to Olympus."

I was too muddled to reply. Apart from what I had seen, there was whirling in my head the question of what threat my choice of Aphrodite might pose to me when carried back to Priam. Hermes took my hand and led me like a child back to the women. They faced me as upright as pillars, seemingly intent upon my verdict, though two must already have known it was not them. I assumed the stance of a herald and opened my mouth, but there was still no speech within me, so I raised my arm, pointed towards Aphrodite, and pitched senseless to the ground. When I revived, they were gone—like Oenone at our last meeting, I recalled to little purpose—and the sun had regained its rightful power from the stellar illusions of before.

Collecting myself as best I could, I resumed my journey. It was a slow trudge. More than once, I almost stopped and turned back; only the thought of Oenone kept me pointed toward Troy. My head pounded with the question of who the man and women had been, and what their purpose was. I still did not believe they were gods come down from Olympus. The curious struggle of sun and stars had been but a freak of nature: the mountain was noted for its weather-borne mirages. Neither the man nor the women had demanded anything of me, save the judgment of beauty, so what advantage was there for them in the performance? Perhaps they were merely mad, a crazed foursome roaming the land in search of a fulfillment that lay forever beyond them? No, that was the stuff of mummers. I came back to my first interpretation, a scheme of Aesacus to blacken me in the eyes of Priam. If so, should I tell my tale upon return and risk ridicule, or say nothing and so invite suspicion? Yet I could not see what part the promise of Helen's beauty might play in such a design. Perhaps there was some matter from the past of which I stood in deadly ignorance? Could Helen be an old love of Priam, fled or snatched from him?

Then I had it. Oenone. It was her doing. A farce she had urgently organized to drive me from my wits as punishment for leaving her, or to terrify me back to my shepherd's life. Oenone. She was capable of anything, and she knew me well enough to coach the man and the women to play their parts to the greatest effect. The shimmering light that had assailed my being must have been the product of one of her potions, designed to bring madness to my mind and apparitions to my eyes. Oenone! A great soundless shout of laughter shook my frame, my fears fell from me, and I stepped out with spirit and speed toward holy Ilium.

Near the end of the banquet that celebrated my return, Priam announced, "Paris, although it grieves my heart to bid you farewell yet again, I wish you to undertake a journey for me; no, not for me alone, but for all of Troy."

This news caused my brothers to cast baleful glances at me, though I could see that Aesacus was torn between fury at my being honored over him and joy at the thought of my absence, during which he might further distill his venom into the royal ear. I deemed it prudent to say nothing beyond a meaningless "My Lord?"

"For some years now, we have enjoyed peace with the Mariandryans, Mygdonians, Phrygians, and all the other tribes that dwell alongside us. And the reputation of our city's walls has kept pirates and foreign enemies at bay. But I have recent intelligence from my friends across the sea that for all of this the Greeks would like nothing better than to bring war to our land. So far, their disunity restrains them; they have been happy killing each other, and without good cause they will not risk the wrath of the gods by attacking us. But good causes can be manufactured, and they are jealous of the name and wealth of Troy, so much so that some of their kings are seeking to end their feuds and combine against us."

Priam counted out three names on his age-flecked fingers. "Odysseus, Agamemnon, and Menelaus stand above the rest. Odysseus, though he is the craftiest of men, I reckon least, confined as he is to that small island of Ithaca and forever at odds with his fellows. Why, they say he but recently went to war over the loss of a flock of sheep.

"Agamemnon I fear the most. A proud and cruel man, and Mycenae is the most powerful kingdom in their land. Stay well away from him, Paris.

"I place my best hopes in Menelaus. It is never difficult to excite brother against brother." Priam gave his own serried ranks of sullen sons a meaningful look. "Their father Atreus was always at odds with his brother Thyestes; he ended by killing his children and serving them up for dinner. A Greek delicacy indeed. Go to Sparta, Paris, ingratiate yourself with him, inflame his mind, turn him against Agamemnon, assure him of our favor and support. They say he is an uncouth creature himself, but his city glories in its women, and Helen is without peer."

Helen. The name pierced me like a javelin. I bowed my head as though mulling over Priam's words, as indeed I was, but not in the way he was thinking.

"Yes, Helen." Priam was oddly beginning to prattle. "Be attentive to her, talk with her, work on her that she may work on her husband. There is no love lost between her and her sister Clytemnestra, Agamemnon's wife. But what can you expect of two women hatched from a swan's egg? Be sure you bake the right words for her to feed him. But keep your hands from her. You are quite the handsomest of my sons, Paris, and Helen may look upon you with more than kindness. We do not want to give the Greeks a pretext for sailing against Troy."

"Exactly!" Aesacus burst in; I wondered how he had managed to hold his tongue so far. "My lord, with all respect for your wisdom and years, Paris of all your sons is not the one for this most delicate of missions. He is, I concede (it was a measure of Aesacus' emotion that he should bring himself to say this in public), the best-looking, if that be a recommendation among men, and the queen may well entertain thoughts that she should not, but he is in his prime, has no woman of his own, and has only just become known to us again. How can we be certain that he would not succumb to her wiles and bring death to us all?"

As the others murmured in agreement, Aesacus added, "They say that in the Greek language the name Helen means 'destroyer.'"

I thought, *The name Oenone suggests 'wine,' but a bitterer draught could not be imagined.* I could think of no ill-omened meaning for Aesacus and did not need to, for Priam rose and said, "We are not here for instruction in the niceties of Greek, Aesacus. It is decided. Paris shall go to Sparta. The mission may be dangerous as well as delicate, and as you have noted, Paris has no one to bewail him, should he not return."

Aesacus, I later heard, gained urgent audience with Priam the next morning and begged him to reconsider. But our father would not bend, and was encouraged in his obduracy by Hecuba, not out of love for me so much as she never forgot that Aesacus was not from her belly but that of Arisbe. Then, I was informed through that most reliable source, the tattle of slave girls, Aesacus laid out his wealth on a variety of seers to shout around the city that Ilium was doomed if Paris went to Sparta. But others, possibly enriched by Priam himself, or by some other brother who wished me out of the way, cried the opposite, and when my sister Cassandra added her wild doomsayings, the cause of Aesacus was lost.

Although Priam would doubtless have preferred a quiet departure, the people turned out to give me a tumultuous farewell. I thought I heard one or two curses. A last bid by Aesacus, perhaps, to sway opinion against me. But crowds are carried more by emotions, and although they were far from sure about the purpose of my enterprise, they were seized with a frenzy for it. None more so than Phereclus, son of Tecton, the best carpenter in all the city, who had worked night and day to get ready my good deepwater ship for the voyage. Ah, Phereclus, his fate was to perish on the plain of Troy, stricken clean through the right buttock by the spear of Meriones the Cretan; as the head drove through the bladder under the bone, his scream was such that the men around him stopped their fighting to watch him writhe. But that lay far in the future, as did a myriad of other deaths, including my own. On the morning we left, Phereclus was among those who made libations of wine from cups of gold supplied by the royal palaces and raised their voices in the common hymn of well-being, which they sang under the direction of a herald.

Before reaching Greece, we put in at various cities of Asia at the instructions of Priam, who thought thereby to lull the suspicions of any Greeks who might learn of our sailing and wonder as to its purpose. At Sidon, I went ashore to explore its bazaars and purchased six fine robes from the local women, who are famous for such work. I had the idea that I would present these to Helen as a first token of goodwill, and ordered that each dress be of a different size that one at least might fit her fabled frame.

During the journey, I had time enough and more to contemplate the chain of events that were sweeping me towards some kind of destiny. It now seemed that the performance in the clearing must after all be the doing not of Oenone but of Aesacus; or if not Aesacus, then Priam himself, to kindle my heart for the adventure he was planning to lay on me. I was still unable to believe in the divinity of the little man and his ladies. Yet the moment I fixed upon the one solution, the others crowded back until my head reeled and my stomach heaved in spite of the calm sea with which our voyage was blessed. At last, I was resolved to have done with it, and persuaded myself that whatever the truth, it was now no matter, I could not draw back, nor did I wish to. What was done was done; what was in the stars was in the stars. So, although I did not fail to be the leader of my men, kept an eye on the crew, bargained bravely with the women of Sidon, and dutifully admired whatever sights were pointed out by hosts along the way, there was but one sound, one word, one thing that consumed me by day and by night: Helen.

There would be one last surge of unease. On the eve of our landing on Greek soil, the captain reported to me that a merchant who had asked to come on board at Sidon that he might travel with us, a request whose refusal would have violated the laws of hospitality and aroused questions about our true purpose, had been overheard by a crew member humming a song. The sailor thought it might be Greek, and swore that the name of Helen was in it. I ordered the man to be given over for questioning, then walked away to the far end of the deck, having no stomach for watching that kind of work. After only a short space of time, we learned that our merchant was indeed a Greek; he had thought it prudent to conceal this from Trojan hosts. The song was but a children's roundelay: *Helen, Helen sinks the ships/Cursed be her name on everyone's lips.* He supposed this Helen to be some demon of coastal folklore, most certainly not the fair queen of Sparta. Whether he told the truth I did not know, and convinced myself I did not care. To be on the safe side, I had him thrown overboard, with his tongue torn out first, lest by some whim of Poseidon he should survive the waters.

We put in at Pylos, a city that King Nestor had ruled for as long as anyone could remember. Priam had warned me about the old man's habit of keeping his guests up half the night while he regaled them with tales of his youth. Happily, upon arriving at his palace, I was informed that he was indisposed and could not grant me audience. I delivered a flowery speech of good wishes—he was understood to carry much influence with the other Greek kings, hence Priam's decision that I pay him our respects—to his daughter Polycaste, who undertook my entertainment, a comely girl on whom my eyes rested longer than they need have done. I ate some good roast meat from the spit, though could not admire the Pylian way with wine. My heart rose when a magnificent gold-studded beaker with four handles was brought in, standing on two legs each with a pair of feeding doves picked out in precious stones. The attendant said this was Nestor's own cup, sent down for my pleasure as an apology for his absence. A slave plashed into it some dark red wine called Pramnian, to which he proceeded to add onion scrapings and crumbling goat's cheese. Forcing this mess down was useful practice for my diplomatic talents.

The next morning Polycaste, whose nocturnal attentions were far more diverting than her father's memories ever could have been, furnished a handsome chariot with an equally good-looking squire at the reins of two sleek horses and bade me farewell as we rumbled through the courtyard gates before speeding across the wheat-bearing plains until these yielded to the hills which gave their protection to Sparta. At the palace entrance, I dismissed the squire with orders to return to Pylos. He was barely out of sight before a watchful equerry, politely concealing his surprise at my appearance, was conducting me into the royal buildings. I had not known what to expect of Sparta, and wondered at the size and sunlike sheen of the halls through which I was guided until we came to an ample bathing area where the equerry handed me over to the experienced ministrations of some strangely beautiful slave girls—the reputation of Sparta for its lovely ladies seemed not undeserved. After I had been dried and oiled and given a fresh tunic from the palace store which fitted me remarkably well, while reminding me that I had quite forgotten to bring the Sidonian dresses with me, I was taken to yet another chamber where an older but still handsome woman was laying out platters of meat and bread on a low table of polished wood with enameled legs. I was eyeing these good things when the equerry slipped in and bade me prepare to be greeted by his master. I was then kept waiting as a reminder that I was the unexpected guest from foreign parts, and had just begun to fidget when I heard clattering feet along the corridor and the equerry stiffened even more to attention as my host and prey strode in.

Although of strong build and confident carriage, Menelaus made no great first impression. He was short, had the ruddy face of one who had been singed too closely too often in the daily trimming of the beard, and a shock of unruly red hair. He looked more like a Thracian bandit than a Greek king. And his speech was that of a braggart and brawler, his words coming in a loud rush and deep-throated accent that, serviceable as my Greek is, made him hard at times to understand.

Still, he made me welcome in his own way. The equerry, earlier primed by myself, started to introduce me as royal Paris, noble son of Dardanian Priam, ruler of holy Ilium, and seemed all too capable of continuing in this manner for half the day—had he been my servant, I would have long ago arranged for him to be dropped into the river Scamander one cold high flood morning—but Menelaus impatiently waved him into silence with a large calloused hand and barked, "Let our guest fall to and eat. After coming so far he has more need of food than of words. When he has had his fill of good Spartan fare, bring him to the audience chamber that I and the queen may learn the purpose of his coming here." The equerry bowed with a cold stiffness that to my taste was well beyond the privilege of his station, but Menelaus either did not notice or did not care as he swept out.

When I was done, I washed my hands in the scented water brought to me in a golden ewer by an alert slave girl who bent down without being commanded that I might dry them on her dark tresses. The equerry then led me down more corridors, so many that I might have been in the Labyrinth of King Minos, until we came to the entrance of a large room guarded by two strapping soldiers in gleaming ceremonial armour. As though jerked by invisible cords, they parted to allow the equerry to bow me through.

I was hard put to it not to exclaim over what I saw. Priam's palace is full of splendors, but compared to this it was a farmer's hovel. The great chamber shone as the sun with its appurtenances of amber and copper and gold and silver; it was as though I had stepped into Zeus' own treasury. I was conscious of the equerry shooting glances at me, looking for some sign as I tried to take everything silently in. My indifference was on the brink of collapse when Menelaus boomed across the room that I should approach him.

He had not risen in my honor, being already on his feet, one hand resting on the back of his ample throne. I could understand why: it was as luxuriously appointed as everything else, but looked uncomfortable. His eyes, which I now perceived to be the color of dark wine, gave me a hooded look that did not sit well with the cheerful thunder of his voice.

"Royal Paris, noble son of Dardanian Priam, and so on, I again bid you welcome to my humble halls. I trust you found our Spartan victuals to your liking? Now, I offer you another feast, this one for your eyes: my queen and wife." With an expansive gesture of his arm, he stepped a pace or two away from his throne.

Men will say of some woman or other that words cannot describe her beauty. They are wrong. It is not the beauty that is beyond description, but the first mark it makes on you. So it was with Helen. By themselves, her attributes were not striking. I have seen many snow-white arms, many a head of well-attended fair hair, many large eyes that draw one in like a fish to the bait, many a fine bosom straining under a saffron robe, its elegant concealment so much more a challenging delight than cheap exposure. It was the perfect conjunction of each aspect that gave Helen her matchless radiance. No one element stood out in such a way as to suggest any imperfection in the rest; all cohered as though she were the handiwork of Hephaestus the divine craftsman.

Some argue that perfection is too cold, that a small flaw serves to point up the glory of all else. As I would later know,

Helen's redeeming fault was a tiny mole, the size of a fly's bite, just below the nipple of her left breast, the very orb to whose shape a cup was once molded on the island of Rhodes, where they display it as their greatest treasure. At that moment, though, as I strove to keep all parts of myself under control, bowing as she briefly bade me welcome in a deep yet honeyed voice, there was one thing for which I did not care. Not the fact that she was sitting in an old woman's chair—a sensible alternative to a hard throne—but that she who was young was engaged on an old woman's work: knitting. On a table by her side was a silver work-basket, protruding from which were skeins of deep purple wool, one ball of it skewered by a golden spindle. Knitting is not a skill I have ever wished for in my women; even Oenone was not guilty of that. Over our years together, I would discover that Helen knitted to the point of obsession, at moments of crisis or while upbraiding me, and when we were on a bed together she was more concerned with the stitchwork on the blankets than anything else. But all this was to come. At that moment in the great audience chamber, I persuaded myself that there was not much else in Sparta for a queen to do; elsewhere, living with an ox like Menelaus would have driven most wives well beyond knitting.

My reverie was broken by some loud throat-clearing by Menelaus, so I gave full respectful attention to his long-winded inquiry as to why I had come, and went fluently through the rigmarole in which Priam had coached me. It was difficult to tell what he was taking in, though I fancied his eyes glittered in angry approval as I cast oblique doubts upon the affections and trustworthiness of his brother. Helen never once looked up from her knitting, except to consult with the two women assisting her. When I was done, Menelaus thanked me in profuse but vague terms, then begged my pardon for the fact that he must leave the following day, sailing as he was to the city of Gortyn on Crete, where he had the dolorous duty of burying his grandfather Catreus. I made sounds of sympathy, thinking he did not seem bowed down with grief: no doubt some legacy of power or wealth was uppermost in his mind.

That night, we ate and drank freely in double honor of my coming and his leaving. At one point, a minstrel, blind as so often, was led in and seated on a stool, from which he proceeded to drone interminably about the glorious history of Sparta. It was largely a litany of names: Lelex the Earth-born, eponym of the Leleges, and suchlike, accompanied very badly on the lyre. Happily, Menelaus, who had been paying closer attention, impatient for the song to reach the subject of his own glorious self, also grew bored and jumped up, banged the table, and ordered the fellow out of the room. He then devoted himself to the wine bowls and was presently in the grip of self-absorbed intoxication, giving us a surprisingly tuneful version of his ancestry and deeds. When I judged it safe to do so, I began to hunt Helen with lingering looks and signals with my fingers that meant nothing but might be taken otherwise, exchanging goblets with her on the pretext of an invented Trojan custom that she might see me drink from the same spot her own lips had touched, and finally tracing some figures of love in a pool of spilt wine on the table between us. Yet the presence of her husband, however deep in drink, could not but constrain her, and I well knew the skill of women in concealing their true feelings until they see it is opportune to reveal them. So I was not displeased with the evening, save when two royal infants, Hermione and Nicostratus, were brought in to receive a cool peck from their mother and slobbering kisses from their father. Children have played no part in my own life, except for a couple of erotic experiments and the times when I have idly flicked the chubby chin of Hector's little Astyanax or dipped my finger in the marrow and mutton fat Andromache pushes into him; hence I had not considered the role they might play in that of Helen. At the conclusion of the banquet, when it was nearer dawn than midnight and she had long since withdrawn, Menelaus rose with impressive steadiness, embraced me with uncomfortable tightness, and rumbled, "I must be early from my bed to begin my progress to Crete, but there is no call for you to rise with me. While I am away, I shall weigh your words with due care. The queen will attend to your needs and desires. Farewell, royal Paris, noble son of Dardanian

Priam, and so on; I know in my heart it is the will of the gods that we shall meet again."

On the morrow, and beyond that, there was no token that Helen regarded me with any interest, let alone something more. As a hostess, at the rare times that I glimpsed her in the palace, she was efficiently courteous, making sure that all the ordinary wants of an honored if ambiguous guest were fulfilled, but aloof in manner and remote of countenance. I whiled away my days pleasantly enough: eating, drinking, exercising, hunting with little success in the rolling hills around the city, seeing such sights as there were—local tales of the cold river god Eurotas made me think uncomfortably of Cebren, hence Oenone—and being carefully polite to everyone down to the sightless minstrel who, sensing my true tastes, abandoned his ballads for the finer entertainment of strumming his lyre to set the pace for acrobats to tumble and whirl among us.

Since one way to a queen's heart is through the bellies of her slave girls, I began to look over her retinue to identify her most intimate and thereby useful attendants. I soon had them whittled down to three. Aethra and Clymene I at once discarded: they had been royalty themselves before enslavement, and behaved as though they still were; as servants are so good at doing, they made it discreetly clear how superior they were to myself. So I set my sights on the third, to whom I was in any event already strangely drawn. Astyanassa, the plain one. Plain? She was quite the ugliest girl I had ever seen. I tend to believe that every woman has some setting in which she may appear beautiful; Astyanassa was the exception. On the Greek side—our sentries have heard their jokes—they jeer at Thersites, but he is a Ganymede compared to Astyanassa. Even her name was ugly. Not in sound—it has a certain lilt to it—but in meaning, as she was not embarrassed to remind me: to put it delicately, it suggests a female so devoid of looks that she cannot excite one's manhood. But they say a brilliant vestment may cover a grievous wound; in her case, I fancied the opposite might be true. It was also a challenge. Anybody can make love to a beautiful woman; it takes a real man to rise to the occasion with an ugly one.

I was well rewarded. My nights with Astyanassa were the most memorable I have spent with any woman. I was, to be modest, no novice, but her knowledge of the art of love began where mine ended. She taught me attitudes and movements I had never dreamed of; it was as if she had invented the whole business, Aphrodite in some hideous disguise. Poor Astyanassa will never be sung of in any ballads about the war, though she richly deserves it. But she hopes to compose an instructional song on the subject of love and its ways, so perhaps will gain immortality from that.

I asked her once if Menelaus had ever engaged her services. She gave me the lopsided smile her face compelled and said no; I believe she was telling the truth, though wondered why she then fell upon me with redoubled energy. But it was information about Helen that I wanted, and in this she was abundant. For instance, the business about being born from an egg: was it true? She said that in one mood Helen swore it was; in another she would dismiss it as some bard's nonsense. Astyanassa herself had a simple explanation. As a baby, Helen was reared in an upper chamber, "hyperoon" in Greek, hence the report that she had sprung from an "oon" or egg. She also told me another tale which I wished I had known when feeding Menelaus my litany of poisoned hints about his relatives. As a young girl, Helen was abducted by Theseus, ruffian king of an unimportant town called Athens, who had a knack for getting singers to cry up his scuffles with Amazon women and monsters in labyrinths. She was soon rescued by her brothers and was brought back supposedly still chaste. According to Astyanassa, it was whispered that she had in fact been ravished and impregnated by him, the consequence being Iphigeneia, whom upon her return Helen secretly gave to her sister Clytemnestra to bring up as her own. I doubted the truth of this, partly because I wanted to, partly because some finger-counting put Helen at too tender an age when kidnapped. But it would have been an effective seed to plant in Menelaus' mind.

Astyanassa also brought the family in to explain Helen's mania for knitting. "It runs in the blood. Clytemnestra is besotted with a certain crimson tapestry, and her cousin Penelope spends her days on Ithaca weaving. I find it a great trial, but Aethra and Clymene encourage her in it, so I must pretend to a liking for spindles and wool to preserve my position. If you wish to stand well with Helen, on no account make light of her handiwork. It is this above all that has undone Menelaus. She labored hard and long over an embroidery on which she had picked out scenes from his exploits in war, but when she offered it to him full of pride, he scarcely glanced at it."

It was hard to discern where her sympathies lay in this. All servants must be diplomats, but Astyanassa had a rare knack of seeing both sides of a matter. Thus, in telling me about the mole I had yet to see on Helen's breast, while showing some of the pleasure that a woman always feels when detailing the defects of another, she made less of it than she might—I thought of how Oenone would have recounted such a thing.

Above all, I wished to know of Helen's feelings for myself. With Priam's warnings never far from my thoughts, my pleasure was tinctured with dread. She had given me no sign. Astyanassa reported that she dare not; Aethra and Clymene watched her like hawks circling their prey and would make known any hint of disloyalty to Menelaus when he returned. Moreover, she had divined from my looks and behavior at that first dinner and formal demeanor in the following days that I was well versed in the ways of a woman and would know how to wait. I basked in these words, without ever considering that they might not be her own.

Not that I had long to wait. Helen quite simply came to my chamber very early one morning and said, "Paris, I have tarried until sure that Menelaus was far away on the sea, from which, I pray, he may never return. No, do not speak. You have told me all that I needed to know in other ways. Rise and eat; a slave will bring food. Then go to the courtyard, where I shall be waiting with the best horses from his stable. I have announced that we are riding to Amyclae, which I wish to show you. It was once the greatest city in Laconia. But you will not see it. Instead we shall gallop to wherever your ship is waiting and set sail for Troy."

She was gone before I could answer. When I reached the courtyard, I was downcast to see Aethra and Clymene in mounted attendance, but rejoiced at the absence of the infants and the sight of Astyanassa, who prudently ignored me. We rode fast to the bay near Pylos, where the relieved cheering at my safe return—they had not trusted a Spartan to honor the laws of Zeus—melted away like spring snow when they saw who was with me. None had seen Helen before, but all knew the prophecies.

We set sail at once. The breeze was in our favor, the captain barked at the crew, the hawsers were cast off, the fir-wood mast hauled up and planted in its box, the sail hoisted and made fast with bonds of plaited leather. The first night—at Helen's instruction, so I overruled the protests of the captain, who had wished to get farther from Spartan territory—we dropped anchor at the tiny isle of Kranae, off Gythion. I did not question her choice; no enemies could yet be chasing us, and one island is much like another to me. Astyanassa speculated that it had to do with the presence on the opposite mainland of a shrine honoring Aphrodite Migonitis, which is a polite way of calling her the Goddess of the Bed. Even now I smile at this, since over the years there has grown up a tale that it was I who had the place built as a monument to our dalliance there. Perhaps an earlier pair of fugitive lovers were responsible: from our ship in the mottling moonlight, it looked very old.

Not for one breath were we divided that first night. But I was always aware that her white arms, more marmoreal than ever in the cold lunar light, were not half so tightly clasped around me as mine around her. And no matter how many times or how violently I played the man within her, she uttered no word of affection, no sound of acknowledged pleasure. I might as well have been coupling with Oenone. Well before matters were concluded, I understood that her desire was not for me but to leave Menelaus and find a comfortable protection elsewhere. It also came to me that the Aphrodite on Ida had not promised love. Men blame Paris for abducting Helen; in truth, it was I who was abducted by her.

And so, seized by a deep melancholy of the kind they say the goddess attaches as an aftermath to love, as if regretting the pleasure she has given to mortals and wishing to spoil it, though it was something I had never before felt, I came home to Ilium with Helen standing regally in the prow as she faced the shore, every so often inclining her head in acknowledgment of the scornful reactions to their first sight of my land from the flanking figures of Aethra and Clymene, whilst Astyanassa joked with members of the crew, giving as good as she received, and I alone was alone.

As soon as we were ashore, Aesacus began to rave about the wrath of the gods and the doom that must now fall upon Troy, while Hector, safely returned from his mission, seized the chance to deliver a homily about honor and the holiness of marriage—he had no wife at the time—and how he wished I had never been born and why had Poseidon the Earth-Shaker not pulled my ship down to the bottom of the sea? Most of the brothers joined in, though one or two were so entranced by Helen that they uttered not one word of reproach, above all young Deiphobos on whom her eye seemed briefly to rest, though he is short and stocky and no thing of beauty. Hecuba stood in boot-faced silence, but I was concerned only over Priam and what he would say and do. For a while he was silent, gazing unashamedly at Helen and sparing me only a single glance that betokened more envy than anger. Finally, he summoned up his manners and, purposeless though it was, asked who she was and whence she came. At least, I smiled grimly to myself, he did not go on to ask if she was a pirate, though in some sense she was: she had already taken me prisoner and was come to loot the Trojans of their hospitality and succor.

Helen stepped one pace forward, faced him boldly, and replied, "I am the kinswoman of Paris and of Priam and Hecuba. I am descended from the Sidonians Danaos and Agenor and thus belong to the family of Priam, for Atlas and Electra were the children of Pleisione the daughter of Danaos, and Electra too was the mother of King Dardanus, from whom came Tros and the rulers of Troy. And the descendant of Phoenix, son of

Agenor, was King Dymas, the father of Hecuba, and often did Leda my mother tell me she was of the family of Dymas. I have come to be with my family, bringing only myself, taking nothing from Menelaus."

Everyone was in wonderment at this lofty pedigree which Helen rolled out fluently in her deep voice. I was grateful that her words had for the moment stemmed the fraternal doomsayings, but was as taken aback as the rest since I had not schooled her in them. It occurred to me that they might be the handiwork of Astyanassa, though there was no telling that from her respectfully lowered face, and when I taxed her later she denied it. Then more surprise. While Priam stood bemused, Hecuba had acted, embracing Helen and calling out that she loved her beyond all others, which sat badly with the assembled young royals.

At this, Priam recovered himself, detached Helen from Hecuba's embrace, and threw his own arms around her, maintaining them there until in her turn Hecuba tapped him on the shoulder to disengage, like a ritual dance. From that time, the official story was that Queen Helen had come to visit her Trojan kinfolk while her husband was away fulfilling his own family obligations on Crete. This last detail could have no long existence, and was gradually replaced by references to his infidelities, his spawning of children by a variety of other women ranging from nymphs to slave girls. Although sensible folk care nothing about what receptacles married men plant their seed in, Helen through Priam managed to make his behavior seem an intolerable insult to wives everywhere. Nobody who mattered was deceived by any of this, but it served to bring the commoners over to her side, at least while there was peace. When the war came, they cheered or at least left her alone when things were going well with us, and cursed her when badly. On one occasion, she had to flee back to our house under a rain of stones. I failed to conceal my delight that both Aethra and Clymene were struck on the head and succumbed to their wounds, but something had to be done. The next day, when a hostile crowd gathered to block her passage by the oak tree at the Scaean Gate, its wrath was stayed by a group of our most distinguished graybeards, who pottered forward to make a circle around her and in a twittering chorus exclaimed, "Who can blame Trojans and Greeks for suffering for the sake of such a woman, the very image indeed of an immortal goddess?" The mood of the crowd changed, and it dispersed through the streets singing the praises of the woman whose death it had just been seeking. Wise old men! They were worth all the gold I gave them to say that.

Although Aesacus never ceased his pratings and Hector swerved between railing against my character and snubbing me on public occasions, months and then years passed with no sign of the Greeks. The citizens returned to their normal lives, leaving only Hector and an ever-dwindling band of retainers to practice their swordsmanship and light watch fires and place sentries on the walls and all the rest of it. Hector kept reminding the court that when Helen was given in wedlock to Menelaus, Tyndareus her father, at least when the egg story was in abeyance, had on the advice of Odysseus made all the unsuccessful suitors stand on pieces of a dismembered horse—a detail abhorrent to hippophile Trojans—and swear a mighty oath to avenge any insult done to either bride or groom. But Priam replied that Tyndareus had only done this because he himself feared trouble from the disappointed kings, and true enough, his network of agents sent reports that the Greek leaders continued to be more interested in fighting each other than joining against ourselves. A few were willing, but were disheartened by the prevarications of Agamemnon, who, it was whispered, feared to leave Clytemnestra at home with Aegisthus lest the suspect intentions of his resident kinsman result in him losing his wife as well, and above all by the flat refusal of Odysseus, who had shown his opinion of Helen by courting and marrying her cousin Penelope instead. Few liked Odysseus, and nobody trusted him, but all stood in awe of his cunning and feared to begin such a war without him.

Priam claimed to have anticipated all this. While insisting that my mission to Sparta had been an honest one, he admitted that he thought his injunctions to me to eschew Helen might yield the opposite. Had she not come away with me, Menelaus could have become a useful ally. But now that she had, Troy was viewed with envy and respect as the city she preferred to any other. If the Greeks came, how would they feed themselves in a long siege on foreign soil? How could they ever break down the great walls of Ilium? Who was to say that the Egyptians and Hittites would not rally to our cause, or fall upon Greece itself while its kings were away? For such reasons, the Greeks might never attack us. As to dreams and prophecies, he had obeyed by sending Paris to die and (a new revelation, one that to judge by her face would cost him some uncomfortable time with Hecuba) had given an extra earnest by killing another baby, one born on the same day as myself, spawned in secret from the wife of a nobleman, Thymoites. Since the gods had spared me and sent me back to Troy, might not the curse safely be judged null? Furthermore, he knew that a number of the Greek leaders, including the great Achilles, were supposedly fated to die at Troy, should they come. Why would they not stay at home, preferring to keep their lives rather than give them for the likes of Menelaus? I do not think I was the only one who felt that Priam was attempting to persuade himself as much as others in all of this, especially as a brave man might point to him as the curse of Troy, thanks to the perfidy practiced on its gods by his father Laomedon. But we chose to believe what we wished to hear, myself above all into whose mind there came more than once the idea that Priam had hoped I would return from Sparta with Helen that he might use her for himself: such things are not to be thought.

Nine years went by, during which I built my fine house and grew older, and Helen who never aged a day knitted and wove and was coolly gracious towards all, even Aesacus and Hector, who were unreconciled by Priam's words, and at nights she would come Oenone-like to my bed whenever I sent for her and leave as though nothing had happened between entrance and departure, which became more frequently the case, though I was man enough with Astyanassa, who learned more about the secrets of my heart than I did of hers. But in the eyes of the world, I remained the man whom the fair Helen had followed to Troy; I was still talked about, sung about, pointed out and glanced at jealously in the streets. Even when there is no reality, the illusion has its compensations.

Fates or no fates, the war at last came. We pieced together the chain of events from the news sent by Priam's people. Menelaus' harpings on the theme of family honor, along with increasingly dark hints that if Helen and Paris continued unscathed, who knew what thoughts it might inspire in Clytemnestra and Aegisthus, had finally persuaded Agamemnon to agree to leave Mycenae. The former suitors and other Greek kings were ordered to join in the expedition. Odysseus was for once outdone in trickery. Getting wind of what was coming, he arranged it that when the ambassador arrived he was found ploughing in the fields wearing the headgear of a madman. Unluckily for him, Agamemnon had sent Palamedes, a strange-looking person by all accounts but almost as resourceful as Hephaestus, albeit his most famous invention, the game of dice, has brought more pain than happiness into the world. Sensing what Odysseus was up to, Palamedes snatched up Odysseus' infant son—whom for some reason, perhaps as a further token of lunacy, Odysseus had brought to the field with him—and laid the child directly in front of his father's plough. Odysseus betrayed his sanity by not mincing up his offspring, so had to obey the call. However, being Odysseus, he soon restored his reputation by luring Achilles into the campaign. Achilles was then a young brute from Phthia in the wilds of Greece, but already had a great reputation as a warrior. His mother had long feared the prophecy that he would die at Troy, so she persuaded him to skulk on the island of Scyrus disguised as one of the king's daughters. Odysseus turned up there, waited until he saw the girls together at play, and blew a horn, noting how Achilles' reaction differed from the rest, and so flushed him out and shamed him into joining the war.

This was the only thing some of the other Greeks had been waiting for. And so, one day, their beaked ships began to darken the horizon and crowd into our shore, where they have lain ever since, except when forced to go foraging for supplies. A thousand vessels descended upon Ilium to find Helen. Hector fussily insisted that his scouts had counted one thousand one hundred and eighty-four, but as Astyanassa observed, precision is ever the enemy of romance.

The war has now been dragging on for nine full years. We are outnumbered, and there has been no sign of Priam's fancied Egyptians or Hittites. But we have not stood alone: not everyone welcomes the Greeks. We have sallied forth from the city and burned their ships and engaged them on the plain of Troy alongside Lycians, Paeonians, and Paphlagonians, with men from Ascania, Percote, Sesamon, and a hundred other places of which I had scarcely heard. This was touching enough, but what moved me most was the appearance of a detachment of fighters from Zeleia who dwelt under the lowest spurs of Ida. Some of these I had known in my days on the mountain. They were led by my old comrade and friendly rival in archery, Pandarus, for whose death I wept, in private, more tears than over those of my brothers.

Hector, of course, was in his element, playing the hero on the battlefield—I admit without demur that he was our finest champion—and attacking me when off it. Not just the usual taunts about my curly locks and pretty-boy looks, of which I now retained little enough, and all the woes I had brought upon my people. I did not say much in reply to these, and what I did inflamed him all the more, especially when in answer to his reminding me that we had heard from a captive that their chiefs had pledged that every Greek should take to bed a Trojan wife as reward for all the toil and groans Helen had cost them, I remarked that as far as I could tell this prospect seemed to terrify some of our women less than others. He now for the first time cursed me, stammering as he tended to do when overheated, as a coward who lingered on the edge of battle with a bow instead of engaging in hand-to-hand combat with the sword of a real warrior. I replied that Apollo himself was not ashamed to be the patron of archers and that I had my uses: I had wounded the great Diomedes in the foot and Eurypylos in the thigh and brought down with a very accurate shot between jaw and ear Euchenor the Corinthian, thus fulfilling the prediction that he would fall at Troy. As Pandarus and I used often to complain to each other, men should consider the skill and dexterity needed of a good archer: it is much easier to hack off heads and limbs with a sword. But Hector could not be convinced. I had tried once before, and thought I was making ground, but as ill-luck would have it Aesacus came by and overheard and observed in his rancid way that it was no surprise I was expert with bow and arrows; they were after all the weapons of Eros. Hector gave a short laugh, something hardly ever heard from him, which robbed me of my words and the argument was lost.

Since he could not gainsay my tally of victims, Hector shifted ground and renewed his old demand that I bring the war to an end by giving Helen back. I refused yet again, though for the first time said that I would consider offering a generous portion of my wealth to Menelaus as recompense. I knew this was something neither honor nor the other Greeks—I could hardly afford to buy them all off—would allow him to accept. I knew Hector would not accept it either; I was but trying to distract him and, more than that, to avoid saying that Helen was not mine to give back, that she cared as little for me as for Menelaus, though only Astyanassa and I knew that, and would insist on her kinship and charm Priam with eyes and voice into a declaration that the laws of hospitality would not allow him to send her away against her will.

Other brothers joined with Hector's urgings, though not Aesacus, who did not want me to find so easy a solution. Suddenly, I heard myself proclaiming that I would challenge Menelaus to a duel, the winner to have Helen and all the other's goods: neither Priam nor Helen could counter that. At once I would have given anything to summon back these rash words, but it was too late. Hector jumped at the idea, even praised me, saying I had something of a true warrior inside me after all. Aesacus was radiant: he gave me no chance.

Hector clambered up to where a fig tree stands at the highest point of the ramparts and, keeping his stutter under control, shouted my proposition across to the encamped Greeks. Almost at once, Agamemnon bawled back an acceptance on behalf of his brother. I then retired to my house to prepare for the combat, while priests on both sides diverted the armies with prayers and the slaughtering of animals that the gods are supposed to love so much. I encouraged myself with the thought that perhaps Menelaus for all his bluster and fame was just as apprehensive of this way of accounting, else why had he never issued such a challenge himself, and why had Agamemnon answered for him? Buoyed by these thoughts, I set aside my beloved bow, which could play no part in a formal duel, and also the aging panther skin which I usually draped around my shoulders in battle, and arrayed myself in my finest armour, some of which I had only ever worn for ceremonial occasions, thinking such a display might further unnerve him. I felt a pang as I buckled on the cuirass which had belonged to my brother Lycaon, a fresh-faced lad butchered by Achilles; I had to adjust it to my size. Along with a heavy sword made more grand by its studded hilt, I looked out the stoutest shield I could find, thinking I might have more need of this than any other weapon, then selected the best spear from my arsenal, testing it several times for its grip. Whereupon Astyanassa slipped through the polished doors to send me off with a kiss, placing more value on this than on prayers. There was no sign of Helen. I supposed that she was in her quarters, either conversing with Deiphobos, who Astyanassa had informed me was always in her company these days, or knitting and hoping that the gods would somehow contrive to destroy both Menelaus and myself. Astyanassa bade me kneel, so that she might place on my head, taking care to gather what remained of my locks inside it, a flashing helmet from whose crown there nodded a horsehair plume. "Now," she said, "you look just like Hector; go and fight like him."

Menelaus was already pacing up and down the piece of ground that had been measured out between the two watching armies for our fray when I appeared, a further token (or so I hoped) of his apprehension. I myself trembled when I saw Odysseus was one of the judges, dreading some trick, but concealed my fear and was reassured when Hector not he cast the lots to determine who would first throw his spear at the other, an arrangement I hoped would be to the advantage of an archer like myself rather than a sword-slasher like Menelaus.

One of the lots leapt out of the helmet. After an inspection, Hector and Odysseus announced that it was mine. A great groan went up from the Greeks, answered by Trojan cheering, but it was too soon for any of that. Menelaus and I faced each other across the measured strip. Grasping my spear, I waved it in the air for effect, checked the grip one last time, and hurled it. It was a good direct throw, but he parried it with a small round shield which was so well designed that it bent back the point. This time it was the Greeks who cheered while the Trojans lamented. Then Menelaus, having shouted something which I could not catch, perhaps as well in view of the roar from his side, flung his spear. He was as accurate as I, and to my dismay his weapon tore a way through my shield. My cuirass held it off, but while I was struggling to dislodge it, he bore down upon me with his sword raised high in the air. He moved much more quickly than I had expected, and I thought I was done for, but as though in reproach to the shield my helmet stayed in place—the fancy passed through my mind that I owed this to the loving skill of Astyanassa—and his sword broke into small pieces and showered harmlessly to the ground. Again, Menelaus cried out unintelligibly; then, to my horror, for it was a stratagem we had never been taught to defend against in our young men's drills, he seized the horsehair crest—so much after all for the helmet as my savior—and began to drag me backward toward the enemy side. Astyanassa had fitted the embroidered helmet-strap tightly to ensure it would not desert me, but now it seemed as though her solicitude would be my undoing, for it bit deep into my throat and I started to choke. Then, all of a sudden, my chest was filled with air again: despite being made of the finest leather, the strap broke and Menelaus was left with a tauntingly empty helmet in his hand. And I was twice blessed on that day, for one of those thick mists which the Scamander likes to throw up when men least expect them now rolled across the plain and settled over us. I heard Menelaus cursing as he blundered about in search of me, but instinct for saving my skin and the fact that I was on familiar soil brought me safely back to my own side.

The story spread that the mist was a magical one, sent by

Aphrodite to save her favorite. I did not discourage this tale—it helped me deflect the charge of running away, for how could I be blamed for such divine interference? But I did not believe it. Nor did Helen, who seemed in her own way to materialize out of the air to confront me in my chamber as I was stripping off my armour. A good woman like Andromache would have seen to it that there was a cauldron of hot water ready for me to soothe my limbs. Not Helen. Looking more bitch-faced than I had ever seen her, she both cursed and mocked me: why was I not dead, how had I failed to defeat Menelaus, why was I not already issuing a new challenge? I was angry in my own turn. In truth, Menelaus had not beaten me, our spear throws were about equal, and what shame is there in withdrawing when your shield is damaged and your helmet gone? Blazing with the injustice of her, I laid hold of Helen, dragged her down to the bed, tore aside her robe, saffron as always, and took her more fiercely than I had done since our night on Kranae. Even more than then, she not only remained unmoved and unmoving, she contrived to make me feel that she was not there under me at all. Later, I had my fill of encouragement and solace from Astyanassa. I would never summon Helen to my company again.

Thus I lived to fight another day. But in the eyes of most, the war was lost when Hector, not long after he had given Troy new heart by spearing Patroclus—the tent-companion and, as our men used to shout from the walls, bed-sharer of Achilles—through the belly, was felled by Patroclus' maddened lover. Hector had gone out to fight in the fine bronze armour he had stripped from Patroclus' corpse. He looked invulnerable, but Achilles, who knew every way there is to kill a man, found his one exposed spot, an opening of the gullet where the collarbones come down to the neck. I knew from my training and the physicians that this is a prime place of death, just as between navel and groin is the most painful.

When a man finds the death he would have chosen, he is fortunate indeed; I can say that, who have not. I was not expected to be inconsolable: all knew how things had stood between us. But I put on a well-judged show of grief, not of course as dramatic as

Andromache, the center of attention for once and making full use of baby Astyanax as a howling token of her loss; not even as effective as Helen, who joined in with a lamentation that managed to say more about herself than Hector, but was well received for all that. Over the years I had come to think that Hector was one of the many men better suited to her than myself. My own tears were not all squeezed from a dry sponge. I knew as well as anyone what Hector's death meant to our cause, and its effect on our parents, hence on me. And life would not be the same without his fussy ways and well-meaning lectures.

My standing went down with him. Priam took his death worse even than that of Polydorus. Hecuba too. Talk of the doom I had been prophesied to bring upon Ilium returned, fomented of course by Aesacus, and it now fell on newly receptive ears despite being supported by the shriekings of Cassandra, who at that stage was confined to her quarters but who contrived to escape from time to time to fill the streets with her noise.

But it went up again when I got rid of Achilles with my bow. Achilles. They called him the fleet of foot. Not the most creditable nickname for a warrior, but despite my jests on it I could never shake our men's awe of him. Of course, they believed the tale which made him invulnerable except in the left heel by which his mother, some kind of minor goddess, hung on to him while dipping him in the river Styx to give him this protection. If this was true, why did he need that gorgeous armour of his, especially the shield decorated with pictures that no less than Hephaestus was said to have wrought in his Olympian smithy? He could have run naked around the battlefield without getting a scratch. But Astyanassa suggested to me that Achilles' own belief in this story might be his downfall. I had never thought of this. So one day, while there was a lull in the fighting, when I observed him from the battlements strutting around with a group of his Myrmidons as his private army of cutthroats was called, I fitted a newly crafted arrow to my bow, squinted down its length several times, drew back the ox-gut string to my chest, and let fly. It zoomed straight and true, caught him full in the heel left exposed in the embroidered sandals he always wore. He cried out in disbelief, his ruffians fled, the blood flowed, there was no physician to staunch the wound, and down went great Achilles, son of Peleus, to Hades to join the many of my brothers and comrades he had sent ahead of himself. I recalled what I had been told of how he had taunted my brother Lycaon just before slicing him almost in half and pitching his corpse into the Scamander: "Yes, my friend, you too must die. Why make a song about it?" So I shouted these same words down from the walls. Whether he heard them, I do not know, but the saying of them lifted my heart and those of the Trojans. I had never stood so high in the city as I did at that moment. Even Aesacus muttered a few words of praise.

Yet it was not for long. The bow was my undoing as well as my glory. Another man's. Philoctetes, son of Poeas, king of the Malians, wherever they may dwell. He was said to own the bow and arrows of Heracles himself, but they had done him no good on the way to the war, for on the isle of Tenedos, in the act of sacrificing to Athene, he was bitten by a blasphemous snake. No local physician could heal the wound, it stank to the heavens, and what with the stench and his unheroic screaming his men complained; so Agamemnon, with a rare sense of grim humor, had him dumped on Lemnos, a place uninhabited since the women there banded together to murder their men—quite what happened to them, I do not know—and his fleet sailed on without him. Philoctetes suppurated in Lemnian silence for years; then as his good and my bad luck would have it, one of his friends dredged up an oracle that said Troy would not fall until he was there. So, Odysseus went to the island and fetched him to the Greek camp where one of their medical men mysteriously found a cure, and Philoctetes was restored to full vigor, and one day when I was conferring with my comrades well beyond bow range as I thought, he hit me first in the left hand and then the right thigh. By themselves, these wounds should not have been serious, had they been clean, but with typical lack of honor, or so our physicians claim to justify their failure to heal me, the arrows had been tipped with a poison whose action is slow but whose consequence is final.

Murdered, yet I am still alive to tell the tale, to name the one who has done for me without laying a finger upon my person. No, not Philoctetes: he only provided the way to my death. It is Oenone who has slain me. When it was clear that the doctors had despaired, I ordered that I be carried to Mount Ida, where she would surely cure me with her antidotes and ointments, remembering how she had saved more than one peasant lad from the bite of snakes. There was another break in the fighting—the Greeks were celebrating some festival or other—so a group of my comrades laid me across a horse and conducted me there.

She looked down on me and without expression declared that she would do nothing for me. I was barely conscious after the bumping fatigue of the journey, but in as calm a voice as possible said, "The last time we were together, you promised that if I ever needed you, you would help me."

"No, Paris. What I told you was, should there dawn a day when you have need of my arts, I shall be here. I did not say that I would help you."

I did not remonstrate. Her refusal had to be accepted. I had not loved her, she did not love me, there was no answer to that. She owed me nothing, I could demand nothing. My comrades wanted to kill her on the spot, but I bade them lower their swords and extracted an oath that after my death they were not to return in vengeance; then I had them bring me back to the city and my chamber.

Priam and Hecuba have not been to see me, but I have had one visitor, as unexpected as he was unwelcome: Aesacus. I imagined he had come to gloat, and could have endured that, even welcomed one final round of exchanges with him. But he said only that it was time I knew of Asterope, the wife he had mysteriously acquired between my winning of the bull and return to Troy after judging the beauties in the clearing. Apart from thinking her looks quite wasted upon him, I had never paid her any heed. Now he informed me with much satisfaction that she was none other than the daughter of Cebren, sister of Oenone. For all these years Aesacus, not I, had known that we were kinsmen twice over, by blood and by marriage. For all these years he had been in contact with Oenone, whose existence neither he nor Asterope had betrayed at Troy, feeding her bile and cosseting her fury, hugging to himself a secret that he hoped might one day be turned against me with lethal advantage; and now that day had come.

Pelion piled upon Ossa. As I was being carried from her presence, Oenone burst out into harsh laughter, ridiculing me that I had brought myself and my people to ruin for a woman who was no woman. Yes, I am dealing in riddles again, but this one is not of my making. Had I not heard, she asked, of the story from Egypt, as she had when visiting there to seek out knowledge of its famous drugs? The story that was being whispered throughout the land, that Helen was in the palace of their King Proteus, the real Helen, whilst what had come to Ilium was but a phantom fashioned by Zeus.

Astyanassa poured scorn on this tale; it was nothing but a different kind of poison from Oenone's pharmacy. Why, she smiled, if Helen was just a wraith, perhaps she, Astyanassa, was too. And would a ghost have been caught trying to escape down a rope over the walls, as Helen had lately been reported as doing? A phantom needed no ordinary agency of flight. My reason agreed, but my heart wondered, for if this Helen was unreal there was much that was now explained. Good luck to Deiphobos, I managed to laugh, if she stays long enough for him to succeed me in her spectral embraces. And if our Helen was not flesh and blood, what would I not give to see, though I knew I never should, the expression on Menelaus' ruddy face when he learned for what so many of his countrymen had died. If she and I were the bane of Troy, we were also the bane of Greece. More and more thoughts and questions crowded into my head, so thickly that it ached and spun, and I finally sank back on my pillows in despair: such tangles of reason and phantasm are not for the mind of a dying man.

Astyanassa has been attempting to comfort me with the belief that Oenone, despite her loathing of me and the machinations of Aesacus, will repent, perhaps already had done and was even now hastening to Troy with her remedies, if only to save her own self; for the name of Paris is still loved on the mountain, and unlike my soldiers the peasants had taken no oath to spare her. And had I not said that she could not flee because she had long ago pledged never to desert her father Cebren? If Astyanassa is right, will she get here in time? And do I want her to? Perhaps it is best that I follow Hector and Lycaon and Pandarus and Achilles too for that matter and the countless others down to Hades. At least I shall be spared the sight of Troy in flames and what will happen to my parents and family: the Greeks are famously unkind in victory. Will Menelaus forgive Helen, ghost or reality? Will one glimpse of those white arms or snowy bosom cause him to drop his sword? As for Astyanassa, may Aphrodite whom I may or may not have met in the clearing protect her. The goddess of beauty who married the lame Hephaestus on Olympus can surely see beyond the physical. Yet who can trust the gods to render justice? Perhaps I should order Astyanassa to put a dagger to her heart when she has watched me go, that she may accompany me. I have no doubt that she would obey, indeed welcome, such a command. Unless, unless she herself has been my evil genius, hating Helen and myself and all beauty because of her own lack of it, first an instrument of Menelaus to promote the excuse for war, then an accomplice, even the director, of Aesacus. She might even have contrived in some fashion that I should be the target of Philoctetes, not a bowman to discharge his darts at random. Perhaps I should rather order her death before my own comes, either to discover the truth or ensure that she does not survive to savor the cup of triumph. No, no, the poison in my body is producing its own in my mind. Astyanassa will follow me of her own desire and we shall spend an eternity together. But how shall I cope with an eternity of Hector and, when they come, of Helen and Oenone and Aesacus?

I was born cursed. It is only fit that I should die cursing.